About the Authors

an Air Force officer, **Merline Lovelace** served at
es all over the world. When she hung up her uniform
r the last time, she combined her love of adventure with
a flair for storytelling. She's now produced more than
ninety-five action-packed novels. Over twelve million
copies of her works are in print in thirty countries.
Named Oklahoma's Writer of the Year and Female
Veteran of the Year, Merline is also a recipient of
Romance Writers of America's prestigious RITA® Award.

Jennifer Lewis has always been drawn to fairy tales,
and stories of passion and enchantment. Writing
allows her to bring the characters crowding her
imagination to life. She lives in sunny South Florida
and enjoys the lush tropical environment and spending
time on the beach all year long. Please visit her website
at http://www.jenlewis.com

Leanne Banks is a *New York Times* bestselling author
with over sixty books to her credit. A book lover and
omance fan from even before she learned to read,
eanne has always treasured the way that books allow
to go to new places and experience the lives of
onderful characters. Always ready for a trip to the
each, Leanne lives in Virginia with her family and
er Pomeranian muse.

Royal Rebels

March 2021
The Royal Heir

April 2021
Forbidden to the Crown

May 2021
Royal Weddings

June 2021
His Passionate Duty

July 2021
Seducing the Crown

August 2021
A Convenient Marriage

Royal Rebels: Forbidden to the Crown

MERLINE LOVELACE

JENNIFER LEWIS

LEANNE BANKS

MILLS & BOON

First Published in Great Britain 2021
By Mills & Boon, an imprint of HarperCollins*Publishers* Ltd
1 London Bridge Street, London, SE1 9GF

www.harpercollins.co.uk

HarperCollins*Publishers*
1st Floor, Watermarque Building,
Ringsend Road, Dublin 4, Ireland

ISBN: 978-0-263-29961-8

MIX
Paper from
responsible sources
FSC™ C007454

This book is produced from independently certified FSC™ paper to ensure responsible forest management.

For more information visit: www.harpercollins.co.uk/green

Printed and bound in Spain
by CPI, Barcelona

HER UNFORGETTABLE ROYAL LOVER

MERLINE LOVELACE

To Neta and Dave, friends, travelling buds, and the source of all kinds of fodder for my books. Thanks for the info on research grants and nasty bugs, Neta!

Prologue

Who would have imagined my days would become this rich and full, and at such a late point in my life! My darling granddaughter Sarah and her husband, Dev, have skillfully blended marriage with their various enterprises, their charitable work and their travels to all parts of the world. Yet Sarah still finds time to involve me in the book she's writing on lost treasures of the art world. My input has been limited, to be sure, but I've very much enjoyed being part of such an ambitious undertaking.

And Eugenia, my carefree, high-spirited Eugenia, has surprised herself by becoming the most amazing wife and mother. Her twins are very much like she was at that age. Bright-eyed and lively, with very distinct personalities. And best of all, her husband, Jack, is being considered for appointment as US Ambassador to the United Nations. If he's confirmed, he and Gina and the babies would live only a few blocks away.

Until that happens, I have the company of my longtime friend and companion, Maria. And Anastazia, my lovely, so serious Anastazia. Zia's in her second year of a residency in pediatric medicine and I played shamelessly on our somewhat tenuous kinship to convince her to live with me for the three-year program. She wears herself to the bone, poor dear, but Maria and I see that she eats well and gets at least some rest.

It's her brother, Dominic, I fret about. Dom insists he's not ready to settle down, and why should he with all the women who throw themselves at him? His job worries me, however. It's too dangerous, too high-risk. I do wish he would quit working undercover, and may have found just the enticement to encourage him to do so. How surprised he'll be when I tell him about the document Sarah's clever research assistant has discovered!

From the diary of Charlotte,
Grand Duchess of Karlenburgh

One

August was slamming New York City when Dominic St. Sebastian climbed out of a cab outside the castle-like Dakota. Heat waves danced like demented demons above the sidewalks. Across the street, moisture-starved leaves drifted like yellowed confetti from the trees in Central Park. Even the usual snarl of cabs and limos and sightseeing buses cruising the Upper West Side seemed lethargic and sluggish.

The same couldn't be said for the Dakota's doorman. As dignified as ever in his lightweight summer uniform, Jerome abandoned his desk to hold the door for the new arrival.

"Thanks," Dom said with the faint accent that marked him as European despite the fact that English came as naturally to him as his native Hungarian. Shifting his carry-all to his right hand, he clapped the older man's shoulder with his left. "How's the duchess?"

"As strong-willed as ever. She wouldn't listen to the rest of us, but Zia finally convinced her to forego her daily constitutional during this blistering heat."

Dom wasn't surprised his sister had succeeded where others failed. Anastazia Amalia Julianna St. Sebastian combined the slashing cheekbones, exotic eyes and stunning beauty of a supermodel with the tenacity of a bulldog.

And now his beautiful, tenacious sister was living with

Grand Duchess Charlotte. Zia and Dom had met their long-lost relative for the first time only last year and formed an instant bond. So close a bond that Charlotte had invited Zia to live at the Dakota during her pediatric residency at Mt. Sinai.

"Has my sister started her new rotation?" Dom asked while he and Jerome waited for the elevator.

He didn't doubt the doorman would know. He had the inside track on most of the Dakota's residents but kept a close eye on his list of favorites. Topping that list were Charlotte St. Sebastian and her two granddaughters, Sarah and Gina. Zia had recently been added to the select roster.

"She started last week," Jerome advised. "She doesn't say so, but I can see oncology is hard on her. Would be on anyone, diagnosing and treating all those sick children. And the hospital works the residents to the bone, which doesn't help." He shook his head, but brightened a moment later. "Zia wrangled this afternoon off, though, when she heard you were flying in. Oh, and Lady Eugenia is here, too. She arrived last night with the twins."

"I haven't seen Gina and the twins since the duchess's birthday celebration. The girls must be, what? Six or seven months old now?"

"Eight." Jerome's seamed face folded into a grin. Like everyone else, he'd fallen hard for an identical pair of rose-bud mouths, lake-blue eyes and heads topped with their mother's spun-sugar, silvery-blond curls.

"Lady Eugenia says they're crawling now," he warned. "Better watch where you step and what you step in."

"I will," Dom promised with a grin.

As the elevator whisked him to the fifth floor, he remembered the twins as he'd last seen them. Cooing and blowing bubbles and waving dimpled fists, they'd already developed into world-class heartbreakers.

They'd since developed two powerful sets of lungs,

Dom discovered when a flushed and flustered stranger yanked open the door.

"It's about time! We've been..."

She stopped, blinking owlishly behind her glasses, while a chorus of wails rolled down the marble-tiled foyer.

"You're not from Osterman's," she said accusingly.

"The deli? No, I'm not."

"Then who...? Oh! You're Zia's brother." Her nostrils quivered, as if she'd suddenly caught a whiff of something unpleasant. "The one who goes through women like a hot knife through butter."

Dom hooked a brow but couldn't dispute the charge. He enjoyed the company of women. Particularly the generously curved, pouty-lipped, out-for-a-good-time variety.

The one facing him now certainly didn't fall into the first two of those categories. Not that he could see more than a suggestion of a figure inside her shapeless linen dress and boxy jacket. Her lips were anything but pouty, however. Pretty much straight-lined, as a matter of fact, with barely disguised disapproval.

"Igen," Dom agreed lazily in his native Hungarian. "I'm Dominic. And you are?"

"Natalie," she bit out, wincing as the howls behind her rose to high-pitched shrieks. "Natalie Clark. Come in, come in."

Dom had spent almost seven years now as an Interpol agent. During that time, he'd helped take down his share of drug traffickers, black marketeers and the scum who sold young girls and boys to the highest bidders. Just last year he'd helped foil a kidnapping and murder plot against Gina's husband right here in New York City. But the scene that greeted him as he paused at the entrance to the duchess's elegant sitting room almost made him turn tail and run.

A frazzled Gina was struggling to hang on to a red-faced, furiously squirming infant in a frilly dress and a lacy headband with a big pink bow. Zia had her arms full with the second, equally enraged and similarly attired baby. The duchess sat straight-backed and scowling in regal disapproval, while the comfortably endowed Honduran who served as her housekeeper and companion stood at the entrance to the kitchen, her face screwed into a grimace as the twins howled their displeasure.

Thankfully, the duchess reached her limit before Dom was forced to beat a hasty retreat. Her eyes snapping, she gripped the ivory handle of her cane in a blue-veined, white-knuckled fist.

"Charlotte!" The cane thumped the floor. Once. Twice. "Amalia! You will kindly cease that noise at once."

Dom didn't know whether it was the loud banging or the imperious command that did the trick, but the howls cut off like a faucet and surprise leaped into four tear-drenched eyes. Blessed silence reigned except for the babies' gulping hiccups.

"Thank you," the duchess said coolly. "Gina, why don't you and Zia take the girls to the nursery? Maria will bring their bottles as soon as Osterman's delivers the milk."

"It should be here any moment, *Duquesa*." Using her ample hips, the housekeeper backed through the swinging door to the kitchen. "I'll get the bottles ready."

Gina was headed for the hall leading to the bedrooms when she spotted her cousin four or five times removed. "Dom!" She blew him an air kiss. "I'll talk to you when I get the girls down."

"I, as well," his sister said with a smile in her dark eyes.

He set down his carryall and crossed the elegant sitting room to kiss the duchess's cheeks. Her paper-thin skin carried the faint scent of gardenias, and her eyes were cloudy with age but missed little. Including the wince he couldn't quite hide when he straightened.

"Zia told me you'd been knifed. Again."

"Just nicked a rib."

"Yes, well, we need to talk about these nicked ribs and bullet wounds you collect with distressing frequency. But first, pour us a…" She broke off at the buzz of the doorbell. "That must be the delivery. Natalie, dear, would you sign for it and take the milk to Maria?"

"Of course."

Dom watched the stranger head back to the foyer and turned to the duchess. "Who is she?"

"A research assistant Sarah hired to help with her book. Her name's Natalie Clark and she's part of what I want to talk to you about."

Dominic knew Sarah, the duchess's older granddaughter, had quit her job as an editor at a glossy fashion magazine when she married self-made billionaire Devon Hunter. He also knew Sarah had expanded on her degree in art history from the Sorbonne by hitting every museum within taxi distance when she accompanied Dev on his business trips around the world. That—and the fact that hundreds of years of art had been stripped off walls and pedestals when the Soviets overran the Duchy of Karlenburgh decades ago—had spurred Sarah to begin documenting what she learned about the lost treasures of the art world. It also prompted a major New York publisher to offer a fat, six-figure advance if she turned her notes into a book.

What Dom *didn't* know was what Sarah's book had to do with him, much less the female now making her way to the kitchen with an Osterman's delivery sack in hand. Sarah's research assistant couldn't be more than twenty-five or twenty-six but she dressed like a defrocked nun. Mousy-brown hair clipped at her neck. No makeup. Square glasses with thick lenses. Sensible flats and that shapeless linen dress.

When the kitchen door swung behind her, Dom had to

ask. "How is this Natalie Clark involved in what you want to talk to me about?"

The duchess waived an airy hand. "Pour us a *pálinka*, and I'll tell you."

"Should you have brandy? Zia said in her last email that…"

"Pah! Your sister fusses more than Sarah and Gina combined."

"With good reason, yes? She's a doctor. She has a better understanding of your health issues."

"Dominic." The duchess leveled a steely stare. "I've told my granddaughters, I've told your sister, and I'll tell you. The day I can't handle an aperitif before dinner is the day you may bundle me off to a nursing home."

"The day you can't drink us all under the table, you mean." Grinning, Dom went to the sideboard and lined up two cut-crystal snifters.

Ah, but he was a handsome devil, Charlotte thought with a sigh. Those dark, dangerous eyes. The slashing brows and glossy black hair. The lean, rangy body inherited from the wiry horsemen who'd swept down from the Steppes on their sturdy ponies and ravaged Europe. Magyar blood ran in his veins, as it did in hers, combined with but not erased by centuries of intermarriage among the royals of the once-great Austro-Hungarian Empire.

The Duchy of Karlenburgh had been part of that empire. A tiny part, to be sure, but one with a history that had stretched back for seven hundred years. It now existed only in dusty history books, and one of those books was about to change Dominic's life. Hopefully for the better, although Charlotte doubted he would think so. Not at first. But with time…

She glanced up as the instigator of that change returned to the sitting room. "Ah, here you are, Natalie. We're just about to have an aperitif. Will you join us?"

"No, thank you."

Dom paused with his hand on the stopper of the Bohemian crystal decanter he and Zia had brought the duchess as a gift for their first meeting. Thinking to soften the researcher's stiff edges, he gave her a slow smile.

"Are you sure? This apricot brandy is a specialty of my country."

"I'm sure."

Dom blinked. *Mi a fene!* Did her nose just quiver again? As though she'd picked up another bad odor? What the hell kind of tales had Zia and/or Gina fed the woman?

Shrugging, he splashed brandy into two snifters and carried one to the duchess. But if anyone could use a shot of *pálinka*, he thought as he folded his long frame into the chair beside his great-aunt's, the research assistant could. The double-distilled, explosively potent brandy would set more than her nostrils to quivering.

"How long will you be in New York?" the duchess asked after downing a healthy swallow.

"Only tonight. I have a meeting in Washington tomorrow."

"Hmm. I should wait until Zia and Gina return to discuss this with you, but they already know about it."

"About what?"

"The Edict of 1867." She set her brandy aside, excitement kindling in her faded blue eyes. "As you may remember from your history books, war with Prussia forced Emperor Franz Joseph to cede certain concessions to his often rambunctious Hungarian subjects. The Edict of 1867 gave Hungary full internal autonomy as long as it remained part of the empire for purposes of war and foreign affairs."

"Yes, I know this."

"Did you also know Karlenburgh added its own codicil to the agreement?"

"No, I didn't, but then I would have no reason to," Dom

said gently. "Karlenburgh is more your heritage than mine, Duchess. My grandfather—your husband's cousin—left Karlenburgh Castle long before I was born."

And the duchy had ceased to exist soon after that. World War I had carved up the once-mighty Austro-Hungarian Empire. World War II, the brutal repression of the Cold War era, the abrupt dissolution of the Soviet Union and vicious attempts at "ethnic cleansing" had all added their share of upheavals to the violently changing political landscape of Eastern Europe.

"Your grandfather took his name and his bloodline with him when he left Karlenburgh, Dominic." Charlotte leaned closer and gripped his arm with fingers that dug in like talons. "You inherited that bloodline and that name. You're a St. Sebastian. And the present Grand Duke of Karlenburgh."

"What?"

"Natalie found it during her research. The codicil. Emperor Franz Joseph reconfirmed that the St. Sebastians would carry the titles of Grand Duke and Duchess forever and in perpetuity in exchange for holding the borders of the empire. The empire doesn't exist anymore, but despite all the wars and upheavals, that small stretch of border between Austria and Hungary remains intact. So, therefore, does the title."

"On paper, perhaps. But the lands and outlying manors and hunting lodges and farmlands that once comprised the duchy have long since been dispersed and redeeded. It would take a fortune and decades in court to reclaim any of them."

"The lands and manor houses are gone, yes. Not the title. Sarah will become Grand Duchess when I die. Or Gina if, God forbid, something should happen to her sister. But they married commoners. According to the laws of primogeniture, their husbands can't assume the title of

Grand Duke. Until either Sarah or Gina has a son, or their daughters grow up and marry royalty, the only one who can claim it is you, Dom."

Right, he wanted to drawl. That and ten dollars would get him a half-decent espresso at one of New York's overpriced coffee bars.

He swallowed the sarcasm but lobbed a quick glare at the woman wearing an expression of polite interest, as if she hadn't initiated this ridiculous conversation with her research. He'd have a thing or two to say to Ms. Clark later about getting the duchess all stirred up over an issue that was understandably close to her heart but held little relevance to the real world. Particularly the world of an undercover operative.

He allowed none of those thoughts to show in his face as he folded Charlotte's hand between his. "I appreciate the honor you want to bestow on me, Duchess. I do. But in my line of work, I can hardly hang a title around my neck."

"Yes, I want to speak to you about that, too. You've been living on the edge for too many years now. How long can you continue before someone nicks more than a rib?"

"Exactly what I've been asking him," Zia commented as she swept into the sitting room with her long-legged stride.

She'd taken advantage of her few hours away from the hospital to pull on her favorite jeans and a summer tank top in blistering red. The rich color formed a striking contrast to her dark eyes and shoulder-length hair as black and glossy as her brother's. When he stood and opened his arms, she walked into them and hugged him with the same fierce affection he did her.

She was only four years younger than Dom, twenty-seven to his thirty-one, but he'd assumed full responsibility for his teenage sibling when their parents died. He'd been there, too, standing round-the-clock watch beside her hospital bed when she'd almost bled to death after a uterine cyst ruptured her first year at university. The complications that resulted from the rupture had changed her life in so many ways.

What hadn't changed was Dom's bone-deep protectiveness. No matter where his job took him or what dangerous enterprise he was engaged in, Zia had only to send a coded text and he would contact her within hours, if not minutes. Although he always shrugged off the grimmer aspects of his work, she'd wormed enough detail out of him over the years to add her urging to that of the duchess.

"You don't have to stay undercover. Your boss at Interpol told me he has a section chief job waiting for you whenever you want it."

"You can see me behind a desk, Zia-mia?"

"Yes!"

"What a poor liar you are." He made a fist and delivered a mock punch to her chin. "You wouldn't last five minutes under interrogation."

Gina had returned during their brief exchange. Shoving back her careless tumble of curls, she entered the fray. "Jack says you would make an excellent liaison to the State Department. In fact, he wants to talk to you about that tomorrow, when you're in Washington."

"With all due respect to your husband, Lady Eugenia, I'm not ready to join the ranks of bureaucrats."

His use of her honorific brought out one of Gina's merry, irreverent grins. "Since we're tossing around titles here, has Grandmother told you about the codicil?"

"She has."

"Well then..." Fanning out the skirts of her leafy-green sundress, she sank to the floor in an elegant, if theatrical, curtsy.

Dom muttered something distinctly unroyal under his breath. Fortunately, the Clark woman covered it when she pushed to her feet.

"Excuse me. This is a family matter. I'll leave you to discuss it and go back to my research. You'll call me when it's convenient for us to continue our interview, Duchess?"

"I will. You're in New York until Thursday, is that correct?"

"Yes, ma'am. Then I fly to Paris to compare notes with Sarah."

"We'll get together again before then."

"Thank you." She bent to gather the bulging briefcase that had been resting against the leg of her chair. Straightening, she nudged up her glasses back into place. "It was good to meet you, Dr. St. Sebastian, and to see you again, Lady Eugenia."

Her tone didn't change. Neither did her polite expression. But Dom didn't miss what looked very much like a flicker of disdain in her brown eyes when she dipped her head in his direction.

"Your Grace."

He didn't alter his expression, either, but both his sister and his cousin recognized the sudden, silky note in his voice.

"I'll see you to the door."

"Thank you, but I'll let myself… Oh. Uh, all right."

Natalie blinked owlishly behind her glasses. The smile didn't leave Dominic St. Sebastian's ridiculously handsome face and the hand banding her upper arm certainly wouldn't leave any bruises. That didn't make her feel any less like a suspect being escorted from the scene of a crime, however. Especially when he paused with a hand on the door latch and skewered her with a narrow glance from those dark eyes.

"Where are you staying?"

"I beg your pardon?"

"Where are you staying?"

Good Lord! Was he hitting on her? No, he couldn't

be! She was most definitely not his type. According to Zia's laughing reports, her bachelor brother went for leggy blondes or voluptuous brunettes. A long string of them, judging by the duchess's somewhat more acerbic references to his sowing altogether too many wild oats.

That more than anything had predisposed Natalie to dislike Dominic St. Sebastian sight unseen. She'd fallen for a too-handsome, too-smooth operator like him once and would pay for that stupidity for the rest of her life. Still, she tried, she really tried, to keep disdain from seeping into her voice as she tugged her arm free.

"I don't believe where I'm staying is any of your business."

"You've made it my business with this nonsense about a codicil."

Whoa! He could lock a hand around her arm. He could perp-walk her to the door. He could *not* disparage her research.

Thoroughly indignant, Natalie returned fire. "It's not nonsense, as you would know if you'd displayed any interest in your family's history. I suggest you show a little more respect for your heritage, *Your Grace*, and for the duchess."

He muttered something in Hungarian she suspected was not particularly complimentary and bent an elbow against the doorjamb, leaning close. Too close! She could see herself in his pupils, catch the tang of apricot brandy on his breath.

"My respect for Charlotte is why you and I are going to have a private chat, yes? I ask again, where are you staying?"

His Magyar roots were showing, Natalie noted with a skitter of nerves. The slight thickening of his accent should have warned her. Should have sent her scurrying back into the protective shell she'd lived inside for so long it was now as much a part of her life as her drab hair and clothes. But some spark of her old self tilted her chin.

"You're supposed to be a big, bad secret agent," she said coolly. "Dig out the information yourself."

He would, Dom vowed as the door closed behind her with a small thud. He most definitely would.

Two

All it took was one call to arm Dom with the essential information. Natalie Elizabeth Clark. Born Farmington, Illinois. Age twenty-nine, height five feet six inches, brown hair, brown eyes. Single. Graduated University of Michigan with a degree in library science, specializing in archives and presentation. Employed as an archivist with Centerville Community College for three years, the State of Illinois Civil Service Board for four. Currently residing in L.A. where she was employed by Sarah St. Sebastian as a personal assistant.

An archivist. Christ!

Dom shook his head as his cab picked its way downtown later that evening. He envisioned a small cubicle, her head bent toward a monitor screen, her eyes staring through those thick lenses at an endless stream of documents to be verified, coded and electronically filed. And she'd done it for seven years! Dom would have committed ritual hara-kiri after a week. No wonder she'd jumped when Sarah put out feelers for an assistant to help research her book.

Ms. Clark was still running endless computer searches. Still digging through archives, some electronic, some paper. But at least now she was traveling the globe to get at the most elusive of those documents. And, Dom guessed as his cab pulled up at the W New York, doing that traveling on a very generous expense account.

He didn't bother to stop at the front desk. His phone call had confirmed that Ms. Clark had checked into room 1304 two days ago. And a tracking program developed for the military and now in use by a number of intelligence agencies confirmed her cell phone was currently emitting signals from this location.

Two minutes later Dom rapped on her door. The darkening of the peephole told him she was as careful in her personal life as she no doubt was in her work. He smiled his approval, then waited for the door to open.

When neither of those events happened, he rapped again. Still no response.

"It's Dominic St. Sebastian, Ms. Clark. I know you're in there. You may as well open the door."

She complied but wasn't happy about it. "It's generally considered polite to call ahead for an appointment instead of just showing up at someone's hotel room."

The August humidity had turned her shapeless linen dress into a roadmap of wrinkles, and her sensible pumps had been traded for hotel flip-flops. She'd freed her hair from the clip, though, and it framed her face in surprisingly thick, soft waves as she tipped Dom a cool look through her glasses.

"May I ask why you felt compelled to come all the way downtown to speak with me?"

Dom had been asking himself the same thing. He'd confirmed this woman was who she said she was and verified her credentials. The truth was he probably wouldn't have given Natalie Clark a second thought if not for those little nose quivers.

He'd told himself the disdain she'd wiped off her face so quickly had triggered his cop's instinct. Most of the scum he'd dealt with over the years expressed varying degrees of contempt for the police, right up until they were cuffed and led away. His sister, however, would probably insist those small hints of derision had pricked his male ego. It was true that Dom could never resist a challenge. But despite Zia's frequent assertions to the contrary, he didn't try to finesse *every* female who snagged his attention into bed.

Still, he was here and here he intended to remain until he satisfied his curiosity about this particular female. "I'd like more information on this codicil you've uncovered, Ms. Clark."

"I'm sure you would. I'll be happy to email you the documentation I've..."

"I prefer to see what you have now. May I come in, or do we continue our discussion in the hall?"

Her mouth pursing, she stood aside. Her obvious reluctance intrigued Dom. And, all right, stirred his hunting instincts. Too bad he had that meeting at the National Central Bureau—the US branch of Interpol—in Washington tomorrow. It might have been interesting to see what it would take to get those prim, disapproving lips to unpurse and sigh his name.

He skimmed a glance around the room. Two queen beds, one with her open briefcase and neat stacks of files on it. An easy chair angled to get the full benefit of the high-definition flat-screen. A desk with a black ergonomic chair, another stack of files and a seventeen-inch laptop open to a webpage displaying a close-up of an elaborately jeweled egg.

"One of the Fabergé eggs?" he asked, moving closer to admire the sketch of a gem-encrusted egg nested in a two-wheeled gold cart.

"Yes."

"The Cherub with a Chariot," Dom read, "a gift from Tsar Alexander III to his wife, Maria Fyodorovna for Easter, 1888. One of eight Fabergé eggs currently lost."

He glanced at the researcher hovering protectively close to her work, as if to protect it from prying eyes.

"And you're on the hunt for it?"

"I'm documenting its history."

Her hand crept toward the laptop's lid, as if itching to slam it down.

"What have you found so far?"

The lips went tight again, but Dom was too skilled at interrogations to let her off the hook. He merely waited until she gave a grudging nod.

"Documents show it was at Gatchina Palace in 1891, and was one of forty or so eggs sent to the armory at the Kremlin after the 1917 Revolution. Some experts believe it was purchased in the 1930s by Victor and Armand Hammer. But..."

He could see when her fascination with her work overcame her reluctance to discuss it. Excitement snuck into her voice and added a spark to her brown eyes. Her very velvety, very enticing brown eyes, he thought as she tugged off her glasses and twirled them by one stem.

"I found a reference to a similar egg sold at an antiques shop in Paris in 1930. A shop started by a Russian émigré. No one knows how the piece came into his possession, but I've found a source I want to check when I'm in Paris next week. It may..."

She caught herself and brought the commentary to an abrupt halt. The twirling ceased. The glasses whipped up, and wariness replaced the excitement in the doe-brown eyes.

"I'm not trying to pump you for information," Dom assured her. "Interpol has a whole division devoted to lost, stolen or looted cultural treasures, you know."

"Yes, I do."

"Since you're heading over to Paris, I can set up a meeting for you with the division chief, if you like."

The casual offer seemed to throw her off balance. "I... Uh... I have access to their database but..." Her glance went to the screen, then came back to Dom. "I would appreciate that," she said stiffly. "Thank you."

A grin sketched across his face. "There now. That didn't taste so bad going down, did it?"

Instant alarms went off in Natalie's head. She could almost hear their raucous clanging as she fought to keep her chin high and her expression politely remote. She would *not* let a lazy grin and a pair of glinting, bedroom eyes seduce her. Not again. Never again.

"I'll give you my business card," she said stiffly. "Your associate can reach me anytime at my mobile number or by email."

"So cool, so polite." He didn't look at the embossed card she retrieved from her briefcase, merely slipped it into the pocket of his slacks. "What is it about me you don't like?"

How about everything!

"I don't know you well enough to dislike you." She should have left it there. Would have, if he hadn't been standing so close. "Nor," she added with a shrug, "do I wish to."

She recognized her error at once. Men like Dominic St. Sebastian would take that as a challenge. Hiding a grimace, Natalie attempted some quick damage control.

"You said you wanted more information on the codicil. I have a scanned copy on my computer. I'll pull it up and print out a copy for you."

She pulled out the desk chair. He was forced to step back so she could sit, but any relief she might have gained from the small separation dissipated when he leaned a hand on the desk and bent to peer over her shoulder. His breath stirred the loose tendrils at her temple, moved lower, washed warm and hot against her ear. She managed to keep from hunching her shoulder but it took an iron effort of will.

"So that's it," he said as the scanned image appeared, "the document the duchess thinks makes me a duke?"

"Grand Duke," Natalie corrected. "Excuse me, I need to check the paper feed in the printer."

There was nothing wrong with the paper feed. Her little portable printer had been cheerfully spitting out copies before St. Sebastian so rudely interrupted her work. But it was the best excuse she could devise to get him to stop breathing down her neck!

He took the copy and made himself comfortable in the armchair while he tried to decipher the spidery script. Natalie was tempted to let him suffer through the embellished High German, but relented and printed out a translation.

"I stumbled across the codicil while researching the Canaletto that once hung in the castle at Karlenburgh," she told him. "I'd found an obscure reference to the painting in the Austrian State Archives in Vienna."

She couldn't resist an aside. So many uninformed thought her profession dry and dull. They couldn't imagine the thrill that came with following one fragile thread to another, then another, and another.

"The archives are so vast, it's taken years to digitize them all. But the results are amazing. Really amazing. The oldest document dates back to 816."

He nodded, not appearing particularly interested in this bit of trivia that Natalie found so fascinating. Deflated, she got back to the main point.

"The codicil was included in a massive collection of letters, charters, treaties and proclamations relating to the Austro-Prussian War. Basically, it states what the duchess told you earlier. Emperor Franz Joseph granted the St. Sebastians the honor of Karlenburgh in perpetuity in exchange for defending the borders for the empire. The duchy may not exist anymore and so many national lines have been redrawn. That section of the border between

Austria and Hungary has held steady, however, through all the wars and invasions. So, therefore, has the title."

He made a noise that sounded close to a snort. "You and I both know this document isn't worth the paper you've just printed it on."

Offended on behalf of archivists everywhere, she cocked her chin. "The duchess disagrees."

"Right, and that's what you and I need to talk about."

He stuffed the printout in his pocket and pinned her with a narrow stare. No lazy grin now. No laughter in those dark eyes.

"Charlotte St. Sebastian barely escaped Karlenburgh with her life. She carried her baby in her arms while she marched on foot for some twenty or thirty miles through winter snows. I know the story is that she managed to bring away a fortune in jewels, as well. I'm not confirming the story…"

He didn't have to. Natalie had already pieced it together from her own research and from the comments Sarah had let drop about the personal items the duchess had disposed of over the years to raise her granddaughters in the style she considered commensurate with their rank.

"…but I am warning you not to take advantage of the duchess's very natural desire to see her heritage continue."

"Take advantage?"

It took a moment for that to sink in. When it did, she could barely speak through the anger that spurted hot and sour into her throat.

"Do you think…? Do you think this codicil is part of some convoluted scheme on my part to extract money from the St. Sebastians?"

Furious, she shoved to her feet. He rose as well, as effortlessly as an athlete, and countered her anger with a shrug.

"Not at this point. If I discover differently, however, you and I will most certainly have another chat."

"Get out!"

Maybe after she cooled down Natalie would admit flinging out an arm and stabbing a finger toward the door was overly melodramatic. At the moment, though, she wanted to slam that door so hard it knocked this pompous ass on his butt. Especially when he lifted a sardonic brow.

"Shouldn't that be 'Get out, *Your Grace*'?"

Her back teeth ground together. "Get. Out."

As a cab hauled him back uptown for a last visit with the duchess and his sister, Dom couldn't say his session with Ms. Clark had satisfied his doubts. There was still something he couldn't pin down about the researcher. She dressed like a bag lady in training and seemed content to efface herself in company. Yet when she'd flared up at him, when fury had brought color surging to her cheeks and fire to her eyes, the woman was anything but ignorable.

She reminded him of the mounts his ancestors had ridden when they'd swept down from the Steppes into the Lower Danube region. Their drab, brown-and-dun-colored ponies lacked the size and muscle power of destriers that carried European knights into battle. Yet the Magyars had wreaked havoc for more than half a century throughout Italy, France, Germany and Spain before finally being defeated by the Holy Roman Emperor Otto I.

And like one of those tough little ponies, Dom thought with a slow curl in his belly, Ms. Clark needed taming. She might hide behind those glasses and shapeless dresses, but she had a temper on her when roused. Too bad he didn't have time to gentle her to his hand. The exercise would be a hell of a lot more interesting than the meetings he had lined up in Washington tomorrow. Still, he entertained himself for the rest of the cab ride with various techniques he might employ should he cross paths with Natalie Elizabeth Clark anytime in the near future.

He'd pretty much decided he would make that happen when Zia let him into the duchess's apartment.

"Back so soon?" she said, her eyes dancing. "Ms. Clark didn't succumb to your manly charms and topple into bed with you?"

The quip was so close to Dom's recent thoughts that he answered more brusquely than he'd intended. *"I didn't go to her hotel to seduce her."*

"No? That must be a first."

"Jézus, Mária és József! The mouth on you, Anastazia Amalia. I should have washed it with soap when I had the chance."

"Ha! You would never have been able to hold me down long enough. But come in, come in! Sarah's on FaceTime with her grandmother. I think you'll be interested in their conversation."

FaceTime? The duchess? Marveling at the willingness of a woman who'd been born in the decades between two great world wars to embrace the latest in technology, Dom followed his sister into the sitting room. One glance at the tableau corrected his impression of Charlotte's geekiness.

She sat upright and unbending in her customary chair, her cane close at hand. An iPad was perched on her knees, but she was obviously not comfortable with the device. Gina sat cross-legged on the floor beside her, holding the screen to the proper angle

Sarah's voice floated through the speaker and her elegant features filled most of the screen. Her husband's filled the rest.

"I'm so sorry, Grandmama. It just slipped out."

"What slipped out?" Dom murmured to Zia.

"You," his sister returned with that mischievous glint in her eyes.

"Me?"

"Shh! Just listen."

Frowning, Dom tuned back into the conversation.

"Alexis called with an offer to hype my book in *Beguile*," Sarah was saying. "She wanted to play up both angles." Her nose wrinkled. "My former job at the magazine and my title. You know how she is."

"Yes," the duchess drawled. "I do."

"I told Alexis the book wasn't ready for hype yet. Unfortunately, I also told her we're getting there much quicker since I'd hired such a clever research assistant. I bragged about the letter Natalie unearthed in the House of Parma archives, the one from Marie Antoinette to her sister describing the miniature of her painted by Le Brun that went missing when the mob sacked Versailles. And…" She heaved a sigh. "I made the fatal mistake of mentioning the codicil Nat had stumbled across while researching the Canaletto."

Although the fact that Dom's cousin had mentioned that damned codicil set his internal antennae to vibrating, it didn't appear to upset the duchess. Mention of the Canaletto had brought a faraway look to her eyes.

"Your grandfather bought me that painting of the Grand Canal," she murmured to Sarah. "Right after I became pregnant with your mother."

She lapsed into a private reverie that neither of her granddaughters dared break. When she emerged a few moments later, she included them both in a sly smile.

"That's where it happened. In Venice. We were supposed to attend a *carnival* ball at Ari Onassis's palazzo. I'd bought the most gorgeous mask studded with pearls and lace. But…how does that rather obnoxious TV commercial go? You never know when the mood will hit you? All I can say is something certainly hit your grandfather that evening."

Gina hooted in delight. "Way to go, Grandmama!"

Sarah laughed, and her husband issued a joking curse. "Damn! My wife suggested we hit the carnival in Venice this spring but I talked her into an African photo safari instead."

"You'll know to listen to her next time," the duchess sniffed, although Dom would bet she knew the moment could strike as hot and heavy in the African savannah as it had in Venice.

"I don't understand," Gina put in from her perch on the floor. "What's the big deal about telling Alexis about the codicil?"

"Well..." Red crept into Sarah's cheeks. "I'm afraid I mentioned Dominic, too."

The subject of the conversation muttered a curse, and Gina let out another whoop. "Ooh, boy! Your barracuda of an editor is gonna latch on to that with both jaws. I foresee another top-ten edition, this one listing the sexiest single royals of the male persuasion."

"I know," her sister said miserably. "It'll be as bad as what Dev went through after he came out on *Beguile*'s top-ten list. When you see Dominic tell him I'm so, so sorry."

"He's right here." Hooking a hand, Gina motioned him over. "Tell him yourself."

When Dominic positioned himself in front of the iPad's camera, Sarah sent him a look of heartfelt apology. "I'm so sorry, Dom. I made Alexis promise she wouldn't go crazy with this, but..."

"But you'd better brace yourself, buddy," her husband put in from behind her shoulder. "Your life's about to get really, really complicated."

"I can handle it," Dom replied with more confidence than he was feeling at the moment.

"You think so, huh?" Dev returned with a snort. "Wait

till women start trying to stuff their phone number in your pants pocket and reporters shove mics and cameras in your face."

The first prospect hadn't sounded all that repulsive to Dom. The second he deemed highly unlikely…right up until he stepped out of a cab for his scheduled meeting at Washington's Interpol office the following afternoon and was blindsided by the pack of reporters, salivating at the scent of fresh blood.

"Your Highness! Over here!"

"Grand Duke!"

"Hey! Your lordship!"

Shaking his head at Americans' fixation on any and all things royal, he shielded his face with his hands like some damned criminal and pushed through the ravenous newshounds.

Three

Two weeks later Dominic was in a vicious mood. He had been since a dozen different American and European tabloids had splashed his face across their front pages, trumpeting the emergence of a long-lost Grand Duke.

When the stories hit, he'd expected the summons to Interpol Headquarters. He'd even anticipated his boss's suggestion that he take some of the unused vacation time he'd piled up over the years and lie low until the hoopla died down. He'd anticipated it, yes, but did *not* like being yanked off undercover duty and sent home to Budapest to twiddle his thumbs. And every time he thought the noise was finally dying down, his face popped up in another rag.

The firestorm of publicity had impacted his personal life, as well. Although Sarah's husband had tried to warn him, Dom had underestimated the reaction to his supposed royalty among the females of his acquaintance. The phone number he gave out to non-Interpol contacts had suddenly become very busy. Some of the callers were friends, some were former lovers. But many were strangers who'd wrangled the number out of *their* friends and weren't shy about wanting to get to know the new duke on a very personal level.

He'd turned most of them off with a laugh, a few of the more obnoxious with a curt suggestion they get a life. But one had sounded so funny and sexy over the phone that he'd arranged to meet her at a coffee bar. She turned out to be a tall, luscious brunette, as bright and engaging in person as she was over the phone. Dom was more than ready to agree with her suggestion they get a second cup to go and down it at her apartment or his loft. Before he could put in the order, though, she asked the waiter to take their picture with her cell phone. Damned if she hadn't zinged it off by email right there at the table. Just to a few friends, she explained with a smile. One, he discovered when yet another story hit the newsstands, just happened to be a reporter for a local tabloid.

In addition to the attention from strangers, the barrage of unwanted publicity seemed to make even his friends and associates view him through a different prism. To most of them he wasn't Dominic St. Sebastian anymore. He was Dominic, Grand Duke of a duchy that had ceased to exist a half century ago, for God's sake.

So he wasn't real happy when someone hammered on the door of his loft apartment on a cool September evening. Especially when the hammering spurred a chorus of ferocious barking from the hound who'd followed Dom home a year ago and decided to take up residence.

"Quiet!"

A useless command, since the dog considered announcing his presence to any and all visitors a sacred duty. Bred originally to chase down swiftly moving prey like deer and wolves, the Magyar Agár was as lean and fast as a greyhound. Dom had negotiated an agreement with his downstairs neighbors to dog-sit while he was on assignment, but man and beast had rebonded during this enforced vacation. Or at least the hound had. Dom had yet to reconcile himself to sharing his Gold Fassl with the pilsner-guzzling pooch.

"This better not be some damned reporter," he muttered as he kneed the still-barking hound aside and checked the spy hole. The special lens he'd had installed gave a

180-degree view of the landing outside his loft. The small area was occupied by two uniformed police officers and a bedraggled female Dom didn't recognize until he opened the door.

"Mi a fene!" he swore in Hungarian, then switched quickly to English. "Natalie! What happened to you?"

She didn't answer, being too preoccupied at the moment with the dog trying to shove his nose into her crotch. Dom swore again, got a grip on its collar and dislodged the nose, but he still didn't get a reply. She merely stared at him with a frown creasing her forehead and her hair straggling in limp tangles around her face.

"Are you Dominic St. Sebastian?" one of the police officers asked.

"Yes."

"Aka the Grand Duke?"

He made an impatient noise and kept his grip on the dog's collar. "Yes."

The second officer, whose nametag identified him as Gradjnic, glanced down at a newspaper folded to a grainy picture of Dom and the brunette at the coffee shop. "Looks like him," he volunteered.

His partner gestured to Natalie. "And you know this woman?"

"I do." Dom's glance raked the researcher, from her tangled hair to her torn jacket to what looked like a pair of men's sneakers several sizes too large for her. "What the devil happened to you?"

"Maybe we'd better come in," Gradjnic suggested.

"Yes, yes, of course."

The officers escorted Natalie inside, and Dom shut the dog in the bathroom before joining them. The Agár whined and scratched at the door but soon nosed out the giant chew-bones Dom stored in the hamper for emergencies like this.

Aside from the small bathroom, the loft consisted of a single, barn-like attic area that had once stored artifacts belonging to the Ethnological Museum. When the museum moved to new digs, their old building was converted to condos. Zia had just nailed a full scholarship to medical school, so Dom had decided to sink his savings into this loft apartment in the pricy Castle Hill district on the Buda side of the river. He'd then proceeded to sand and varnish the oak-plank floors to a high gloss. He'd also knocked out a section of the sloping roof and opened up a view of the Danube that usually had guests gasping.

Tonight's visitors were no exception. All three gawked at the floodlit spires, towering dome, flying buttresses and stained-glass windows of the Parliament Building across the river. Equally elaborate structures flanked the massive building, while the usual complement of river barges and brightly lit tour boats cruised by almost at its steps.

Ruthlessly, Dom cut into their viewing time. "Please sit down, all of you, then someone needs to tell me what this is all about."

"It's about this woman," Gradjnic said in heavily accented English when everyone had found a place to perch. He tugged a small black notebook from his shirt pocket. "What did you say her name was?"

Dom's glance shot to Natalie. "You didn't tell them your name?"

"I...I don't remember it."

"What?"

Her frown deepened. "I don't remember anything."

"Except the Grand Duke," Officer Gradjnic put in drily.

"Wait," Dom ordered. "Back up and start at the beginning."

Nodding, the policeman flipped through his notebook. "The beginning for us was 10:32 a.m. today, when dispatch called to report bystanders had fished a woman out of the

Danube. We responded, found this young lady sitting on the bank with her rescuers. She had no shoes, no purse, no cell phone, no ID of any kind and no memory of how she ended up in the river. When we asked her name or the name of a friend or relative here in Budapest, all she could tell us was 'the Grand Duke.'"

"Jesus!"

"She has a lump the size of a goose egg at the base of her skull, under her hair."

When Dom's gaze shot to Natalie again, she raised a tentative hand to the back of her neck. "More like a pigeon's egg," she corrected with a frown.

"Yes, well, the lump suggests she may have fallen off a bridge or a tour boat and hit her head on the way down, although none of the tour companies have reported a missing passenger. We had the EMTs take her to the hospital. The doctors found no sign of serious injury or concussion."

"No blurred vision?" Dom asked sharply. He'd taken—and delivered—enough blows to the head to know the warning signs. "No nausea or vomiting or balance problems?"

"Only the memory loss. The doctor said it's not all that unusual with that kind of trauma. Since we had no other place to take her, it was either leave her at the hospital or bring her to the only person she seems to know in Budapest—the Grand Duke."

Hit by a wicked sense of irony, Dom remembered those quivering nostrils and flickers of disdain. He suspected Ms. Clark would rather have been left at a dog pound than delivered to him.

"I'll take care of her," he promised, "but she must have a hotel room somewhere in the city."

"If she does, we'll let you know." Gradjnic flipped to an empty page and poised his pen. "Now what did you say her name was?"

"Natalie. Natalie Clark."

"American, we guessed from her accent."

"That's right."

"And she works for your cousin?"

"Yes, as research assistant." Angling around, Dom tried a tentative probe. "Natalie, you were supposed to meet with Sarah sometime this week. In Paris, right?"

"Sarah?"

"My cousin. Sarah St. Sebastian Hunter."

Her first response was a blank stare. Her second startled all three men.

"My head hurts." Scowling, she pushed out of her chair. "I'm tired. And these clothes stink."

With that terse announcement, she headed for the unmade bed at the far end of the loft. She kicked off the sneakers as she went. Dom lurched to his feet as she peeled out of the torn jacket.

"Hold on a minute!"

"I'm tired," she repeated. "I need sleep."

Shaking off his restraining hand, she flopped facedown across the bed. The three men watched with varying expressions of surprise and resignation as she buried her face in the pillow.

Gradjnic broke the small silence that followed. "Well, I guess that does it for us here. Now that we have her name, we'll trace Ms. Clark's entry into the country and her movements in Hungary as best we can. We'll also find out if she's registered at a hotel. And you'll call us when and if she remembers why she took that dive into the Danube, right?"

"Right."

The sound of their departure diverted the Agár's attention from the chew-bone he'd dug out of the hamper. To quiet his whining, Dom let him out of the bathroom but kept a close watch while he sniffed out the stranger sprawled sideways across the bed. Apparently deciding she posed no threat, the dog padded back to the living area and stretched out in front of the window to watch the brightly lit boats cruising up and down the river.

Dom had his phone in hand before the hound's speckled pink belly hit the planks. Five rings later, his sleepy-sounding cousin answered.

"Hullowhozzis?"

"It's Dom, Sarah."

"Dom?"

"Where are you?"

"We're in…uh…Dalian. China," she added, sounding more awake…and suddenly alarmed by a call in what had to be the middle of the night on the other side of the globe. "Is everyone okay? Grandmama? Gina? Zia? Oh, God! Is it one of the twins?"

"They're all fine, Sarah. But I can't say the same for your research assistant."

He heard a swift rustle of sheets. A headboard creaking.

"Dev! Wake up! Dom says something's happened to Natalie!"

"I'm awake."

"Tell me," Sarah demanded.

"The best guess is she fell off a bridge or a cruise boat. They fished her out of the river early this morning."

"Is she…? Is she dead?"

"No, but she's got a good-size lump at the base of her skull and she doesn't remember anything. Not even her name."

"Good Lord!" The sheets rustled again. "Natalie's been hurt, Dev. Would you contact your crew and have them prep the Gulfstream? I need to fly back to Paris right away."

"She's not in Paris," Dom interjected. "She's with me, in Budapest."

"In Budapest? But…how? Why?"

"I was hoping you could tell me."

"She didn't say anything about Hungary when we got together in Paris last week. Only that she might drive down to Vienna again, to do more research on the Canaletto." A note of accusation slipped through Sarah's concern. "She was also going to dig a little more on the codicil. Something you said about it seemed to have bothered her."

He'd said a lot about it, none of which he intended to go into at the moment. "So you don't know why she's here in Hungary?"

"I have no clue. Is she there with you now? Let me speak to her."

He flicked a glance at the woman sprawled across his bed. "She's zoned out, Sarah. Said she was tired and just flopped into bed."

"This memory thing? Will she be all right?"

"Like you, I have no clue. But you'd better contact her family just in case."

"She doesn't have any family."

"She's got to have someone. Grandparents? An uncle or aunt stashed away somewhere?"

"She doesn't," Sarah insisted. "Dev ran a detailed background check before I hired her. Natalie doesn't know who her parents are or why she was abandoned as an infant. She lived with a series of foster families until she checked herself out of the system at age eighteen and entered the University of Michigan on full scholarship."

That certainly put a different spin on the basic age-height-DOB info he'd gathered.

"I'll fly to Budapest immediately," Sarah was saying, "and take Natalie home with me until she recovers her memory."

Dom speared another glance at the researcher. His gut

told him he'd live to regret the suggestion he was about to make.

"Why don't you hang loose for now? Could be she'll be fine when she wakes up tomorrow. I'll call you then."

"I don't know..."

"I'll call you, Sarah. As soon as she wakes up."

When she reluctantly agreed, he cut the connection and stood with the phone in hand for several moments. He'd worked undercover too long to take anything at face value...especially a woman fished out of the Danube who had no reason to be in Budapest that anyone knew. Thumbing the phone, he tapped in a number. His contact at Interpol answered on the second ring.

"Oui?"

"It's Dom," he replied in swift, idiomatic French. "Remember the query you ran for me two weeks ago on Natalie Clark?"

"Oui."

"I need you to dig deeper."

"Oui."

The call completed, he contemplated his unexpected houseguest for a few moments. Her rumpled skirt had twisted around her calves and her buttoned-to-the-neck blouse looked as though it was choking her. After a brief inner debate, Dom rolled her over. He had the blouse unfastened and was easing it off when she opened her eyes to a groggy squint and mumbled at him.

"Whatryoudoin?"

"Making you comfortable."

"Mmm."

She was asleep again before he got her out of her blouse and skirt. Her panties were plain, unadorned white cotton but, Dom discovered, covered slender hips and a nice, trim butt. Nobly, he resisted the urge to remove her underwear and merely tucked the sheets around her. That done, he popped the cap on a bottle of a pilsner for himself, opened another for the hound and settled in for an all-night vigil.

He rolled her over again just after midnight and pried up a lid. She gave a bad-tempered grunt and batted his hand away, but not before he saw her pupil dilate and refract with reassuring swiftness.

He woke her again two hours later. “Natalie. Can you hear me?”

“Go away.”

He did a final check just before dawn. Then he stretched out on the leather sofa and watched the dark night shade to gold and pink.

Something wet and cold prodded her elbow. Her shoulder. Her chin. She didn’t come awake, though, until a strap of rough leather rasped across her cheek. She blinked fuzzily, registered the hazy thought that she was in bed, and opened her eyes.

“Yikes!”

A glistening pink mouth loomed only inches from her eyes. Its black gums were pulled back and a long tongue dangled through a set of nasty-looking incisors. As if in answer to her startled yip, the gaping mouth emitted a blast of powerful breath and an ear-ringing bark.

She scurried back like a poked crab, heart thumping and sheets tangling. A few feet of separation gave her a better perspective. Enough to see the merry eyes above an elongated muzzle, a broad forehead topped with one brown ear and one white, and a long, lean body with a wildly whipping tail.

Evidently the dog mistook her retreat for the notion that she was making space for him in the bed. With another loud woof, he landed on the mattress. The tongue went to work again, slathering her cheeks and chin before she could hold him off.

"Whoa! Stop!" His joy was contagious and as impossible to contain as his ecstatically wriggling body. Laughing now, she finally got him by the shoulders. "Okay, okay, I like you, too! But enough with the tongue."

He got in another slurp before he let her roll him onto his back, where he promptly stuck all four legs into the air and begged for a tickle. She complied and raised quivers of ecstasy on his short-haired ribs and speckled pink-and-brown belly.

"You're a handsome fellow," she murmured, admiring his sleek lines as her busy fingers set his legs to pumping. "Wonder what your name is?"

"He doesn't have one."

The response came from behind her. Twisting on the bed, she swept her startled gaze across a huge, sparsely furnished area. A series of overhead beams topped with A-frame wooden trusses suggested it was an attic. A stunningly renovated attic, with gleaming oak floors and modern lighting.

There were no interior walls, only a curved, waist-high counter made of glass blocks that partitioned off a kitchen area. The male behind the counter looked at home there. Dark-haired and dark-eyed, he wore a soccer shirt of brilliant red-and-black stripes with some team logo she didn't recognize emblazoned on one breast. The stretchy fabric molded his broad, muscular shoulders. The wavy glass blocks gave an indistinct view of equally muscular thighs encased in running shorts.

She watched him, her hand now stilled on the dog's belly, while he flicked the switch on a stainless-steel espresso machine. Almost instantly the machine hissed out thick, black liquid. Her eyes never left him as he filled two cups and rounded the glass-block counter.

When he crossed the huge room, the dog scrambled to sit up at his approach. So did she, tugging the sheet up with her. For some reason she couldn't quite grasp, she'd slept in her underwear.

He issued an order in a language she didn't understand. When he repeated it in a firmer voice, the dog jumped off the bed with obvious reluctance.

"How do you feel?"

"I…uh… Okay."

"Head hurt?"

She tried a tentative neck roll. "I don't… Ooh!"

Wincing, she fingered the lump at the base of her skull.

"What happened?"

"Best guess is you fell off a bridge or tour boat and hit your head. Want some aspirin?"

"God, yes!"

He handed her one of the cups and crossed to what she guessed was a bathroom tucked under one of the eaves. She used his brief absence to let her gaze sweep the cavernous room again, looking for something, *anything* familiar.

Panic crawled like tiny ants down her spine when she finally accepted that she was sitting cross-legged on an unmade bed. In a strange apartment. With a hound lolling a few feet away, grinning from ear to ear and looking all too ready to jump back in with her.

Her hands shaking, she lifted the china cup. The rim rattled against her teeth and the froth coated her upper lip as she took a tentative sip.

"Ugh!"

Her first impulse was to spit the incredibly strong espresso back into the cup. Politeness—and the cool, watchful eyes of the bearer of aspirin—forced her to swallow.

"Better take these with water."

Gratefully, she traded the cup for a glass. She was

reaching for the two small white pills in his palm when she suddenly froze. Her heart slamming against her chest, she stared down at the pills.

Oh, God! Had she been drugged? Did he intend to knock her out again?

A faint thread of common sense tried to push through her balled-up nerves. If he wanted to drug her, he could just as easily have put something in her coffee. Still, she pulled her hand back.

"I…I better not. I, uh, may be allergic."

"You're not wearing a medical alert bracelet."

"I'm not wearing much of anything."

"True."

He set the pills and her cup on a low bookshelf that doubled as a nightstand. She clutched the water glass, looked at him, at the grinning dog, at the rumpled sheets, back at him. Ants started down her spine again.

"Okay," she said on a low, shaky breath, "who *are* you?

Four

"I'm Dominic. Dominic St. Sebastian. Dom to my friends and family."

He kept his eyes on her, watching for the tiniest flicker of recognition. If she was faking that blank stare, she was damned good at it.

"I'm Sarah's cousin," he added.

Nothing. Not a blink. Not a frown.

"Sarah St. Sebastian Hunter?" He waited a beat, then decided to go for the big guns. "She's the granddaughter of Charlotte, Grand Duchess of Karlenburgh."

"Karlenburgh?"

"You were researching a document pertaining to Karlenburgh. One with a special codicil."

He thought for a moment he'd struck a chord. Her brows drew together, and her lips bunched in an all-too-familiar moue. Then she blew out a breath and scooted to the edge of the bed, pulling the sheet with her.

"I don't know you, or your cousin, or her grandmother. Now, if you don't mind, I'd like to get dressed and be on my way."

"On your way to where?"

That brought her up short.

"I...I don't know." She blinked, obviously coming up empty. "Where...? Where am I?"

"Maybe this will help."

Dom went to the window and drew the drapes. Morning light flooded the loft. With it came the eagle's-eye view of the Danube and the Parliament's iconic red dome and forest of spires.

"Ooooh!" Wrapping the sheet around her like a sari, she stepped to the glass wall. "How glorious!"

"Do you recognize the building?"

"Sort of. Maybe."

She sounded anything but sure. And, Dom noted, she didn't squint or strain as she studied the elaborate structure across the river. Apparently she only needed her glasses for reading or close work. Yet…she'd worn them during both their previous meetings. Almost like a shield.

"I give up." She turned to him, those delicate nostrils quivering and panic clouding her eyes. "Where *am* I?"

"Budapest"

"Hungary?"

He started to ask if there was a city with that same name in another country but the panic had started to spill over into tears. Although she tried valiantly to gulp them back, she looked so frightened and fragile that Dom had to take her in his arms.

The sobs came then. Big, noisy gulps that brought the Agár leaping to all fours. His ears went flat and his long, narrow tail whipped out, as though he sensed an enemy but wasn't sure where to point.

"It's all right," Dom said, as much to the dog as the woman in his arms. She smelled of the river, he thought as he stroked her hair. The river and diesel spill and soft, trembling female still warm from his bed. So different from the stiff, disdainful woman who'd ordered him out of her New York hotel room that his voice dropped to a husky murmur.

"It's all right."

"No, it's not!"

The tears gushed now, soaking through his soccer shirt and making the dog whine nervously. His claws clicked on the oak planking as he circled Dom and the woman clinging to his shirt with one hand and the sheet with her other.

"I don't understand any of this! Why can't I remember where I am? Why can't I remember *you*?" She jerked back against his arm and stared up at him. "Are we…? Are we married?"

"No."

Her glance shot to the bed. "Lovers?"

He let that hang for a few seconds before treating her to a slow smile.

"Not yet."

Guilt pricked at him then. Her eyes were so huge and frightened, her nose red and sniffling. Gentling his voice, he brushed a thumb across her cheek to wipe the tears.

"Do you remember the police bringing you here last night?"

"I…I think so."

"They took you to a hospital first. Remember?"

Her forehead wrinkled. "Now I do."

"A doctor examined you. He told the police that short-term memory loss isn't unusual with a head injury."

She jumped on that. "How short?"

"I don't know, *drágám*."

"Is that my name? *Drágám*?"

"No, that's a nickname. An endearment, like 'sweetheart' or 'darling.' Very casual here in Hungary," he added when her eyes got worried again. "Your name is Natalie. Natalie Elizabeth Clark."

"Natalie." She rolled it around in her head, on her tongue. "Not a name I would pick for myself," she said with a sniffle, "but I guess it'll do."

The brown-and-white hound poked at her knee then, as if demanding reassurance that all was well. Natalie eased out of Dom's arms and knuckled the dog's broad, intelligent forehead.

"And who's this guy?"

"I call him *kutya*. It means 'dog' in Hungarian."

Her eyes lifted to his, still watery but accusing. "You just call him 'dog'?"

"He followed me home one night and decided to take up residence. I thought it would be a temporary arrangement, so we never got around to a baptismal ceremony."

"So he's a stray," she murmured, her voice thickening. "Like me."

Dom knew he'd better act fast to head off another storm of tears. "Stray or not," he said briskly, "he needs to go out. Why don't you shower and finish your coffee while I take him for his morning run? I'll pick up some apple pancakes for breakfast while I'm out, yes? Then we'll talk about what to do next."

When she hesitated, her mouth trembling, he curled a knuckle under her chin and tipped her face to his. "We'll work this out, Natalie. Let's just take it one step at a time."

She bit her lip and managed a small nod.

"Your clothes are in the bathroom," Dom told her. "I rinsed them out last night, but they're probably still damp." He nodded to the double-doored wardrobe positioned close to the bath. "Help yourself to whatever you can find to fit you."

She nodded again and hitched the sheet higher to keep from tripping over it as she padded to the bathroom. Dom waited until he heard the shower kick on before dropping into a chair to pull on socks and his well-worn running shoes.

He hoped to hell he wasn't making a mistake leaving her alone. Short of locking her in, though, he didn't see how he could confine her here against her will. Besides which, they needed to eat and Dog needed to go out. A point the hound drove home by retrieving his leash from its hook by the door and waiting with an expression of acute impatience.

Natalie. Natalie Elizabeth Clark.

Why didn't it feel right? Sound right?

She wrapped her freshly shampooed hair in a towel and stared at the steamed-up bathroom mirror. The image it reflected was as foggy as her mind.

She'd stood under the shower's hot, driving needles and tried to figure out what in the world she was doing in Budapest. It couldn't be her home. She didn't know a word of Hungarian. Correction. She knew two. *Kutya* and… What had he called her? *Dragon* or something.

Dominic. His name was Dominic. It fit him, she thought with a grimace, much better than Natalie did her. Those muscled shoulders, the strong arms, the chest she'd sobbed against, all hinted at power and virility and, yes, dominance.

Especially in bed. The thought slipped in, got caught in her mind. He'd said they weren't lovers. Implied she'd slept alone. Yet heat danced in her belly at the thought of lying beneath him and feeling his hands on her breasts, his mouth on her…

Oh, God! The panic came screaming back. She breathed in. Out. In. Then set her jaw and glared at the face in the mirror.

"No more crying! It didn't help before! It won't help now."

She snatched up a dry washcloth and had started to scrub the fogged glass when she caught the echo of her words. Her fist closed around the cloth, and her chest squeezed.

"Crying didn't help before *what*?"

Like the steam still drifting from the shower stall,

the mists in her mind seemed to curl. Shift. Become less opaque. Something was there, just behind the thin gray curtain. She could almost see it. Almost smell it. She spun around and hacked out a sound halfway between a sob and a laugh.

She could smell it, all right. The musty odor emanated from the wrinkled items hanging from hooks on the door. The steam from the hot shower must have released the river stink.

Her nose wrinkling, she fingered the shapeless jacket, the unadorned blouse, the mess that must once have been a skirt. Good grief! Were these really her clothes? They looked like they'd come from a Goodwill grab bag. The bra and panties she'd discarded before getting in the shower were even worse.

He—Dominic—said he'd rinsed her things out. He should have tossed them in a garbage sack and hauled them to a dumpster.

"Well," she said with a shrug, "he told me to help myself."

The helping included using his comb to work the tangles from her wet hair and squirting a length of his toothpaste onto her forefinger to scrub her teeth. It also included poking her head through the bathroom door to make sure he was still gone before she raided his closet.

It was a European-style wardrobe, with mirror double doors and beautiful carving. The modern evolution of the special room in a castle where nobles stored their robes in carved wooden chests. Called an armoire in French, a shrunk in German, this particular wardrobe wasn't as elaborate as some she'd seen but…

Wait! How did she know about castles and nobles and shrunks? What other, more elaborate armoires had she seen? She stared at the hunting scene above the doors, feeling as though she was straining every brain cell she possessed through a sieve, and came up empty.

"Dammit!"

Angry and more than a little scared, she yanked open the left door. Suits and dress shirts hung haphazardly from the rod, while an assortment of jeans, T-shirts and sporting gear spilled from the shelves below. She plucked out a soccer shirt, this one with royal-blue and white stripes but with the same green-and-gold emblem on the right sleeve. The cool, slick material slithered over her hips. The hem hung almost to her knees.

Curiosity prompted her to open the right door. This side was all drawers. The top drawer contained unmatched socks, tangled belts, loose change and a flashlight.

The middle drawer was locked. Securely locked, with a gleaming steel mechanism that didn't give a hair when she tested it.

She slid the third drawer out and eyed the jumble of jock straps, Speedos and boxers. She thought about appropriating a Speedo but couldn't quite bring herself to climb into his underwear.

"Not the neatest guy in the world, are you?" she commented to the absent Dominic.

She started to close the drawer, intending to go back to the bathroom and give her panties a good scrubbing, when she caught a glimpse of delicate black lace amid boxers.

Oh, Lord! Was he into kink? Cross-dressing? Transgender sex play? Did that locked drawer contain whips and handcuffs and ball gags?

She gulped, remembering her earlier thought about strength and power and dominance, and used the tip of a finger to extract a pair of lace-trimmed silk hipsters. A new and very expensive pair of hipsters judging by the embossed tag still dangling from the band. Natalie's eyes widened when she saw the hand-lettered price.

Good grief! Three hundred pounds? Could that be right?

When she recovered from sticker shock, she found it interesting that the price was displayed in British pounds and not in Hungarian…Hungarian whatever. Also interesting, the light-as-air scrap of silk had evidently been crafted by an "atelier" who described her collection as feminine and ethereal, each piece a limited edition made to measure for the client. The matching garter belt and triangle bra, the tag advised, would put the cost for the complete ensemble at just over a thousand pounds.

Well, she thought with a low whistle, if he was into kink, he certainly did it up right. She was about to stuff the panties back in the drawer when she noticed handwriting on the back of the tag.

I stuck these in your suitcase so you'll know what I won't be wearing next time you're in London.
Kiss, kiss, Arabella.

Oh, yuck! Her lip curling, she started to stuff the hipsters back in the drawer. Common sense and a bare butt made her hesitate several seconds too long. She still had the panties in hand when the front door opened and the hound burst in. Sweat darkened the honey-brown patches on the dog's coat. Similar damp splotches stained Dominic's soccer shirt.

"Find everything you need?" he asked as he dropped a leash and a white paper sack on the kitchen counter.

"Almost everything." She lifted her hand. The scrap of silk and lace dangled from her forefinger. "Do you think Arabella will mind if I borrow her knickers?"

"Who?"

"Arabella. London. Kiss, kiss."

"Oh. Right. That Arabella." He eyed the gossamer silk

with a waggle of his brow. "Very nice. Where'd you find them?"

"In with your socks," she drawled. "There's a note on the back of the tag."

He flipped the tag over and skimmed the handwriting. She could smell the sharp tang of his sweat, see the bristles darkening his cheeks and chin. See, too, the smile that played at the corners of his mouth. He managed to keep it from sliding into a full grin as he handed back the panties.

"I'm sure Arabella wouldn't mind you borrowing them," he said solemnly.

But *he* would. The realization hit Dom even before she whirled and the hem of his soccer shirt flared just high enough to give him a glimpse of her nicely curved butt.

"That might have been a mistake," he told the hound when the bathroom door shut. "Now I'm going to be imagining her in black silk all day."

The Agár cocked his head. The brown ear came up, the white ear folded over, and he looked as though he was giving the matter serious consideration.

"She's fragile," Dom reminded the dog sternly. "Confused and frightened and probably still hurting from her dive into the Danube. So you refrain from slobbering all over her front and I'll keep my mind off her rear."

Easier said than done he discovered when she reemerged. She wore a cool expression, the blue crew shirt and, as Dom could all-too-easily visualize, a band of black silk around her slender hips.

And here he'd thought her nondescript back in New York. She certainly looked different with her face flushed and rosy from the shower and her damp hair showing streaks of rich, dark chestnut. The oversize glasses had dominated her face in New York, distracting from those cinnamon-brown eyes and the short, straight nose. And, he remembered, her full lips had been set in such thin, disapproving lines for most of their brief acquaintance. They were close to that now but still looked very kissable.

Not that he should be thinking about her eyes or her lips or the length of bare leg visible below the hem of his shirt. She's vulnerable, he had to remember. Confused.

"I bought some apple pancakes from my favorite street seller," he told her, indicating the white sack on the counter. "They're good cold, if you're hungry now, but better when crisped a bit in the oven. Help yourself while I take my turn in the shower."

"I'll warm them up."

Rounding the glass counter, she stooped to study the knobs on the stovetop. The soccer shirt rode up again. Barely an inch. Two at the most. All it showed were the backs of her thighs, but Dom had to swallow a groan as he grabbed a pair of jeans and a clean shirt and hit the bathroom.

He didn't take long. A hot, stinging shower and a quick shampoo. He scraped a palm over his three or four days' worth of bristles, but a shave lost out to the seductive scent of warm apples.

She was perched on one of the counter stools, laughing at the shivering bundle of ecstasy hunkered between her bare legs. "No, you idiot! Don't give me that silly grin. I'm not feeding you another bite."

She glanced up, her face still alight, and spotted Dom. The laughter faded instantly. He felt the loss like a hard right jab to the solar plexus.

Jézus, Mária és József! Did she dislike all men, or just him? He couldn't tell but sure as hell intended to find out.

The woman represented so many mysteries. There was the disdain she'd treated him to in New York. That ridiculous codicil. The memory loss. The yet-to-be-explained reason she was here in his loft, swathed in his soccer shirt. Dom couldn't remember when a woman had challenged him in so many ways. He was about to tell her so when the cell phone he'd left on the counter buzzed.

"It's Sarah," he said after a quick glance at the face that came up on the screen. "My cousin and your boss. Do you want to talk to her?"

"I...uh... All right."

He accepted the FaceTime call and gave his anxious cousin the promised update. "Natalie's still here with me. Physically she seems okay but no progress yet on recovering her memory. Here, I'll put her on."

He positioned the phone so the screen captured Natalie still seated on the high stool. Both he and Sarah could see the desperate hope and crushing disappointment that chased across the researcher's features as she stared at the face on the screen.

"Oh, Nat," Sarah said with a tremulous smile, "I'm so, so sorry to hear you've been hurt."

Her hand crept to her nape. "Thank you."

"Dev and I will fly to Budapest today and take you home."

Uncertainty flooded her eyes. "Dev?"

Sarah swallowed. "Devon Hunter. My husband."

The name didn't appear to register, which caused Natalie such obvious dismay that Dom intervened. Leaning close, he spoke into the camera.

"Why don't you and Dev hold off for a while, Sarah? We haven't spoken to the police yet this morning. They were going to trace Natalie's movements in Hungary and might have some information for us. Also, they might have found her purse or briefcase. If not, we'll need to go to the American Embassy and get a replacement passport before she can leave the country. That could take a few days."

"But..."

Sarah struggled to mask her concern. Dom guessed she felt personally responsible for her assistant being hurt and stranded in a foreign country.

"Are you good with remaining in Hungary a little while yet, Nat?"

"I..." She looked from the screen to Dom to the hound, who now sat with his head plopped on her knee. "Yes."

"Would you feel better staying at a hotel? I can make a reservation in your name today."

Once again Dom felt compelled to intercede. Natalie was in no condition to be left on her own. Assuming, of course, her memory loss was real. He had no reason to believe otherwise but the cop in him went too deep to take anyone or anything at face value.

"Let's leave that for now, too," he told Sarah. "As I said, we need to talk to the police and start the paperwork for a replacement passport if necessary. While we're working things at this end, you could make some inquiries back in the States. Talk to the duchess and Zia and Gina. Maybe the editor you're working with on your book. Find out if anyone's called inquiring about Natalie or her research. It might help jog her memory if we can discover what brought her to Budapest from Vienna."

"Of course. I'll do that today." She hesitated, clearly distressed for her assistant. "You'll need money, Natalie. I'll arrange a draft... No, we'd better make it cash since you don't have any ID. I'll have it delivered to Dom's address this afternoon. Just an advance on your salary," she added quickly when Natalie looked as though she'd been offered charity.

Dom considered telling his cousin that the money could wait, too. He was more than capable of covering his unexpected guest's expenses. More to the point, it might be better to keep her dependent on him until they sorted out her situation. On reflection, though, he decided the leash was short enough.

The brief conversation left Natalie silent for several long moments. She scratched the hound's head, obviously dismayed over not recognizing the woman she worked for and with. Dom moved quickly to head off another possible panic attack.

"Okay, here's today's agenda," he said with brisk cheerfulness. "First, we finish breakfast. Second, we hit the shops to buy you some shoes and whatever else you need. Third, we visit police headquarters to find out what, if anything, they've learned. We also get a copy of their incident report and contact the embassy to begin the paperwork for a replacement passport. Finally, and most important, we arrange a follow-up with the doctor you saw yesterday. Or better yet, with a specialist who has some expertise dealing with amnesia cases."

"Sounds good to me," she said, relief at having a concrete plan of action edging aside the dismay. "But do you really think we can swing an appointment with a specialist anytime soon? Or even find one with expertise in amnesia?"

"I've got a friend I can call."

He didn't tell her that his "friend" was the internationally renowned forensic pathologist who'd autopsied the victims of a particularly savage drug cartel last year. Dom had witnessed each autopsy, groaning at the doc's morbid sense of humor as he collected the evidence Interpol needed to take down key members of the cartel.

He made the call while Natalie conducted another raid on his wardrobe. By the time she'd dug out a pair of Dom's flip-flops and running shorts with a drawstring waist, one of Budapest's foremost neurologists had agreed to squeeze her in at 11:20 a.m.

Five

The short-notice appointment with the neurologist necessitated a quick change in the day's agenda. Almost before Natalie had downed her last bite of apple pancake, Dom hustled her to the door of the loft and down five flights of stairs to the underground garage.

It'd been dark when she'd arrived the previous evening, so she'd caught only glimpses of the castle dominating the hill on the Buda of the river. The bright light of morning showed the royal palace in its full glory.

"Oh, look!" Her glance snagged on the bronze warrior atop a muscled warhorse that guarded the entrance to the castle complex. "That's Prince Eugene of Savoy, isn't it?"

Dominic slanted her a quick look. "You know about *Priz Eugen*?"

"Of course." She twisted in her seat to keep the statue in view as they negotiated the narrow, curving streets that would take them down to the Danube. "He was one of the greatest military leaders of the seventeenth century. As I recall, he served three different Holy Roman Emperors and won a decisive victory against the Ottoman Turks in 1697 at..."

She broke off, her eyes rounding. "Why do I know that?"

She sank back against her seat and stared through the windshield at the tree-dappled street ahead. Dom said nothing while she struggled to jam together the pieces of the puzzle.

"Why do I know the Hapsburgs built this palace on the site of the Gothic castle originally constructed by an earlier Holy Roman Emperor? Why do I know it was reconstructed after being razed to the ground during World War II?" Her fists bunched, drummed her thighs. "Why can I pull those details out of my head and not know who I am or how I ended up in the river?"

"Recalling those details has to be a good sign. Maybe it means you'll start to remember other things, as well."

"God, I hope so!"

Her fists stayed tight through the remainder of the descent from Castle Hill and across the majestic Chain Bridge linking Buda and Pest.

Their first stop was a small boutique, where Natalie traded Dom's drawstring shorts, soccer shirt and flip-flops for sandals, slim designer jeans, a cap-sleeved tank in soft peach and a straw tote. A second stop garnered a few basic toiletries. Promising to shop for other necessities later, Dom hustled her back to the car for her appointment with Dr. Andras Kovacs.

The neurologist's suite of offices occupied the second floor of a gracious nineteenth-century town house in the shadow of St. Stephen's Basilica. The gray-haired receptionist in the outer office confirmed Natalie's short-notice appointment, but showed more interest in her escort than the patient herself.

"I read about you in the paper," she exclaimed to Dom in Hungarian. "Aren't you the Grand Duke of…of…something?"

Swallowing a groan, he nodded. "Of Karlenburgh, but the title is an empty one. The duchy doesn't exist any longer."

"Still, it must be very exciting to suddenly find yourself a duke."

"Yes, very. Is Dr. Kovacs running on time for his appointments?"

"He is." She beamed. "Please have a seat, Your Highness, and I'll let his assistant know you and Ms. Clark are here."

When he led Natalie to a set of tall wingback chairs, she sent him a quick frown. "What was all that about?"

"She was telling me about a story she'd read in the paper."

"I heard her say 'Karlenburgh.'"

He eyed her closely. "Do you recognize that name?"

"You mentioned it this morning. I thought for a moment I knew it." Still frowning, she scrubbed her forehead with the heel of her hand. "It's all here, somewhere in my head. That name. That place. You."

Her eyes lifted to his. She looked so accusing, he had to smile.

"I can think of worse places to be than in your head, *drágám*."

He wasn't sure whether it was the lazy smile or the casual endearment or the husky note to his voice that brought out the Natalie Clark he'd met in New York. Whatever the reason, she responded with a hint of her old, disapproving self.

"You shouldn't call me that. I'm not your sweetheart."

He couldn't help himself. Lifting a hand, he brushed a knuckle over the curve of her cheek. "Ah, but we can change that, yes?"

She pulled away, and Dom was cursing himself for the mix of wariness and confusion that came back to her face when a slim, thirtysomething woman in a white smock coat emerged from the inner sanctum.

"Ms. Clark? I'm Dr. Kovacs's assistant," she said in Hungarian. "Would you and your husband please follow me?"

"Ms. Clark is American," Dom told her. "She doesn't speak our language. And we're not married."

"Oh, my apologies."

Switching to English, she repeated the invitation and advised Natalie it was her choice whether she wished to have her friend join her for the consult. Dom half expected her to refuse but she surprised him.

"I'd better have someone with me who knows who I am."

The PA showed them to a consultation room lined with mahogany bookshelves displaying leather-bound volumes and marble busts. No desk, just high-backed wing chairs in Moroccan leather arranged around a marble-topped pedestal table. The physician fit his surroundings. Tall and lean, he boasted an aristocratic beak of a nose and kind eyes behind rimless glasses.

"I reviewed the computer results of your examination at the hospital yesterday," he told Natalie in flawless English. "I would have preferred a complete physical exam with diagnostic imaging and cognitive testing before consulting with you, of course. Despite the limited medical data available at this point, however, I doubt your memory loss resulted from an organic issue such as a stroke or brain tumor or dementia. That's the good news."

Natalie's breath hissed softly on the air. The sound made Dom reach for her hand.

"What's the bad?" she asked, her fingers closing around his.

"Despite what you see in movies and on television, Ms. Clark, it's very rare for persons suffering from amnestic syndrome to lose their self-identity. A head injury such as the one you sustained generally leads to confusion and problems remembering *new* information, not old."

"I'm starting to remember things." Her fingers curled tighter, the nails digging into Dom's palm. "Historical dates and facts and such."

"Good, that's good. But for you to have blocked your sense of self…"

Kovacs slid his rimless glasses to the tip of his nose. Dom found himself wondering again about Natalie's glasses, but pushed the thought to the back of his mind as the doctor continued.

"There's another syndrome. It's called psychogenic, or dissociative, amnesia. It can result from emotional shock or trauma, such as being a victim of rape or some other violent crime."

"I don't think…" Her nails gouged deeper, sharper. "I don't remember any…"

"The hospital didn't run a rape kit," Dom said when she stumbled to a halt. "There was no reason to. Natalie—Ms. Clark—doesn't have any defensive wounds or bruises other than the swelling at the base of her skull."

"I'm aware of that. And I'm not suggesting the trauma is necessarily recent. It could have happened weeks or months or years ago." He turned back to Natalie. "The blow to your head may have triggered a memory of some previous painful experience. Perhaps caused you to throw up a defensive shield and block all personal memories."

"Will…" She swiped her tongue over her lower lip. "Will these personal memories come back?"

"They do in most instances. Each case is so different, however, it's impossible to predict a pattern."

Her jaw set. "So how do I pry open Pandora's box? Are there drugs I should take? Mental exercises I can do?"

"For now, I suggest you just give it a little time. You're a visitor to Budapest, yes? Soak in the baths. Enjoy the opera. Stroll in our beautiful parks. Let your mind heal along with the injury to your head."

The neurologist's parting advice didn't sit well with Natalie.

"Hit the opera," she huffed as they exited the town house. "Soak in the baths. Easy for him to say!"

"And easy for us to do."

The drawled comment brought her up short. Coming to a dead stop in the middle of the wide, tree-shaded sidewalk, she cocked her head.

"How can you dawdle around Budapest with me? Don't you have a job? An office or a brickyard or a butcher shop wondering where you are?"

"I wish I worked in a butcher shop," he replied, laughing. "I could keep the hound in bones for the rest of his life."

"Don't dodge the question. Where do you work?"

"Nowhere at the moment, thanks to you."

"Me?" A dozen wild possibilities raced through her head but none of them made any sense. "I don't understand."

"No, I don't suppose you do." He hooked a hand under her elbow and steered her toward a café a short distance away. "Come, let's have a coffee and I'll explain."

If Budapest's many thermal springs and public baths had made it a favorite European spa destination since Roman times, the city owed its centuries-old café culture to the Turks. Suleyman the Magnificent first introduced coffee to Europe when he invaded Hungary in the 1500s.

Taste for the drink grew during the Austro-Hungarian Empire. Meeting friends for coffee or just claiming a table to linger over a book or newspaper became a time-honored tradition. Although Vienna and other European cities developed their own thriving café cultures, Budapest remained its epicenter and at one time boasted more than six hundred *kávébáz*.

Hungarians still loved to gather at cafés. Most were small places with a dozen or so marble-topped tables, serving the inevitable glass of water along with a pitcher of milk and a cup of coffee on a small silver tray. But a few of the more elegant nineteenth-century cafés still remained. The one Dom escorted Natalie to featured chandeliers dripping with Bohemian crystal and a monstrous brass coffeemaker that took up almost one whole wall.

They claimed an outside table shaded by a green-and-white-striped awning. Dom placed the order, and Natalie waited only until they'd both stirred milk and sugar into their cups to pounce.

"All right. Please explain why I'm responsible for you being currently unemployed."

"You uncovered a document in some dusty archives in Vienna. A codicil to the Edict of 1867, which granted certain rights to Hungarian nobles. The codicil specifically confirmed the title of Grand Duke of Karlenburgh to the house of St. Sebastian forever and in perpetuity. Does any of this strike a chord?"

"That name. Karlenburgh. I know I know it."

"It was a small duchy, not much larger than Monaco, that straddled the present-day border between Austria and Hungary. The Alps cut right through it. Even today it's a place of snow-capped peaks, fertile valleys and high mountain passes guarded by crumbling fortresses."

"You've been there?"

"Several times. My grandfather was born at Karlenburgh Castle. It's just a pile of rubble now, but Poppa took my parents, then my sister and me back to see it."

"Your grandfather was the Grand Duke?"

"No, that was Sarah's grandfather. Mine was his cousin." Dom hesitated, thinking about the blood ties that had so recently and dramatically turned his life upside down. “I suppose my grandfather could have tried to claim the title when the last Grand Duke was executed.”

He stirred his coffee again and tried to imagine those long ago days of terror and chaos.

“From what he told me, that was a brutal time. The Soviet invasion leveled everyone—or elevated them, depending on how you looked at it—to the status of comrade. Wealth and titles became dangerous liabilities and made their holders targets. People tried to flee to the West. Neighbors spied on neighbors. Then, after the 1956 Uprising, the KGB rounded up thousands of nationalists. Charlotte, Sarah’s grandmother, was forced to witness her husband’s execution, and barely escaped Hungary with her life.”

The history resonated somewhere in Natalie’s mind. She’d heard this story before. She knew she had. She just didn’t know how it connected her and the broad-shouldered man sitting across from her.

“So this dusty document you say I uncovered? It links you to the title?”

“Charlotte thinks it does. So, unfortunately, do the tabloids.” His mouth twisted. “They’ve been hounding me since news of that damned document surfaced.”

“Well, excuse me for making you aware of your heritage!”

His brows soared. He stared at her with such an arrested expression that she had to ask.

“What?”

“You said almost the same thing in New York. While you were tearing off a strip of my hide.”

The revelation that she’d taken him down a peg or two did wonders for her self-confidence. “I’m sure you deserved it,” she said primly.

This time he just laughed.

“What?” she demanded again.

"That's you, *drágám*. So proper. So prissy. That's the Natalie who made me ache to tumble her to the bed or a sofa and kiss the disapproval from those luscious lips. I hurt for an hour after I left you in New York."

Her jaw dropped. She couldn't speak. Could barely breathe. Some distant corner of her mind warned that she would lose, and lose badly, if she engaged Dominic St. Sebastian in an exchange of sexual repartee.

Yet she couldn't seem to stop herself. Forcing a provocative smile, she leaned her elbows on the table and dropped her voice to the same husky murmur Dom had employed in Dr. Kovacs's reception area.

"Ah, but we can fix that, yes?"

His blank astonishment shot her ego up another notch. For the first time since she'd come awake and found herself eye to eye with a grinning canine, Natalie was able to shelve her worry and confusion.

The arrival of a waiter with their lunch allowed her to revel in the sensation awhile longer. Only after she'd forked down several bites of leafy greens and crunchy cucumber did she return to their original topic.

"You still haven't explained how inheriting the title associated with a long-defunct duchy put you on the rolls of the unemployed."

He swept the café with a casual glance. So casual she didn't realize he was making sure no one was close enough to overhear until he delivered another jaw-dropper.

"I'm an undercover agent, Natalie. Or I was until all this Grand Duke business hit."

"Like…?" She tried to get her head around it. "Like James Bond or something?"

"Closer to something. After my face got splashed across the tabloids, my boss encouraged me to take a nice, long vacation."

"So that explains the drawer!"

He leaned back in his chair. Slowly. Too slowly. Although the September sun warmed the cozy space under the awning and the exhaust from the cabs clogging the boulevard shimmered on the afternoon air, Natalie had the eerie sensation that the temperature around their table had dropped at least ten degrees.

"What drawer?"

"The locked one in your wardrobe. You store all your 007-type gadgets in there, don't you? Poison pens and jet-propelled socks and laser-guided minimissiles?"

He didn't answer for several moments. When he did, her brief euphoria at being in control evaporated.

"This isn't about me, Nat. You're the one with the empty spaces that need filling. Let's finish our coffee, yes? Then we'll swing by police headquarters. With any luck, they will have found the answers to at least some of your questions."

Dom called before they left the café to make sure Officer Gradjnic, his partner or their supervisor would be available to speak with them. Natalie didn't say a word during the short drive. Budapest traffic was nerve-racking enough to tie anyone in knots. The possibility that the police might lift a corner of the curtain blanketing her mind only added to her twist of nerves.

The National Police Department occupied a multistory, glass-and-steel high-rise on the Pest side of the Danube. Command and control of nationwide operations filled the upper stories. The Budapest PD claimed the first two floors. Officer Gradjnic's precinct was crammed into a corner of the second floor.

Natalie remembered Gradjnic from yesterday. More or less. Enough to smile when he asked how she was feeling, anyway, and thank him for their help yesterday.

"So, Ms. Clark. Do you remember how you ended up in the Danube?"

"No."

"But you might, yes?"

"The doctor we consulted this morning said that was possible." She swiped her tongue over suddenly dry lips. "What have you discovered?"

"A little."

Computers sat on every desk in the office but Officer Gradjnic tugged out his leather notepad, licked his finger and flipped through the pages.

"We've verified that you flew from Paris to Vienna last week," he reported. "We've also learned that you rented a vehicle from the Europcar agency in Vienna three days ago. We had the car rental company retrieve the GPS data from the vehicle and discovered you crossed into Hungary at Pradzéc."

"Where's Pradzéc?"

"It's a small village at the foot of the Alps, straddling the border between Austria and Hungary."

Her glance shot to Dom. They'd been talking about the border area less than an hour ago. He didn't so much as flick an eyelid but she knew he'd made the connection, just as she had.

"According to the GPS records, you spent several hours in that area, then returned to Vienna. The next day you crossed into Hungary again and stopped in Győr. The vehicle is still there, Ms. Clark, parked at a tour dock on the Danube. We called the tour office and verified that a woman matching your description purchased a ticket for a day cruise to Budapest. Do you recall buying that ticket, Ms. Clark?"

"No."

"Do you remember boarding the tour boat? Watching the scenery as you cruised down the Danube, perhaps?"

"No."

He shrugged and closed his notebook. "Well, that's all I have for you, I'm afraid. You'll have to make arrangements to return the rental car."

Dom nodded. "We'll take care of it. In the meantime, we'd like a copy of your report."

"Of course."

When they walked out into the afternoon sunshine, Natalie couldn't wait to ask. "Was Győr part of the duchy of Karlenburgh?"

"At one time."

"Is Karlenburgh Castle anywhere in that vicinity?"

"It's farther west, guarding a mountain pass. Or was. It's just a pile of ruins now."

"I need to retrace my steps, Dominic. Maybe if I see the ruins or the towns or the countryside I drove through, I'll remember why I was there."

"We'll go tomorrow."

A part of her cringed a bit at being so dependent on this man, who was still almost a stranger to her. Yet she couldn't help feeling relieved he would accompany her.

"We can have someone from Europcar meet us in Győr with a set of master keys," he advised. "That way you can retrieve any luggage you might have left locked in the trunk."

"Assuming it's still there. Rental cars are always such targets."

"True. Now we'd better see about getting you a replacement passport."

He pulled up the necessary information from the US Embassy's consular services on his iPhone. "As I thought. You'll need proof of US citizenship. A birth certificate, driver's license or previous passport."

"None of which I have."

"I can help there. I'll have one my contacts obtain a copy of your driver's license."

"You can do that?"

When he just smiled, she slapped the heel of her hand against her forehead. "Of course you can. You're 007."

They walked to the car and he opened the passenger door for her. Before she slid into the seat, Natalie turned. "You're a man of many different personas, Dominic St. Sebastian. Grand Duke. Secret agent. Rescuer of damsels in distress."

His mouth curved. "Of the three, I enjoy the last most."

"Hmm." He was so close, almost caging her in, that she had to tip her chin to look up at him. "That comes naturally to you, doesn't it?"

"Rescuing damsels in distress?"

"No, that slow, sexy, let's-get-naked grin."

"Is that the message it sends?"

"Yes."

"Is it working?"

She pursed her lips. "No."

"Ah, *drágám*," he said, laughter springing into his eyes, "every time you do that, I want to do this."

She sensed what was coming. Knew she should duck under his arm, drop into her seat and slam the door. Instead she stood there like an idiot while he stooped, placed his mouth over hers and kissed the disapproval off her lips.

Six

It was just a kiss. Nothing to get all jittery about. And certainly no reason for a purr to start deep in Natalie's throat and heat to ball in her belly. She could feel both, though, right along with the sensual movement of Dominic's lips over hers.

She'd thought it would end there. One touch. One pass of his mouth over hers. It *should* have ended there. Traffic was coursing along the busy street, for pity's sake. A streetcar clanged by. Yet Natalie didn't move as his arm went around her waist, drawing her closer, while her pulse pounded in her veins.

She was breathing hard when Dominic raised his head. He was, too, but recovered much quicker than she did.

"There," he teased. "That's better. You don't want to walk around with your mouth all pruned up."

She couldn't think of an appropriate response, so she merely sniffed and ducked into the car.

She struggled to regain her equilibrium as the car negotiated the narrow, winding streets of Castle Hill. Yet with every turn of the wheels she could feel Dominic's mouth on hers, still taste him.

She snuck a sideways glance, wondering if he was experiencing any aftershocks. No, of course not. He was supercool Mr. Secret Agent. Sexy Mr. Grand Duke, who had women slipping outrageously expensive panties into his carryall. The thought of him cuddling with Kissy Face Arabella struck a sour note in Natalie's mind. Not that it was any of her business *who* he cuddled with, she reminded herself sternly. She certainly had no claim on the man, other than being dropped on his doorstep like an abandoned baby.

That thought, in turn, triggered alternating ripples of worry and fear. She had to battle both emotions as Dom pulled into his parking space in the underground garage and they climbed the five flights of stairs. The enclosed stairwell blocked any glimpse of the river but it did afford a backside view of the uniformed delivery man trudging up ahead of them.

When they caught up with him at the landing outside the loft, Dom gestured to the large envelope in his hand. "Is that for me?"

"It is if you're Dominic St. Sebastian."

He signed for the delivery, noting the address of the sender. "It's from Sarah."

He pulled the tab on the outer envelope and handed Natalie the one inside. She fingered the bulging package before slipping it into her new straw tote. She didn't know the currency or the denomination of the notes her employer had sent but it felt like a fat wad. More than enough, she was sure, to repay Dom for her new clothes and the consult with Dr. Kovacs.

The money provided an unexpected anchor in her drifting world. When Dom unlocked the door to the loft and stood aside for her to enter, the hound provided another. Delirious with joy at their return, he woofed and waggled and whirled in ecstatic circles.

"Okay, Dog, okay." Laughing, Natalie dropped to her knees and fondled his ears. "I missed you, too."

He got in a few quick licks on her cheeks and chin

before she could dodge them. The silly grin on his face tugged at her heart.

"You can't keep calling him 'Dog,'" she scolded Dom. "He needs a proper name."

"What do you suggest?"

She studied the animal's madly whipping tail and white coat with its saddle-brown markings. "He looks a lot like a greyhound, but he's not, is he?"

"There may be some greyhound in him but he's mostly Magyar Agár."

"Magyar Agár." She rolled the words around in her head but drew a blank. "I'm not familiar with that breed."

"They're long-distance-racing and hunting hounds. In the old days, they would run alongside horsemen, often for twenty miles or more, to take down fast game like deer or hare. Anyone could own one, but big fellows like this one normally belonged to royalty."

"Royalty, huh. That settles it." She gave the cropped ears another tug. "You have to call him Duke."

"No."

"It's perfect," she insisted with a wicked glint in her eyes.

"No, Natalie."

"Think of the fun you can have if some pesky reporter wants to interview the duke."

Even better, think of the fun *she* could have whistling and ordering him to heel. "What do you say?" she asked the hound. "Think you could live with a royal title?"

Her answer was an ear-rattling woof.

"There, that settles the matter." She rose and dusted her hands. "What happens to Duke here when you're off doing your James Bond thing?"

"There's a girl in the apartment downstairs who looks after him for me."

Of course there was. Probably another Arabella-From-

London type. Natalie could just imagine what kind of payment she demanded for her dog-sitting services.

The thought was small and nasty and not one she was proud of. She chalked it up to these bizarre circumstances and the fact that she could still feel the imprint of Dom's mouth on her.

"I'd better take his highness out," he said. "Do you want to walk with us?"

She did, but she couldn't get the memory of their kiss out of her head. It didn't help that Dom was leaning against the counter, looking at her with those bedroom eyes.

"You go ahead," she said, needing some time and space. As an excuse she held up the straw tote with its cache of newly purchased toiletries. "Do you mind if I put some of these things in your bathroom?"

"Be my guest, *drágám*."

"I asked you not to call me that."

Nerves and a spark of temper made her sound waspish even to her own ears. He noted the tone but shrugged it off.

"So you did. I'll call you Natushka, then. Little Natalie."

That didn't sound any more dignified but she decided not to argue.

When he left with the dog, she emptied the tote. The toothbrush came out of its protective plastic sleeve first. A good brushing made up for her earlier finger-work, but she grimaced when she tried to find a spot in the bathroom for the rest of her purchases.

The sink area was littered with shaving gear, a hairbrush with a few short hairs that might or might not belong to the dog, dental floss and a dusty bottle of aftershave with the cap crusted on. The rest of the bathroom wasn't much better. Her wrinkled clothes occupied the towel rack. A shampoo bottle lay tipped on its side in the shower. The damp towels from their morning showers were draped over the shower door.

When she swept her skirt, blouse and jacket from the rack, her nose wrinkled at the faint but still-present river smell. They were too far gone to salvage. Not that Natalie wanted to. She couldn't believe she'd traipsed around the capitals of Europe in such a shapeless, ugly suit. Wadding it into a ball, she took it to the kitchen and searched for a wastebasket.

She found one in the cupboard under the sink, right next to some basic cleaning supplies. The suit and blouse went in. A sponge, a bottle of glass cleaner and a spray can of foaming disinfectant came out. Since Dominic was letting her crash at his loft, the least she could do was clean up a little.

The bathroom was small enough that it didn't take her long to get it gleaming and smelling like an Alpine forest. On a roll, she attacked the kitchen next. The coffee mugs and breakfast plates hit the dishwasher. The paper napkins and white bag with its grease stains from the apple pancakes joined her clothes in the trash. The stovetop and oven door got a scrubbing, as did the dog dish in a corner next to a cupboard containing a giant-size bag of dried food. She opened the refrigerator, intending to wipe down the shelves, and jumped back.

"Omig…!"

Gulping, she identified the gory objects in the gallon-size plastic bag as bones. Big bones. Belonging, she guessed, to a cow or boar. The kind of bones a Hungarian hunting dog would gnaw to sharpen his teeth.

The only other objects in the fridge were a to-go carton from an Asian restaurant and a dozen or so bottles of beer with labels touting unfamiliar brands. Curiosity had her opening the cupboards above the sink and stove. She found a few staples, some spices and a half loaf of bread keeping company with a dusty bottle of something called

Tokaji. Dominic St. Sebastian, she decided, was not into cooking at home.

Abandoning the cupboards, she turned her attention to the stainless-steel sink. The scrubbing gave Natalie a sense of fierce satisfaction. She might not be a James Bond type but she knew how to take out sink and shower grunge!

The kitchen done, she attacked the sitting area. Books got straightened, old newspapers stacked. The sleek little laptop nested next to a pair of running shoes on the floor was moved to the drop-down shelf that doubled as a desk. Natalie ran her fingers over the keyboard, gripped by a sudden urge to power up the computer.

She was a research assistant, according to Dom. An archivist. She probably spent most of her waking hours on the computer. What would she find if she went online and researched one Natalie Clark? Or had Dom already done that? She'd have to ask him.

She was dusting the black-and-glass stand of the widescreen TV when he and the hound returned. The dog burst in first, of course, his claws tattooing on the oak floor. Dominic followed and placed a brown paper sack on the counter. Lifting a brow, he glanced at the now spotless kitchen.

"You've been busy."

"Just straightened up a bit. I hope you don't mind."

"Why would I mind?" Amusement glinted in his eyes. "Although I can think of better ways for both of us to work off excess energy than cleaning and dog walking."

She didn't doubt it for a moment. She was wearing proof of one of his workouts in the form of black silk hipsters. No doubt Kiss Kiss Arabella would supply an enthusiastic endorsement of his abilities in that area.

Not that Natalie required a second opinion. He'd already given her a hint of just how disturbing he could be to her equanimity if she let him. Which she wouldn't. She couldn't! Her life was in enough turmoil without adding the complication of a wild tumble between the sheets with Dominic St. Sebastian. The mere thought made her so nervous that she flapped the dust cloth like a shield.

"What's in the bag?"

"I stopped by the butcher shop and picked up our supper."

"I hope you've got more than bones in there," she said with a little grimace.

"You found those, did you?"

"They were hard to miss."

"Not to worry. Dog will take care of those, although I'm sure he would much rather share our goulash."

Natalie eyed the tall, round carton he extracted dubiously. "The butcher shop sells goulash?"

"No, but Frau Kemper, the butcher's wife, always makes extra for me when she cooks up a pot."

"Oh?" She caught the prune before it formed but couldn't quite keep the disdain from her tone. "It must be a burden having so many women showering you with gifts."

"It is," he said sadly. "A terrible burden. Especially Frau Kemper. If she keeps forcing stews and cakes on me, I'll soon match her weight of a hundred and fifty kilos or more."

"A hundred and fifty kilos?" Natalie did the math. "Ha! I'd like to see you at three hundred plus pounds."

"No, you would not." He cocked his head. "But you did that calculation very quickly."

"I did, didn't I?" Surprise gave way to panic. "How can I remember metric conversions and not my name? My past? Anything about my family?"

Dom hesitated a fraction of a second too long. He knew something. Something he didn't want to reveal.

"Tell me!" she said fiercely.

"Sarah says you have no family."

"What?" Her fist bunched, crumpling the cloth she'd forgotten she still held. "Everyone has family."

"Let me put the goulash on to simmer, and I'll tell you what I know. But first..." He reached into the bag again and produced a gold-labeled bottle. "I'll open this and we'll drink a glass while we talk, yes?"

A vague memory stirred. Something or someone splashing pale gold liquid into crystal snifter. A man? This man? Desperately, she fought to drag the details to the front of her mind.

"What's in the bottle?"

"A chardonnay from the Badacsony vineyards."

The fragments shifted, realigned, wouldn't fit together. "Not...? Not apple brandy?"

"*Pálinka*? No," he said casually. Too casually. "That's what the duchess and I drank the last time I visited her in New York. You chose not to join us. This is much less potent."

He retrieved two wineglasses and rummaged in a drawer for an opener. She held up a hand before he poured. "None for me, thanks."

"Are you sure? It's light and crisp, one of Hungary's best whites."

"I'm not a drinker." As soon as the words were out, she sensed they were true. "You go ahead. I'm good with water."

"Then I'll have water, also."

With swift efficiency, he poured the goulash into a pot that had seen much better days. Once it was covered and set on low heat, he retrieved a bone for the hound and left him happily gnawing on the mat strategically placed under one of the eaves. Then he added ice to the two wineglasses and filled them with water.

"Let's take them to the balcony."

"Balcony," Natalie discovered when he held aside the

drapes on one side of the windows and opened an access door, was a grandiose term for the narrow platform that jutted out from the steep, sloping roof. Banded by a wrought-iron safety rail, it contained two bar chairs and a bistro-style table. Dominic edged past the table and settled in the farther chair.

Natalie had to drag in a deep breath before feeling her way cautiously to the closer chairs. She hitched up and peered nervously at the sheer drop on the other side of the railing.

"You're sure this is safe?"

"I'm sure. I built it myself."

Another persona. How many was that now? She had to do a mental recap. Grand Duke. Secret agent. Sex object of kissy-faced Englishwomen and full-bodied butcher's wives. General handyman and balcony-builder. All those facets to his personality, and hers was as flat and lifeless as a marble slab. More lifeless than she'd realized.

"You said I don't have any family," she prompted.

His glance strayed to the magnificence across the river. The slowly setting sun was gilding the turrets and spires and towering dome. The sight held him for several seconds. When it came back to her, Natalie braced herself.

"Sarah ran a background check on you before she hired you. According to her sources, there's no record of who your parents were or why they abandoned you as an infant. You were raised in a series of foster homes."

She must have known. On some subconscious level, she must have known. She'd been tossed out like trash. Unwanted. Unwelcome.

"You said a 'series' of foster homes. How many? Three? Five?"

"I don't have a number. I'll get one if you want."

"Never mind." Bitterness layered over the aching emptiness. "The total doesn't really matter, does it? What does is that in a country with couples desperate to adopt, apparently no one wanted me."

"You don't know that. I'm not familiar with adoption laws in the United States. There may have been some legal impediment."

He played with his glass, his long fingers turning the stem. There was more coming, and she guessed it wouldn't be good. It wasn't.

"We also have to take into account the fact that no one appears to have raised an alarm over your whereabouts. The Budapest police, my contacts at Interpol, Sarah and Dev…none of them have received queries or concerns that you may have gone missing."

"So in addition to no family, I have no friends or acquaintances close enough to worry about me."

She stared unseeing at the stunning vista of shining river and glittering spires. "What a pathetic life I must lead," she murmured.

"Perhaps."

She hadn't been fishing for a shoulder to cry on, but the less-than-sympathetic response rankled…until it occurred to her that he was holding something back.

The thought brought her head up with a snap. She scowled at him, sitting so calm and relaxed on his tiny handkerchief of a balcony. The slanting rays of the late-afternoon sun highlighted the short, glossy black hair, the golden oak of his skin, the strong cheekbones and chin. The speculative look in his dark eyes…

"What do you know that you're not telling me?" she snapped.

"There," he said, tipping his glass toward her in mock salute. "That's what I know."

"Huh?"

"That spark of temper. That flash of spirit. You try so

hard to hide them behind the prim, proper facade you present to the world but every so often they slip out."

"What are you talking about? What facade?"

He parried her questions with one of his own. "Do you see the ironmonger's cast there, right in front of you, stamped into the balcony railing?"

"What?"

"The cast mark. Do you see it?"

Frowning, she surveyed the ornate initial entwined with ivy. The mark was worn almost smooth but still legible. "You mean that *N*?"

He gestured with his glass again, this time at the panorama view across the river. "What about the Liberation Monument, high on that hill?

"Dominic…"

"Do you see it?"

She speared an impatient glance at the bronze statue of a woman holding a palm leaf high aloft. It dominated the hill in the far distance and could obviously be seen from anywhere in the city.

"Yes, I see it." The temper he'd commented on earlier sparked again. "But I'm in no mood for games or quizzes, Mr. Grand Duke. What do you know that I don't?"

"I know you wore glasses in New York," he replied evenly. "Large, square glasses with thick lenses that you apparently don't require for near or distance vision. I know you scraped your hair back most unattractively instead of letting it fall loose to your shoulders, as it does now. I know you chose loose clothes in an attempt to disguise your slender hips and—" his glance drifted south, and an appreciative gleam lit his eyes "—very delightful breasts."

Her mouth had started sagging at the mention of glasses. It dropped farther when he got to her hair, and snapped shut at the mention of her breasts. Fighting the urge to cross her arms over her chest, she tried to make sense of his observations.

She couldn't refute the part about the clothes. She'd questioned her fashion sense herself before she'd tossed the garments in the trash this morning. But the glasses? The hair?

She scrubbed her palms over her thighs, now encased in the formfitting designer jeans she'd purchased at the boutique. The jeans, the sandals, the short-sleeve T-shirt didn't feel strange or uncomfortable. From what Dom had said, though, they weren't her.

"Maybe what you saw in New York is the real me," she said a little desperately. "Maybe I just don't like drawing attention to myself."

"Maybe," he agreed, his gaze steady on her face. "And maybe there's a reason why you don't."

She could think of several reasons, none of them particularly palatable. Some were so far out she dismissed them instantly. She just couldn't see herself as a terrorist in training or a bank robber on the run. There was another explanation she couldn't shrug off as easily. One Dom brought up slowly, carefully.

"Perhaps your desire to hide the real you relates to a personal trauma, as Dr. Kovacs suggested this morning."

She couldn't deny the possibility. Yet…

She didn't *feel* traumatized. And she'd evidently been doing just fine before her dive into the Danube. She had a job that must have paid very well, judging by the advance on her salary Sarah had sent. She'd traveled to Paris, to Vienna, to Hungary. She must have an apartment back in the States. Books, maybe. Framed prints on the wall or a pen-and-ink sketch or a…

Her thoughts jerked to a stop. Rewound. Focused on a framed print. No, not a print. A painting. A canal scene with strong, hazy colors and a light so natural it looked as though the sun was shimmering on the water.

She could see it! Every sleek black gondola, every window arch framed by mellow stone, every ripple of the green waters of the lagoon.

"Didn't Sarah tell you I went to Vienna to research a painting?" she asked Dom eagerly.

"She did."

"A Venetian canal scene." She clung to the mental image with a fierce effort of will. "By…by…"

"Canaletto."

"Yes!" She edged off the tall chair and kept a few careful inches away from the iron railing. "Let's go inside. I need to use your laptop."

Seven

The spicy scent of paprika and simmering beef filled the loft when they went inside. Natalie sniffed appreciatively but cut a straight line for the laptop.

"Do I need a password to power up?"

"Just hit the on switch."

"Really?" She dropped into the leather armchair and positioned the laptop on her knees. "I would have thought 007 would employ tighter security."

Dom didn't bother to explain that all electronic and digital communications he received from or sent to Interpol were embedded with so many layers of encryption that no one outside the agency could decipher them. He doubted she would have heard him in any case. She was hunched forward, her fingers hovering over the keys.

"I hope you have Wi-Fi," she muttered as the screen brightened to display a close-up of the hound. All nose and bright eyes and floppy ears, the image won a smile from Natalie. The real thing plopped down on his haunches before Dom and let his tongue loll in eager anticipation of a libation.

Idly, Dom tipped some lager into his dish and watched as Natalie skimmed through site after site relating to the eighteenth-century Italian painter. The cop in him kept returning to their conversation outside on the balcony. He wasn't buying her quick dismissal of the suggestion she'd tried to downplay her natural beauty.

She most definitely had, and the ploy hadn't worked. Not with Dom, anyway. Despite her disdainful sniffs, daunting glasses and maiden-aunt clothes, she'd stirred his interest from the moment she'd opened the door of the duchess's apartment. And she'd damned near tied him in knots when she'd paraded out of the shower this morning with that crew shirt skimming her thighs.

Now…

His fist tightened on the dew-streaked pilsner bottle. She should see herself through his eyes. The shoulder-length, honey-streaked brown hair. The fierce concentration drawing her brows into a straight line. The lips pooched into a tight rosebud.

Jézus, Mária és József! Those lips!

Swallowing a groan, Dom took another pull of the lager and gave the rest to the ecstatic hound.

"You shouldn't let him have beer."

He glanced over to find her looking all prudish and disapproving again. Maybe it wasn't a disguise, he thought wryly. Maybe there was room in that sexy body for a nun, a shower scrubber and a wanton.

God, he hoped so!

It didn't take her long to find what she was looking for. Dom was still visualizing a steamy shower encounter when she whooped.

"This is it! This is the painting I was researching. I don't know how I know it, but I do."

He crossed the room and peered over her shoulder. Her scent drifted up to him, mingling with that of the goulash to tease his senses. Hair warmed by the sun. Skin dusted from their day in the city. The faint tang of cleaning solutions. Excitement radiated from her as she read him the details she'd pulled up on the laptop.

"It's one of Canaletto's early works. Commissioned by a Venetian doge and seized by Napoleon as part of the spoils of war after he invaded Venice in 1797. It reportedly hung in his study at the Tuileries Palace, then disappeared sometime before or during a fire in 1871."

She scrolled down the page. She was in full research mode now, inhaling every detail with the same eagerness the hound did pilsner.

"The painting disappeared for almost a half a century, until it turned up again in the early '30s in the private collection of a Swiss industrialist. He died in 1953 and his squabbling heirs auctioned off his entire collection. At that point… Look!"

She stabbed a finger at the screen. Dom bent closer.

"At that point," she recited eagerly, "it was purchased by an agent acting for the Grand Duke of Karlenburgh."

She swiveled around, almost tilting the laptop off her knees in her eagerness. Her face was alive, her eyes bright with the thrill of discovery.

"The Grand Duke of Karlenburgh," she repeated. "That was you, several times removed."

"*Many* times removed."

Despite his seeming insouciance, the connection couldn't be denied. It wove around him like a fine, silken thread. Trapping him. Cocooning him.

"The painting was a gift from the duke to his duchess," he related, remembering the mischievous look in Charlotte's eyes. "To commemorate a particularly pleasant visit to Venice."

Natalie's face went blank for a moment, then lit with excitement. "I remember hearing that story! Venice is where she got pregnant, right? With her only child?"

"Right."

They were so close, her mouth just a breath away from

his, that Dom couldn't help himself. He had to drop a kiss on those tantalizing lips.

He kept it light, playful. But when he raised his head confusion and a hint of wariness had replaced the excitement. Kicking himself, he tried to coax it back.

"Charlotte said the painting hung in the Red Salon at Karlenburgh Castle. Is there reference to that?"

"I, uh… Let me look."

She ducked her head and hit the keys again. Her hair feathered against her cheek like a sparrow's wing, shielding her face. He knew he'd lost serious ground when she shook her head and refused to look at him.

"No mention here. All it says is that the painting was lost again in the chaos following the Soviet suppression of the 1956 Hungarian Uprising."

"The same uprising that cost the Grand Duke his life and forced his wife to flee her homeland."

"How sad." With a small sigh, Natalie slumped against the chair back. "Charlotte's husband purchased the painting to celebrate one of the most joyous moments of their lives. And just a little more than a year later, both he and the painting were lost."

Her voice had gone small and quiet. She was drawing parallels, Dom guessed. Empathizing with the duchess's tragic losses. Feeling the emptiness of her own life.

The thought of her being a forgotten, helpless cog in a vast social welfare bureaucracy pulled at something deep inside him. He'd known her for such a short time. Had spoken to her twice in New York. Spent less than twenty-four hours with her here in Budapest. Yet he found himself wanting to erase the empty spaces in her heart. To pull her into his arms and fill the gaps in her mind with new, happy and extremely erotic memories. The urge was so powerful it yanked him up like a puppet on a twisted string.

Christ! He was a cop. Like all cops, he knew that trust

could—and too often did—shift like the sand on a wave-swept shore. Identities had to be validated, backgrounds scrubbed with a wire brush. Until he heard back from his contact at Interpol, he'd damned well better keep his hands to himself.

"The duke was executed," he said briskly, "but Charlotte survived. She made a new life for herself and her baby in New York. Now she has her granddaughters, her great-grandchildren. And you, Ms. Clark, have the finest goulash in all of Budapest to sample."

The abrupt change in direction accomplished precisely what he'd intended. Natalie raised her head. The curtain of soft, shiny hair fell back, and a tentative smile etched across her face.

"I'm ready."

More than ready, she realized. They hadn't eaten since their hurried breakfast and it was now almost seven. The aroma filling the loft had her taste buds dancing in eagerness.

"Ha!" Dom said with a grin. "You may think you're prepared, but Frau Kemper's stew is in a class by itself. Prepare for a culinary tsunami."

While he sniffed and stirred the goulash, Natalie set the counter with the mismatched crockery and cutlery she'd found during her earlier explorations of the kitchen cupboards.

Doing the homey little task made her feel strange. Strange and confused and nervous. Especially when her hip bumped Dominic's in the narrow kitchen area. And when he reached for a paper towel the same time she did. And…

Oh, for pity's sake! Who was she kidding? It wasn't the act of laying out bowls and spoons that had her mind and nerves jumping. It was Dominic. She couldn't look at him without remembering the feel of his mouth on hers.

Couldn't listen to him warning the dog—Duke!—to take himself out of the kitchen without thinking about how he'd called her sweetheart in Hungarian. And not just in Hungarian. In a husky, teasing voice that seemed so intimate, so seductive.

She didn't really know him. Hell, she didn't even know herself! Yet when he went to refill her glass with water she stopped him.

"I'd like to try that wine you brought home."

He looked up from the spigot in surprise. "Are you sure?"

"Yes."

She was. She really was. Natalie had no idea what lay at the root of her aversion to alcohol. A secretive, guilt-ridden tasting as a kid? An ugly drunk as a teen? A degrading experience in college? Whatever had caused it remained shrouded in her past. Right here, though, right now, she felt safe enough enjoy a glass of wine.

Safe?

The word echoed in her mind as Dom worked the cork on the chilled bottle and raised his glass to eye level. *"Egészségére!"*

"I'll drink to that, whatever it means."

"It means 'to your health.' Unless you mispronounce it," he added with a waggle of his brows. "Then it means 'to your arse.'"

She didn't bother to ask which pronunciation he'd used, just took a sip and waited for some unseen ax to fall. When the cool, refreshing white went down smoothly, she started to relax.

The goulash sped that process considerably. The first spoonful had her gasping and reaching desperately for the wineglass. The second, more cautious spoonful went down with less of an assault by the paprika and garlic. By the third, she'd recovered enough to appreciate the subtle flavors of caraway seed, marjoram and sautéed onions. By the fourth, she was spearing the beef, pork and potatoes with avid enthusiasm and sopping up gravy with chunks of dark bread torn from the loaf Frau Kemper had thoughtfully included with her stew.

She limited her wine intake to a single glass but readily agreed to a second helping of goulash. The Agár sat on his haunches beside her stool as she spooned it down. When she didn't share, his liquid brown eyes filled with such reproach that she was forced to sneak him several dripping morsels. Dom pretended not to notice, although he did mention drily that he'd have to take the hound for an extralong run before bed to flush the spicy stew out of his system.

As casual as it was, the comment started Natalie's nerves jumping again. The loft boasted only one bed. She'd occupied it last night. She felt guilty claiming it again.

"Speaking of bed..."

Dom's spoon paused in midair. "Yes?"

Her cheeks heating, she stirred the last of her stew. He had to be wondering why she hadn't taken Sarah up on her offer of a hotel room. At the moment, she couldn't help wondering the same thing.

"I don't like ousting you out of yours."

"Oh?" His spoon lowered. "Are you suggesting we share?"

She was becoming familiar with that slow, provocative grin.

"I'm suggesting," she said with a disdainful sniff, "I sleep on the sofa tonight and you take the bed."

She hadn't intended her retort as a challenge, but she should have known Dom would view it that way. Laughter leaped into his face, along with something that started Natalie's breath humming in her throat.

"Ah, sweetheart," he murmured, his eyes on her mouth.

"You make it very difficult for me to ignore the instincts bred into me by my wild, marauding ancestors."

Even Duke seemed to sense the sudden tension that arced through her. The dog wedged closer to Natalie and propped his head on her knee. She knuckled his forehead and tried desperately to blank any and all thought of Dom tossing her over his shoulder. Carrying her to his bed. Pillaging her mouth. Ravishing her body. Demanding a surrender she was all too willing to…

"Don't look so worried."

The wry command jolted her back to the here and now. Blinking, she watched Dom push off his stool.

"My blood may run as hot as my ancestors', but I draw the line at seducing a woman who can't remember her name. Come, Dog."

Still racked by the erotic images, Natalie bent her head to avoid looking at Dom as he snapped the Agár's lead to his collar. She couldn't avoid the knuckle he curved under her chin, however, or the real regret in his eyes when he tipped her face to his.

"I'm sorry, Natushka. I shouldn't tease you. I know this is a frightening time for you."

Oh, sure. Like she was going to tell him that fright was *not* what she was feeling right now? Easing her chin from his hold, she slid off her stool and gathered the used utensils.

"I'll wash the dishes while you're gone."

"No need. Just stick them in the dishwasher."

"Go!" She needed to do something with her hands and her overactive, overheated mind. "I'll take care of the kitchen."

She did the dishes. Spritzed the sink and countertop. Drew the drapes. Fussed with paperbacks she'd stacked earlier that afternoon. Curled up in the chair and reached for the laptop. And grew more annoyed with each passing moment.

Her glance kept darting from the wide sofa with its worn leather cushions to the bed tucked under the eaves at the far end of the loft. She didn't understand why she was so irritated by Dom's assurance that he wouldn't seduce her. Those brief moments of fantasy involving marauding Magyars aside, she didn't really *want* him to. Did she?

Lips compressed, she tried to balance her contradictory emotions. On the one hand, Dominic St. Sebastian constituted the only island in the empty sea of her mind. It was natural that she would cling to him. Not want to antagonize him or turn him away.

Yet what she was feeling now wasn't mental. It was physical, and growing more urgent by the moment. She wanted his hands on her, dammit! His mouth. She wanted that hard, muscled body pinning hers to the wall, the sheets, even the floor.

The intensity of the hunger pumping through her veins surprised her. It also generated an enormous relief. All that talk about a possible past trauma had raised some ugly questions in her mind. In Dom's, too, apparently, judging by his comment about her deliberately trying to downplay her looks. The realization that she could want a man as much as she appeared to want this one was as reassuring as it was frustrating.

Which brought her right back to square one. She threw another thoroughly annoyed look at the bed. She should have taken Sarah up on her offer to arrange a hotel room, she thought sourly. If she had, she wouldn't be sitting here wondering whether she should—or could!—convince Dom to forget about being all noble and considerate.

Shoving out of the chair, she stalked to the wardrobe and reclaimed the shirt she'd slept in last night. She took it into the bathroom to change, and her prickly irritation ratcheted up another notch when she found the hand towel she'd left folded neatly over the rack tossed in a damp pile atop the counter. Worse, the toiletries she'd carefully arranged to make room for her few purchases were once again scattered haphazardly around the sink.

Muttering, she stripped off her new jeans and top. She didn't think she was obsessive-compulsive. And even if she was, what was so wrong with keeping things neat and orderly?

The sight of her borrowed undies didn't exactly improve her mood. Dom obviously hadn't suffered from an excess of scruples with Kissy Face Arabella. Natalie would have dumped the black silk hipsters in the trash if she'd had another pair to step into. She'd have to do more shopping tomorrow.

Yanking the crew shirt over her head, she scrubbed her face and teeth. Then she carefully refolded *her* towel and scooped up her jeans and top. Just as she exited the bathroom, the front door opened and Duke bounded in. His ecstatic greeting soon had her laughing. Hard to stay in a snit with a cold nose poking her bare thighs and a pink tongue determined to slather her with kisses.

"Okay, enough, stop." She fended off a determined lunge and pointed a stern finger at the floor. "Duke! Sit!"

He looked a little confused by the English command but the gesture got through to him. Ears flopping, he dropped onto his haunches.

"Good boy." She couldn't resist sending his master a smug look. "See, he recognizes his name."

"I think he recognized your tone."

"Whatever." She chewed on her lower lip for a moment. "We didn't resolve the issue of the bed earlier. I don't feel right consigning you to the sofa. I'll sleep there tonight."

"No, you won't."

"Look, I'm very grateful for all you've done for me. I

don't want to inconvenience you any more than I already have."

Dom managed not to snort. If she had any idea of just how badly she was "inconveniencing" him at this moment, she'd shimmy back into her jeans and run like hell. Instead she just stood there while his gaze gobbled up the long, slender legs showing below the hem of his shirt. The mere thought of those legs tangled with his started an ache in his groin.

He damned well better not fantasize about what was *under* the shirt. If he did, neither one of them would make it to the bed. They might not even make it to the sofa.

"I've fallen asleep more nights than I can count in front of the TV," he bit out. "You've got the bed."

He could tell from the way her mouth set that he'd come across more brusque than he'd intended. Tough. After just a little more than twenty-four hours in her company, Ms. Clark had him swinging like a pendulum. One moment his cop's instincts were reminding him that things weren't always what they seemed. The next, he ached to take her in his arms and kiss away the fear she was doing her best to disguise.

Now he just plain ached, and he wasn't happy about the fact that he couldn't—wouldn't!—do anything to ease the hurt. And why was she tormenting him like this, anyway?

"You're not going to bed now, are you?" he asked her.

"It's almost ten."

He managed to keep his jaw from sagging, but it took a heroic effort. He could understand her crashing facedown on the bed last night. She'd been hurt. She'd spent who knew how long in the Danube, and had a lump the size of a softball at the base of the skull.

She'd seemed to recover today, though. Enough for him to make an incautious comment. "At ten o'clock most Hungarians are trying to decide where to go for coffee and dessert."

Her chin tilted. "If you want to go out for coffee and dessert, please don't let me stop you."

Whoa! He'd missed something here. When he left to take out the dog twenty minutes ago, Natalie had been all soft and shy and confused. Now she was as stiff and prickly as a horsehair blanket.

Dom wanted to ask what happened in that short time span but he'd learned the hard way to keep his mouth shut. He'd guided his sister through her hormone-driven teen years. He'd also enjoyed the company of his fair share of women. Enough, anyway, to know that any male who attempted to plumb the workings of the female mind had better be wearing a Kevlar vest. Since he wasn't, he quickly backpedaled.

"Probably just as well we make it an early night. We have a full day tomorrow."

She acknowledged his craven retreat with a regal dip of her head. "Yes, we do. Good night."

"Good night."

Dom and the hound both watched as she made her way to the far end of the loft and arranged her jeans and tank top into neat folds before placing them on the table beside the bed. Dom didn't move while she turned back the comforter and slid between the sheets.

The dog didn't exercise the same restraint. His claws scrabbling on the oak floorboards, he scrambled across the open space and made a flying leap. He landed on the bed with paws outstretched and announced his arrival with a happy woof. Natalie laughed and eased to one side to make room for him.

With a muttered curse, Dom turned away from the sight of the Agár sprawled belly-up beside her.

Eight

The next day dawned achingly bright and gloriously cool. The first nip of fall had swept away the exhaust-polluted city air and left Budapest sparkling in the morning light.

Dom woke early after a restless night. Natalie was still hunched under the featherbed when he took the hound for his morning run. Halfway through their usual five miles he received a text message with a copy of her driver's license. He saved the attachment to print out at the loft and thumbed his phone to access the US Embassy website. Once he'd downloaded the application to replace a lost passport, he made a note to himself to call the consular office and set up an appointment.

He was tempted to make another call to his contact at Interpol. When he'd asked Andre to dig deeper, he hadn't expected the excavation to take more than a day. Two at the most. But he knew Andre would get back to him if he uncovered anything of interest.

Dom also knew he belonged in the field! He'd taken down vicious killers, drug traffickers, the remorseless sleaze who sold children to the highest bidders. He didn't claim to be the best at what he did, but he'd done his part. This extended vacation was pure crap.

Or had been, until Natalie had dropped into his life. If Dom hadn't been at such loose ends he might not have been so quick to assume complete responsibility for her.

Now that he had, he felt obligated to keep her close until her memory returned.

It was already trickling back. Bits and pieces had started to pierce the haze. And when the fog dissipated completely, he thought with a sudden tightening of his belly, he intended to do his damnedest to follow up on that one, searing kiss. He'd spent too many uncomfortable hours on the sofa last night, imagining just that eventuality.

A jerk on the leash checked his easy stride. He glanced down to see the hound dragging his rear legs and glaring at him reproachfully.

"Don't look at me like that. You're already in bed with her."

Still the dog wouldn't move.

"Oh, all right. Have at it."

Dom jogged in place while the Agár sniffed the interesting pile just off the track, then majestically lifted a leg to spray it.

As soon as Dom and the hound entered, they were hit with the aroma of sizzling bacon and freshly baked cinnamon bread. The scents were almost as tantalizing as the sight of Natalie at the stove, a spatula in hand and a towel tucked apronlike around her slim hips. Dom tried to remember the last woman who'd made herself at home in his kitchen. None of those who'd come for a drink and stayed for the night, as best he could recall. And certainly not his sister. Even as a child, Anastazia had always been too busy splinting the broken wings of sparrows or feeding baby squirrels with eyedroppers to think about nourishing herself or her brother.

"I went down to the grocery shop on the corner," Natalie said by way of greeting. "I thought we should have breakfast before we took off for Karlenburgh Castle."

"That sounds good. How long before it's ready?"

"Five minutes."

"Make it ten," he begged.

He snagged a cup of coffee and had to hide a grimace. She'd made it American style. Closer to colored water than the real thing. The weak brew provided barely enough punch to get him through a quick shower and shave.

He emerged eager for a taste of the bacon laid out in crisp strips on a paper towel. The fluffy eggs scrambled with mushrooms and topped with fresh-grated Gruyère cheese had his tongue hanging out almost as far as the hound's. But the warm cinnamon rolls tucked in a napkin made him go weak at the knees. Groaning, he sank onto a stool at the counter.

"Do you cook breakfast for yourself every morning?"

She paused with the spatula hovering above the platter of eggs. "I don't know."

"No matter," Dom said fervently. "You're doing fine."

Actually, she was doing great. Her movements concise and confident, she set out his mismatched plates and folded paper napkins into neat, dainty triangles. Amused, he saw that she'd purchased a small bouquet of flowers during her quick trip to the grocers. The purple lupines and pink roses now sprouted from his prized beer stein. He had to admit they added a nice touch of color to the otherwise drab kitchen area.

So did she. She wore the jeans she'd purchased yesterday and had borrowed another of his soccer shirts. The hem of the hunter-green shirt fell well below her hips, unfortunately, but when she leaned across the counter to refill his coffee mug, the deep-V neckline gave him a tantalizing glimpse of creamy slopes.

Promising the hopeful hound he would be fed later, she perched on the stool beside Dom and served them both. The eggs tasted as good as they looked. He was halfway through his when he gave her an update.

"While I was out jogging, I got a text with a copy of your driver's license attached. I also downloaded the application form for a replacement passport. I'll print both after breakfast, then we'll make an appointment with the consular office."

Natalie nodded. The bits and pieces of her life seemed to be falling into place. She just wished they would fall faster. Maybe this excursion to Karlenburgh Castle would help. Suddenly impatient, she hopped off her stool and rinsed her dish in the sink.

"Are you finished?" she asked.

He relinquished his plate but snagged the last cinnamon bun before she could whisk the basket away. She did a quick kitchen cleanup and changed back into her red tank top. Her straw tote hooked over her shoulder, she waited impatiently while Dom extracted a lightweight jacket from his wardrobe.

"You'll need this. It can get cool up in the mountains."

She was disappointed when he decreed the hound wouldn't join them on the expedition...and surprised when he introduced her to the girl in the apartment downstairs who looked after the animal during his frequent absences.

The dog-sitter wasn't the sultry, predatory single Natalie had imagined. Instead she looked to be about nine or ten, with a splash of freckles across her nose and a backpack that indicated she'd been just about to depart for school.

When she dropped to her knees to return the hound's eager kisses, her papa came to the door. Dom introduced Natalie and explained that they might return late. "I would appreciate it if Katya would walk him after school, as per our usual agreement."

The father smiled fondly at his daughter and replied in heavily accented English. "But of course, Dominic. They will both enjoy the exercise. We still have the bones and bag of food you left last time. If you are late, we'll feed him, yes?"

"We should not call him Dominic anymore, Papa." The girl sent Dom an impish grin. "We should address you as Your Grace, shouldn't we?"

"You do," he retorted, tugging on her ear, "and I won't let you download any more songs from my iTunes account."

Giggling, she pulled away and reminded him of a promise he looked as though he would prefer to forget. "You're coming to my school, aren't you? I want to show off my important neighbor."

"Yes, yes. I will."

"When?"

"Soon."

"When?"

"Katya," her father said in gentle reproof.

"But Dom's on vacation now. He told us so." Her arm looped around the dog's neck, she turned accusing eyes on her upstairs neighbor. "So when will you come?"

Natalie had to bite the inside of her lip to keep from laughing. The kid had him nailed and knew it.

"Next week," he promised reluctantly.

"When next week?"

"Katya, enough!"

"But, Papa, I need to tell my teacher when to expect the Grand Duke of Karlenburgh."

Groaning, Dom committed to Tuesday afternoon if her teacher concurred. Then he grasped Natalie's elbow and steered her toward the garage stairs.

"Let's get out of here before she makes me promise to wear a crown and a purple robe."

"Yes, Your Grace."

"Watch yourself, woman."

"Yes, Your Grace."

She knew him well enough now to laugh off his bad-tempered growl. As they started down the winding streets of Castle Hill, though, she added another facet to his growing list of alter egos. Undercover Agent. Grand Duke. Rescuer of damsels in distress. Loving older brother. Adopter of stray hounds. And now friend to an obviously adoring preteen.

Then there was that other side to him. The hot, sexy marauder whose ancestors had swept down from the Steppes. Sitting right next to her, so close that all she had to do was slide a glance at his profile to remember his taste and his scent and the feel of all those hard muscles pressed against her.

Natalie bit her lip in dismay when she realized she couldn't decide which of Dom's multiple personalities appealed to her most. They were all equally seductive, and she had the scary feeling that she was falling a little bit in love with each one of them.

Lost in those disturbing thoughts, she didn't see they'd emerged onto a broad boulevard running parallel to the Danube until Dom pointed out an impressive complex with an elaborate facade boasting turrets and fanciful wrought-iron balconies.

"That's Gellért Hotel. Their baths are among the best in Budapest. We'll have to follow Dr. Kovacs's advice and go for a soak tomorrow, yes?"

Natalie couldn't remember if she'd been to a communal bath before. Somehow it didn't seem like her kind of thing. "Do the spa-goers wear bathing suits?"

"In the public pools." He tipped her a quick grin. "But we can book a private session, where suits are optional."

Like that was going to happen! Natalie could barely breathe sitting here next to him fully clothed. She refused to think about the two of them slithering into a pool naked.

Hastily, she shoved her thoughts in a different direction. "How far did you say it was to where I left the rental car?"

"Győr's only a little over a hundred kilometers."

"And Pradzéc, where I crossed over from Austria?"

"Another sixty or seventy kilometers. But the going will be slower as we get closer to the border. The road winds as it climbs into the Alps."

"Where it reaches Karlenburgh Castle," she murmured.

She'd been there. She *knew* she'd been there. Dom claimed the castle was nothing but a pile of tumbled rock now but something had pulled Natalie to those ruins. Even now, she could feel the tug. The sensation was so strong, so compelling, that it took her some time to let go of it and pay more attention to the countryside they passed through.

They zipped along the M1 motorway as it cut through the region that Dom told her was called Northern Transdanubia. Despite its bloody history as the traditional battleground between Hungary and the forces invading from the west, the region was one of gentle hills, green valleys and lush forests. The international brown signs designating a significant historic landmark flashed by with astonishing frequency. Each town or village they passed seemed to boast an ancient abbey or spa or fortified stronghold.

The city of Győr was no exception. When Dom pointed out that it was located exactly halfway between Vienna and Budapest, she wondered how many armies had tramped through its ancient, cobbled streets. Natalie caught only a glimpse of Old Town's battlements, however, before they turned north. Short moments later they reached the point where two smaller rivers flowed into the mighty Danube.

A double-decker tour boat was just departing the wharf. Natalie strained every brain cell in an effort to identify with the day-trippers crowding the rails on the upper decks. Nothing clicked. Not even when Dom turned into the parking lot and parked next to the motorized matchbox she'd supposedly rented in Vienna almost two days ago.

Dom had arranged for a rental agency rep to meet them. When the agent popped the trunk with a spare set of keys a tingle began to feather along her nerves. The tingle surged to a hot, excited rush the moment she spotted a bulging leather briefcase.

"That's mine!"

Snatching the case out of the trunk, she cradled it against her breasts like a long-lost baby. She allowed it out of her arms only long enough for Dom to note the initials embossed in gold near the handle…and the fact that it wasn't locked. Her heart pounding, she popped the latch and whooped at the sight of a slim laptop jammed between stacks of fat files.

"This must be yours, too," the rental agency rep said as he lifted out a weekender on wheels.

She didn't experience the same hot rush when the ID tag on the case verified the case was, in fact, hers. Maybe because when she opened it to inspect the contents they looked as though they belonged to an octogenarian. Everything was drab, colorless and eminently sensible. She tried to pump herself up with the realization that she now had several sets of clean undies in her possession. Unfortunately, they were all plain, unadorned undies that Kiss Kiss Arabella wouldn't be caught dead in!

A check of the vehicle's interior produced no purse, passport, ID or credit cards. Nor was there any sign of the glasses Dominic insisted she hadn't really needed. They must have gone into the river with her. Hugging the briefcase, she watched as Dom transferred the weekender to his own car and provided a copy of the police report to the rep from the rental agency. In view of her accident and injury and the fact that there was no apparent damage to the vehicle, the rep agreed to waive the late return charges.

Natalie almost shivered with impatience to delve into the files in the briefcase but Dom wanted to talk to the people at the tour office first on the off-chance they might remember her. They didn't, nor could they provide any more information than the police had already gleaned by tracking her credit card charges.

Natalie stood with Dom next to the ticket booth and stared at the sleek boat now little more than a speck in the distance. "This is so frustrating! Why did I take a river cruise? I don't even like boats."

"How do you know?"

She blinked. "I'm not sure. I just don't."

"Maybe we'll find a clue in your briefcase."

She glanced around the wharf area, itching to get into those fat files, but knew they couldn't spread their contents out on a picnic table where the breeze off the river might snatch them away. Dom sensed her frustration and offered a suggestion.

"We're less than an hour from Karlenburgh Castle. There's an inn in the village below the castle ruins. We can have lunch and ask Frau Dortmann for the use of her parlor to lay everything out."

"Let's go!"

She couldn't resist extracting a few of the files and skimming through them on the way. Each folder was devoted to a lost treasure. A neat table of contents listed everything inside—printed articles from various computer sources, copies of handwritten documents, color photos, black-and-whites, historical chronologies tracing last known ownership, notes Natalie had made to herself on additional sources to check.

"Ooh," she murmured when she flipped to a sketch of jewel-studded egg nested in a gold chariot pulled by a winged cherub. "How beautiful."

Dom glanced at the photo. "Isn't that the Fabergé egg Tsar Alexander gave his wife?"

"I…uh…" She checked her notes and looked up in surprise. "It is. How do you know that?"

"You were researching it in the States. You told me about it when we got together in your hotel room in New York."

"We got together in New York? In my hotel room?"

Dom was tempted, really tempted, but he stuck with the truth. "I thought you might be scheming to rip off the duchess with all that business about the codicil so I came to warn you off. You," he added with a quick grin, "kicked me out on my ass."

The Natalie he knew and was beginning to seriously lust after emerged. "I'm sure you deserved it."

"Ah, Natushka. Don't go all prim and proper on me. We might not make it to the inn."

He said it with a smile but they both knew he was only half kidding. Cheeks flushed, Natalie dug into the file again.

She saw the castle ruins first. She could hardly miss them. The tumbled walls and skeletal remains of a single square tower were set high on a rocky crag and visible from miles away. As they got closer, Natalie could see how the road cut through the narrow pass below—the only pass connecting Austria and Hungary for fifty miles in either direction, Dom informed her.

"No wonder the Habsburgs were so anxious to have your ancestors hold it for the Empire."

Only after they'd topped a steep rise did she see the village at the base of the cliffs. The dozen or so structures were typically Alpine, half-timbered and steep-roofed to slough off snow. A wooden roadside shrine housing a statue of the Virgin Mary greeted them as they approached the village. In keeping with the mingled heritage of the residents, the few street signs and notices were in both German and Hungarian.

The gasthaus sat at the edge of the village. Its mossy shingles and weathered timbers suggested it had welcomed wayfarers for centuries. Geraniums bloomed in every window box and an ivy-covered beer garden beckoned at one side of the main structure.

When Natalie and Dom went up the steps and entered the knotty-pine lobby, the woman who hustled out to greet them didn't match her rustic surroundings. Dom's casual reference to Frau Dortmann had evoked hazy images of an apron-clad, rosy-cheeked matron.

The fortysomething blonde in leggings and a tiger-striped tunic was as far from matronly as a woman could get. And if there was a Herr Dortmann hanging around anywhere, Natalie was certain he wouldn't appreciate the way his wife flung herself into Dom's arms. Wrapping herself around him like a half-starved boa constrictor, she kissed him. Not on both cheeks like any other polite European, but long and hard and full on the lips.

He was half laughing, half embarrassed when he finally managed to extricate himself. With a rueful glance at Natalie, he interrupted the blonde's spate of rapid Hungarian liberally interspersed with German.

"Lisel, this is Natalie Clark. A friend of mine from America."

"America!" Wide, amethyst eyes turned to Natalie. Eager hands reached out to take both of hers. "*Wilkommen!* You must come in. You'll have a lager, *ja*? And then you will tell me how you come to be in the company of a rogue such as Dominic St. Sebastian." Her laughing glance cut back to Dom. "Or do I address you as 'Your Grace'? *Ja, ja,* I must. The whole village talks of nothing else but the stories about you in the papers."

"You can thank Natalie for that," he drawled.

The blonde's brows soared. "How so?"

"She's an archivist. A researcher who digs around in musty old ledgers. She uncovered a document in Vienna that appears to grant the titles of Grand Duke and Duchess of Karlenburgh to the St. Sebastians until the Alps crumble. As we all know, however, it's an empty honor."

"Ha! Not here. As soon as word gets around that the Grand Duke has returned to his ancestral home, the taproom will be jammed and the beer will flow like a river. Just wait. You will see."

They didn't have to wait long. Dom had barely finished explaining to Frau Dortman that he'd only come to show Natalie the ruins and aid her in her research when the door opened. A bent, craggy-faced gentleman in worn leather pants hobbled in and greeted Dom with the immense dignity of a man who'd lived through good times and bad. This, Natalie soon grasped, was a good time. A very good time, the older man indicated with a wide smile.

He was followed in short order by a big, buff farmer who carried the sharp tang of the barn in with him, two teenagers with curious eyes and earbuds dangling around their necks and a young woman cradling a baby on her hip. Natalie kept waiting for Herr Dortmann to make an appearance. When he didn't show, a casual query revealed Lisel had divorced the lazy good-for-nothing and sent him packing years ago.

Dom tried his best to include Natalie in the conversations that buzzed around them. As more and more people arrived, though, she edged out of the inner circle and enjoyed the show. St. Sebastian might downplay this whole royalty thing, she mused as she settled on a bar stool and placed her briefcase on a counter worn smooth by centuries of use, but he was a natural. It wasn't so much that he stood two or three inches above the rest of the crowd. Or that he exuded such an easy self-confidence. Or, she thought wryly, that he had already informed Lisel that he would pay for the beer that flowed as freely as the innkeeper had predicted.

He also, Natalie guessed, paid for the platters piled with sausages and spaetzle and fried potatoes and pickled beets that emerged in successive waves from the kitchen. The feasting and toasts and storytelling lasted through the afternoon and into the evening. By then, Dom had downed too much beer to get behind the wheel again.

Lisel had anticipated just such an eventuality. "You will stay here tonight," she announced and drew an old-fashioned iron key from the pocket of her tiger-striped tunic. "The front bedroom has a fine view of the castle," she confided to Natalie. "You and Dominic can see it as you lie in bed."

"It sounds wonderful." She plucked the room key out of the innkeeper's hand. "But Dominic will need other sleeping arrangements."

After Lisel Dortmann's enthusiastic welcome, Natalie preferred not to speculate on what those arrangements might be. All she knew was that she wasn't going to share a bed with the man—as much as she wanted to.

Nine

She took the narrow wooden stairs to the second floor and found the front bedroom easily enough. It contained a good-size bath and an alcove tucked under the slanting eaves that housed a small desk and overstuffed easy chair. The beautifully carved wooden headboard and washstand with its porcelain pitcher and bowl provided antique touches, while the flat-screen TV and small placard announcing the inn offered free Wi-Fi were welcome modern conveniences.

As Lisel had promised, the lace-draped windows offered an unimpeded view of the ruins set high atop the rocky promontory. The early evening shadows lent them a dark and brooding aspect. Then the clouds shifted, parted, and the last of the sun's rays cut like a laser. For a few magical moments what remained of Karlenburgh Castle was bathed in bright gold.

She'd seen these ruins before! Natalie knew it! Not all shimmery and ethereal and golden like this but…

A rap on the door interrupted her tumultuous thoughts. Dom stood in the hall with the weekender he'd brought in from the car.

"I thought you might need your case."

"Thanks." She grabbed his arm and hauled him toward the window. "You've got to see this."

He glanced through the windows at the sight she pointed

to but almost immediately his gaze switched back to Natalie. Her eyes were huge, her face alive with excitement. She could hardly contain it as she turned to him.

"Those ruins… That setting… I went up there, Dom."

Her forehead scrunched with such an intense effort to dredge up stubborn memories that it hurt him to watch. Aching for her, he raised his hand and traced his thumb down the deep crease in her brow. He followed the slope of her nose, the line of her tightly folded lips.

"Ah, Natushka." The husky murmur distracted her, as he'd intended. "You're doing it again."

"Doing wh…? Oh."

He couldn't help himself. He had to coax those lips back to lush, ripe fullness. Then, of course, he had to take his fill of them. To his delight, she tilted her head to give him better access.

He wasn't sure when he knew a mere taste wouldn't be enough. Maybe when she gave a little sigh and leaned into him. Or when her hands slid up and over his shoulders. Or when the ache he'd felt when he'd watched her struggling to remember dropped south. Hard and heavy and suddenly hurting, he tried to disentangle.

"No!"

The command was breathy and urgent. She tightened her arms around his neck, dragging him in for another kiss. This time she gave, and Dom took what she offered. The eager mouth, the quick dance of her tongue against his, the kick to his pulse when her breasts flattened against his chest.

He dropped his hands, cupped her bottom and pulled her closer. A serious mistake, he realized the instant her hip gouged into his groin. Biting down a groan, he eased back an inch or two.

"I want you, Natalie. You can see it. Feel it. But…"

"I want you, too."

"But," he continued gruffly, "I'm not going to take advantage of your confusion and uncertainty."

She leaned back in his arms and considered that for several moments while Dom shifted a little to one side to ease the pressure of her hip.

"I think it's the other way around," she said at last. "I'm the one taking advantage. You didn't have to let me stay at the loft. Or go with me to Dr. Kovacs, or get a copy of my driver's license, or come with me today."

"So I was just supposed to set you adrift far from your home with no money and no identity?"

"The point is, you didn't set me adrift." Her voice softened, and her eyes misted. "You're my anchor, Dominic. My lifeline." She leaned in again and brushed his mouth with hers. "Thank you."

The soft whisper sliced into him like a double-bladed ax. Wrapping his hands around her upper arms, he pushed her away. Surprise left her slack-jawed and gaping up at him.

"Is that what this is about, Natalie? You're so grateful you feel you have to respond when I kiss you? Perhaps sleep with me in payment for services rendered?"

"No!" Indignation sent a tide of red to her cheeks. "Of all the arrogant, idiotic…"

She stopped, dragged in a breath and tilted her chin to a dangerous angle.

"I guess you didn't notice, St. Sebastian, but I happen to like kissing you. I suspect I would also like going to bed with you. But I'll be damned if I'll do it with you thinking I'm so pathetic that I should be grateful for any crumbs that you and the hound and Kissy Face Arabella and…" She waved an irate hand. "And all your other friends toss my way."

The huffy speech left Dom swinging from anger to amusement. He didn't trust himself to address her comment about Arabella. Just the thought of Natalie wearing the Londoner's black silk put another kink in his gut. The hound was a different matter.

"This is a first," he admitted. "I've never been lumped in the same category as a dog before."

"You're not in the same category," she retorted. "Duke at least recognizes honest emotions like friendship and loyalty and affection."

"Affection?" His ego dropped another notch. "That's what you feel for me?"

"Oh, for….!" Exasperated, she twisted out of his arms and planted both fists on her hips. "What do you want, *Your Highness*? A written confession that I lay awake last night wishing it was you snuffling beside me instead of Duke? An engraved invitation to take his place?"

He searched her face, her eyes, and read only indignation and frustration. No subliminal fear stemming from a traumatic past event. No prim, old-maidish reluctance to get sweaty and naked. No confusion about what she wanted.

His scruples died an instant death as hunger rushed hot and greedy through his veins. "No engraved invitation required. I'll take this." He reached for her again and found her mouth. "And this," he murmured, nipping at her throat. "And this," he growled as his hand found her breast.

When he scooped her into his arms several long, mind-drugging moments later, his conscience fought through the red haze for a last, desperate battle. She was still lost, dammit! Still vulnerable. Despite her irate speech, he shouldn't carry her to the bed.

Shouldn't, but did. Some contrary corner of his mind said it was her very vulnerability that made him want to strengthen the lifeline she mentioned. Anchor her even more securely.

The last thought shook him. Not enough to stop him,

though. Especially with the moonlight spilling through the windows, bathing her face and now well-kissed lips in a soft glow.

His hunger erupted in a greedy, gnawing need. He stood her on her feet beside the bed and peeled away her clothes with more haste than finesse. Impatience made him clumsy but fired a similar urgency in Natalie. She tugged his shirt over his head and dropped hungry kisses on his chest as she fumbled with the snap of his jeans.

When he dragged back the thick, down-filled featherbed and tumbled her to the sheets, her body was smooth and warm, a landscape of golden lights and dark shadows. And when she hooked a calf around one of his, he had to fight the primal need to drive into her. He had to get something straight between them first. Thrusting his hands into her hair, he delivered a quick kiss and a wry confession.

"Just so you don't think this is your idea, you should know I was plotting various ways to get you into bed when I came to your hotel room in New York."

Natalie's heart kicked. In a sudden flash, she could see the small hotel room. Two double beds. An open laptop. Herself going nose to nose with Dom about… About…

"You thought I was some kind of schemer, out to fleece the duchess."

He went still. "You remember that?"

"Yes!" She clung to the image, sorting through the emotions that came with it. One proved especially satisfying. "I also remember slamming the door in your face," she said gleefully.

"You do, huh?" He got even for that with a long, hard kiss that left her gasping. "Remember anything else?"

"Not at the moment," she gulped.

He released her hair and slid his hands down her neck, over her shoulders, down her body. "Then I guess we'd better generate a few new memories."

Natalie gasped again as he set to work exploring her body. Nipping her earlobe. Kneading her breasts. Teasing her nipples. Tracing a path down her belly to the apex of her thighs. She was quivering with delight when he used a knee to part her legs.

His hair-roughened thigh rasped against hers. His breathing went fast and harsh. And his hand—his busy, diabolical hand—found her center. She was hot and wet and eager when he slid a finger in. Two. All the while his thumb played over the tight bud at her center and his teeth brought her nipples to taut, aching peaks. As the sensations piled one on top of the other, she arched under him.

"Dom! Dom, I… Ooooooh!"

The cry ripped from deep in her throat. She tried to hold back but the sensations spiraling up from her belly built to a wild, whirling vortex. Shuddering, she rode them to the last, gasping breath.

Minutes, maybe hours later, she pried up eyelids that felt as heavy as lead. Dom had propped his weight on one elbow and was watching her intently. He must be thinking of Dr. Kovacs's hypothesis, she realized. Worrying that some repressed trauma in her past might make her wig out.

"That," she assured him on a ragged sigh, "was wonderful."

His face relaxed into a smile. "Good to hear, but we're not done yet."

Still boneless with pleasure, she stretched like a cat as he rolled to the side of the bed and groped among the clothes they'd left in a pile on the floor. Somehow she wasn't surprised when he turned back with several foil-wrapped condoms. By the time he'd placed them close at hand on the table beside the bed, she was ready for round two.

"My turn," she murmured, pushing up on an elbow to

explore his body with the same attention to detail he'd explored hers.

God, he was beautiful! That wasn't an adjective usually applied to males but Natalie couldn't think of any other to categorize the long, lean torso, the roped muscle at shoulder and thigh, the flat belly and nest of thick, dark hair at his groin. His sex was flaccid but came to instant, eager attention when she stroked a finger along its length.

But it was the scar that caught and held her attention. Healed but still angry in the dim glow of the moon, it cut diagonally along his ribs. Frowning, she traced the tip of her finger along the vicious path.

"What's this?"

"A reminder not to trust a rookie to adequately pat down a seasoned veteran of the Cosa Nostra."

She spotted another scar higher on his chest, this one a tight, round pucker of flesh.

"And this?"

"A parting gift from an Albanian boat captain after Interpol intercepted the cargo of girls he was transporting to Algeria."

He said it with a careless shrug, as if knife wounds and kidnappings were routine occurrences in the career of a secret agent. Which they probably were, Natalie thought with a swallow. Suddenly the whole James Bond thing didn't seem quite so romantic.

"Your employer's brother-in-law took part in that op," Dom was saying. "Gina's husband, Jack Harris."

"He's undercover, too?"

"No, he's a career diplomat. He was part of a UN investigation into child prostitution at the time."

"Have I met him?"

"I don't know."

"Hmm."

It was hard to work up an interest in her employer's

brother-in-law while she was stretched out hip-to-naked-hip with Dominic St. Sebastian. Aching for the insults done to his body, she kissed the puckered scar on his shoulder.

One kiss led to another, then another, as she traced a path down his chest. When she laved her tongue along the scar bisecting his stomach, his belly hollowed and his sex sprang to attention again. Natalie drew a nail lightly along its length and would have explored the smooth satin further but Dom inhaled sharply and jerked away from her touch.

"Sorry! I want you too much."

She started to tell him there was no need for apologies, but he was already reaching for one of the condoms he'd left so conveniently close at hand. Heat coiled low in her belly and then, when he turned back to her, raced through her in quick, electric jolts. On fire for him, she took his weight and welcomed him eagerly into her body.

There was no slow climb to pleasure this time. No delicious heightening of the senses. He drove into her, and all too soon Natalie felt another climax rushing at her. She tried desperately to contain it, then sobbed with relief and sheer, undiluted pleasure when he pushed both her and himself over the edge.

She sprawled in naked abandon while the world slowly stopped spinning. Dom lay next to her, his eyes closed and one arm bent under his head. As she stared at his profile in the dim light of the moon, a dozen different emotions bounced between her heart and her head.

She acknowledged the satisfaction, the worry, the delight and just the tiniest frisson of fear. She hardly knew this man, yet she felt so close to him. *Too* close. How could she tell how much of that was real or the by-product of being too emotionally dependent on him?

As if to underscore her doubts, she glanced over his shoulder at the open window. Silhouetted against a midnight-blue sky were the ruins that had brought her to Hungary and to Dom.

Somehow.

The need to find the missing pieces of the puzzle put a serious dent in the sensual satisfaction of just lazing next to him. She bit her lip and shifted her attention to the desk tucked in the alcove under the eaves. Her briefcase lay atop the desk, right where she'd placed it. Anticipation tap-danced along her nerves at the thought of attacking those fat files and getting into her laptop.

Dom picked up on her quiver of impatience and opened his eyes. "Are you cold?"

"A little," she admitted but stopped him before he could drag up the down-filled featherbed tangled at their feet. "It's early yet. I'd like to go through my briefcase before we call it a night."

Amusement colored his voice. "Do you think we're done for the night?"

"Aren't we?"

"Ah, Natushka, we've barely begun. But we'll take a break while you look through your files." He rolled out of bed with the controlled grace of a panther and pulled on his clothes. "I'll go down and get us some coffee, yes?"

"Coffee would be good."

While he was gone she made a quick trip to the bathroom, then dug into her suitcase. She scrambled into clean panties but didn't bother with a bra. Or with either of the starched blouses folded atop a beige linen jumper that had all the grace and style of a burlap sack. Frowning, she checked the tag and saw the jumper was two sizes larger than the clothes she'd bought in Budapest.

Was Dom right? Had she deliberately tried to disguise her real self in these awful clothes? Was there something in her past that made her wary of showing her true colors? If so, she might find a clue to whatever it was in the briefcase. Impatient to get to it, she stuffed the jumper back in the case and slipped on the soccer shirt she'd appropriated from Dom to use as a sleep shirt. It hung below her hips but felt soft and smooth against her thighs.

She lifted the files out of her briefcase and arranged them in neat stacks. She was flipping through one page by page when Dom returned with two mugs of foaming latte.

"Finding anything interesting?" he asked as he set a mug at her elbow.

"Tons of stuff! So far it all relates to missing works of art, like that Fabergé egg and a small Bernini bronze stolen from the Uffizi Gallery in Florence. I haven't found information on the Canaletto painting yet. It's got to be in one of these files, though."

He nodded to the still-closed laptop. "You probably cross-indexed the paper files on your computer. Why don't you check it?"

"I tried." She blew out a frustrated breath. "The laptop's password-protected."

"And you can't remember the password."

"I tried a dozen different combinations, but none worked."

"Do you want me to get into it?"

"How can you…? Oh. Another useful skill you picked up at Interpol, right?"

He merely smiled. "Do you have a USB cord in your briefcase? Good. Let me have it."

He deposited the latte on the table beside the easy chair and settled in with the computer on his lap. It booted up to a smiley face and eight blinking question marks in the password box. Dom plugged one end of the USB cord into the laptop, the other into his cell phone. He tapped a series of numbers on the phone's keypad and waited to connect via a secure remote link to a special program developed by Interpol's Computer Crimes Division for use by agents in the field. The handy-dandy program whizzed through hundreds of thousands of letter/number/character combinations at the speed of light.

Scant minutes later, the password popped up letter by letter. Dom made a note of it and hit Return. The smiley face on Natalie's laptop dissolved and the home screen came up. The icons were arranged with military precision, he saw with an inner smile. God forbid his fussy archivist should keep a messy electronic filing cabinet. He was about to tell Natalie that he was in when a message painted across the screen.

D—I see you're online. Don't know whose computer you're using. Contact me. I have some info for you. A.

About time! Dom erased the message and de-linked before passing the laptop to Natalie. "You're good to go."

She took it eagerly and wedged it onto the desk between the stacks of paper files. Fingers flying, she conducted a quick search.

"Here's the Canaletto folder!"

A click of the mouse opened the main file. When dozens of subfolders rippled down the screen, Natalie groaned.

"It'll take all night to go through these."

"You don't have all night," Dom warned, dropping a kiss on her nape. "Just till I get back."

"Where are you going?"

"I need to let Katya and her father know we won't be home tonight. I'll get a stronger signal outside."

It wasn't a complete lie. He did need to call his downstairs neighbors. That bit about the stronger signal shaded the truth, but the habit of communicating privately with his contacts at headquarters went too deep to compromise.

He slipped on a jacket and went downstairs. The bar was still open. Lisel waved, inviting him in for another coffee or a beer, but he shook his head and held up his phone to signal his reason for going outside.

He'd forgotten how sharp and clean and cold the nights could be here in the foothills of the Alps. And how bright the stars were without a haze of smog and city lights to blur them. Hiking up the collar of his jacket, he contacted Andre.

"What have you got for me?"

"Some interesting information about your Natalie Elizabeth Clark."

Dom's stomach tightened. "Interesting" to Andre could mean anything from an unpaid speeding ticket to enrollment in a witness protection program.

"It took a while, but the facial recognition program finally matched to a mug shot."

Hell! His gut had told him Natalie was hiding her real self. He almost didn't want to hear the reason behind the disguise now but forced himself to ask.

"What were the charges?"

"Fraud and related activities in connection with computers."

"When?" he bit out.

"Three years ago. But it looks like the charges were dropped and the arrest record expunged. Someone missed the mug shot, though, when they wiped the slate."

Dom wanted to be fair. The fact that the charges had been dropped could mean the arrest was a mistake, that Natalie hadn't done whatever the authorities thought she had. Unfortunately, he'd seen too many sleazy, high-priced lawyers spring their clients on technicalities.

"Do you want me to contact the feds in the US?" Andre asked. "See what they've got on this?"

Dom hesitated, his gaze going to the brightly illuminated window on the second floor of the gasthaus. Had he just made love to a hacker? Had she tracked him down, devised a ploy to show up at his loft dripping wet and helpless? Was this whole amnesia scene part of some elaborate sting?

Every one of his instincts screamed no. She couldn't have faked the panic and confusion he'd glimpsed in her eyes. Or woven a web of lies and deceit, then flamed in his arms the way she had. The question now was whether he could trust his instincts.

"Dom? What do you want me to do?"

He went with his gut. "Hang loose, Andre. If I need more, I'll get back to you."

He disconnected, hoping to hell he wasn't thinking with the wrong head, and made a quick call to his downstairs neighbors.

Ten

Natalie was still hard at it when Dom went back upstairs. Her operation had spread from the desk to the armchair and the bed, which was now neatly remade. With pillows fluffed and the corners of the counterpane squared, he noted wryly. He also couldn't help noticing how her fingers flew over the laptop's keyboard.

"How's it coming?" he asked.

"So-so. The good news is I'm now remembering many of these details. The bad news is that I went through the Canaletto folder page by page. I also searched its corresponding computer file. I didn't find an entry that would explain why I drove down from Vienna, nor any reference to Győr or Budapest. Nothing to tell me why I hopped on a riverboat and ended up in the Danube." Sighing, she flapped a hand at the stacks now spread throughout the room. "I hope I find something in one of those."

Dom eyed the neat array of files. "How have you separated them?"

"The ones on the chair contain paper copies of documents and reports of lost art from roughly the same period as the Canaletto. The ones on the bed detail the last known locations of various missing pieces from other periods."

"Sorted alphabetically by continent and country, I see."

She looked slightly offended. "Of course. I thought I might have stumbled across something in reports from a gallery or museum or private collection that gained a new acquisition at approximately the same time the Canaletto disappeared from Karlenburgh Castle."

"What about information unrelated to missing art treasures? Any personal data in the files or on the computer that triggered memories?"

"Plenty," she said with a small sigh. "Apparently I'm as anal about my personal life as I am about professional matters. I've got everything on spreadsheets. The service record for my car. The books I've read and want to read. Checking and savings accounts. A household inventory with purchase dates, cost, serial numbers where appropriate. Restaurants I've tried, sorted by type of food and my rating. In short," she finished glumly, "my entire existence. Precise, well-organized and soulless."

She looked so frustrated, so dejected and lost, that Dom had to fight the urge to take her in his arms. He'd get into the computer later, when she was asleep, and check out the household inventory and bank accounts. Right now he was more interested in her responses to his careful probing.

"How about your email? Find anything there?"

"Other than some innocuous correspondence from people I've tagged in my address book as 'acquaintances,' everything relates to work." Her shoulders slumped. "Is my life pathetic, or what?"

If she was acting, she was the best he'd ever seen. To hell with fighting the urge. She needed comforting. Clearing the armchair, he caught her hand and tugged her into his lap.

"There's more to you than spreadsheets and color-coded files, Ms. Clark."

With another sigh, she laid her head on his shoulder. "You'd think so."

"There are all your little quirks," he said with a smile,

stroking her hair. "The lip thing, the fussiness, the questionable fashion sense."

"Gee, thanks."

"Then there's your rapport with the Agár."

"Ha! I suspect he bonds instantly with everyone."

"And there's tonight," he reminded her. "You, me, this gasthaus."

She tipped her head back to search his face. He supported her head, careful of the still-tender spot at the base of her skull.

"About tonight… You, me, this place…"

"Don't look so worried. We don't have to analyze or dissect what happened here."

"I'm thinking more along the lines of what happens after we leave. Next week. Next month."

"We let them take care of themselves."

As soon as he said it, he knew it was a lie. Despite the mystery surrounding this woman—or maybe because of it—he had no intention of letting her drop out of his life the same way she'd dropped into it. She was under his skin now.

That last thought made him stop. Rewind. Take a breath. Think about the other women he'd been with. The hard, inescapable fact was that none of them had ever stirred this particular mix of lust, tenderness, worry, suspicion and fierce protectiveness.

He might have to change his tactics if and when Natalie's memory fully returned, Dom acknowledged. At the moment she considered him an anchor in a sea of uncertainty. He couldn't add to that uncertainty by demanding more than she was ready to give.

"For now," he said with a lazy smile, "this is good, isn't it?"

"Oh, yes."

She leaned in, brought her mouth to his, gave him a

promise of things to come. He was ready to take her up on that promise when she made a brisk announcement.

"Okay, I'm done wallowing in self-pity. Time to get back to work."

"What do you want me to do?"

She glanced at the files on the bed and caught her lower lip between her teeth. Dom waited, remembering how antsy she'd been about letting him see her research when he'd shown up unannounced at her New York hotel room. He'd chalked that up to a proprietary desire to protect her work. With Andre's call still fresh in his mind, he couldn't help wondering if there was something else in those fat folders she wanted to protect.

"I guess you could start on those," she said with obvious reluctance. "There's an index and a chronology inside each file. The sections are tabbed, the documents in each section numbered. That's how I cross-reference the contents on the computer. So keep everything in order, okay?"

Dom's little bubble of suspicion popped. The woman wasn't nervous about him digging into her private files, just worried that he'd mess them up. Grinning, he pushed out of the chair with her still in his arms and deposited her back at the desk.

"I'll treat every page with care and reverence," he promised solemnly.

She flushed at little at the teasing but stood her ground. "You'd better. We archivists don't take kindly to anyone who desecrates our files."

It didn't take Dom long to realize Natalie could land a job with any investigative agency in the world, including Interpol. She hadn't just researched facts about lost cultural treasures. She'd tracked every rumor, followed every thread. Some threads were so thin they appeared to have no relation to the object of her research. Yet in at least two of the files he dug through, those seemingly unrelated, unconnected tidbits of information led to a major find.

"Jesus," Dom muttered after following a particularly convoluted trail. "Do you remember this?"

She swiveled around and frowned at a scanned photo depicting a two-inch-long cylinder inscribed with hieroglyphics. "Looks familiar. It's Babylonian, isn't it? About two thousand years old, I'd guess."

"You'd guess right."

"What's the story on it?"

"It went missing in Iraq in 2003, shortly after Saddam Hussein was toppled."

"Oh, I remember now. I found a reference to a similar object in a list of items being offered for sale by a little-known dealer. Best I recall, he claimed he specialized in Babylonian artifacts."

She rubbed her forehead, trying to dredge up more detail. Dom helped her out.

"You sent him a request for a more detailed description of that particular item. When it came in, you matched it to a list the US Army compiled of Iraqi antiquities that were unaccounted for."

"I can't remember…did the army recover the artifact?"

He flipped through several pages of notes and correspondence. "They did. They also arrested the contractor employee who'd lifted it during recovery efforts at the Baghdad Archeological Museum."

"Well! Maybe I'm not so pathetic after all."

She turned back to the laptop with a smug little smile that crushed the last of Dom's doubts. Those two inches of inscribed Babylonian clay were damned near priceless. If Natalie was into shady deals, she wouldn't have alerted the army to her find. The fact that she had convinced Dom. Whatever screwup had led to her arrest, she was no hacker or huckster.

He dug into the next folder and soon found himself absorbed in the search for a thirteenth-century gold chalice studded with emeralds that once graced the altar of an Irish abbey. He was only halfway through the thick file when he glanced up and saw Natalie's shoulders drooping again, this time with fatigue. So much for his anticipation of another lively session under the featherbed. He closed the folder, careful not to dislodge any of its contents, and stretched.

"That's it for me tonight."

She frowned at the remaining files. "We've still got a half dozen to go through."

"Tomorrow. Right now, I need bed, sleep and you. Not necessarily in that order, although you look as whipped as I feel."

"I might be able to summon a few reserves of energy."

"You do that," he said as he headed for the bathroom.

His five-o'clock shadow had morphed into a ten-o'clock bristle. He'd scraped Natalie's tender cheeks enough the first time around. He better shave and go a little more gentle on her this time. But when he reentered the bedroom a scant ten minutes later, she was curled in a tight ball under the featherbed and sawing soft, breathy Z's.

Taking advantage of the opportunity, he settled at the desk. His conscience didn't even ping as he powered up her laptop. Forty minutes later he'd seen everything he needed to. His skills weren't as honed as those of the wizards in Interpol's Computer Crimes Division, but they were good enough for him to feel confident she wasn't hacking into unauthorized databases or shifting money into hidden accounts. Everything he saw indicated she'd lived well within her salary as an archivist for the State of Illinois and was now socking most of the generous salary Sarah paid her into a savings account.

Satisfied and more than a little relieved to have his instincts validated, Dom shed his clothes and slid in beside her lax, warm body. He was tempted to nudge her awake and treat himself to a celebration of his nonfindings. He restrained himself but it required a heroic effort.

Natalie woke to bright morning sunshine, the distant clang of cowbells and a feeling of energy and purpose. She ascribed the last to a solid night's sleep—until she tried to roll over and realized she probably owed it more to the solid wall of male behind her.

God, he felt good! What's more, he made *her* feel good. Just lying nested against his warmth and strength generated all kinds of wild possibilities. Like maybe waking up in the same nest for the next few weeks or months. Or even, her sneaky little subconscious suggested, years.

The thought struck her that Dominic St. Sebastian might be all she needed to feel complete. All she would ever need. Apparently, she had no family. Judging by the dearth of personal emails on her laptop, she didn't have a wide circle of friends. Yet lying here with Dom, she didn't feel the lack of either.

Maybe that's why the details of her personal life were so slow returning. Her life was so empty, so blah, she didn't *want* to remember it. That made her grimace, which must have translated into some small movement because a lazy voice sounded just behind her ear.

"I've been waiting for you to wake up."

Sheets rustling, she angled a look over her shoulder and sighed. "It's not fair."

"What isn't?"

"My eyes feel goopy from sleep, my hair's probably sticking out in all directions and I know my teeth need brushing. You, on the other hand, look fresh and wide-awake and good enough to eat."

Good enough to gobble whole, actually. Those black

eyes and hair, the golden-oak hue of his skin, the square chin and chiseled cheekbones…the whole package added up to something really spectacular to start the day with. Only the nicks and scars of his profession marred the perfection.

"In fact," she announced, "I think I'll have you for breakfast."

She rolled onto her side, trying not to treat him to a blast of morning breath, and wiggled down a few inches. She started with the underside of his jaw and slowly worked her way south. Teasing, tasting, nibbling the cords in his neck, dropping kisses on alternate ribs, circling his belly button with her tongue. By the time she dragged the sheets down to his hips, he was stiff and rampant.

Her own belly tight and quivering now, she circled him with her palm. The skin was hot and satin smooth, the blood throbbing in his veins. She slid her hand up, down, up again, delighted when he grunted and jerked involuntarily.

"Okay," she told him, her voice throaty with desire, "I need a little of that action."

All thought of ratty hair and goopy eyes forgotten, she swung a leg over his thighs and raised her hips. Dom was straining and eager but held her off long enough to tear into another foil package.

"Let me," she said, brushing his hands aside.

She rolled on the condom, then positioned her hips again. Together they rode to an explosive release that had him thrusting upward and her collapsing onto his chest in mindless, mewling pleasure.

Natalie recovered first. Probably because she had to pee really, really bad. She scooped up her jeans and the green-and-white-striped rugby shirt she now claimed as her own on the way to the bathroom. When she emerged, she found Dom dressed and waiting for his turn.

"Give me five minutes and I'll be ready to go."

Since she wasn't sure whether they would return to the gasthaus, she stuffed the files and laptop back into her briefcase and threw her few miscellaneous items into her weekender. The sight of those plain, sensible, neatly folded blouses made her wrinkle her nose. Whatever happened when—*if*—she regained her memory, she was investing in an entire new wardrobe.

Dom agreed that it was probably better to check out of the gasthaus and head back to Budapest after going up to the castle. "But first, we'll eat. I guarantee you've never tasted anything like Lisel's *bauernfrühstück*."

"Which is?"

"Her version of a German-Austrian-Hungarian farmer's breakfast."

Their hostess gave them a cheerful smile when they appeared in the dining room and waved them to a table. She was serving two other diners, locals by the looks of them, and called across the room.

"Frühstück, ja?"

"Ja," Dom called back as he and Natalie helped themselves to the coffee and fresh juice set out on an elaborately carved hutch.

A short time later Lisel delivered her special. Natalie gaped at the platter-size omelette bursting with fried potatoes, onions, leeks, ham and pungent Munster cheese. The Hungarian input came from the pulpy, stewed tomatoes flavored with red peppers and the inevitable paprika.

When their hostess returned with a basket of freshly baked rolls and a crock of homemade elderberry jam, she lingered long enough to knuckle Dom's shoulder affectionately.

"So you leave us today?"

His mouth full, Dom nodded.

"You must come again soon." The blonde's amethyst eyes twinkled as she included his companion in the invitation. "You, as well. You and Dominic found the bed in my front room comfortable, yes?"

Natalie could feel heat rushing into her cheeks but had to laugh. "Very comfortable."

With a respectable portion of her gargantuan breakfast disposed of and the innkeeper's warm farewells to speed them on their way, Natalie's spirits rose with every twist and turn of the road that snaked up to the mountain pass. Something had drawn her to the ruins dominating the skyline ahead. She felt it in her bones, in the excitement bubbling through her veins. Impatience had her straining against her seat belt as Dom turned off the main road onto the single lane that led to what was left of Karlenburgh Castle.

The lane had once been paved but over the years frost heaves had buckled the asphalt and weeds now sprouted in the cracks. The weedy approach took nothing away from the dramatic aspect of the ruins, however. They rose from a base of solid granite, looking as though they'd been carved from the mountain itself. To the west was a breath-stealing vista of the snow-covered Austrian Alps. To the east, a series of stair-stepping terraces that must once have contained gardens, vineyards and orchards. The terraces ended abruptly in a sheer drop to the valley below.

Natalie's heart was pounding by the time Dom pulled up a few yards from the outer wall. The wind slapped her in the face when she got out of the car and knifed through the rugby shirt.

"Here, put this on."

Dom held up the jacket he'd retrieved from the backseat. She slid her arms into the sleeves and wrapped its warmth around her gratefully.

"Watch your step," he warned as they approached a gap in the outer ring of rubble. "A massive portcullis used to guard this gate, but the Soviets claimed the iron for scrap—along with everything else of any value. Then," he said, his voice grim, "they set charges and destroyed the castle itself as a warning to other Hungarians foolish enough to join the uprising."

Someone had cleared a path through the rubble of the outer bailey. "My grandfather," Dom explained, "with help from some locals."

Grasping her elbow to guide her over the rough spots, he pointed out the charred timbers and crumpled walls of the dairy, what had been the kitchens in earlier centuries, and the stables-turned-carriage house and garage.

Another gate led to what would have been the inner courtyard. The rubble was too dense here to penetrate but she could see the outline of the original structure in the tumbled walls. The only remaining turret jutted up like a broken tooth, its roof blown and stone staircase exposed to the sky. Natalie hooked her arm through Dom's and let her gaze roam the desolation while he described the castle he himself had seen only in drawings and family photographs.

"Karlenburgh wasn't as large as some border fortresses of the same era. Only thirty-six rooms originally, including the armory, the great hall and the duke and duchess's chambers. Successive generations of St. Sebastians installed modern conveniences like indoor plumbing and electric lights, but for comfort and luxury the family usually wintered in their palazzos on the Italian Riviera or the Dalmatian Coast." A smile lightened his somber expression. "My grandfather had a photo of him and his cousin dunking each other in the Mediterranean. They were very close as children, he and the last Grand Duke."

"Except," Natalie said, squeezing his arm with hers, "he wasn't the last Grand Duke."

For once Dominic didn't grimace or shrug or otherwise downplay his heritage. He couldn't, with its very dramatic remains staring him in the face.

"I've told the duchess she should come back for a visit," he murmured almost to himself. "But seeing it like this…"

They stood with shoulders hunched against the wind, Dom thinking of the duchess and Natalie searching the ruins for something to jog her memory. What had drawn her here? What had she found among the rubble that propelled her from here to Győr and onto that damned boat?

It was there, just behind the veil. She knew it was there! But she was damned if she could pull it out. Disappointment ate into her, doubly sharp and bitter after her earlier excitement.

Dom glanced down and must have read the frustration in her face. "Nothing?" he asked gently.

"Just a sort of vague, prickly sensation," she admitted, "which may or may not be goose bumps raised by the cold."

"Whichever it is, we'd best get you out of the wind."

Dejected and deflated and feeling dangerously close to tears, she picked her way back through the rubble. She'd been so sure Karlenburgh Castle was the key. So certain she'd break through once she stood among the ruins.

Lost in her glum thoughts, her eyes on the treacherous path, it took a moment for a distant, tinny clanging to penetrate her preoccupation. When it did, her head jerked up. That sound! That metallic tinkling! She'd heard it before, and not long ago.

Her heart started pumping. Her mouth went dry. Feeling as though she was teetering on the edge of a precipice, she followed the clanging to a string of goats meandering along the overgrown lane in their direction. A gnarled gnome of a man trailed the flock. His face was shadowed by the wide brim of his hat and he leaned heavily on a burled wood staff.

"That's old Friedrich," Dom exclaimed. "He helped tend the castle's goats as a small boy and now raises his own. Those are *cou noirs*—black necks—especially noted for their sweet milk. My grandfather always stopped by Friedrich's hut to buy cheese when he brought Zia and me back for a visit."

Natalie stood frozen as Dom forged a path through the goats to greet their herder. She didn't move, couldn't! Even when the lead animals milled inquisitively around her knees. True to their name, their front quarters were black, the rest of their coat a grayish-white. The does were gentle creatures but some instinct told Natalie to keep a wary eye on the buck accompanying them.

A bit of trivia slipped willy-nilly into her mind. She'd read somewhere that Alpine goats were among the earliest domesticated animals. Also that their adaptability made them good candidates for long sea voyages. Early settlers in the Americas had brought this breed with them to supply milk and cheese. And sea captains would often leave a pair on deserted islands along their trade routes to provide fresh milk and meat on return voyages.

Suddenly, the curtains in her mind parted. Not all the way. Just far enough for her to know she hadn't picked up that bit of trivia "somewhere." She'd specifically researched Alpine goats on Google after… After…

Her gaze shot to the herder hobbling alongside Dom, a smile on his wrinkled walnut of a face. Excitement rushed back, so swift and thrilling she was shaking with it when Friedrich smiled and greeted her in a mix of German and heavily accented English.

"*Guten tag, fraülein. Es gut* to see you again."

Eleven

Natalie had spent all those hours soul- and mind- and computer-searching. She'd tried desperately to latch on to something, *anything*, that would trigger her memory. Never in her wildest dreams would she have imagined that trigger would consist of a herd of smelly goats and a wizened little man in a floppy felt hat. Yet the moment Friedrich greeted her in his fractured English, the dam broke.

Images flooded the empty spaces in her mind. Her, standing almost on this same spot. The goatherd, inquiring kindly if she was lost. These same gray-white does butting her knees. The buck giving her the evil eye. A casual chat that sent her off on a wild chase.

"*Guten tag*, Herr Müller." Her voice shook with excitement. "*Es gut* to see you again, too."

Dom had already picked up on the goatherd's greeting to Natalie. Her reply snapped his brows together. "When did you and Friedrich meet?"

"A week ago! Right here, at the castle! I remember him, Dom. I remember the goats and the bells and Herr Müller asking if I was lost. Then…then…"

She was so close to hyperventilating she had to stop and drag in a long, hiccuping breath. Müller looked confused by the rapid-fire exchange, so Natalie forced herself to slow down, space the words, contain the hysterical joy that bubbled to the surface.

"Then we sat there, on that wall, and you told me about the castle before the Soviets came. About the balls and the hunting parties and the tree-lighting ceremony in the great hall. Everyone from the surrounding villages was invited, you said. On Christmas Eve. Uh...*Heiliger Abend*."

"Ja, ja, Heiliger Abend."

"When I mentioned that I'd met the duchess in New York, you told me that you remember when she came to Karlenburgh Castle as a bride. So young and beautiful and gracious to everyone, even the knock-kneed boy who helped tend the goats."

She had to stop and catch her breath again. She could see the scene from last week so clearly now, every detail as though etched in glass. The weeds poking from the cracks in the road. The goats wandering through the rubble. This hunched-shouldered man in his gray felt hat, his gnarled hands folded atop the head of his walking stick, describing Karlenburgh Castle in its glory days.

"Then," she said, the excitement piling up again, "I told you I was searching for a painting that had once hung in the Red Salon. You gave me a very hard look and asked why I, too, should want to know about that particular room after all these years."

Everything was coming at her so fast and furiously and seemingly in reverse, like a DVD rewound at superhigh speed. The encounter with Herr Müller. The drive down from Vienna. A burning curiosity to see the castle ruins. The search for the Canaletto. Sarah and Dev. The duchess and Gina and the twins and Anastazia and meeting Dom for the first time in New York.

The rewind came to a screeching halt, stuck at that meeting with Dom. She could see his laughing eyes. His lazy grin. Hear his casual dismissal of the codicil and the title it conferred on him.

That was one of the reasons she'd returned to Vienna!

Why she'd decided to make a day trip to view the ruins of Karlenburgh Castle, and why she'd been so blasted determined to track the missing Canaletto. She'd wanted to wipe that cynical smile off Dominic St. Sebastian's face. Prove the validity of her research. Rub his nose in it, in fact. And, oh, by the way, possibly determine what happened to a priceless work of art.

And why, when the police tried to determine who she was and what she was doing in Budapest, the only response she could dredge from her confused mind was the Grand Duke of Karlenburgh!

With a fierce effort of will, she sidelined those tumultuous memories and focused on the goatherd. "I asked you who else had enquired about the Red Salon. Remember? You told me someone had come some months ago. And told you his name."

"Ja." His wrinkled face twisting in disgust, Müller aimed a thick wad of spittle at the ground. "Janos Lagy."

Dom had been listening intently without interruption to this point, but the name the goatherd spit out provoked a startled response. "Janos Lagy?"

Natalie threw him a surprised glance but he whipped up a palm and stilled the question he saw quivering on her lips.

"Ja," Müller continued in his thick, accented English. "Janos Lagy, a banker, he tells me, from Budapest. He tells me, too, he is the grandson of a Hungarian who goes to the military academy in Moscow and becomes a *mladshij lejtenant* in the Soviet Army. And I tell him I remember this lieutenant," the goatherd related, his voice shaking with emotion. "He commands the squad sent to destroy Karlenburgh Castle after the Grand Duke is arrested."

Dom mumbled something in Hungarian under his breath. Something short and terse and sounding very unnice to Natalie. She ached to ask him what he knew about

Lagy but Herr Müller was just getting to the crux of the story he'd shared with her less than a week ago.

"When I tell this to the grandson, he shrugs. He shrugs, the grandson of this traitorous lieutenant, as if it's of no matter, and asks me if I am ever in the Red Salon!"

The old man quivered with remembered rage. Raising his walking stick, he shook it in the air.

"I threatened to knock his head. He leaves very quickly then."

"Jézus," Dom muttered. "Janos Lagy."

Natalie couldn't contain herself. "You know him?"

"I know him."

"How!"

"I'll explain in the car, and you can tell me what you did with the information Friedrich gave you. But first..."

He probed for more information but when it was clear the goatherd had shared all he knew, he started to take a gracious leave. To his surprise and acute embarrassment, the old man grabbed his hand and kissed it.

"The Grand Duke and Duchess, they are still missed here," he said with tears swimming in his eyes. "It's good, what I read in the papers, that you are now duke. You'll come back again? Soon?"

"I will," he promised. "And perhaps I can convince the duchess to come, too."

"Ahhhh, I pray that I live to see her again!"

They left him clinging to that hope and picked their way through the weeds back to the car. Natalie was a quivering bundle of nerves but the deep crease between Dom's eyes kept her silent while he keyed the ignition, maneuvered a tight turn and regained the road that snaked up and over the pass. Neither of them spoke until he pulled into a scenic turnout that gave an eagle's-eye view of the valley below.

When Dom swung toward her, his face was still tight. "Start at the beginning. Tell what you remember."

She rewound the DVD again. She focused her growing absorption with both the codicil and Canaletto but glossed over the ignoble desire to rub a certain someone's nose in her research.

"I was there in Vienna, only a little over an hour away. I wanted to see the castle the duchess had told me about during our interviews, perhaps talk to some locals who might remember her."

"Like Friedrich Müller."

"Like Friedrich Müller," she confirmed. "I'd done a review of census records and knew he was one of only a handful of people old enough to have lived through the 1956 Uprising. I intended to go to the address listed as his current residence, but met him by chance there at the ruins instead."

"What a string of coincidences," Dom muttered, shaking his head. "Incredible."

"Not really," she countered, defensive on behalf of her research. "Pretty much everything one needs to know is documented somewhere. You just have to look for it."

He conceded the point. "So you met Friedrich, and he told you about Lagy. What did you do then?"

"I researched him on Google as soon as I got back to my hotel in Vienna. Took me a while to find the right Lagy. It's a fairly common name in Hungary. But I finally tracked him to his office at his bank. His secretary wouldn't put me through until I identified myself as Sarah St. Sebastian Hunter's research assistant and said I was helping with her book dealing with lost works of art. Evidently Janos is something of a collector. He came on the line a few minutes later."

"Did you tell him you were trying to track the Canaletto?"

"Yes, and he asked why I'd contacted him about it. I didn't want to go into detail over the phone, just said I thought I'd found a possible link through his grandfather that I'd like to pursue with him. He asked if I'd discussed this link with anyone else and I told him no, that I wanted to verify it first. I offered to drive to Budapest but he generously offered to meet me halfway."

"In Győr."

"On the tour boat," she confirmed. "He said cruising the Danube was one of his favorite ways to relax, that if I hadn't taken a day trip on the river before I would most certainly enjoy it. I knew I wouldn't. I hate boats, loathe being on the water. But I was so eager to talk to him I agreed. I drove down to Győr the next day."

"And you met Lagy aboard?"

"No. He called after the damned boat had left the dock and said he'd been unavoidably detained. He apologized profusely and said he would meet me when it docked in Budapest instead."

She made a moue of distaste, remembering the long, queasy hours trying not to fixate on the slap of the current against the hull or the constant engine vibration under her feet.

"We didn't approach Budapest until late afternoon. By then I was huddled at the rail near the back of the boat, praying I wouldn't be sick. I remember getting another call. Remember reaching too fast for my phone and feeling really dizzy. I leaned over the rail, thinking I was going to puke." Frowning, she slid her hand under her hair and fingered the still tender spot at the base of her skull. "I must have banged my head on one of the support poles because there was pain. Nasty, nasty pain. And the next thing I know someone's leaning on my chest, pumping water out of my lungs!"

"You never saw Janos Lagy? Never connected with him?"

"Not unless he was one of the guys who fished me out of the river. Who *is* he, Dom? How do you know him?"

"We went to school together."

"You're friends with him?" she asked incredulously.

"Acquaintances. My grandfather was not one to forgive or forget old wrongs. He knew Jan's grandfather had served in the Soviet Army and didn't want me to have anything to do with the Lagy family. He didn't know the bastard had commanded the squad that leveled Karlenburgh Castle, though. I didn't either, until today."

Natalie had been certain that once she regained her memory, every blank space would fill and every question would have an answer. Instead, all new questions were piling up.

"This is so frustrating." She shook her head. "Like a circle that doesn't quite close. You, me, the duchess, the castle, the painting, this guy Lagy. They're all connected, but I can't see how they come together."

"Nor do I," he said, digging his cell phone out of his jeans pocket, "but I intend to find out."

She watched wide-eyed as he pressed a single key and was instantly connected. She understood just enough of his fluid French to grasp that he was asking someone named Andre to run a check on Janos Lagy.

Their return sent the hound into a paroxysm of delight. When Natalie laughed and bent to accept his joyous adulation, he got several quick, slurpy kisses past her guard before she could dodge them.

As a thank-you to the dog-sitters, Dom gave Katya the green light to purchase the latest Justin Bieber CD on his iTunes account and download it to her iPod—with her father's permission, he added. The indulgent papa received the ten-pound Westphalia ham that Dom had picked up at the butcher's on the way home. The hound got a bag of bones, which tantalized him all the way up to the loft.

When Dom unlocked the front door and stood aside for Natalie to precede him, she was hit with a sudden attack of nerves. Now that she'd remembered her past, would it overshadow the present? Would the weight of all those months and years in her "real" life smother the brief days she'd spent here, with Dom?

Her heart thumping, she stepped inside and felt instant relief. And instantly at home...despite the dust motes dancing on a stray sunbeam and the rumpled bedcovers she'd straightened so meticulously before the hound had pounced on them. She knew she was just a guest, yet the most ridiculous sense of belonging enveloped her. The big fat question mark now was how long she'd stay camped out here. At least until she and Dom explored this business with Lagy, surely.

Or not. Doubt raised its ugly head when she glanced over her shoulder and saw him standing just inside the still-open door.

"Aren't you coming in?"

He gave himself a little shake, as if dragging his thoughts together, and dredged up a crooked smile.

"We left your case in the car. I'll go get it."

She used his absence to open the drapes and windows to let in the crisp fall air. Conscious of how Dom had teased her about her neat streak, she tried to ignore the rumpled bed but the damned thing pulled her like a magnet. She was guiltily smoothing the cover when he returned.

Propping her roller case next to the wardrobe, he made for the fridge. "I'm going to have a beer. Would you like one? Or wine, or tea?"

"Tea sounds good. Why don't I brew a fresh pitcher while you check with your friend to see what he's turned up on Lagy?"

Dom took the dew-streaked pilsner and cell phone out to the balcony. Not because he wanted privacy to make the call to Andre. He'd decided last night to trust Natalie in spite of that unexplained arrest and nothing had happened since to change his mind. Unless whatever he learned about Lagy was classified "eyes only," he intended to share it with her. No, he just needed a few moments to sort through everything that had happened in the past twenty-four hours.

Oh hell, who was he kidding?

What he needed was, first, a deep gulp of air. Second, a long swallow of Gold Fassl. And third, a little more time to recover from the mule kick that'd slammed into his midsection when he'd opened the door to the loft and Natalie waltzed in with the Agár frisking around her legs.

He liked having her here. Oddly, she didn't crowd him or shrink his loft to minuscule proportions the way Zia did whenever she blew into Budapest on one of her whirlwind visits, leaving a trail of clothes and scarves and medical books and electronic gadgets in her wake. In fact, Natalie might lean a bit too far in the opposite direction. She would alphabetize and color-code his life if he didn't keep a close eye on her.

He would have to loosen her up. Ratchet her passion for order and neatness down to human levels. He suspected that might take some work but he could manage it. All he had to do was take her to bed often enough—and keep her there long enough—to burn up any surplus energy.

As he gazed at the ornate facades on the Pest side of the river, he could easily envision fall rolling into winter while he lazed under the blankets with Natalie and viewed these same buildings dusted with snow. Or the two of them exercising the hound when the park below was tender and green with spring.

The problem was that he wasn't sure how Natalie felt

about resuming her real life now that she'd remembered it. He suspected she wasn't sure, either. Not yet, anyway. His conscience said he should stick to the suggestion he'd made last night to take things between them slowly, step-by-step. But his conscience couldn't stand up to the homey sounds of Natalie moving around inside the loft, brewing her tea, laughing at the hound's antics.

He wanted her here, with him. Wanted to show her more of the city he loved. Wanted to explore that precise, fascinating mind, hear her breathy gasps and groans when they made love.

And, he thought, his eyes going cold and flat, he wanted to flatten whoever'd hurt her. He didn't believe for a moment she'd hit her head on a support pole and tumbled into the Danube. Janos Lagy had lured her onto that tour boat and Dom was damned well going to find out why.

For once Andre didn't have the inside scoop. Instead, he referred Dom back to the Hungarian agency that conducted internal investigations. The individual Dom spoke to there was cautious and closemouthed and unwilling to share sensitive information with someone she didn't know. She did, however, agree to meet with him and Natalie in the morning.

That made two appointments for tomorrow—one at the US Embassy to obtain a replacement passport and one at the National Tax and Customs Administration.

"Tax and Customs?" Natalie echoed when he told her about the appointments. "Is that like the Internal Revenue Service in the US?"

"More like your IRS and Department of the Treasury combined. The NTCA is our focus for all financial matters, including criminal activities like money laundering and financing terrorist activities."

Her eyes rounded. "And they have something on Lagy?"

"They wouldn't say, but they're interested in talking to you."

"I can't tell them any more than I told you."

"No, but they can tell us what, if anything, Lagy's involved in."

"Well, this has been an amazing day. Two days, actually." Her eyes met his in a smile. "And a pretty amazing night."

The smile clinched it. No way was he letting this woman waltz out of his life the same way she'd waltzed in. Dom thought seriously about plucking the glass out of her hand and carrying her to the bed. Which he would, he promised himself. Later. Right now, he'd initiate a blitz-style campaign to make her develop a passion for all things Hungarian—himself included.

"Did you bring a bathing suit?"

She blinked at the abrupt change of topic. "A bathing suit?"

"Do you have one in your suitcase?"

"I packed for business, not splashing around in hotel pools."

"No matter. We can rent one."

"Rent a bathing suit?" Her fastidious little nose wrinkled. "I don't think so."

"They're sanitized and steam-cleaned. Trust me on this. Stuff a couple of towels in your tote while I feed the hound and we'll go."

"Dom, I don't think public bathing is really my thing."

"You can't leave Budapest without experiencing what gives this city its most distinctive character. Why do you think the Romans called their settlement here Aquincum?"

"Meaning water something?"

"Meaning abundant waters. All they had to do was poke a stick in the ground and a hot spring bubbled up. Get the towels."

* * *

Natalie was even less sure about the whole communal spa thing when they arrived at the elegant Gellért Hotel. The massive complex sat at the base of Gellért Hill, named, Dom informed her, for the unfortunate bishop who came from Venice at the request of King Istivan in 1000 A.D.

"My rebellious Magyar ancestors took exception to the king's conversion to Christianity," Dom related as he escorted her to the columned and colonnaded entrance. "They put the bishop in a barrel, drove long spikes in it and rolled him down the hill."

"Lovely."

"Here we go."

He ushered her into a grand entry hall two or three stories high. A long row of ticket windows lining one side of the hall offered a bewildering smorgasbord of options. Dom translated a menu that included swimming pools, thermal baths with temperatures ranging from a comfortable 86 degrees to a scorching 108 degrees, whirlpools, wave pools, saunas and steam rooms. And massages! Every sort of massage. Natalie gave up trying to pick out options and left the choice to him.

"Don't you need to know what bathing suit size I need?" she asked as they approached a ticket booth.

He cut her an amused glance. "I was with you when you bought those jeans, remember? You're a size forty-two."

Ugh! She hated European sizing. She stood beside him while he purchased their entry and noted that a good number of people passed through the turnstiles with just a flash of a blue card.

"They don't have to pay?"

"They have a medical pass," he explained as he fastened a band around her wrist. "The government operates all spas in Hungary. They're actually part of our health care system. Doctors regularly send patients here for massage or hot soaks or swimming laps."

Impressed but still a little doubtful, Natalie accompanied him into a gloriously ornate lobby, then to a seemingly mile-long hall with windows offering an unimpeded view of a sparkling swimming pool. Swimmers of all ages, shapes and sizes floated, dog-paddled or cut through the water with serious strokes.

"Here's where we temporarily part ways," Dom told her, extracting one of the towels from her tote. "The men's changing area is on the right, the women's on the left. Just show the attendant your wristband and she'll fix you up with a suit. Then hold the band up to the electronic pad and it'll assign you a changing cabin and locker. Once you've changed, flash the band again to enter the thermal baths. I'll meet you there."

That sounded simple enough—until Natalie walked through the entrance to the women's area. It was huge, with marble everywhere, stairs leading up and down, and seemingly endless rows of massage rooms, saunas, showers and changing rooms. A friendly local helped her locate the alcove containing the suit rental desk.

She still harbored distinct doubts about shimmying into a used bathing suit. But when she slid the chit Dom had given her across the desk, the attendant returned with a sealed package containing what looked like a brand-new one-piece. She held her wristband up to the electronic pad as Dom had instructed and got the number of a changing room. Faced with long, daunting rows of cubicles, she had to ask another local for help locating hers. Once they'd found it, the smiling woman took Natalie's wrist and aimed the band at the electronic lock.

"Here, here. Like this."

The door popped open, and her helpful guide added further instructions.

"It locks behind you, yes? You leave your clothes and towels in the cabin, then go through to the thermal pool."

"Thank you."

"Szívesen."

The room was larger than Natalie had expected, with a bench running along one wall and a locker for her clothes and tote. She was still leery of the rented bathing suit but a close inspection showed it to be clean and fresh-smelling.

And at least one size too small!

Cut high on the thighs and low in the front, the sleek black Spandex revealed far more skin than Natalie wanted to display. She tried yanking up the neck but that only pulled the Spandex into an all-too-suggestive V at her crotch. She tugged it down again, determined not to give Dom a peep show.

Not that he would object. The man was nothing if not appreciative of the opposite sex. Kiss Kiss Arabella and lushly endowed Lisel were proof of that. And, Natalie now remembered, his sister Zia and Sarah's sister Gina had both joked about how women fell all over him. And why not? With that sexy grin and too-handsome face, Dominic St. Sebastian could have his pick of…

She froze, her fingers still tugging at the bottom of the suit, as another handsome face flashed into her mind.

Oh, God!

She dropped onto the bench. Blood drained from her heart and gathered like a cold, dead pool in her belly.

Oh God, oh God, oh God!

Wrapping her arms around her middle, she rocked back and forth on the bench. She remembered now the "traumatic" event she'd tried to desperately to suppress. The ugly incident that had caused her to lose her sense of self.

How could she have forgotten for a day—an hour!—the vicious truth she'd kept buried for more than three years? Tears stung her eyes, raked her throat. Furiously, she fought them back. She'd cried all the tears she had in her three years ago. She was damned if she'd shed any more for the bastard who destroyed her life then. And would now destroy it again, she acknowledged on a wave of despair.

How could she have let herself believe last night could lead to something more between her and Dominic St. Sebastian? When she told him about her past, he'd be so disappointed, so disgusted. She sat there, aching for what might have been, until the urge to howl like a wounded animal released its death grip on her throat. Then she got off the bench and pushed through the door at the other end of the changing room.

The temperature in the marble hall shot up as she approached the first of the thermal pools. Dom was there, waiting for her as promised. Yesterday, even this morning, she would have drooled at the sight of his tall, muscled torso sporting a scant few inches of electric-blue Speedo. Now all she could do was gulp when he got a look at her face and stiffened.

"What's wrong?"

"I…I…"

"Natalie, what is it? What's happened?"

"I have to tell you something." She threw a wild look around the busy spa. "But not here. I'll…I'll meet you at the car."

Whirling, she fled back to her changing room.

Twelve

Her mind drowning in a cesspool of memories, Natalie scrambled into her clothes and had to ask for directions several times before she emerged from the maze of saunas and massage rooms.

Dom waited at the entrance to the women's changing rooms instead of at the car. His face was tight with concern and unspoken questions when she emerged. He swept a sharp glance around the hall, as though checking to see if anyone lingered nearby or appeared to be waiting or watching for Natalie, then cut his gaze back to her.

"What happened in the changing area to turn your face so pale?"

"I remembered something."

"About Janos Lagy?"

"No." She gnawed on her lower lip. "An incident in my past. I need to tell you about it."

Something flickered in his eyes. Surprise? Caution? Wariness? It came and went so quickly she couldn't have pinned a label on it even if her thoughts weren't skittering all over the place.

"There's a café across the street. We can talk there."

"A café? I don't think… I don't know…"

"We haven't eaten since breakfast. Whatever you have to tell me will go down easier with a bowl of goulash."

Natalie knew nothing could make it go down easier,

but she accompanied him out of the hotel and into the fall dusk. Lights had begun to glow on the Pest side of the Danube. She barely registered the glorious panorama of gold and indigo as Dom took her arm and steered her to the brightly lit café.

Soon—too soon for her mounting dread—they were enclosed in a high-backed booth that afforded both privacy and an unimpeded view of the illuminated majesty across the river. Dom ordered and signaled for her to wait until the server had brought them both coffee and a basket of thick black bread. He cut Natalie's coffee with a generous helping of milk to suit her American taste buds, then nudged the cup across the table.

"Take a drink, take a breath and tell me what has you so upset."

She complied with the first two instructions but couldn't find a way to broach the third. She stirred more milk into her coffee, fiddled with her spoon, gnawed on her lower lip again.

"Natalie. Tell me."

Her eyes lifted to his. "The scum you hunt down? The thieves and con artists and other criminals?" Misery choked her voice. "I'm one of them."

She'd dreaded his reaction. Anticipated his disgust or icy withdrawal. The fact that he didn't even blink at the anguished confession threw her off for a moment. But only a moment.

"Oh, my God! You know?" Shame coursed through her, followed almost immediately by a scorching realization. "Of course you do! You've known all along, haven't you?"

"Not all along, and not the details." His calm, even tone countered the near hysteria in hers. "Only that you were arrested, the charges were later dropped and the record wiped clean."

Her laugh was short and bitter. "Not clean enough, apparently."

The server arrived then with their goulash. The brief interruption didn't give her nearly enough time to swallow the fact that Dom had been privy to her deepest, darkest, most mortifying secret. The server departed, but the steaming soup sat untouched while Natalie related the rest of her sorry tale.

"I'm not sure how much you know about me, but before Sarah hired me I worked for the State of Illinois. Specifically, for the state's Civil Service Board. I was part of an ongoing project to digitize more than a hundred years' worth of paper files and merge them with current electronic records. I enjoyed the work. It was such a challenge putting all those old records into a sortable database."

She really *had* loved her job, she remembered as she plucked a slice of coarse black bread from the basket and played with it. Not just the digitizing and merging and sorting, but the picture those old personnel records painted of previous generations. Their work ethic, their frugal saving habits, their large numbers of dependents and generous contributions to church and charity. For someone like Natalie with no parents or grandparents or any known family, these glimpses into the quintessential American working family were fascinating.

"Then," she said with a long, slow, thoroughly disgusted sigh, "I fell in love."

She tore a thick piece off the bread, squeezed it into a wad, rolled it around and around between her fingers.

"He was so good-looking," she said miserably. "Tall, athletic, blue-eyed, always smiling."

"Always smiling? Sounds like a jerk."

Her lips twisted. "I was the jerk. I bought his line about wanting to settle down and start a family. Actually started weaving fantasies about a nursery, a minivan with car seats, the whole baby scene. I should've known I wasn't the type to interest someone as smooth and sophisticated as Jason DeWitt for longer than it took for him to hack into my computer."

Dom reached out and put his palm over the fingers still nervously rolling the bread. His grip was strong and warm, his eyes glinting with undisguised anger.

"We'll discuss what type you are later. Right now, I can pretty well guess what came next. Mr. Smooth used your computer to access state records and mine thousands of addresses, dates of birth and social security numbers."

"Try hundreds of thousands."

"Then he sold them, right? I'm guessing to the Russians, although the marketplace is pretty well wide-open these days. And when the crap hit the fan, the feds tracked the breach to you."

"He hadn't sold them yet. They caught him with his hand still in my cookie jar."

Shame and misery engulfed her again. Tears burned as the images from that horrible day played through her head.

"Oh, Dom, it was so awful! The police came to my office! Said they'd been after Jason—the man I *knew* as Jason DeWitt—for over a year. They'd decoded his electronic signature and knew he'd hacked into several major databases. They'd finally penetrated his shields and not only pinpointed his exact location, they kicked in the door to my apartment and nailed him in the act. Then they charged me with being an accomplice to unauthorized access to public records with intent to commit fraud. They arrested me right there in front of all my coworkers and… and…"

She had to stop and gulp back the stinging tears. "Then they hauled me downtown in handcuffs."

"At which point they discovered you weren't a party to the hacking and released you."

Dom's unquestioned acceptance of her innocence should have soothed her raw nerves. Instead, it made it even tougher to finish the sordid tale.

"Not quite."

Writhing inside, she tried to pull her hand away but he kept it caged.

"Jason tried to convince the police it was all my idea. He said I'd teased and taunted him with sex. That would have been laughable," she said, heat surging into her cheeks, "if the police hadn't found a closet full of crotch-high leather skirts, low-cut blouses and peek-a-boo lingerie. Jason kept pestering me to wear that kind of…of slut stuff when we went out. It was enough to make the investigators wring me inside out before they finally released me."

Dom played his thumb over the back of her hand and fought to keep his fury in check. It wasn't enough that the hacker had played on Natalie's lonely childhood and craving for a family. The bastard had also cajoled her into decking herself out like a whore. No wonder she'd swung to the opposite extreme and started dressing like a refugee from a war zone.

Even worse, she'd had no one to turn to for help during what had to be one of the most humiliating moments of her life. No parents to rush downtown and bail her out. No sister to descend like an avenging angel, as Zia would have done. No brother to pulverize the man who'd set her up.

She wasn't alone now, though. Nor would she be alone in the future. Not as long as Dominic had a say in the matter. The absolute certainty of that settled around his heart like a glove as he quietly prompted her to continue.

"What did you do then?"

"I hired a lawyer and got the arrest expunged. Or so I thought," she amended with a frown. "Then I had the lawyer negotiate a deal with my boss. Since the state records hadn't actually been compromised, I said I would quietly disappear if he agreed that my employment record would contain no reference to the whole sorry mess. After some weeks of wrangling with the state attorney general's office, I packed up and left town. I worked at odd jobs for a while until..."

"Until you went to work for Sarah," he finished when she didn't.

Guilt flooded her face. "I didn't lie to her, Dom. I filled out my employment history truthfully. I knew she would check my references, knew my chances were iffy at best. But my former boss stuck to his end of the deal, and my performance reports before...before that big mess were so glowing and complimentary that Sarah hired me after only one interview."

She turned away, shamefaced.

"I know you think I should have told her. I wanted to. I really did. And I intended to. I just thought...maybe if I tracked down the Canaletto first...helped return it to its rightful owner...Sarah and Dev and the duchess would know I wasn't a thief."

"You're not a thief. Natalie, look at me. You're not a thief or a con artist or a criminal. Trust me, I've been around the breed enough to know. Now I have two questions for you before we eat the soup that's been sitting here for so long."

"Only two?"

Her voice was wobbly, her eyes still tear-bright and drenched with a humiliation that made Dom vow to pulverize the scum who'd put it there.

"Where is this Jason character now?"

"Serving five to ten at the Danville Correctional Facility."

"Well, that takes him off my hit list. For now."

An almost smile worked through her embarrassment. "What's question two?"

"How long are you going to keep mashing that piece of bread?"

She blinked and looked down in surprise at the pulpy glob squishing through her fingers.

"Here." He passed her a napkin. "Eat your soup, *drágám*. Then we'll go home and get back to work on finding your painting."

Home. The word reverberated in Natalie's mind when Dom opened the door to the loft and Duke treated them to an ecstatic welcome. She clung to the sound of it, the thought of it, like a lifeline while man and dog took a quick trip downstairs and she went to unpack the roller suitcase still propped next to the wardrobe.

Her toiletries went into the bathroom, her underwear onto the corner of a shelf in the wardrobe. When she lifted the neatly folded blouses, her mouth twisted.

Natalie knew she'd never been a Princess Kate. She wasn't tall or glamorous or as poised as a supermodel. But she'd possessed her own sense of style. She'd preferred a layered look, she now remembered. Mostly slim slacks or jeans with belted tunics or cardigans over tanks…until Jason.

He'd wanted sexier, flashier. She cringed, remembering how she'd suppressed her inner qualms and let him talk her into those thigh-hugging skirts and lace-up bustiers. She'd burned them. The leather skirts, the bustiers, the stilettos and boob tubes and garter belts and push-up bras. Carted the whole lot down to the incinerator in her building, along with every other item in her apartment that carried even a whiff of Jason's scent or a faint trace of his imprint.

Then she'd gone out and purchased an entire new wardrobe of maiden aunt blouses and shapeless linen dresses. She'd also stopped using makeup and began scraping her hair back in a bun. She'd even resorted to wearing glasses she didn't need. Paying penance, she now realized, for her sins.

She was still staring at the folded blouses when Dom and the hound returned. When he saw what she was holding, he dropped the dog's lead on the kitchen counter and crossed the room.

"You don't need these anymore." He took the blouses and dumped them back in the case. "You don't need any of this."

When he zipped the case and propped it next to the wardrobe again, Natalie experienced a heady sense of freedom. As though she'd just shed an outer skin that'd felt as unnatural and uncomfortable as the one she'd tried to squeeze into for Jason.

Buoyed by the feeling, she flashed Dom a smile. "If you don't want me to continue raiding your closet, you'll have to take me shopping again."

"You're welcome to wear anything of mine you wish. Although," he confessed with a quick grin, "I must admit I prefer when you wear nothing at all."

The need that splintered through her was swift and clean and joyous. The shame she'd tried to bury for three long years was still there, just below the surface. She suspected traces of it would linger there for a long while. But for now, for this moment, she could give herself completely to Dom and her aching hunger for his touch.

She looped her arms around his neck and let the smile in his eyes begin healing the scars. "I must admit I prefer you that way, too."

"Then I suggest we both shed some clothes."

They made it to the bed. Barely. A stern command prevented Duke from jumping in with them, but Natalie had to force herself not to look at the hound's reproachful face until Dom's mouth and teeth and busy, busy hands made her forget everything but him.

She was boneless with pleasure and half-asleep when he tucked her into the curve of his body and murmured something in Hungarian.

"What does that mean?"

"Sleep well, my darling."

Her heart tripped, but she didn't ask him to expand on that interesting translation. She settled for snuggling closer to his warmth and drifting into a deep, dreamless sleep.

Natalie woke the next morning to the sound of hammering. She pried one eye open and listened for several moments before realizing that was rain pounding against the roof. Burrowing deeper under the featherbed, she resurfaced again only when an amused voice sounded just over her shoulder.

"The dog and I are going for our run. Coffee's on the stove when you're ready for it."

She half rolled over. "You're going out in the rain?"

"That's one of the penalties of being adopted by a racing hound. He needs regular exercise whatever the weather. We both do, actually."

Natalie grunted, profoundly thankful that she wasn't invited to participate in this morning ritual.

"I'll bring back apple pancakes for breakfast," Dom advised as he and the joyously prancing Agár headed for the door. "Then we'll need to leave for the appointments at the embassy and the Tax and Customs Administration."

"And shopping," Natalie called to his back. "I need to shop!"

The prospect of replenishing her wardrobe with bright colors and soft textures erased any further desire to burrow. By the time Dom and Duke returned she'd showered and dressed in her one pair of jeans and tank top. She'd also made the bed, fussed with the folds in the drapes and dust-mopped the loft's wood-plank floors.

Her welcome smile slipped a little when the runners tracked wet foot- and paw-prints across the gleaming floors. She had to laugh, though, and hold up her hands against a flying spray when the hound planted all four paws and shook from his nose to his tail.

She and Dom feasted on the pancakes that he'd somehow protected from the rain. Then he, too, got ready for the morning's appointments. He emerged from the bathroom showered and shaved and looking too scrumptious for words in jeans and a cable-knit fisherman's sweater.

"You'd better bring the Canaletto file," he advised.

"I have it," she said, patting her briefcase. "I made copies of the key documents, just in case."

"Good." He held up the jacket she'd pretty much claimed as her own. "Now put this on and we'll go."

Natalie was glad of its warmth when they went down to the car. The rain had lessened to a misty drizzle but the damp chill carried a bite. Not even the gray weather could obscure the castle ramparts, though, as Dom negotiated the curving streets of Castle Hill and joined the stream of traffic flowing across Chain Bridge.

The US Embassy was housed in what had once been an elegant turn-of-the century palazzo facing a lush park. High metal fencing and concrete blocks had turned it into a modern-day fortress and long lines waited to go through the security checkpoint. As Dom steered Natalie to a side entrance with a much shorter line, she noted a bronze plaque with a raised relief religious figure.

"Who's that?"

"Cardinal József Mindszenty, one of the heroes of modern Hungary. The communists tortured and imprisoned him for speaking out against their brutal regime. He got a temporary reprieve during the 1956 Revolution, but when the Soviets crushed the uprising, the US Embassy granted him political asylum. He remained here for more than fifteen years.

"Fifteen *years*?"

"Cardinal Mindszenty is one of the reasons Hungary and the United States enjoy such close ties today."

Dom's Interpol credentials got them into the consular offices through the side entrance. After passing through security and X-ray screening, they arrived at their appointment right on time

Replacing Natalie's lost passport took less than a half hour. She produced the copy of her driver's license Dom's contact had procured and the forms she'd already completed. After signing the form in front of a consular officer and having it witnessed by another official, the computer spit out a copy of her passport's data page.

She winced at the photo, taken when she'd renewed her passport just over a year ago, but she thanked the official and slipped the passport into her tote with an odd, unsettled feeling. She should have been relieved to have both her memory and her identity back. She could leave Hungary now. Go home to the States, or anywhere else her research took her. How stupid was she for wishing this passport business had taken weeks instead of minutes?

Their second appointment didn't go as quickly or as well. Dom's Interpol credentials seemed to have a negative effect on the two uniformed officers they met with at the NTCA. One was a spare, thirtysomething woman who introduced herself as Patrícia Czernek, the other a graying older man who greeted Natalie with a polite nod before engaging Dom in a spirited dialogue. It didn't take a genius or a working knowledge of Hungarian to figure out they were having a bit of a turf war. Natalie kept out of the line of fire until the female half of the team picked up the phone and made a call that appeared to settle the matter.

With a speaking glance at her partner, Officer Czernek turned to Natalie. "So Ms. Clark, we understand from Special Agent St. Sebastian that you may have knowledge of a missing painting by a Venetian master. One taken from Karlenburgh Castle during the 1956 Uprising. Will you tell us, please, how you came by this knowledge?"

"Certainly."

Extracting the Canaletto file, she passed each of the officers a copy of the chronology she'd run earlier. "This summarizes my research, step-by-step. As you can see, it began three months ago with a computer search."

The NTCA officers flipped through the four-sheet printout and exchanged looks. Dom merely smiled.

"If you'll turn to page three, line thirty-seven," Natalie continued briskly, "you'll see that I did a search of recently declassified documents from the Soviet era relating to art treasures owned by the state and found an inventory of items removed from Karlenburgh Castle. The inventory listed more than two dozen near priceless works of art, but not the Canaletto. Yet I knew from previous discussions with Grand Duchess Charlotte that the painting *was* hanging in the Red Salon the day the Soviets came to destroy the castle."

She walked them through her search step-by-step. Her decision to drive down from Vienna to interview local residents. Her stop at the ruins and meeting with Friedrich Müller. His reference to an individual who'd inquired previously at the Red Salon.

"Janos Lagy," the older of the two officers murmured. He skimmed down several lines and looked up quickly. "You spoke with him? You spoke with Lagy about this painting?"

"I did."

"And arranged to meet with him on a riverboat?"

"That was his idea, not mine. Unfortunately, he didn't show."

"Do you have a recording of this conversation?" Officer Czernek asked hopefully. "On your cell phone, perhaps?"

"I lost my purse and phone when I went overboard."

"Yes, Special Agent St. Sebastian told us about your accident." A frown etched between her brows. "We also reviewed a copy of the incident report from the metropolitan police. It's very strange that no one saw you fall from the boat or raised an alarm."

"I was at the back of the ship and not feeling very well. Also, this happened in the middle of the week. There weren't many other passengers aboard."

"Still…"

She and her partner engaged in a brief exchange.

"We, too, have a file," she said, turning back to Natalie. "Would you be so kind as to look at some pictures and tell me if you recognize any of the people in them?"

She produced a thin folder and slid out three eight-by-tens. One showed a lone figure in a business suit and tie. The second picture was of the same individual in a tux and smiling down at the svelte beauty on his arm. In the third, he strolled along a city street wearing an overcoat and smart fedora.

"Do you recognize that man?" Czernek asked, her gaze intent on Natalie.

She scrutinized the lean features again. The confident smile, the dark eyes and fringe of brown hair around a head going bald on top. She'd never seen him before. She was sure of it.

"No, I don't recognize him. Is it Lagy?"

The police officer nodded and blew out an obviously disappointed breath. When she reached over to gather the pictures, Natalie had to battle her own crushing disappointment. Lagy's link to the Canaletto had been tenuous at best but she'd followed thinner threads. Suddenly, she frowned and took another look at the street shot.

"Him!" She stabbed a finger at a figure trailing a little way behind Lagy. "I recognize this man. He was on the boat."

"Are you sure?"

"Very sure. When I got sick, he asked if he could help but I waved him away. I didn't want to puke all over his shoes." She looked up eagerly. "Do you know who he is?"

"He's Janos Lagy's bodyguard."

The air in the small office suddenly simmered with rigidly suppressed excitement. Natalie looked from Czernek to her partner to Dom and back again. All of them, apparently, knew something she didn't.

"Clue me in," she demanded. "What have you got on Janos Lagy?"

The officer hesitated. A cop's natural instinct to hold her cards close to her chest, Natalie guessed. Tough! She wasn't leaving the NTCA until she got some answers.

"Look," she said mutinously, "I've chased all over Europe tracking the Canaletto. I've spent weeks digging through musty records. I whacked my head and took an unplanned swim in the Danube. I didn't know who I was for almost a week. So I think I deserve an answer. What's the story on Lagy?"

After another brief pause, Czernek relented. "We've had him under surveillance for some time now. We suspect he's been trafficking in stolen art and have unsubstantiated reports of a private collection kept in a secret vault in his home."

"You're kidding!"

"No, I am not. Unfortunately, we haven't been able to gather enough evidence to convince a judge to issue a search warrant." Patrícia Czernek's lips parted in a knife blade of a smile. "Based on what you've told us, we may be able to get that warrant."

Thirteen

After all she'd done, all she'd been through, Natalie considered it a complete and total bummer that she was forced to sit on the sidelines during the final phase of the hunt that had consumed her for so many weeks.

The task force gathered early the morning after Natalie had ID'd the bodyguard. As tenuous as that connection was to Lagy and the missing Canaletto, when combined with other evidence NCTA had compiled on the banker, it proved sufficient for a judge to grant a search warrant. Dom left the loft before dawn to join the team that would hit the banker's villa on the outskirts of Budapest. Natalie was left behind with nothing to do but walk the hound, make another excursion to the butcher shop, scrub the shower stall, dust-mop the floors again and pace.

"This is the pits," she complained to the hound as the morning dragged by.

The Agár cocked his head but didn't look particularly sympathetic.

"Okay, okay! It's true I don't have any official standing that could have allowed them to include me in the task force. And I guess I don't really want to see anyone hauled off in handcuffs. That would cut a little too close to the bone," she admitted with a grimace. "Still," she grumbled, shooting another glance at the kitchen clock, "you'd think certain people would find a way to let me know what's happening."

Dominic couldn't contact her directly. She knew that. Natalie's phone was at the bottom of the Danube and the loft didn't have a landline. He could've called his downstairs neighbors, though, and asked Katya or her father to relay a message.

Or not. There was probably some rule or protocol that prohibited disseminating information about an ongoing investigation to civilians.

"That better not include me."

The bad-tempered comment produced a nervous whine from the hound. Natalie stooped to scratch behind his ear.

"Sorry, Duke'ums. I'm just a little annoyed with your alter ego."

Annoyed and increasingly worried as morning crawled toward noon, then into the afternoon, she was seriously contemplating going downstairs to ask Katya if she could use her phone when she heard the heavy tread of footsteps on the outside stairs.

"Finally!"

She rushed to the door, startling the dog into a round of excited barking. One look at Dom's mile-wide grin sent all her nasty recriminations back down her throat. She could only laugh when he caught her by the waist and swung her in wide circles. The hound, of course, went nuts. Natalie had to call a halt before they all tripped over each other and tumbled down five flights of stairs.

"Dom, stop! You're making me dizzy."

He complied with a smooth move that shifted her from mostly vertical to horizontal. Still wearing a cheek-splitting grin, he carried her over the threshold and kicked the door shut as soon as the three of them were inside.

"I assume you got your man," she said.

"You assume right. Hold on."

He opened the fridge and dipped her almost vertical again. Squealing, she locked her arms around his neck while he retrieved two frosty bottles from the bottom shelf, then carried her to the sofa. He sank onto the cushions with Natalie in his lap and thumped his boots up on the coffee table.

She managed to keep from pelting him with questions while he offered her one of the dew-streaked bottles of pilsner. When she shook her head, he popped the cap and tilted his head. She watched, fascinated, as he downed half the contents in long, thirsty swallows. He hadn't had time to shave before he'd left. The beginnings of a beard shadowed his cheeks and chin. And his knuckles, she noted with a small gasp, had acquired a nasty set of scrapes and bruises.

"What happened to your knuckles?"

"Lagy's bodyguard ran into them." Something dark and dangerous glinted in his eyes. "Several times."

"What? Why?"

"We had a private discussion about your swim in the Danube. He disavowed any responsibility for it, of course, but I didn't like the way his lip curled when he did."

She gaped at him, her jaw sagging. She'd been alone so long. And so sickened by the way Jason had tried to pin the blame for his illegal activities on her. The idea that Dom had set himself up as her protector and avenger cut deep into her heart. Before she could articulate the chaotic emotions those bruised knuckles roused, however, the hound almost climbed into her lap.

She held him off, but it took some effort. "You'd better give him some of your beer before he grabs the bottle out of your hand, and tell me the rest of the story!"

He tipped the bottle toward the Agár's eager jaws. Natalie barely registered an inward cringe as pale gold lager slopped in all directions. Duke dropped the empty bottle on the floor and was scooting it across the oak planks to extract the last drops when Dom launched into a detailed account.

"We hit the villa before Lagy had left for the bank. When Czernek showed him the search warrant, he wouldn't let us proceed until his high-priced lawyer arrived on the scene."

"Did Lagy recognize you?"

"Oh, yeah. He made some crack about the newspaper stories, but I could tell the fact that a St. Sebastian had showed up at his door with an armed squad made him nervous. Especially when I flashed my Interpol credentials."

"Then what happened?"

"We cooled our heels until his lawyer showed up. Bastard had the nerve to play lord of the manor and offer us all coffee."

"Which you accepted," she guessed, all too mindful of the Hungarian passion for the brew.

"Which we accepted," he confirmed. "By the time his lawyer arrived, though, we'd all had our fill of acting polite. His attorney tried to posture and bluff, but folded like an accordion when Czernek waved the search warrant under his nose. Apparently he'd gotten crosswise of this particular judge before and knew he couldn't fast-talk his client out of this one. Then," Dom said with savage satisfaction, "we tore the villa apart. Imagine our surprise when infrared imaging detected a vault hidden behind a false wall in Lagy's study."

When he paused to pop the cap on the second bottle, Natalie groaned in sheer frustration.

"Don't you dare drink that before you tell me what was in the vault!"

"See for yourself." Shifting her on his lap, he jammed a hand in the pocket of his jeans and extracted a folded printout. "That's just a preliminary inventory. Each piece has to be examined and authenticated by a team of experts."

Her hands shaking with excitement, Natalie unfolded the printout and skimmed the fourteen entries.

"Omigod!"

The list read like a who's who of the art world. Edgar Degas. Josef Grassi. Thomas Gainsborough. And there, close to the bottom, Giovanni Canaletto.

"Did you see the Canaletto?" she asked breathlessly. "Is it the one from Karlenburgh Castle?"

"Looked like it to me."

"I can't believe it!"

"Lagy couldn't, either, when Czernek called for a team to crate up his precious paintings and take them in evidence."

She skimmed the list again, stunned by its variety and richness. "How incredible that he managed to amass such an extensive collection. It must be worth hundreds of millions."

"He may have acquired some of it through legitimate channels. As for the rest..." Dom's jaw hardened. "I'm guessing he inherited many of those paintings from his grandfather. Karlenburgh Castle wasn't the only residence destroyed in retribution for their owners' participation in the '56 Uprising. *Mladshij Lejtenant* Lagy's company of sappers would have been only too eager help take them down. God knows how many treasures the bastards managed to appropriate for themselves in the process."

Natalie slumped against his chest and devoured the brief descriptions of the paintings removed from Lagy's villa. Several she recognized immediately from Interpol's database of lost or stolen art. Others she would need more detail on before she could be sure.

"This," she said, excitement still singing through her veins, "is going make a fantastic final chapter in Sarah's book. Her editors will eat up the personal angle. A painting purchased for a young duchess, then lost for decades. The hunt by the duchess's granddaughter for the missing masterpiece. The raid that recovered it, which just happened to include the current Grand Duke."

"Let's not forget the part you played in the drama."

"I'm just the research assistant. You St. Sebastians are the star players."

"You're not 'just' anything, Natushka."

To emphasize the point, he tugged on her hair and tilted her head back for a long, hard kiss. Neither of them held back, taking and giving in both a welcome release of tension and celebration.

Natalie was riding high when Dom raised his head. "I can't wait to tell Sarah about this. And the duchess! When do you think her painting will be returned to her?"

"I have no idea. They'll have to authenticate it first, then trace the provenance. If Lagy can prove he purchased it or any of these paintings in good faith from a gallery or another collector, the process could take weeks or months."

"Or longer," she said, scrunching her nose. "Can't you exert some royal influence and hurry the process along?"

"Impatient little thing, aren't you?"

"And then some!" She scooted off his lap and onto the cushion next to him. "Let's contact Sarah via FaceTime. I want to see her reaction when we tell her."

They caught Sarah in midair aboard Dev's private jet. The moment Dom made the connection, her employer fired an anxious query.

"How's Natalie? Has her memory returned?"

"It has."

"Thank God! Where is she now?"

"She's here, with me. Hang on."

He angled the phone to capture Natalie's eager face. "Hello, Sarah."

"Oh, Natalie, we've been so worried. Are you really okay?"

"Better than okay. We've located the Canaletto!"

"What?" Sarah whipped her head to one side. "Dev, you're not going to believe this! Natalie's tracked down Grandmama's Canaletto."

"I didn't do it alone," Natalie protested, aiming a quick smile at Dom. "It was a team effort."

When she glanced back at the screen, Sarah's brows had inched up. "Well," she said after a small pause, "if I was going to team with anyone other than my husband, Dominic would certainly top my list."

A telltale heat rushed into Natalie's cheeks but she didn't respond to the curiosity simmering just below the surface of her employer's reply. Mostly because she wasn't really sure how to define her "teaming" with Dom, much less predict how long it would last. But she couldn't hold back a cheek-to-cheek grin as she related the events of the past few days. Sarah's eyes grew wider with the telling, and at the end of the recital she echoed Natalie's earlier sentiments.

"This is all so incredible. I can't wait to tell Grandmama the Canaletto's been recovered."

Dom leaned over Natalie's shoulder to issue the same warning he had earlier. "They'll have to assemble a team of experts to authenticate each painting and validate its provenance. That could take several months or more."

Dev's face crowded next to his wife's on the small screen. "We'll see what we can do to expedite the process, at least as far as the Canaletto is concerned."

"And I'll ask Gina to get Jack involved," Sarah volunteered. "He can apply some subtle pressure through diplomatic channels."

"I also suggested to the Grand Duke here that he should exercise a little royal muscle," Natalie put in.

"Good for you. With all three of our guys weighing in, I'm sure we can shake Grandmama's painting loose without too long a delay."

The reference to "our" guys deepened the heat in Natalie's cheeks. She floundered for a moment, but before she could think of an appropriate response to the possessive pronoun, Sarah had already jumped ahead.

"We need to update the chapter on the Canaletto, Nat. And if we put our noses to the grindstone, we ought to be able to finish the final draft of the book in two or three weeks. When can you fly back to L.A.?"

"I, uh…"

"Scratch that. Instead of going straight home, let's rendezvous in New York. I'd like you to personally brief my editor. I know she'll want to take advantage of the publicity all this is going to generate. We can fly to L.A. from there."

She could hardly say no. Sarah St. Sebastian Hunter had offered her the job of a lifetime. Not only did Natalie love the work, she appreciated the generous salary and fringe benefits that came with it. She owed her boss loyalty and total dedication until her book hit the shelves.

"No problem. I can meet you in New York whenever it works for you."

"I'll call my editor as soon as we hang up. I'll try to arrange something on Thursday or Friday. Did you get a replacement passport? Great. You should probably fly home tomorrow, then. I'll have a ticket waiting for you at the airport."

She disconnected with a promise to call back as soon as she'd nailed down the time and place of the meeting. Dominic tossed his phone on the coffee table and turned to Natalie.

She couldn't quite meet his eyes. She felt as though

she'd just dropped down an elevator shaft. Mere moments ago she'd been riding a dizzying high. In a few short seconds, she'd plunged back into cold, hard reality. She had a job, responsibilities, a life back in the States, such as it was. And neither she nor Dom had discussed any alternative. Still, the prospect of leaving Hungary drilled a hole in her heart.

"Sarah's been so good to me," she said, breaking the small silence. "I need to help put the final touches on her book."

"Of course you do. I, too, must go back to work. I've been away from it too long."

She plucked at the hem of her borrowed shirt. She should probably ask Dom to take her on a quick shopping run. She could hardly show up for a meeting with Sarah's editor in jeans and a tank top, much less a man's soccer shirt. Yet she hated to spend her last hours in Budapest cruising boutiques.

She tried to hide her misery at the thought of leaving, but Dom had to see it when he curled a knuckle under her chin and tipped her face to his.

"Perhaps this is for the best, *drágám.* You've had so much thrown at you in such a short time. The dive into the Danube. The memory loss. Me," he said with a crooked grin. "You need to step back and take a breath."

"You're probably right," she mumbled.

"I know I am. And when you've helped Sarah put her book to bed, you and I will decide where we go from there, yes?"

She wanted to believe him. Ached all over with the need to throw herself into his arms and make him *swear* this wasn't the end. Unfortunately, all she could think of was Kiss Kiss Arabella's outrageously expensive panties and Lovely Lisel's effusive greeting and Gina's laughing comments about her studly cousin and…

Dominic cut into those lowering thoughts by tugging her up and off the sofa with him. "So! Since this is your last night in Budapest for a while at least, we should make it one to remember."

For a while at least. Natalie clung to the promise of that small phrase as Dom scooped up his phone and stuffed it in his jeans pocket. Taking time only to pull on the red-and-black soccer shirt with its distinctive logo on the sleeve, he insisted she throw on the jacket she'd pretty much claimed as her own before hustling her to the door.

"Where are we going?"

"My very favorite place in all the city."

Since the city boasted spectacular architecture, a world-class opera house, soaring cathedrals, palatial spas and a moonlit, romantic castle perched high on its own hill, Natalie couldn't begin to guess which was Dom's favorite spot. She certainly wouldn't have picked the café/bar he ushered her into on the Pest side of the river. It was tiny, just one odd-shaped room, and noisy and crammed with men decked out in red-and-black-striped shirts. Most were around Dom's age, although Natalie saw a sprinkling of both freckles and gray hair among the men. Many stood with arms looped over the shoulders or around the waists of laughing, chatting women.

They were greeted with hearty welcomes and backslaps and more than one joking "His Grace" or "Grand Duke." Dom made so many introductions Natalie didn't even try to keep names and faces matched. As the beer flowed and his friends graciously switched to English to include her in the lively conversation, she learned she would have a ringside seat—via satellite and high-definition TV—at the World Cup European playoffs. Hungary's team had been eliminated in the quarterfinals, much to the disgust of everyone in the bar, but they'd grudgingly shifted their allegiance to former rival Slovakia.

With such a large crowd and such limited seating, Natalie watched the game, nestled on Dom's lap. Hoots and boos and foot-stomping thundered after every contested call. Cheers and ear-splitting whistles exploded when Slovakia scored halfway through the first quarter. Or was it the first half? Third? Natalie had no clue.

She was deafened by the noise, jammed knee to knee with strangers, breathing in the tang of beer and healthy male sweat, and she loved every minute of it! The noise, the excitement, the color, the casually possessive arm Dom hooked around her waist. She filed away every sensory impression, every scent and sound and vivid visual image, so she could retrieve them later. When she was back in New York or L.A. or wherever she landed after Sarah's book hit the shelves.

She refused to dwell on the uncertain future during the down-to-the-wire game. Nor while she and Dom took the hound for a romp through the park at the base of the castle. Not even when they returned to the loft and he hooked his arms around her waist as she stood in front of the wall of windows, drinking in her last sight of the Parliament's floodlit dome and spires across the river.

"It's so beautiful," she murmured.

"Like you," he said, nuzzling her ear.

"Ha! Not hardly."

"You don't see what I see."

He turned her, keeping her in the circle of his arms, and cradled her hips against his. His touch was featherlight as he stroked her cheek.

"Your skin is so soft, so smooth. And your eyes reflect your inner self. So intelligent, so brave even when you were so frightened that you would never regain your memory."

"Terrified" was closer to the mark, but she wasn't about to interrupt this interesting inventory.

Smiling, he threaded his fingers through her hair.

"I love how this goes golden-brown in the sunlight. Like thick, rich honey. It's true, your chin hints at a bit of a stubborn streak but your lips… Ah, Natushka, your lips. Have you any idea what that little pout of yours does to me?"

"Children pout," she protested. "Sultry beauties with collagen lips pout. I merely express…"

"Disapproval," he interjected, nipping at her lower lip. "Disdain. Disgust. All of which I saw in your face the first time we met. I wondered then whether I could make these same lips quiver with delight and whisper my name."

The nipping kisses achieved the first of his stated goals. Pleasure rippled across the surface of Natalie's skin even as Dom's husky murmur sent up a warning flag. She'd represented a challenge. She'd sensed that from the beginning. She remembered, too, how his sister and cousins had teased him about his many conquests. But now? Was the slow heat he stirred in her belly, the aching need in her chest, merely the by-product of a skilled seduction? Had she tumbled into love with the wrong man again?

She knew the answer before the question even half formed. Dominic St. Sebastian was most definitely the right man. The *only* man she wanted in her heart. In her life. She couldn't tell him, though. Her one and only previous foray into this love business had left her with too much baggage. Too many doubts and insecurities. And she was leaving in the morning. That more than anything else blocked the words she ached to say.

It didn't keep her from cradling his face in her palms while she kissed him long and hard. Or undressing him slowly, savoring every taut muscle, every hollow and hard plane of his body. Or groaning his name when he drove them both to a shattering climax.

Fourteen

Natalie couldn't classify the next five weeks as totally miserable.

Her first priority when she landed in New York was refurbishing her wardrobe before the meeting with Sarah and her editors. After she'd checked into her hotel she made a quick foray to Macy's. Sarah had smiled her approval at her assistant's conservative but nicely tailored navy suit and buttercup-yellow blouse.

Her smile had morphed to a wide grin when she and Natalie emerged from the meeting at Random House. Her editors were enthusiastic about how close the manuscript was to completion and anxious to get their hands on the final draft.

After a second meeting to discuss advance promo with Sarah's former boss at *Beguile* magazine, the two women flew back to California and hit the ground running. They spent most of their waking hours in Sarah's spacious, glass-walled office on the second floor of the Pacific Palisades mansion she shared with Dev. The glorious ocean view provided no distraction as they revised and edited and polished and proofed.

The final draft contained twenty-two chapters, each dedicated to a specific lost treasure. The Fabergé egg rated one chapter, the Bernini bronze another. The final chapter was devoted to the Canaletto, with space left for a photograph of the painting being restored to its rightful owner. *If* it was ever restored!

The authentication and provenance process was taking longer than any of the St. Sebastians had hoped. Several big-time insurance companies were now involved, anxious to recoup the hundreds of thousands of dollars they'd paid out over the years.

The Canaletto didn't fall into that category. It *had* been insured, as had many of the valuable objects in Karlenburgh Castle, but the policy contained exclusions for loss due to war and/or acts of God. By categorizing the 1956 Uprising as war, the insurer had wiggled out of compensating the duchess for St. Sebastian heirlooms that had either disappeared or made their way into private collections. Still, with so many conflicting claims to sort out, the team charged with verifying authenticity and rightful ownership had its hands full.

Dominic, Dev Hunter and Jack Harris had done what they could to speed the process. Dev offered to fund part of the effort. Jack helped facilitate coordination between international agencies asserting conflicting claims. Much to his disgust, Dom didn't return to undercover work. Instead, his boss at Interpol detailed him to act as their liaison to the recovery team. He grumbled about that but provided the expertise to link Lagy to several black marketeers and less reputable galleries suspected of dealing in stolen art.

He kept Sarah and Natalie apprised of the team's progress by email and texts. The personal calls came in the evenings, after Natalie had dragged back to her rented one-room condo. They'd spoken every couple of nights when she'd first returned, less frequently as both she and Dom got caught up in their separate tasks. But just the sound of his voice could make her hurt with a combination of hunger and loneliness.

The doubts crept in after she'd been home for several weeks. Dom seemed distracted when he called. After almost a month, it felt to Natalie as though he was struggling to keep any conversation going that didn't deal directly with the authentication effort.

Sarah seemed to sense her assistant's growing unease. She didn't pry, but she had a good idea what had happened between her cousin and Natalie during their time together in Budapest. She got a far clearer picture when she dropped what she thought was a casual question one rainy afternoon.

"Did Dom give you any glimmer of hope when the team might vet the Canaletto the last time he called?"

Natalie didn't look up from the dual-page layout on her computer screen. "No."

"Damn. We're supposed to fly to New York for another meeting with Random House next week. I hate to keep putting them off. Maybe you can push Dom a little next time you talk to him."

"I'm…I'm not sure when that will be."

From the corner of her eye Natalie saw Sarah's head come up. Swiveling her desk chair, she met her employer's carefully neutral look.

"Dom's been busy… The time difference… It's tough catching each other at home and…"

The facade crumbled without a hint of warning. One minute she was faking a bright smile. Two seconds later she was gulping and swearing silently that she would *not* cry.

"Oh, Natalie." Sympathy flooded Sarah's warm brown eyes. "I'm sure it's just as you say. Dom's busy, you're busy, you're continents apart…"

"And the tabloids have glommed on to him again," Natalie said with a wobbly smile.

"I know," Sarah said with a grimace. "One of these days I'll learn not to trust Alexis."

Her former boss had sworn up and down she didn't leak the story. Once it hit the press, though, *Beguile* followed almost immediately with a four-page color spread featuring Europe's sexiest single royal and his role in the recovery of stolen art worth hundreds of millions. Although the story stopped short of revealing that Dom worked for Interpol, it hinted at a dark and dangerous side to the duke. It even mentioned the Agár and obliquely suggested the hound had been trained by an elite counterterrorist strike force to sniff out potential targets. Natalie might have chuckled at that if the accompanying photo of Dom and Duke running in the park below the castle hadn't knifed right into her heart.

As a consequence, she was feeling anything but celebratory when she joined Sarah and Dev and Dev's extraordinarily efficient chief of operations, Pat Donovan, at a dinner to celebrate the book's completion. She mustered the requisite smiles and lifted her champagne flute for each toast. But she descended into a sputtering blob of incoherence when Sarah broached the possibility of a follow-on book specifically focused on Karlenburgh's colorful, seven-hundred-year history.

"Please, Natalie! Say you'll work with me on the research."

"I, uh…"

"Would you consider a one-year contract, with an option for two more? I'll double what I'm paying you now for the first year, and we can negotiate your salary for the following two."

She almost swallowed her tongue. "You're already paying me twice what the average researcher's services are worth!"

Dev leaned across the table and folded his big hand around Natalie's. "You're not just a researcher, kid. We consider you one of the family."

"Th-Thank you."

She refused to dwell on her nebulous, half-formed thoughts of actually becoming a member of their clan. Those silly hopes had faded in the past month…to the point where she wasn't sure she could remain on the fringe of Sarah's family orbit.

Her outrageously expensive dinner curdled at the thought of bumping into Dom at the launch of Sarah's book six or eight months from now. Or crossing paths with him if she returned to Hungary to research the history of the St. Sebastians. Or seeing the inevitable gossip put out by the tabloids whenever the sexy royal appeared at some gala with a glamorous female looking suspiciously like Natalie's mental image of Kissy Face Arabella.

"I'm overwhelmed by the offer," she told Sarah with a grateful smile. "Can I take a little time to think it over?"

"Of course! But think fast, okay? I'd like to brief my editors on the concept when we meet with them next week."

Before Natalie could even consider accepting Sarah's offer, she had to come clean. The next morning she burned with embarrassment as she related the whole sorry story of her arrest and abrupt departure from her position as an archivist for the State of Illinois. Sarah listened with wide eyes but flatly refused to withdraw her offer.

"Oh, Nat, I'm so sorry you got taken in by such a conniving bastard. All I can say is that he's lucky he's behind bars. He'd damned well better keep looking over his shoulder when he gets out, though. Dev and Dominic both have long memories."

Relieved by Sarah's unqualified support but racked with doubts about Dom, Natalie was still agonizing over her decision the following Tuesday, when a taxi delivered her and Sarah to the tower of steel and glass housing her publisher. Spanning half a block in downtown Manhattan, the mega-conglomerate's lobby was walled with floor-to-ceiling bookcases displaying the hundreds of books put out each month by Random House's many imprints.

It was Natalie's third time accompanying Sarah to this publishing cathedral but the display of volumes hot off the press still awed her book-lover soul. While Sarah signed them both in and waited for an escort to whisk them up to the thirty-second floor, Natalie devoured the jacket and back-cover copy of a new release detailing the events leading to World War I and its catastrophic impact on Europe. Germany and the Austro-Hungarian Empire were major players in those cataclysmic events.

Karlenburgh sat smack in the juxtaposition of those cultures and epic struggles. Natalie itched to get her hands on the book. She was scrambling for her iPhone to snap a shot of the book jacket when a shrill bark cut through the low-level hum of the busy lobby. She spun around, her jaw dropping as a brown-and-white bullet hurtled straight toward her.

"Duke!" She took two front paws hard in the stomach, staggered back, dropped to her knees. "What…? How…? Whoa! Stop, fella! Stop!"

Laughing, she twisted her head to dodge the Agár's ecstatic kisses. The sight of Dom standing at the lobby entrance, his grin as goofy as the hound's, squeezed the air from her lungs. The arms fending the dog off collapsed, Duke lunged, and they both went down.

She heard a scramble of footsteps. A frantic voice shouting for someone to call 911 or animal control or whoever. A strangled yelp as a would-be rescuer grabbed Duke's collar and yanked him off her. Sarah protesting the rough handling. Dom charging across the lobby to take control of the situation.

By the time the chaos finally subsided, he'd hauled Natalie to her feet and into his arms. "Ah, Natushka," he said, his eyes alight with laughter, "the hound and I hoped to surprise you, not cause a riot."

"Forget the riot! What are you doing in here?"

"I called Sarah's office to speak with you and was told you'd both flown to New York."

"But...but..." She couldn't get her head and her heart to work in sync. "How did you know we'd be here, at the publisher? Oh! You did your James Bond thing, didn't you?"

"I did."

"I still don't understand. You? Duke? Here?"

"We missed you."

The simple declaration shimmered like a rainbow, breathing color into the hopes and dreams that had shaded to gray.

"I planned to wait until I could bring the Canaletto," he told her, tipping his forehead to hers. "I wanted you with me when we restored the painting and all the memories it holds for the duchess. But every day, every night away from you ate at my patience. I got so restless and bad-tempered even the hound would snarl or slink away from me. The team's infuriatingly slow pace didn't help. You probably didn't notice when I called but..."

"I noticed," she drawled.

"But it all boiled down to frustration," he finished with a rueful smile. "Pure, unadulterated frustration."

She started to tell him he wasn't the only one who'd twisted and turned and tied themself up in knots but he preempted any reply by cradling her face in his palms.

"I wanted to wait before I told you that I love you, *drágám*. I wanted to give you time, let you find your feet again. I was worried, too, about the weeks and months my job would take me away. Your job, as well, if you accept the offer Dev told me about when I called to speak with you. I know your work is important to you, as mine is to me. We can work it out, yes?"

She pretty much stopped listening after the "I love you" part but caught the question in the last few words.

"Yes," she breathed with absolutely no idea what she was agreeing to. "Yes, yes, yes!"

"Then you'll take this?"

She glanced down, a laugh gurgling in her throat as Dom pinned an enameled copy of his soccer club's insignia to the lapel of her suit jacket.

"It will have to do," he told her with a look in those dark eyes that promised the love and home and family she'd always craved, "until we find an engagement ring to suit the fiancée of the Grand Duke of Karlenburgh, yes?"

"Yes!"

As if that weren't enough to keep Natalie dancing on a cloud and completely delight his sister, Sarah and the duchess, Gina and her husband arrived with the twins the next afternoon.

They were house hunting, they informed the assembled family. Jack's appointment as US Ambassador to the UN still needed to be confirmed by the Senate but the chairman of the Foreign Affairs Committee had assured him the vote was purely pro forma.

"How wonderful!" Her eyes bright with tears of joy, the duchess thumped her cane and decreed this called for a toast. "Dominic, will you and Jack pour *pálinka* for us all?"

Charlotte's heart swelled with pride as she watched her tall, gold-haired grandson-in-law and darkly handsome young relative move to the sideboard and line up an array of Bohemian cut-crystal snifters. Her gaze roamed the sitting room, lingering on her beautiful granddaughters and the just-crawling twins tended by a radiant Natalie and a laughing, if somewhat tired-looking, Zia. When Maria joined them with a tray of cheese and olives, the only one missing was Dev.

"I've been thinking," Jack said quietly as he and Dom stood shoulder to shoulder, filling delicate crystal aperitif glasses with the potent apricot brandy. "Now that your face has been splashed across half the front pages of Europe, your days as an undercover operative must be numbered."

Dom's mouth twisted. "My boss agrees. He's been trying to convince me to take over management of the organized-crimes division at Interpol Headquarters."

"A desk job in Lyon couldn't be all that bad, but why not put all this hoopla about your title and involvement in the recovery of millions of dollars in stolen art to good use?" Jack's blue eyes held his. "*My* soon-to-be boss at the UN thinks the Grand Duke of Karlenburgh would make a helluva cultural attaché. He and his lovely wife would be accepted everywhere, have access to top-level social circles—and information."

Dom's pulse kicked. He'd already decided to take the promotion and settle in Lyon. He couldn't subject Natalie to the uncertainties and dangers associated with his current occupation. But deep inside he'd been dreading the monotony of a nine-to-five job.

"Cultural attaché?" he murmured. "What exactly would that involve?"

"Whatever you wanted it to. And you'd be based here in New York, surrounded by family. Which may not always be such a good thing," Jack added drily when one of his daughters grabbed a fistful of her sister's hair and gleefully yanked.

"No," Dom countered, watching Natalie scoop the howling twin into her arms to nuzzle and kiss and coo her back to smiles. "Family is a very good thing. Especially for someone who's never had one. Tell your soon-to-be boss that the Grand Duke of Karlenburgh would be honored to accept the position of cultural attaché."

Yesterday was one of the most memorable days in my long and incredibly rich life. They were all here, my ever-increasing family. Sarah and Dev. Gina and Jack and the twins. Dominic and Natalie. Zia, Maria, even Jerome, our vigilant doorman who insisted on escorting the Brink's couriers up to my apartment. I'm not ashamed to admit I cried when they uncrated the painting.

The Canaletto my husband gave me so long ago now hangs on my bedroom wall. It's the last thing I see before I fall asleep, the first thing I see when I wake. And, oh, the memories that drift in on gossamer wings between darkness and dawn! Dominic wants to take me back to Hungary for a visit. As Natalie and Sarah delve deeper into our family's history, they add their voice to his. I've said I'll return if Dom will agree to let me formally invest him with the title of Grand Duke at the black-tie affair Gina is so eager to arrange.

Then we'll settle in until Zia finishes her residency. She works herself to the bone, poor darling. If Maria and I didn't force her to eat and snatch at least a few hours' rest, she'd drop where she stands. Something more than determination to complete the residency drives her. Something she won't speak about, even to me. I tell myself to be patient. To wait until she's ready to share the secret she hides behind her seductive smile and stunning beauty. Whatever it is, she knows I'll stand with her. We are, after all, St. Sebastians.

From the diary of Charlotte
Grand Duchess of Karlenburgh

* * * * *

AT HIS MAJESTY'S CONVENIENCE

JENNIFER LEWIS

For Lulu, a gracious lady and a powerful communicator who's encouraged me to slow down and see the big picture.

One

He won't ever forgive you.

Andi Blake watched her boss from the far end of the grand dining room. Dressed in a black dinner jacket, dark hair slicked back, he looked calm, composed and strikingly handsome as usual, while he scanned the printed guest list she'd placed on the sideboard.

Then again, maybe he wouldn't care at all. Nothing rattled Jake Mondragon, which was why he'd transitioned easily from life as a successful Manhattan investor to his new role as king of the mountainous nation of Ruthenia.

Would her departure cause even a single furrow in his majestic brow? Her heart squeezed. Probably not.

Her sweating palms closed around the increasingly crumpled envelope containing her letter of resignation. The letter made it official, not just an idle threat or even a joke.

Do it now, before you lose your nerve.

Her breath caught in her throat. It didn't seem possible to just walk up to him and say, "Jake, I'm leaving." But if she didn't she'd soon be making arrangements for his wedding.

She'd put up with a lot of things in the three years since she'd moved from their lofty office in Manhattan to this rambling Ruthenian palace, but she could not stand to see him marry another woman.

You deserve to have a life. Claim it.

She squared her shoulders and set out across the room, past the long table elegantly set for fifty of his closest friends.

Jake glanced up. Her blood heated—as always—when his dark eyes fixed on hers. "Andi, could you put me next to Maxi Rivenshnell instead of Alia Kronstadt? I sat next to Alia last night at the Hollernsterns and I don't want Maxi to feel neglected."

Andi froze. How could it have become her job to cultivate his romances with these women? Ruthenia's powerful families were jostling and shoving for the chance to see their daughter crowned queen, and no one cared if little Andi from Pittsburgh got trampled in the stampede.

Least of all Jake.

"Why don't I just put you between them?" She tried to keep her tone even. Right now she wanted to throw her carefully typed letter at him. "That way you can kiss up to both of them at once."

Jake glanced up with a raised brow. She never spoke to him like this, so no wonder he looked surprised.

She straightened her shoulders and thrust the letter out at him. "My resignation. I'll be leaving as soon as the party's over."

Jake's gaze didn't waver. "Is this some kind of joke?"

Andi flinched. She'd known he wouldn't believe her.

"I'm totally serious. I'll do my job tonight. I'd never leave you in the lurch in the middle of an event, but I'm leaving first thing tomorrow." She couldn't believe how calm she sounded. "I apologize for not giving two weeks' notice, but I've worked day and night for the last three years in a strange country without even a week's vacation so I hope you can excuse it. The Independence Day celebrations are well under way and everything's been delegated. I'm sure you won't miss me at all." She squeezed the last words out right as she ran out of gumption.

"Not miss you? The Independence Day celebrations are the biggest event in the history of Ruthenia—well, since the 1502 civil war, at least. We can't possibly manage without you, even for a day."

Andi swallowed. He didn't care about her at all, just about the big day coming up. Wasn't it always like this? He was all business, all the time. After six years working together he barely knew anything about her. Which wasn't fair, since she knew almost everything about him. She'd eaten, slept and breathed Jake Mondragon for the past six years and in the process fallen utterly and totally in love with him.

Shame he didn't even notice she was female.

He peered down at her, concern in his brown eyes. "I told you to take some vacation. Didn't I suggest you go back home for a few weeks last summer?"

Home? Where was home anymore? She'd given up her apartment in Manhattan when she moved here. Her parents both worked long hours and had moved to a different suburb since she left high school, so if she went to see them she'd just end up hanging around their house—probably pining for Jake.

Well, no more. She was going to find a new home and start over. She had an interview for a promising job as an event planner scheduled for next week in Manhattan, and that was a perfect next step to going out on her own.

"I don't want to be a personal assistant for the rest of my life and I'm turning twenty-seven soon so it's time to kick-start my career."

"We can change your title. How about..." His dark eyes narrowed. She couldn't help a slight quickening in her pulse. "Chief executive officer."

"Very funny. Except that I'd still be doing all the same things."

"No one else could do them as well as you."

"I'm sure you'll manage." The palace had a staff of nearly thirty including daytime employees. She was hardly leaving him in the lurch. And she couldn't possibly stand to be here for Independence Day next week. The press had made a big deal of how important it was for him to choose a bride; the future of the monarchy depended on it. He'd jokingly given their third Independence Day as his deadline when he'd assumed the crown three years ago.

Now everyone expected him to act on it. Being a man of his word, Andi knew he would. Maxi, Alia, Carina, there were plenty to choose from, and she couldn't bear to see him with any of them.

Jake put down the guest list, but made no move to take her letter of resignation. "I know you've been working hard. Life in a royal palace is a bit of a twenty-four-hour party, but you do get to set your own hours and you've never been shy about asking for good compensation."

"I'm very well paid and I know it." She did pride herself on asking for raises regularly. She knew Jake respected that, which was probably half the reason she'd done it. As a result she had a nice little nest egg put aside to fund her new start. "But it's time for me to move on."

Why was she even so crazy about him? He'd never shown the slightest glimmer of interest in her.

Her dander rose still higher as Jake glanced at his watch. "The guests will be here any minute and I need to return a call from New York. We'll talk later and figure something out." He reached out and clapped her on the arm, as if she was an old baseball buddy. "We'll make you happy."

He turned and left the room, leaving her holding her letter of resignation between trembling fingers.

Once the door had closed behind him, she let out a growl of frustration. Of course he thought he could talk her down and turn everything around. Isn't that exactly what he was known for? And he even imagined he could make her "happy."

That kind of arrogance should be unforgivable.

Except that his endless confidence and can-do attitude were possibly what she admired and adored most in him.

The only way he could make her happy was to sweep her off her feet into a passionate embrace and tell her he loved her and wanted to marry her.

Except that kings didn't marry secretaries from Pittsburgh. Even kings of funny little countries like Ruthenia.

"The vol-au-vents are done, cook's wondering where to send them."

Andi started at the sound of the events assistant coming through another doorway behind her.

"Why don't you have someone bring them up for the first guests? And the celery stalks with the cheese filling." She tucked the letter behind her back.

Livia nodded, her red curls bobbing about the collar of her white shirt, like it was just another evening.

Which of course it was, except that it was Andi's last evening here.

"So did they ask you in for an interview?" Livia leaned in with a conspiratorial whisper.

"I cannot confirm or deny anything of that nature."

"How are you going to manage an interview in New York when you're imprisoned in a Ruthenian palace?"

Andi tapped the side of her nose. She hadn't told anyone she was leaving. That would feel too much like a betrayal of Jake. Let them just wake up to find her gone.

Livia put her hands on her hips. "Hey, you can't just take off back to New York without me. I told you about that job."

"You didn't say you wanted it."

"I said I thought it sounded fantastic."

"Then you should apply." She wanted to get away. This conversation was not productive and she didn't trust Livia to keep her secrets.

Livia narrowed her eyes. "Maybe I will."

Andi forced a smile. "Save a vol-au-vent for me, won't you?"

Livia raised a brow and disappeared back through the door.

Who would be in charge of choosing the menus and how the food should be served? The cook, probably, though she had quite a temper when she felt pressured. Perhaps Livia? She wasn't the most organized person in the palace and she'd been skipped over for promotion a few times. Probably why she wanted to leave.

Either way, it wasn't her problem and Jake would soon find someone to replace her. Her heart clenched at the thought, but she drew in a steadying breath and marched out into the hallway toward the foyer. She could hear the hum of voices as the first guests took off their luxurious coats and handed them to the footmen to reveal slinky evening gowns and glittering jewels.

Andi smoothed the front of her black slacks. It wasn't appropriate for a member of staff to get decked out like a guest.

All eyes turned to the grand staircase as Jake descended to greet the ladies with a kiss on each cheek. Andi tried to ignore the jealousy flaring in her chest. How ridiculous. One of these girls was going to marry him and she had no business being bothered in any way.

"Could you fetch me a tissue?" asked Maxi Rivenshnell. The willowy brunette cast her question in Andi's direction, without actually bothering to meet her gaze.

"Of course." She reached into her pocket and withdrew a folded tissue from the packet she kept on her. Maxi snatched it from her fingers and tucked it into the top of her long satin gloves without a word of thanks.

She didn't exist for these people. She was simply there to serve them, like the large staff serving each of their aristocratic households.

A waiter appeared with a tray of champagne glasses and she helped to distribute them amongst the guests, then ushered people into the green drawing room where a fire blazed in a stone fireplace carved with the family crest.

Jake strolled and chatted with ease as the room filled with well-dressed Ruthenians. Several of them had only recently returned after decades of exile in places like London, Monaco and Rome, ready to enjoy Ruthenia's promised renaissance after decades of failed socialism.

So far the promise was coming true. The rich were getting richer, and—thanks to Jake's innovative business ideas—everyone else was, as well. Even the staunch anti-monarchists who'd opposed his arrival with protests in the streets now had to admit that Jake Mondragon knew what he was doing.

He'd uncovered markets for their esoteric agricultural

products, and encouraged multinational firms to take advantage of Ruthenia's strategic location in central Europe and its vastly underemployed workforce. The country's GDP had risen nearly 400% in just three years, making eyeballs pop all across the globe.

Andi stiffened as Jake's bold laugh carried through the air. She'd miss that sound. Was she really leaving? A sudden flash of panic almost made her reconsider.

Then she followed the laugh to its source and her heart seized as she saw Jake with his arm around yet another Ruthenian damsel—Carina Teitelhaus—whose blond hair hung in a silky sheet almost to her waist.

Andi tugged her gaze away and busied herself with picking up a dropped napkin. She would not miss seeing him draped over other women one bit. He joked that he was just trying to butter up their powerful parents and get them to invest in the country, but right now that seemed like one more example of how people were pawns to him rather than living beings with feelings.

He'd marry one of them just because it was part of his job. And she couldn't bear to see that.

She needed to leave tonight, before he could use his well-practiced tongue to… Thoughts of his tongue sent an involuntary shiver through her.

Which was exactly why she needed to get out of here. And she wasn't going to give him a chance to talk her out of it.

Jake pushed his dessert plate forward. He'd had all the sticky sweetness he could stand for one night. With Maxi on one side and Alia on the other, each vying to tug his attention from the other, he felt exhausted. Andi knew he liked to have at least one decent conversationalist seated next to him, yet she'd followed through on her threat to stick him between two of the most troublesome vixens in Ruthenia.

Speaking of which, where was Andi?

He glanced around the dining room. The flickering light from the candles along the table and walls created deep shadows, but he didn't see her. Usually she hovered close by in case he needed something.

He summoned one of the servers. "Ulrike, have you seen Andi?"

The quiet girl shook her head. "Would you like me to find her, sir?"

"No, thanks, I'll find her myself." At least he would as soon as he could extricate himself from yet another eight-course meal. He couldn't risk offending either of his bejeweled dinner companions with an early departure since their darling daddies were the richest and most powerful men in the region. Once things were settled, he wouldn't have to worry so much about currying their favor, but while the economy was growing and changing and finding its feet in the world, he needed their flowing capital to oil its wheels.

He could see how men in former eras had found it practical to marry more than one woman. They were both pretty—Maxi a sultry brunette with impressive cleavage and Alia a graceful blonde with a velvet voice—but to be completely honest he didn't want to marry either of them.

Carina Teitelhaus shot him a loaded glance from across the table. Her father owned a large factory complex with a lot of potential for expansion. And she didn't hesitate to remind him of that.

Ruthenia's noblewomen were becoming increasingly aggressive in pursuing the role of queen. Lately he felt as if he were juggling a bevy of flaming torches and the work of keeping them all in the air was wearing on his nerves.

He'd committed to choosing a bride before Independence Day next week. At the time he'd made that statement the deadline had seemed impossibly far off and none of them were sure Ruthenia itself would even still be in existence.

Now it was right upon them, along with the necessity of choosing his wife or breaking his promise. Everyone in the room was painfully aware of each glance, every smile or laugh he dispensed in any direction. The dining table was a battlefield, with salvos firing over the silver.

Usually he could count on Andi to soothe any ruffled feathers with careful seating placements and subtly coordinated private trysts. Tonight, though, contrary to her promise, she'd left him in the lurch.

"Do excuse me, ladies." He rose to his feet, avoiding all mascara-laden glances, and strode for the door.

Andi's absence worried him. What if she really did leave? She was the anchor that kept the palace floating peacefully in the choppy seas of a changing Ruthenia. He could give her any task and just assume it was done, without a word of prompting. Her tact and thoughtfulness were exemplary, and her organizational skills were unmatched. He couldn't imagine life without her.

After a short walk over the recently installed plum-colored carpets of the west hallway, he glanced into her ever-tidy office—and found it dark and empty. He frowned. She was often there in the evenings, which coincided with business hours in the U.S. and could be a busy time.

Her laptop was on the desk, as usual. That was a good sign.

Jake headed up the west staircase to the second floor, where most of the bedrooms were located. Andi had a large "family" bedroom rather than one of the pokey servants' quarters on the third floor. She was family, dammit. And that meant she couldn't pick up and leave whenever she felt like it.

A nasty feeling gripped his gut as he approached her closed door. He knocked on the polished wood and listened for movement on the other side.

Nothing.

He tried the handle and to his surprise the door swung open. Curiosity tickling his nerves, he stepped inside and switched on the light. Andi's large room was neat and free of clutter—much like her desk. It looked like a hotel room, with no personal touches added to the rather extravagant palace décor. The sight of two black suitcases—open and packed—stopped him in his tracks.

She really was leaving.

Adrenaline surged through him. At least she hadn't gone yet, or the bags would be gone, too. The room smelled faintly of that subtle scent she sometimes wore, almost as if she was in the room with him.

He glanced around. Could she be hiding from him?

He strode across the room and tugged open the doors of the massive armoire. His breath stopped for a second and he half expected to see her crouched inside.

Which of course she wasn't. Her clothes were gone, though, leaving only empty hangers on the rod.

Anger warred with deep disappointment that she intended to abandon him like this. Did their six years together mean nothing to her?

She couldn't leave without her suitcases. Perhaps he should take them somewhere she couldn't find them. His room, for example.

Unfamiliar guilt pricked him. He didn't even like the idea of her knowing he'd entered her room uninvited, let alone taken her possessions hostage. Andi was a stickler for honesty and had kept him aboveboard more times than he cared to remember. Taking her bags just felt wrong.

She'd said she'd leave as soon as the party was over. A woman of her word, she'd be sure to wait until the last guest was gone. As long as he found her before then, everything would be fine. He switched off the light and left the room as he'd found it.

He scanned the east hall as he headed for the stairs, a sense of foreboding growing inside him. The packed bags were an ominous sign, but he couldn't really believe she'd abandon Ruthenia—and him.

"Jake, darling, we were wondering what happened to you," Maxi called to him from the bottom of the stairs. "Colonel Von Deiter has volunteered to play piano while we dance." She stretched out her long arm, as if inviting him to share the first dance with her.

Since coming to Ruthenia he sometimes felt he'd stepped into a schnitzel-flavored Jane Austen story, where people waltzed around ballrooms and gossiped behind fans. He was happier in a business meeting than on a dance floor, and right now he'd much rather be dictating a letter to Andi than twirling Maxi over the parquet.

"Have you seen Andi, my assistant?"

"The little girl who wears her hair in a bun?"

Jake frowned. He wasn't sure exactly how old Andi was—mid-twenties, maybe?—but it seemed a bit rude for someone of twenty-two to call her a little girl. "She's about five foot seven," he said, with an arched brow. "And yes, she always wears her hair in a bun."

Come to think of it, he'd literally never seen her hair down, which was pretty odd after six years. A sudden violent urge to see Andi with her hair unleashed swept through him. "I've looked all over the palace for her, but she's vanished into thin air."

Maxi shrugged. "Do come dance, darling."

His friend Fritz appeared behind her. "Come on, Jake. Can't let the ladies down. Just a twirl or two. I'm sure Andi has better things to do than wait on you hand and foot."

"She doesn't wait on me hand and foot. She's a valued executive."

Fritz laughed. "Is that why she's always hovering around taking care of your every need?"

Jake stiffened. He never took Andi for granted. He knew just how dependent on her he was. Did she feel that he didn't care?

Frowning, he descended the stairs and took Maxi's offered hand. He was the host, after all. Two waltzes and a polka later he managed to slip out into the hallway.

"Any idea where Andi is?" he asked the first person he saw, who happened to be the night butler.

He shrugged in typical Ruthenian style. "Haven't seen her in hours. Maybe she went to bed?"

Unlikely. Andi never left a party until the last guest had rolled down the drive. But then she'd never quit before, either. He was halfway up the stairs before he realized he was heading for her bedroom again.

Jake stared at her closed door. Was she in there? And if not, were her bags still there?

He knocked, but heard no movement from inside. After checking that the corridor was deserted, he knelt and peered through the keyhole. It was empty—no key on the inside—which suggested she was out. On the other hand, the pitch darkness on the other side meant he couldn't see a thing.

He slipped in—didn't she know better than to leave her door unlocked?—and switched on the light. The suitcases were still there. Closer inspection revealed that one of them had been partially unpacked, as if an item was removed. Still, there were no clues as to Andi's whereabouts.

Frustration pricked his muscles. How could she just disappear like this?

At the foot of the stairs, Fritz accosted him, martini in hand. "When are you going to choose your bride, Jake? We're all getting impatient."

Jake growled. "Why is everyone so mad for me to get married?"

"Because there are precious few kings left in the world and you're up for grabs. The rest of us are waiting to see who's left. None of the girls dare even kiss us anymore, let alone do anything more rakish, in case they're making themselves ineligible for a coronet. They're all fighting for the chance to be called Your Majesty."

"Then they're all nuts. If anyone calls *me* 'Your Majesty,' I'll fire 'em."

Fritz shoved him. "All bluster. And don't deny you have some of the loveliest women in the world to choose from."

"I wish the loveliest women in the world would take off for the night. I'm ready to turn in." Or rather, ready to find and corner Andi.

Fritz cocked his head. "Party pooper. All right. I'll round up the troops and march 'em out for you."

"You're a pal."

Jake watched the last chauffeured Mercedes disappear down the long driveway from the east patio. He needed some air to clear his head before tackling Andi—and watching from here ensured that she couldn't leave without him seeing her.

Could he really stand to marry Maxi or Alia or any of these empty-headed, too-rich, spoiled brats? He'd been surrounded by their kind of women all his life, even in New York. Just the circle he'd been born into. You'd think a king would have more choices than the average Joe, but that was apparently not the case.

Something moving in the darkness caught his eye. He squinted, trying to make out what was crossing the lawn. An animal? Ruthenia had quite large deer that he was supposed to enjoy hunting.

But this creature was lighter, more upright, and moved with a kind of mystical grace. He stepped forward, peering into the gloom of a typical moonlit but cloudy night. The figure whirled and twirled on the lawn, pale fabric flowing around it.

A ghost? His back stiffened. The palace was nearly three hundred years old and built over a far more ancient structure. Tales of sieges and beheadings and people imprisoned in the dungeons rattled around the old stone walls.

Long, pale arms extended sideways as the figure twirled again. A female ghost.

Curiosity goaded him across the patio and down the stone stairs onto the lawn. He walked silently across the damp grass, eyes fixed on the strange apparition. As he drew closer he heard singing—soft and sweet—almost lost in the low breeze and the rustling of the trees.

Entranced, he moved nearer, enjoying the figure's graceful movements and the silver magic of her voice.

He stopped dead when he realized she was singing in English.

"Andi?"

Despite the hair streaming over her shoulders and the long, diaphanous dress, he recognized his assistant of six years, arms raised to the moon, swaying and singing in the night.

He strode forward faster. "Are you okay?"

She stopped and stared at him and the singing ceased. Her eyes shone bright in the darkness.

"What are you doing out here?" He walked right up to her, partly to prove to himself that she was real and not a figment of his imagination. His chest swelled with relief. At least now he'd found her and they could have that talk he'd been rehearsing in his head all night.

"Why don't we go inside?" He reached out for her hand, almost expecting his own to pass through it. She still looked so spectral, smiling in the cloud-veiled moonlight.

But the hand that seized his felt warm. Awareness snapped through him as her fingers closed around his. Her hair was longer than he'd imagined. Almost to the peaks of her nipples, which jutted out from the soft dress. He swallowed. He'd never noticed what…luxurious breasts Andi had. They were usually hidden under tailored suits and crisp blouses.

He struggled to get back on task. "We need to talk."

Andi's grip tightened on his, but she didn't move. Her face looked different. Transfixed, somehow. Her eyes sparkling and her lips glossy and parted. Was she drunk?

"You must be cold." On instinct he reached out to touch her upper arm, which was bare in the floaty evening gown she wore. As he drew closer, her free arm suddenly wrapped around his waist with force.

Jake stilled as she lifted her face to his. She smelled of that same soft scent she always wore, not a trace of alcohol, just flowers and sweetness. He groped for words, but failed to find any as her lips rose toward his.

Next thing he knew he was kissing her full—and hard—on the mouth.

Two

Jake let his arms wind around her waist. The movement was as instinctive as breathing. Their mouths melted together and her soft body pressed against his. Desire flared inside him, hot and unexpected, as the kiss deepened. His fingers ached to explore the lush curves she'd kept hidden for so long.

But this was Andi—his faithful and long-suffering assistant, not some bejeweled floozy who just wanted to lock lips with a monarch.

He pulled back from the kiss with great difficulty, unwinding himself from the surprisingly powerful grip of her slim arms. A momentary frown flashed across her lovely face—why had he never noticed she was so pretty?—then vanished again as a smile filled her soft eyes and broadened her mouth.

She lifted a hand and stroked his cheek. "You're beautiful."

Shocked, Jake struggled for a response. "*You're* beautiful. I'm handsome." He lifted a brow, as if to assure himself they were both kidding.

She giggled—in a most un-Andi-like way—and tossed her head, which sent her hair tumbling over her shoulders in a shimmering cascade. She twirled again, and the soft dress draped her form, allowing him a tantalizing view of her figure. He'd certainly never seen her in this dress before. Floor-length and daringly see-through, it was far dressier and more festive than her usual attire.

"Happiness is glorious joy," she sang, as she turned to face him again.

"Huh?" Jake frowned.

"Mysterious moonlight and wonderful wishes." Another silver peal of laughter left her lips—which looked quite different than he remembered, bare of their usual apricot lipstick and kissed to ruby fullness.

Unless she'd suddenly turned to poetry—very bad poetry at that—she must be intoxicated. He didn't smell anything on her breath, though. And didn't she always insist she was allergic to alcohol? He couldn't remember ever seeing her with a real drink.

Drugs?

He peered at her eyes. Yes, her pupils were dilated. Still, Andi experimenting with illegal substances? It seemed impossible.

"Did you take something?"

"Steal? I'd never steal from you. You're my true love." She gazed at him as she spoke the words, eyes clear and blue as a summer sky.

Jake groped for words. "I meant, did you take any pills?"

You're my true love? She was obviously tripping on something. He'd better get her inside before she tried to fly from the parapets or walk on the water in the moat. "Let's go inside."

He wrapped his arm around her, and she squeezed against him and giggled again. This was not the Andi he knew. Perhaps the stress of threatening to leave had encouraged her to take some kind of tranquilizer. He had no idea how those things worked, but couldn't come up with any other explanation for her odd behavior.

"You smell good." She pressed her face against him, almost tripping him.

Jake's eyes widened, but he managed to keep walking. Her body bumping against his was not helping his own sanity. Now she'd slid an arm around his waist and her fingers fondled him as they walked. His blood was heating in a most uncomfortable way.

Maybe he could bring both of them back down to earth.

"It was cold of you to seat me between Maxi and Alia."

"Who?" She marched gaily along over the lawn, still clinging to him. No reaction to the names.

"Maxi and Alia. Both of them fighting over me was a bit much to take on top of the cook's roulade."

"Pretty names. We haven't met. You must introduce me sometime." She pulled her arm from his waist and took off skipping across the damp lawn.

Jake paused and stared for a moment, then strode after her.

Since he didn't particularly want any of the other staff to see Andi in this compromising state, Jake hustled her into his private chambers and locked the door. That was the accepted signal that he was off duty for the night and not to be disturbed.

Andi made herself quite at home, curling up on one

of the sofas, with a languid arm draping along the back. "Happiness is as happiness does," she said dreamily.

Jake resisted the urge to pour himself a whisky. "Listen, what you said about leaving. I saw your bags—"

"Leave? I would never leave you, my love." Her face rested in a peaceful smile.

Jake swallowed. "So you're staying."

"Of course. Forever and ever and ever." Her eyes sparkled.

"Ah. That's settled then." He moved to the liquor cabinet, deciding to have that whisky after all. "I am relieved. The thought of managing without you was quite frightening."

Andi had risen from the sofa and was now waltzing around the room by herself, singing, "Someday my prince will come." She twirled, sweeping her pale evening dress about her like smoke. "Some day I'll love someone." Her radiant smile was almost infectious.

Almost. Jake took a swig of his drink. Did she really think they were having some kind of relationship outside their well-established professional one? As much as the idea appealed right this second, he knew it would really mess things up once she snapped out of whatever chemical induced trance she was in.

He'd better remind her of that. "We've worked together a long time."

She stopped twirling for a moment, and frowned. "I don't think I do work."

"You're a lady of leisure?"

She glanced down at her evening gown. "Yes." She frowned; then her expression brightened. "I must be. Otherwise why would I be dressed like this?"

Had she temporarily forgotten that she was his assistant? "Why are you dressed like that?" She'd certainly never worn anything so festive before.

"It's pretty, isn't it?" She looked up at him. "Do you like it?"

"Very much." He allowed his eyes to soak up the vision of it draped over her gorgeous body. Desire licked through him in tiny, tormenting flames.

Andi reached out and tugged at his shirt. Even that made his synapses flash and his groin tighten.

"Why don't you come sit with me." She stroked the sofa cushion next to her.

"I'm not sure that's a good idea." His voice came out gruff.

"Why not?"

"It's late. We should get to bed." The image of her in his bed flooded his brain, especially as it was right there in the next room. But caution tightened his muscles.

"Oh, don't be silly—" She frowned. "How odd." She glanced up at him. "I can't think of your name right now."

Jake was about to tell her, but something made him stop. "You don't know my name?"

She looked up for a few moments, as if searching her brain. "No, I don't seem to know it."

Panic tightened his chest. "What's your name?"

She looked toward the ceiling, scrunched up her brow and clenched her fists. When she finally looked back at him, her expression had changed from glee to confusion. "I'm not sure."

"I think we should call for a doctor." He pulled his phone out.

"A doctor? What for? I feel fine."

He hesitated. "Let me look at you. Did you bump your head?"

She shrugged. "I don't think so."

He put his phone back in his pocket and touched her temples with his thumbs. Her eyes sparkled as she looked up at him and her scent was a torment. He worked his fingers gently back into her hair—which was soft and luxurious to touch. "Hey, I feel a lump."

"Ouch!"

"You have a bruise." He touched it gently. A big goose egg. That explained a whole lot. "We're definitely calling the doctor. You could have a concussion." He dialed the number. "Listen, sorry it's so late, Gustav, but Andi's taken a fall and bumped her head. She's not talking too much sense and I think you should look at her."

Gustav replied that he'd be there in the ten minutes it took to drive from the town, and to keep her awake until he got there.

After letting the staff know to expect Gustav, Jake sat down on the sofa opposite her. It made sense to find out just how much of her memory had vanished. "How old are you?" Odd that he didn't know that.

"Over twenty-one." She laughed. Then frowned. "Other than that, I'm not too sure. How old do I look?"

Jake smiled. "I'd be a damned fool if I answered a question like that from a woman." He decided he'd be better off following the lawyer's strategy of only asking questions he knew the answer to. It was pretty embarrassing that he really didn't know how old she was. "How long have you lived here?"

She stared at him, mouth slightly open, then looked away. "Why are you asking me these silly questions? I've lived here a long time. With you."

Her gaze—innocent yet needy—ate into him. She stroked the sofa arm with her fingers and his skin tingled in response. She seemed to have lost her memory, and, in its absence, assumed they were a couple.

Jake sucked in a long breath. They'd never had any kind of flirtation, even a playful one. She always seemed so businesslike and uninterested in such trivial matters. He'd never really looked at her that way, either. Much simpler to keep business and pleasure separate, especially when a really good assistant was so hard to find and keep.

Right now he was seeing a different aspect of Andi—alarming, and intriguing.

She rose and walked a few steps to his sofa, then sank down next to him. Her warm thigh settled against his, causing his skin to sizzle even through their layers of clothing. He stiffened. Was it fair to offer a man this kind of temptation?

At least it was keeping her awake.

Her fingers reached up to his black bow tie and tugged at one end. The knot came apart and the silk ribbons fell to his starched shirtfront.

"Much better." She giggled again, then pulled the tie out from his collar and undid the top button of his shirt. Jake watched, barely breathing, trying to suppress the heaving tide of arousal surging inside him.

After all, it would be rude to push her away, wouldn't it? Especially in her delicate and mysterious condition.

When her fingers roamed into his hair, causing his groin to ache uncomfortably, he had to take action. He stood up rapidly. "The doctor will be here any minute. Can I get you a glass of water?"

"I'm not thirsty." Her hurt look sent a pang to his heart.

"Still, it's good to keep hydrated." He busied himself with filling a glass at the bar, and took care not to accidentally brush her fingertips as he handed it to her. Her cheeks and lips were flushed with pink, which made her look aroused and appealing at the same time.

She took the glass and sipped cautiously. Then looked up at him with a slight frown. "I do feel odd."

Jake let out a sigh of relief. This seemed more like the real Andi than the one spouting loopy epithets. "You'll probably feel better in the morning, but it can't hurt to have the doctor take a look."

Alarm filled him as tears welled in her eyes. "It's just so strange not being able to remember anything. How could I not even know my own name?" A fat tear rolled down her soft cheek.

Disturbing that he now knew how soft her cheek was.

"Your name is Andi Blake."

"Andi." She said it softly. Then frowned again. "Is that short for something?"

Jake froze. Was it? He had no idea. He didn't remember ever calling her anything else, but it had been six long years since he'd seen her résumé and frankly he couldn't remember the details. "Nope. Just Andi. It's a pretty name."

He regretted the lame comment, something you might say to a six-year-old. But then he didn't have experience in dealing with amnesiacs, so maybe it wasn't all that inappropriate.

"Oh." She seemed to mull that over. She wiped her eyes. "At least I know my own name now." Then she bit her lip. "Though it doesn't sound at all familiar." Tears glistened in her eyes. "What if my memory doesn't come back?"

"Don't worry about that, I'm sure—" A knock on the door announced the arrival of the doctor, and Jake released a sigh of relief. "Please send him in."

Andi's tearful trembling subsided as the doctor checked her over, peering into her eyes with a light, checking her pulse and breathing, and taking her temperature.

As the local doctor, he'd been to the palace before and knew Andi. She showed no sign of recognizing or remembering him. His questions revealed that while she remembered general concepts, like how to tie a knot, she recalled nothing about her own life.

"Andi, would you excuse us a moment?" The doctor ushered Jake out into the hallway. "Is she exhibiting mood changes?"

"Big time. She's not like herself at all. She seemed happy—silly even—when I first found her. Just now she was crying. I think the reality of what's going on is setting in."

"Sounds like a pretty textbook case of temporary memory loss, if there is such a thing." The older man snapped his briefcase closed. "Lots of emotion. Mood swings. Loss of long-term memory. I've never seen it before, myself, but in most cases the memory eventually starts to come back."

"When? How long will she be like this?"

The doctor gave a Ruthenian shrug. "Could be days, could be weeks. There's a slim possibility she won't ever recall everything. She's certainly had a good bump to her head, but no signs of concussion or other injury. Do you have any idea what happened?"

Jake shook his head. "I found her out dancing on the lawn. I didn't see anything happen at all."

"Make sure she gets plenty of sleep, and encourage her with questions to bring back her memory." The doctor hoisted his bag onto his shoulder. "Call me anytime, of course."

"Thanks." Jake frowned. "Can we keep this amnesia thing between us? I think Andi would be embarrassed if people knew what was going on. She's a very private person."

The doctor's brow furrowed even more than usual. "Of course." *Your Highness*. The unspoken words hovered in the air. Jake sensed slight disapproval at his request for secrecy, but he knew the physician would honor it. "Please keep me posted on her progress."

Jake went back into his suite and locked the door. Andi was sitting on the sofa and her mood seemed to have brightened. Her tears were gone, and a smile hovered in her eyes as she looked up at him. "Will I live?"

"Without a doubt. It's late. How about some sleep?"

"I'm not at all sleepy." She draped herself over the sofa, eyes heavy-lidded with desire. "I'd rather play."

Jake's eyes widened. Could this really be the same Andi he'd worked with all these years? It was shocking to imagine that this flirtatious person had been lurking inside her the whole time. Unless it was just a mood swing caused by her condition.

She rose from the sofa and swept toward him, then threw her arms around his waist. "I do love you."

Gulp. Jake patted her cautiously on the back. This could last for days. Or weeks. Or longer.

His skin tingled as her lips pressed against his cheek. "I'm so glad we're together." Her soft breath heated his skin as she breathed the words in his ear.

And this was the woman who'd announced, only a few hours before, that she was leaving for good, that night.

At least that was off the agenda for now.

His phone rang and he tensed. What now? "Excuse me." He extricated himself from her embrace and pulled it from his pocket.

A glance at the number revealed the caller was Maxi. She'd formed a new habit of calling him at bizarre times like the crack of dawn or during his morning workout. This call in the wee hours was a new and even more unappealing attempt to monopolize his time.

Still, maybe there was some kind of emergency.

"Hi, Maxi."

"Jake, are you still awake?" Her breathy voice grated on his nerves.

"I am now." He glanced at Andi, who was twirling around the room doing the dance of the seven veils, or something. "What do you want?"

"So impatient. I just wanted to chat. About you and me."

He shoved a hand through his hair. Maxi was definitely not The One. In fact she could be voted Least Likely to be Queen of Ruthenia, since she was firmly in his "keep your enemies closer" circle. He'd been drawing her in and inviting her confidence on purpose. Not because he loved her, or was even attracted to her. He'd found evidence that her family was involved in weapons dealing and possibly worse, but he didn't have enough proof to do anything about it yet.

None of the other girls dealt in arms or drugs, as far as he knew, but they were all empty-headed and silly. Right now he was more attracted to his own assistant than to any of Ruthenia's pampered beauties.

An idea crept into his brain.

Since Andi seemed to assume they were a couple, why not make it a reality? He had to marry someone. He could announce to the press tomorrow that his chosen bride was his own assistant.

A chill of sangfroid crept over him. Could he really arrange his own marriage so easily? Andi was agreeable, intelligent and practical, perfectly suited to life in the spotlight. She'd worked just outside it for years and knew the whole routine of palace life perfectly. Apart from her presumably humble origins—he really didn't know anything about her origins, but since he'd never met her parents at a ball, he was guessing—she'd be the ideal royal wife.

They'd known each other for years and he could simply

announce that they'd been involved for a long time but kept their relationship secret.

The announcement would send the long-fingernailed wolves away from his door for good. He and Andi could marry, produce an heir and a spare or two, and live a long, productive life in the service of the citizens of Ruthenia—wasn't that what was really important?

Andi had wandered into the bedroom and a quick glance revealed that she now lay sprawled on his bed.

Heat surged through him like a shot of brandy.

Her dress draped over her, displaying her inviting curves like an ice-cream sundae with whipped cream on top. Her gaze beckoned him, along with her finger. His muscles itched to join her on the bed and enjoy discovering more of Andi's wickedly intriguing sensual side.

"Maxi, I have to go. Have a good night."

"I can think of a way to have a much better night."

Jake's flesh crawled. "Sleep knits up the raveled sleeve of care."

"Is that Moby?"

"Shakespeare. Goodnight, Maxi."

"When are you going to choose your wife?" Jake flinched at the blunt question, and the shrill voice that asked it. "Daddy wants to know. He's not sure whether to contribute funds for the new hydroelectric project."

Jake stiffened. This is what it all boiled down to. Money and power. Well, he didn't want to build Ruthenia with ill-gotten gains from the black market, and he'd rather share his life with a hardworking woman than one who thought she could buy her way into a monarchy. "I've already chosen my wife."

"What do you mean?" she gasped.

He moved across the room, away from the bedroom where Andi now sprawled enticingly on the bed. She was humming again, and wouldn't hear him. "I intend to marry Andi Blake, my longtime assistant."

"You're joking."

"Not in the slightest. She and I have had a close relationship for six years. We intend to enjoy each other's company for many more."

Already his pronouncement had an official ring to it. Marriage to Andi was a perfectly natural and practical course of action. He was confident Andi would agree, especially since she seemed to have romantic feelings toward him.

"People are going to be very, very..." She paused, apparently struggling for words.

"Happy for us. Yes. Of course you'll be invited to the wedding." He couldn't help a tiny smile sneaking across his mouth. Maxi had clearly intended to be the featured host of the event.

"Invited to the wedding?" Her growl made him pull the phone away from his ear. "You're impossible!"

The dial tone made a satisfying noise. And now he wouldn't have to even make an announcement. Maxi would do all the legwork for him.

All he had to do was tell Andi.

Three

Morning sunlight streamed through the gap between heavy brocade curtains. Hot and uncomfortable, Andi looked down to find herself wearing a long evening dress under the covers. Weirdest thing, she had no idea why.

She sat bolt upright. Where was she?

His room. She remembered the soft touch of his lips on her cheek. Her skin heated at the memory. "Good night, Andi," he'd said. So she was Andi.

Andi.

Who was Andi? She racked her brain, but the racks were empty. She couldn't even remember the name of the handsome man who'd put her to bed, though she knew they were close.

How could her whole reality just slip away? Her heart pounded and she climbed out of bed. Her chiffon-y dress was horribly wrinkled and had made an uncomfortable nightgown, leaving lines printed on her skin.

She moved to the window and pulled one of the heavy drapes aside. The view that greeted her was familiar—rolling green hills dotted with grazing sheep, rising to fir-covered mountains. The village in the middle distance, with its steep clay-tiled roofs and high church steeple.

Looking down she saw the long rectangular fishpond in the walled courtyard. She didn't recall seeing it from this angle before.

But then she didn't recall much.

Andi what? She pressed a hand to her forehead. Blake, he'd said. How could even her own last name sound alien and unfamiliar?

She walked to the door and cautiously pulled it open. She caught her breath at the sight of him, standing in front of the mirror, buttoning his collar. Thick black-brown hair swept back from the most handsome face she'd ever seen. Warm, dark eyes reflected in the glass. Mouth set in a serious but good-humored line. Heat flooded her body and she stood rooted to the spot.

He turned. "Morning, Andi. How are you feeling?"

His expression looked rather guarded.

"Okay. I think. I…I can't seem to remember much." Had she slept with him last night? Her fully dressed state seemed to suggest not. Her body was sending all kinds of strange signals, though—pulsing and throbbing and tingling in mysterious places—so she couldn't tell.

"What can you remember?" He didn't look surprised at her announcement. Did he know what was going on?

"Why can't I remember?"

He took a few steps toward her and put his hand on her arm. Arousal flashed through her at his touch. "You bumped your head. The doctor says you're not concussed."

"How long have I been like this?" Fear twisted in her stomach.

"Just since last night. The doc said your memory will come back soon. A few weeks at most."

"Oh." Andi frowned, feeling ridiculously vulnerable, standing there in her wrinkled dress with no idea of who or where she was. Except that she was very—very—attracted to this man. "What should I do in the meantime?"

"Don't worry about a thing. I'll take care of you." He stroked her cheek. The reassuring touch of his fingers made her breath catch and sent tingles of arousal cascading through her.

She frowned. How should she put a question like this? "Are we…intimate?"

His gaze flickered slightly, making her stomach tighten. Had she said the wrong thing? She felt sure there must be something between them. She remembered kissing him last night, and the memory of the kiss made her head grow light.

"Yes, Andi. We're going to be married." He looked down at her hands, gathering them in his.

"Oh." She managed a smile. "What a relief that I have you to take care of me until my memory comes back." If it did come back. "It's embarrassing to ask, but how long have we been together?"

"Oh, years." He met her gaze again.

"It seems impossible, but I don't remember your name."

"Jake." He looked slightly flustered, and why wouldn't he? "Jake Mondragon."

"Jake Mondragon." She smiled dreamily, allowing herself to relax in his sturdy presence. And his face was kind, despite the proud, sculpted features. Totally gorgeous, too. She was very lucky. "So I'm going to be Andi Mondragon."

Jake's eyes widened. "Uh, yes. Yes, you are."

Why did he seem surprised by the idea? It was hardly an odd one if they'd been together for years. "Or was I going to keep my original surname?" Curiosity pricked her.

He smiled. "I don't think we'd discussed whether you would change it or not."

"Oh." Funny they hadn't talked about that. After all, what would the children be called? "How long have we been engaged?"

He lifted his chin slightly. "Just since yesterday. We haven't even told anyone yet."

Yesterday? Her eyes widened. "How odd that I would lose my memory on the same day. I can't even remember the proposal."

She watched his Adam's apple move as he swallowed. He must be upset that she couldn't even remember such a momentous and important moment. "I'm sure it will come back eventually."

An odd sensation started forming in the pit of her stomach. Something felt…off. How could she have forgotten her own fiancé? It was disorienting to know less about her own life than someone else did. "I think I should lay low for a few days. I don't really want to see anyone until I know who I am."

Jake grimaced. "I'm afraid that's going to be hard. The media will probably want an interview."

"About my memory?"

"About our engagement."

"Why would we tell the media?"

Jake hesitated for a moment. "Since I'm the king of this country, everything I do is news."

Andi's mouth fell open. "You're the king?" She was pretty sure she wasn't some kind of royal princess or aristocrat. She certainly didn't feel like one. But maybe that explained the long evening gown. She glanced down at its crumpled folds. "How did we meet?"

Jake's lids lowered slightly. "You're my longtime assistant. We just decided to marry."

She blinked. That explained all the sizzling and tingling in her body—she'd been intimate with this man for a long time. How bizarre that she had to hear about her own life from someone else. From the man she'd apparently dated for years and planned to marry.

Then again, if she'd been seeing this man for years, why did his mere presence send shivers of arousal tingling over her skin and zapping through her insides?

A deep breath didn't help clear the odd mix of confusion and emptiness in her brain. She hoped her memory would return before she did anything to embarrass him. "I guess I should get changed. I feel silly asking this, but where are my clothes?"

Jake froze for a moment, brow furrowed. "You wait here. I'll bring some for you."

"It's okay, I don't want to put you to any trouble. If you'll just tell me where they are." She hated feeling so helpless.

"It's no trouble at all. Just relax on the sofa for a bit. I'll be right back."

She shrugged. "I suppose you probably know what I like to wear better than I do. Still, I could come with you. I need to figure out where everything is."

"Better that you get dressed first. I'll be right back."

He left the room abruptly, leaving Andi uneasy. Why was he so anxious for her to stay here? Like he didn't want anyone to see her. Maybe he didn't want people to know about her loss of memory.

She glanced around the room, already feeling alone and worried without him. Did he have to leave? As the king, you'd think he'd just call for a servant to bring her clothes.

Or did things not work that way anymore? When your memory had taken flight it was hard to distinguish between fairy tales and ordinary life.

She lay back on the sofa and tried to relax. She was engaged to a handsome and caring man that she was fiercely attracted to. Maybe her real life was a fairy tale?

Jake strode along the corridor, hoping he wouldn't run into anyone—which was an unfamiliar feeling for him. Usually he prided himself on being up-front and open, but right now he didn't want anyone to know Andi had been about to leave.

That felt…personal.

He was confident she'd keep it to herself until she'd squared things with him. She'd proved over the years that she was the soul of discretion and confided in no one.

Her job was her life. At least it had been until she decided she'd had enough of it. Hurt flared inside him that she could even consider abandoning him and Ruthenia, especially now he'd realized she was the ideal wife for him. This odd memory loss would give him a chance to turn things around and keep her here for good.

He reached her door and slipped into the room with a sense of relief. Her packed suitcases still sat on the floor next to the bed. He closed the door and began to unpack, hanging the clothes back in the closet and placing some items in the large dresser. He intended to make it look as if she'd never thought of leaving.

Some things startled him. A lacy pink nightgown. A pair of black stockings and garters. When had she had occasion to wear these? He didn't think she had been on a single date since they'd moved to Ruthenia.

Guilt speared him at the thought. She was so busy working she had no life at all outside of her job. Why had he assumed that would be enough for her?

He placed her toiletries back in the bathroom. Handling her shampoo bottle and deodorant felt oddly intimate, like he was peeking into her private life. She had a lot of different lipsticks and he tried to arrange them upright on the bathroom shelf, though really he had no idea how she kept them.

She looked a lot prettier without all that lipstick on. Maybe he should just ditch them and she'd be none the wiser?

No. These were her possessions and that would be wrong.

He arranged her eyeliner pencils and powders and bottles of makeup on the shelf, too. Did all women have so much of this stuff? She had a ridiculous assortment of hair products, too—gels and sprays and mousses—which was funny since her hair was almost always tied back in a bun.

It took a full twenty minutes to get her bags unpacked and rearranged in some sort of convincing order. He shoved the bags under the bed and stood back to admire his handiwork.

Too perfect. He pulled a pair of panty hose from a drawer and draped them over the bed. Better.

He was about to leave when he remembered he was supposed to bring her back something to wear. Hmm. Mischief tickled his insides. What would he like to see her in? Not one of those stiff, bright suits she always wore.

He pulled a pair of jeans from one of the drawers. He'd never seen her in those, so why not? A blue long-sleeved T-shirt seemed to match, and he pulled some rather fetching black lace underwear—tags still attached—from the drawer.

He removed the tags. Why not let her think she wore stuff like this every day?

He rolled the items in a soft blue-and-gray sweater and set off down the corridor again, glancing left and right, glad that the palace was still quiet at this hour.

Andi's uncharacteristically anxious face greeted him as he returned to his rooms. She seemed quite different from last night, when she was spouting garbled poetry and dancing around the room. Now she sat curled up on the sofa, clutching her knees.

"How are you feeling?" Her rigid posture made him want to soothe and relax her.

"Nervous. It's odd not knowing anything about myself or my life. More than odd. Scary."

Jake tried to ignore the trickle of guilt that slid down his spine. He had no intention of telling her the truth about her plans to leave. And come to think of it, he hadn't seen any tickets or itineraries in her room. Maybe her plans weren't all that firm, anyway. "Don't worry. It'll all come back eventually. In the meantime, we'll just carry on as usual. Does that sound okay?"

She nodded.

"I brought some clothes." He set them down on the sofa beside him.

She unrolled the sweater and her eyes widened briefly at the sight of the lacy bra and panties. "Thanks."

She glanced up at him, and then at the pile of clothes again.

He resisted a powerful urge to see her slip into that sexy underwear. "You can change in the bedroom if you want some privacy. There are fresh towels in the bathroom if you'd like to take a shower."

Andi closed the bedroom door behind her. If Jake was her fiancé, why did the thought of changing in front of him make her want to blush crimson? She'd probably done it numerous times in the past. This whole situation was so weird. Her own fiancé felt—not like a stranger, but not like an intimate companion, either.

Must be pretty uncomfortable for Jake, too, though he didn't seem too flustered. Maybe he was just the sort to take things in stride. He had a reassuring air of composure, which was probably a good thing in a king.

Andi slipped out of her crumpled evening gown and climbed into a luxurious marble shower that could accommodate about six people. Unlike the scenery outside the window, and even the dressing room/sitting area, which felt at least somewhat familiar, everything in the bathroom suite seemed totally strange, like she'd literally never been there before. Maybe the memory was selective like that in its recall.

The warm water soothed and caressed her and she dried off feeling fresher.

She managed to arrange her hair into some semblance of order using a black comb, and applied some rather masculine-scented deodorant. They obviously didn't share this bathroom as there were no girly items in here at all. Unease pricked her skin again. No real reason for it though. Probably plenty of engaged couples slept in separate rooms. And one would expect extra attention to propriety in a royal household.

The black underwear he'd brought made her want to blush again. Why? It was her own, so why did it feel too racy for her? The bra fit perfectly, and the panties, while very low-cut, were comfortable, too. She was glad to quickly cover them with the practical jeans and blue T-shirt. No socks or shoes? Well, she could go retrieve those herself. She tied the soft sweater around her shoulders and stepped outside.

Jake's mouth broadened into a smile at the sight of her. "You look great." His dark eyes shone with approval.

She shrugged. Something about the ensemble felt funny. Too casual, maybe. It didn't seem right to wear jeans in a royal palace.

"You didn't bring any shoes." She pointed to her bare feet.

"Maybe I wanted to admire your pretty toes."

Heat flared inside her as his gaze slid down her legs to the toes in question. She giggled, feeling suddenly lighthearted. "My toes would still like to find some shoes to hide in. Why wasn't I wearing any last night? I looked in the bedroom and the dressing room, but I didn't see any."

"I don't know." Jake's expression turned more serious. "You were twirling barefoot on the lawn when I found you."

Andi's skin prickled with unease again. "So we decided to get engaged, and then I lost my memory?"

Jake nodded. His guarded expression didn't offer much reassurance.

He took a step toward her. "Don't worry, we'll get through this together." He slid his arms around her waist. Heat rippled in her belly. His scent stirred emotions and sensations and she softened into his embrace. She wondered if he was going to say he loved her, but he simply kissed her softly on the mouth.

Pleasure crept over her. "I guess I'm lucky it happened right here, and that I'm not wandering around some strange place with no idea who I am like those stories you see on the news."

"It is fortunate, isn't it?" He kissed her again. This time both their eyes slid closed and the kiss deepened. Colors swirled and sparkled behind Andi's eyelids and sensation crashed through her, quickening her pulse and making her breath come in unsteady gasps. Her fingers itched to touch the skin under his starched shirt.

She stepped back, blinking, once they managed to pull apart. Were their kisses always this intense?

Jake smiled, relaxed and calm. Apparently this was all par for the course. Andi patted her hair, wishing she could feel half as composed as he looked. Terror snapped through her at the prospect of facing strangers and trying to pretend everything was normal. "Can we keep our engagement a secret for now?"

Jake's eyes widened for a second. "Why?"

"Just so I don't have to answer a lot of questions when I don't even know who I am."

He frowned. "I'm afraid it's too late. I told someone on the phone last night."

"Who?" Not that she'd even know the name.

"Maxi Rivenshnell. She's a…friend of the family."

Andi paused. The name had a nasty ring to it. Maybe it was the way he pronounced it, like something that tasted bad. "Maybe she won't tell anyone."

"I suspect she'll tell everyone." He turned and strode across the room. Shoved a hand through his dark hair. Then he turned and approached her. "But nothing's going to stop me buying you a ring today, and you're going to choose it. First, let me summon your shoes."

Jake parked his Mercedes in his usual reserved spot in the town's main square. No need for chauffeurs and armed escorts in tiny Ruthenia. He rushed around the car to help Andi out, but she was already on her feet and closing the door by the time he got there.

She'd devoured her breakfast of fruit and pastries in the privacy of his suite. At least he knew what she liked to eat. Despite obvious confusion over little things like how to find her way around, she seemed healthy and relatively calm, which was a huge relief.

Of course her reluctance to announce their engagement was a slight hitch in his plans to unload his unwanted admirers, but word would get out soon enough. Ruthenia had more than its share of gossiping busybodies, and for once they'd be working in his favor.

He took her arm and guided her across the main square. Morning sunlight illuminated the old stone facades of the shops and glinted off the slate tiles of the church steeple. Pigeons gathered near the fountain, where a little girl tossed bread crumbs at them and two dogs barked a happy greeting as their owners stopped for a chat.

"The local town," murmured Andi.

"Does it look familiar?"

"A little. Like I've seen it in a dream rather than in real life. It's so pretty."

"It is lovely. You and I saw it together for the first time three years ago."

She paused. "You didn't grow up here?"

"No, I grew up in the States, like you. I didn't come here until the socialist government collapsed in a heap of corruption scandals and people started agitating for the return of the royal family. At first I thought they were nuts, then I realized I could probably help put the country back on its feet." He looked at her, her clear blue eyes wide, soaking in everything he said. "I couldn't have done it without you."

His chest tightened as he spoke the words. All true. Andi's quiet confidence and brisk efficiency made almost anything possible. The prospect of carrying on without her by his side was unthinkable.

"Was I good at being your assistant?" Her serious gaze touched him. "I don't remember anything about my job."

"Exemplary. You've been far more than my assistant. My right-hand woman is a better description."

She looked pleased. "I guess that's a good thing, since we're getting married."

"Absolutely." Jake swallowed. How would she react when her memory returned and she realized they were never romantically involved? He drew in a breath. She wasn't in love with him. Still, she was sensible enough to see that marriage between them would be in the best interests of Ruthenia.

And that kiss had been surprisingly spicy. In fact, he couldn't remember experiencing anything like it in his fairly substantial kissing experience.

Maybe it was the element of the forbidden. He'd never considered kissing his assistant and it still felt…wrong. Probably because it was wrong of him to let her think they'd been a couple. But once a ring was on her finger, they really would be engaged and everything would be on the up and up.

At least until her memory came back.

"The jeweler is down this street." He led her along a narrow cobbled alley barely wide enough for a cart. The kind of street he'd have to fold in his wing mirrors to drive down without scraping the ancient walls on either side. Thick handblown glass squares glazed the bowed window of the shop, giving a distorted view of the luxurious trinkets inside.

Despite its old-world ambience—or maybe because of it—this jeweler was one of the finest in Europe and had recently regained its international reputation as part of Jake's Rediscover Ruthenia campaign. He'd bought quite a few pieces here—gifts for foreign diplomats and wealthy Ruthenian acquaintances. Why had it never occurred to him to buy something lovely for Andi?

He opened the heavy wood door and ushered her in, unable to resist brushing her waist with his fingers as he coaxed her through. The formally attired proprietor rushed forward to greet them. "Welcome, sir." Jake was grateful the man remembered his aversion to pompous titles. "How can we assist you today? A custom commission, perhaps?"

Jake hesitated. Andi might well like a ring designed to her exact specifications—but he needed a ring on her finger right now to make an honest man of him. He certainly didn't want her memory coming back before the setting was tooled. "I suspect you have something lovely in the shop already."

He took Andi's hand in his. It was warm, and he squeezed it to calm her nerves. "We're looking for an engagement ring."

The elderly jeweler's eyes opened wide. His gaze slid to Andi, then back again. He seemed unsure what to make of the situation. Perhaps he'd been following the local gossip columns and was already designing one with Maxi or Alia in mind. "Should I be offering you my congratulations?"

"Most certainly." Jake slid his arm around Andi.

"Wonderful." The jeweler bowed his head slightly in Andi's direction. "My best wishes for you both. And in time for Independence Day, too." A smile creased his wrinkled face. "The whole nation will be overjoyed. I do think a custom creation would be most appropriate. Perhaps with the family crest?"

"Why don't we take a look at what you have in stock?" He tightened his arm around Andi's waist, then loosened it, suddenly aware of how intent he was to hold on to her. Not that she was resisting. She leaned into him, perhaps seeking reassurance he was happy to provide.

A large tray of sparkling rings appeared from a deep wooden cabinet. Jake glanced at Andi and saw her eyes widen.

"See if anything appeals to you." He spoke softly,

suddenly feeling the intimacy of the moment. The first step in their journey through life as a married couple. The rings were nearly all diamonds, some single and some triple, with a large stone flanked by two smaller stones. A few more had clusters of diamonds and there was a large sapphire and a square cut ruby.

Andi drew in a long breath, then reached for a small single diamond in a carved platinum band. She held it for a moment, then extended her fingers to try it on. "Wow, this feels weird. Like you should be doing it, or something." She glanced shyly at him.

Jake swallowed. He took the ring from her—the diamond was too small, anyway—and gingerly slid it onto her slender finger. His skin tingled as he touched hers and a flutter of something stirred in his chest. The ring fit well and looked pretty on her hand.

"What do you think?" She turned her hand, and the stone sparkled in the light.

"Nice." He didn't want to criticize, if that was her choice.

The jeweler frowned. "It's a fine ring, but for the royal family, perhaps something a bit more…extravagant?" He lifted a dramatic large stone flanked by several smaller stones. The kind of ring that would make people's eyes pop. Jake had to admit it was more appropriate under the circumstances.

Andi allowed the older man to slide her choice off her finger and push the big sparkler onto it. His face creased into a satisfied smile as it slid perfectly into place. "Lovely. Much more suitable for a royal bride, if you don't mind my saying."

She tilted her hand to the side and studied the ring. Despite the large size of the stones it also looked elegant on her graceful hands. Jake wondered how he'd never noticed what pretty hands she had. He'd been watching them type his letters and organize his files for years.

"It's a bit over the top...." She paused, still staring at it. "But it is pretty." She looked up at Jake. "What do you think?"

"Very nice." He intended to buy her many more trinkets and baubles to enjoy. It was worth it to see the sunny smile on her face, and they were supporting the local economy. "Let's buy it and go get a hot chocolate to celebrate."

She hesitated for a moment more, studying the ring on her finger. When she looked up, confusion darkened the summer-blue of her eyes. She seemed like she wanted to say something, but hesitated in front of the jeweler. The shop owner tactfully excused himself and disappeared through a low door into a back room.

"I guess he trusts us alone with the merchandise." Jake grinned. "There must be a million dollars worth of rocks on this tray."

"I'd imagine a crown inspires a certain amount of trust." She looked up at him, eyes sparkling. "I'm still getting used to the idea that you're a king."

"Me, too. I'm not sure I'll ever be completely used to it, but at least it's starting to feel like a suit that fits. How does the ring feel?"

Andi studied the ring again. "It is lovely, but it's just so... big."

"He's right, though. It makes sense to go dramatic. Do you want people muttering that I'm a cheapskate?" He raised a brow.

Andi chuckled. "I guess you have a good point." Then she frowned. "Are people going to be shocked that you're marrying your assistant?" She bit her lip for a moment. "I mean...did they know that we're...intimate?"

Jake inhaled. "We kept it all pretty private."

"Did anyone know?" Her serious expression tugged at him.

"A few people may have guessed something." Who knew what people might imagine, even if there had never been anything to guess? "But on the whole, we were discreet so it'll be a surprise."

Andi's shoulders tightened a bit. "I hope they won't be too upset that you're not marrying someone more… important."

"No one's more important than you, Andi. I'd be lost without you." It was a relief to say something honest, even if he meant it in a business sense, rather than a romantic one.

"I guess I should get the fancy one. If they're going to talk, let's give them something to talk about."

"That's the attitude." Jake rang the bell on the counter and the jeweler appeared again like Rumpelstiltskin. "We'll take it."

The old man beamed. "An excellent choice. I wish you both a lifetime of happiness."

Me, too, thought Jake. He'd need to think on his feet when Andi snapped out of this thing.

Four

Andi blinked as they stepped out of the dark shop into bright morning sunlight that reflected off everything from the gray cobbles to the white-crested mountain peaks that loomed over the town. The cold air whipped at her skin and she drew her warm coat about her. Out in the open she felt violently self-conscious about the huge ring on her finger, and gratefully tucked it into her coat pocket.

"The coffeehouse is just up the road." Jake took her arm. "You may not remember, but they have the best hot chocolate in the known world and you love it."

Andi's muscles tightened at the reminder that he knew more about her than she did. "Do you go there often?" It seemed odd for a king to frequent a local café. Then again she had no idea what was normal. Very strange how she remembered things like old fairy tales but not her own life.

"Of course. Got to support the local businesses."

He certainly was thoughtful. That cozy feeling of being protected and cared for warmed her as he slid his arm through hers again. How lucky she was! No doubt her memory would come back soon and—

A moped skidded past them on the narrow street. Its rider, a man in a black leather jacket, stopped and leaped off, camera in hand. "Your Highness, is it true you are engaged?" he asked, in a French accent.

Jake paused. "It is true." Andi stared in surprise at his polite demeanor.

"May I take your picture?"

Jake took Andi's hands in his. "What do you say, Andi? He's just doing his job."

Andi cringed inwardly. She didn't want anyone seeing her in her confused state, let alone photographing her. She also didn't want to make a fuss in front of a stranger. That might give the game away.

She swallowed. "Okay, I guess." She pushed a lock of hair self-consciously off her face. She hadn't had time to style it—not that she even remembered what style she usually wore—but Jake had assured her it looked lovely.

The man took about fifty pictures from different angles through a long, scary-looking lens that would probably show every pore on her face. Jake was obviously used to the attention and remained calm and pleasant. He even adjusted them into several dignified romantic poses as if they were at a professional shoot.

Almost as if he'd planned this encounter.

She fought the urge to frown, which certainly wouldn't be a good idea for the pictures. How did the photographer know they were engaged when it had only happened last night?

Jake managed to politely disengage them from the impromptu photo session and continue down the road.

He smiled and nodded at passersby, all of whom seemed quite comfortable rubbing shoulders with their monarch. But when they reached the main square she saw two more reporters, a woman with a tiny microphone clipped to her jacket and a tall man with a notepad. They greeted Jake with warm smiles and asked if congratulations were in order.

Andi tried to maintain a pleasant expression while unease gnawed at her gut.

"How does it feel to marry a king?" asked the woman, in soft Ruthenian tones.

"I'm not sure yet," admitted Andi. "Since we're not married. I'll have to let you know after the ceremony."

"When will that be?" asked the man. Andi glanced at Jake.

"We'll make an announcement when we have all the details sorted out. A royal wedding isn't something you rush into."

"Of course." The reporter was a middle-aged woman with soft blond hair. "And you've kept your promise of choosing your bride before Ruthenia's third Independence Day next week."

"The people of Ruthenia know I'm a man of my word."

Andi only just managed not to frown. He'd become engaged to her at the last minute because of some promise he made? That was awfully convenient. The knot in the pit of her stomach tightened.

The woman asked if she could see Andi's ring. Andi pulled it out and was alarmed to see it looked even bigger and brighter out here in daylight. The camera flashed several times before she could hide her hand back in her pocket again.

When Jake finally excused them, her heart was pounding and her face flushed. She let out a silent sigh of relief as he guided her into the warm and inviting coffee shop. She removed her coat and hung it on a row of iron hooks that looked hundreds of years old.

"I'm glad they didn't ask any questions I couldn't answer."

"The paparazzi are polite here." Jake took her hand and led her to a secluded table. "They know I can have them clapped in irons if they're not."

She glanced up to see if he was kidding and was relieved to see a sparkle of humor in his eye.

"The press has been helpful in letting the world know about my efforts to bring the country into the twenty-first century. It pays to keep them happy."

"How could they know about our engagement already? Did that girl you spoke to phone them?" Andi sat in the plush upholstered chair. A small fire snapped and sizzled nearby. The coffee shop had dark wood paneling and varied antique tables and chairs clustered around the low-ceilinged space that looked unchanged since the 1720s—which it probably was.

"I doubt it. They seem to know everything. It's a bit spooky at first, but you get used to it. Maybe they saw us inside the jeweler's?"

"Or maybe he tipped them off." Andi gingerly pulled her be-ringed hand from her pocket to take a menu from the elegantly attired waiter.

"Old Gregor is the soul of discretion." Jake studied his menu. Andi wondered for a second how he knew to trust Old Gregor. Had he commissioned gems for other women? But he said they'd been dating for years.

She cursed the hot little flame of jealousy that had flickered to life inside her. Why were they suddenly engaged after years of dating? Was it somehow precipitated by this promise he'd made, or had she previously refused?

For a moment Andi was hyperaware of people at tables all around them, sipping their drinks and eating. Could they tell she was missing a huge part of her life?

He shrugged. "It's their job. We live in the public eye." He reached across the table and took her hand. His strong fingers closed around hers. She squeezed his hand back and enjoyed the sense of reassurance she got from him. "You'll get used to it again."

"I suppose I will." She glanced warily about the interior of the intimate coffeehouse. "It's so unnerving not to even know what's normal. Then you can't figure out what's odd and unusual."

"It would certainly be odd for us to sit here without drinking hot chocolate." He summoned the waiter and ordered a pot of hot chocolate and a dish of cream. "And, just so you know, the waffles with summer berries are your favorite."

"Did we eat here together a lot?" The place didn't look especially familiar.

"Yes. We often brought business associates and visitors from the States here, since it's so quaint and unchanged. Now that we're engaged..." He stroked her hand inside his and fixed his dark eyes on hers. "It's just the two of us."

Andi's insides fluttered as his gaze crept right under her skin. If only she could remember what their relationship was like. It didn't sound as if they ate out unless in company, which was a bit odd. A secret affair.

It must be strange and unsettling for him to have her behaving like a different person.

Then again, he didn't seem rattled by the situation. His handsome face had an expression of calm contentment. The chiseled features were steady as the mountains outside and it was hard to imagine him getting upset or bothered by anything. Jake was obviously the kind of man who took things in stride. Her hand felt totally comfortable in his, as if he was promising her that he'd take care of her and make sure only good things happened.

Why did it feel so bizarre that such a gorgeous and successful man was all hers?

Well, of course she had to share him with a small nation, but after the lights went out he was hers alone. Hope and excitement rose through her, along with a curl of desire that matched the steam rising off the hot chocolate.

Jake kept his gaze on her face as the waiter poured the fragrant liquid into two wide round cups and then dropped a dollop of thick whipped cream on top of each one. When the waiter moved away, Jake lifted her hand to his lips and kissed it. Sensual excitement flashed through her body at the soft touch of his mouth on her skin, a promise of what would come when they were alone together.

Andi fought the urge to glance around to see if anyone had witnessed the intimate moment. She drew in a deep breath and forced herself to display the kind of cool that Jake possessed naturally. She'd better get used to being in the public eye, since she'd be spending the rest of her life in it.

If she really was marrying Jake. The idea still seemed too far-fetched and outrageous to truly believe. He gently let go of her hand and she moved it quickly to her cup and covered her confusion with a sip. The rich and delicious chocolate slid down her throat and heated her insides. Perfect.

Everything was perfect. Too perfect.

So why couldn't she escape the niggling feeling that when she got her memory back she'd discover something was horribly wrong?

Andi grew increasingly nervous as they drove back to the palace. None of the other staff knew about their engagement—at least as far as she knew. How would they react?

She climbed out of the car on shaky legs. Did she have a best friend here in whom she confided? Or was that person Jake? Tears hovered very close to the surface, but she tried hard to put on a brave face as they approached the grand doorway up a flight of wide steps.

"Good morning, sir." A black-attired man opened the door before they even reached it. "And may I offer you congratulations."

Andi cringed. They all knew already? Word spread around this tiny country like a plague.

"Congratulations, Andi. I'm not sure whether it's appropriate to tell you that, as usual, the mail is in your office."

She didn't even know she had an office, let alone where it was. She gulped, realizing that she'd be expected to do her job, regardless of whether or not she could remember how.

Either that or tell everyone that her mind had been wiped blank, and she couldn't face that. "Thanks," she managed.

She kept her hand buried deep in the pocket of her wool coat as they crossed the marble-floored entrance hall. Faces looked vaguely familiar, but she couldn't remember names or if they were friends as well as coworkers. Jake stopped to answer some questions about a phone call they'd received, and Andi hesitated, unsure which direction to walk in, or where to even hang her coat. Worse yet, a girl with lots of red hair rushed up to her, wide-eyed. "Why am I the last to know everything?"

Andi managed a casual shrug.

The redhead leaned in and lowered her voice. "I see you decided not to leave after all?"

Andi's eyes widened. "Leave?" She glanced up to see if

Jake had heard, but he was still deep in conversation several yards away.

"Stop acting innocent. I saw the suitcases you bought in town. Still, obviously something better than a new job came up."

"I don't know what you're talking about." Truer words were never spoken. Anxiety churned the hot chocolate in her stomach. Suitcases? A new job? That was odd. She needed to get to her room and see if she could find something to jog her memory.

If only she knew where her room was.

She remembered the way back to Jake's suite, and was tempted to head that way without him just to get away from the inquisitive redhead. Then again, he was apparently her boss, so that might look odd.

The ring practically burned her finger, still hidden deep inside her coat. "Let me take that for you." An older man with neat white hair crossed the floor. Andi stared. "Your coat," he continued, demonstrating the hanger in his hand. "I wonder if it's premature to call you Your Majesty?" he asked with a kind expression.

"Probably." She managed a smile while shrugging the coat off. She looked up at Jake and their eyes met. He must have seen the plea in her face as he detached himself from his questioner and strode to her side. "Let's head for my office."

As soon as they were on the stairs, she whispered that she didn't know where her room was. He frowned for a second, then smiled. "We'll go there right now."

The hallway was empty. "I don't even know anyone's name. It's the most awkward feeling. People must think I'm so rude."

"That was Walter. Worked here back when it was a hotel

and always the first to know every bit of gossip. He probably spread the word."

"This building was a hotel?"

"For a while. It had a few different lives while my family was in exile in the States. It took a lot of work to get it looking like this, and you were in charge of most of it."

Andi bit her lip, walking along carpet she may even have selected. Jake pointed to the third polished wood door in a long hallway, only a few yards from his. "That's yours. It wasn't locked when I came to get your clothes."

She tried the handle and it swung open. A neat, hotel-like room greeted her, with heavy brocade curtains and a small double bed. The dark wood furniture looked antique and impressive. She cringed at the sight of a pair of panty hose draped over the bed.

"Um, maybe I should spend a little time alone here. See if anything jogs my memory."

"Sure." Jake stroked her back softly. Her skin heated under her T-shirt as he turned her toward him and lowered his face to hers. All worries and fears drifted way for a few seconds as she lost herself in his soft and gentle kiss.

"Don't worry about anything." He pointed to a dresser. "Your phone's right there and you've always told me I'm programmed in as number one." He winked. "I'll head for my office to deal with this electrical supply situation that's cropped up. Call me if you need anything, and even if you don't."

Her fingers felt cold as he released them from his, but she couldn't help a sigh of relief as she closed the door behind him and found herself alone in the room. At last she could… fall apart.

Part of her wanted to run to the bed and collapse on it, sobbing. But another, apparently more influential, part wanted to pull open the drawers and search for signs of who she was. She tucked the stray panty hose back into their drawer, wondering if she'd taken them out when she was dressing in her evening gown. She wasn't wearing any when she'd woken up in the morning.

The drawer was rather disorganized, as if everything was just shoved in there without much thought. What did this tell her about herself? She frowned and pulled open the drawer above it. Three carelessly folded blouses and some socks gave no further encouragement about her organizational skills.

The closet door was slightly ajar and she pulled it open. An array of colorful suits hung from the hangers, along with several solid-colored dresses and skirts. At least it didn't look as messy as her drawers. She pushed some hangers apart and pulled down one of the suits. A medium blue, it was tailored but otherwise quite plain. She tried to smooth out a horizontal crease that ran just below the lapels. Another crease across the skirt made her frown. Why would a suit hanging in a closet have creases running across it?

She pulled out another suit and saw that it too had lines running through the middle. A forest-green dress also showed signs of having been folded recently, and a navy skirt and… She stopped and frowned. All the items in the closet had crease marks running across them. Not deep, sharp creases, but soft ones, as if they'd been folded only for a short time. What could that mean?

After she hung the suit back in the closet, she walked into the attached bathroom. A floral smell hovered in the air and felt reassuringly familiar. Her favorite scent? She recognized it—which meant it was a memory. Cheered, she examined the cosmetics arranged on a low shelf. There were a lot of lipsticks. She pulled one open and applied it. A rather garish orangey-pink that didn't do her complexion any favors. She put it back on the shelf and wiped her lips with a tissue.

She found the bottle of scent and removed the cap. Warmth suffused her as she sprayed some on her wrists and inhaled the familiar smell. Relief also swept through her that at least something around here felt familiar.

The scent…and Jake.

Excitement mixed with apprehension tickled her insides. How odd that they'd become engaged and she'd lost her memory in the same night. She couldn't help wondering if the two things were related.

Jake was lovely, though. He'd been so sweet and encouraging with her since she'd lost her memory. She was lucky to be engaged to such a kind and capable man. A bit odd that he was a king, but that was just one facet of him. Just a job, really. No doubt she wasn't bothered by his royal status or she wouldn't have become romantically involved with him in the first place.

She picked up her hand and looked at her big diamond ring. It was beautiful and fit her perfectly. She'd feel comfortable wearing it once she got used to it.

Once she got used to any of this.

A knock on the door made her jump. "It's me, Livia."

Andi gulped. Apparently she was supposed to know who Livia was. So far no one seemed to know about her memory except Jake and the doctor, but that was bound to change unless it came back soon. She smoothed her hair and went to open the door.

It was the same red-haired girl from downstairs. The one who'd talked about her leaving. She had a huge grin on her freckled face. "You are a dark horse."

Andi shrugged casually, as if admitting it, even though she didn't know exactly whether Livia referred to the engagement or her memory loss.

"You never breathed a word. How long have the two of you been…?" Her conspiratorial whisper sounded deafening in the quiet hallway.

"Come in." Andi ushered her into the room. Livia glanced around. Andi got the idea that she hadn't been here before, so they probably weren't the closest of friends, but maybe she could learn something from her. She managed a smile. "We didn't really want anyone to know. Not until we were sure."

Livia seemed satisfied with that answer. "How romantic. And after working together all these years. I never suspected a thing!"

"I hardly believe it myself."

"So the suitcases were for your honeymoon." Livia grinned and shook her head. "Where are you going?"

"Not sure yet." Jake hadn't said anything about a honeymoon. Surely they had to have a wedding first.

"This time make sure I'm not the last person in the palace to know. I know you're always insisting that it's part of your job to keep mum about things, but I can't believe I had to learn about your engagement on the radio."

"What did they say?"

"That you and Jake were out ring shopping in town this morning, and you told reporters you were getting married. Hey, let's see the rock!" She reached out and grabbed Andi's hand. "Wow. That's some ring. I wouldn't go on the New York City subway in that."

So Livia had come from New York, as well? That meant they'd probably known each other at least three years. Andi felt awful that she didn't even remember her.

Livia sighed. "And just imagine what your wedding dress will be like. You could probably get anyone in the world to design it for you. Some people have all the luck."

Andi was sorely tempted to point out that she had the

bad luck to not even know who she was, but a gut instinct told her not to confide in Livia. She sensed an undercurrent of jealousy or resentment that made her reluctant to trust her.

"Oh, there are the suitcases, under your bed." Livia pointed. Andi could see the edges of two black rolling cases.

"You're very obsessed with those."

"I thought you were going to take off and leave us. At least to do that interview."

Andi frowned. Had she planned a job interview somewhere?

"I was even starting to think that if we both went back to New York we could share an apartment or something. Guess I was wrong." She widened her eyes, which fell again to Andi's hand.

"You were. I'll be staying here." She smiled, and conviction filled her voice. How nice it was to be sure of something.

"I bet you will."

A million questions bounced around Andi's brain, as many about Jake and life at the palace as about herself. But she couldn't think of any way to ask them without giving the game away, and she wasn't ready to do that yet. On the other hand, at least Livia could help her find her way to her own office. That would be one less problem for her to bother Jake with.

"Why don't you walk to my office with me?"

Livia looked curious. Andi worried that she'd made a misstep. She had no idea what Livia did at the palace, and her clothing, dark pants and a blue long-sleeved peasant shirt, didn't offer any clues. "Sure."

They set out, Andi lagging a fraction behind so that Livia could lead the way without realizing it. They went along the hallway in the opposite direction from Jake's suite, and up a flight of stairs to the third floor. At the top of the stairs a blond man hurried up to them. "Goodness, Andi. Congratulations."

"Thanks." She blushed, mostly because she had no idea who he was. Luckily it was an appropriate response.

"Cook wanted me to ask you whether we should do duck or goose on Thursday for the Finnish ambassador."

"Whichever she prefers would be fine." She froze for an agonizing second while it occurred to her that Cook might be a he.

His eyes widened. "I'll let her know. I suspect you have a lot on your plate right now, what with, well, you know." He smiled. "We're all very happy for you, Andi."

She forced another smile. He'd looked surprised by her lack of decisiveness. She must usually be a very take-charge person. At least the engagement gave her an excuse to be out to lunch—literally and figuratively. She was "preoccupied."

They reached a door halfway down a corridor on the third floor, and Livia hesitated. Andi swallowed, then reached out a hand and tried the door. The handle turned but didn't open it. "Oh no. I forgot my key! You go on with what you're doing and I'll go back and get it. See you later."

Livia waved a cheery goodbye and Andi heaved a sigh. She counted the doors along the hallway so she could find her way here alone next time. Back in her room she searched high and low for the key. When she found a black handbag at the bottom of her closet, her heart leapt.

She'd already discovered that the phone in her bedroom was for business only. Not a single personal number was stored in it. She'd called each one with hope in her heart, only to find herself talking to another bank or supplier. She must have another phone somewhere.

Eager to see her wallet and find out some more about herself, she dove into the bag with her hands. A neat, small wallet contained very few clues. A New York driver's license, with an 81st Street address, about to expire. A Ruthenian driver's license ornamented with a crest featuring two large birds. A Visa credit card from an American bank, and a MasterCard from a European one.

She seemed to be living a double life—half American and half Ruthenian. But that wasn't unusual among expats. She probably kept her accounts open, figuring she'd go back sooner or later.

The bag did contain a keychain containing two keys—her bedroom and office? Other than that there was a small packet of tissues and two lipsticks. No phone. Disappointment dripped through her. Maybe she just had no life.

Except Jake.

She glanced at the business phone on the dresser and her nerves sizzled with anticipation at the thought of calling him. She felt a lot safer in his large, calm presence.

But she didn't want to be a bother. She'd wait until she really needed him.

Keys and phone in the pocket of her jeans, she set off back for the locked office. Her instincts proved correct and the smaller key opened the door. Like her bedroom, her office was neat and featureless, no photos or mementos on the desk. She'd be worried that she was the world's dullest person, except that apparently she was intriguing enough for a king to want to marry her.

She opened a silver laptop on the desk. Surely this would reveal a wealth of new information about her life—her work, anyway. But the first screen asked her to enter her password.

Andi growled with frustration. She felt like she was looking for the password to her own life and it was always just out of reach. Password, password. She racked her brain for familiar words. *Blue,* she typed in. The screen was blue. Nothing happened. *Jake?* Nothing doing. *Love?*

Nada. Apparently her computer, like her memory, was off-limits for now.

Irritation crackled through her veins. She pulled open the drawers in the antique desk and was disappointed to find nothing but a dull collection of pens, paper clips, empty notebooks. The entire office revealed nothing about her. Almost as if every trace of her individuality had been stripped away.

The way you might do if you were leaving a job.

A pang of alarm flashed through her at the thought. Had she stripped her office bare in preparation for abandoning it? She could see how getting engaged to Jake could mean her leaving her job as his assistant, or at least changing it dramatically. But surely Jake would have mentioned it?

She picked up her phone and punched in his number. Feelings of helplessness and anxiety rose inside her as she heard it ring, but she fought them back.

"Hi, Andi. How are you doing?"

A smile rose to her lips at the sound of his deep, resonant voice. "Confused," she admitted. "I'm in my office and feeling more lost than ever."

"I'll meet you there."

She blew out a long breath as she put the phone back in her pocket. It was embarrassing to feel lost without Jake at her side, but wonderful that she could call him to it at any moment. She glanced at the ring on her finger. The big diamond sparkled in the sunlight, casting little shards of light over her skin, a symbol of his lifelong commitment to her.

At least she knew what it felt like to be loved.

She flew to the door at the sound of a knock. A huge smile spread over her face at the sight of him, tall and gorgeous, with a twinkle in his dark eyes.

"I missed you," he murmured, voice low and seductive.

"Come in." Her belly sizzled with arousal and her nipples tightened just at the sight of him. "Do you always knock on my office door?" It seemed oddly formal if they'd worked together and dated for years.

A shadow of hesitation crossed his face for a split second. "I suppose I do. Would you prefer me to barge right in?"

"I don't know." She giggled. Nothing seemed to matter all that much now that Jake was here. "I guess it depends on if I'm trying to keep secrets from you."

"Are you?" His brow arched.

"I have no idea." She laughed again. "Hopefully if I do, they're not very dark ones."

"Dark secrets sound rather intriguing." He moved toward her and lifted his hand to cup her cheek. Her skin heated under his palm. "I might have fun uncovering them."

Their lips met, hot and fast, and his tongue in her mouth drove all thoughts away. She pressed herself against him and felt his arms close around her. *Much better.* Wrapping herself up in Jake was the best medicine for anything that ailed her.

His suit hid the hard muscle beneath it, but that didn't stop her fingers from exploring his broad back and enjoying the thickness of his toned biceps. Her fingertips were creeping into his waistband when a sharp knock on the door made them jump apart.

She blushed. "Do we get carried away like that often?"

Jake shot her a crooked smile. "Why not?"

A glance at the door sent her cheer scattering. "I won't recognize the person."

"I'll help you out."

She drew in a deep breath as she approached the door. "Who is it?"

"Domino." A male voice. "Just wanted to take a peek at Jake's calendar for tomorrow."

She glanced back at Jake and whispered, "I have no idea where your calendar is."

"You can peek at it in my head, Dom." Jake's voice boomed across the room.

A compact, dark-haired man in a gray suit flung the door open and entered. "Sorry, Mr. Mondragon, I didn't know you were in here. I just wondered if there was a set time for the Malaysian High Commission's arrival."

Andi listened while Jake rattled off a few planned events for the following day and tried to keep them filed in her brain in case anyone else asked her. It couldn't hurt to practice using her memory again. Still, she didn't truly breathe again until Domino backed out with a slight bow.

"I feel like the world's most incompetent assistant. Is the calendar on the computer?"

"Yup."

"It's password protected and I don't know the password. Do you know it?"

Jake looked thoughtful. "No."

"Any ideas what it might be?"

"None whatsoever. I guess there are some dark secrets between us." He lifted a brow playfully. "Maybe you have it written down somewhere."

"That's another thing." She frowned, apprehension twisting her gut as she prepared to tell him. "There's nothing personal in here at all. It's all business all the time, as if all the personal effects had been removed."

Jake blinked and his gaze swept the room. A furrow deepened between his brows; then he shrugged. "I'm not much for personal knickknacks in the office, either. Why don't we take a break and go stroll around the palace? Then at least you'll know where everything is."

Andi was a bit alarmed by the brusque way he changed the subject. One question burned in her mind. "Am I still your assistant? I mean, now that we're engaged."

"Yes, of course." Jake looked startled for a second. "I'd be lost without you arranging my life."

"Then prepare to get lost, since I can't arrange my own computer desktop right now." Tears loomed again. Apparently they'd never been very far away. "I still don't remember anything at all."

Jake took her into his arms again. His scent, familiar and enticing, wrapped around her as his embrace gave her strength. "The doctor said it would take time for your memory to return. Come on, let's go for that walk. There's no point getting upset over something you can't control."

The palace was so large that probably no one knew exactly how many rooms it had or how to get to all of them. As Jake explained, it had been the home of several dynasties of Ruthenian royals, all of whom had left their own stylistic stamp, so the building had everything from fortified turrets to elegant rows of French windows opening out onto a terrace for alfresco dancing.

As they walked about, on the pretext of discussing the decor, everyone stopped to offer their congratulations on their engagement. Some people hid their surprise, but Andi could tell it was a startling occurrence. Could they really have not noticed a romance occurring—over several years—right beneath their noses?

Five

"Jake, congratulations on your engagement." The silvery tones emerging from his phone dripped with acid. Jake glanced across his suite to where Andi reclined on the sofa looking through a tourist brochure about Ruthenia.

"Thanks, Carina." Lucky thing she couldn't see how happy he was not to be marrying her.

"Quite a surprise." Her tone was cool. "I had no idea you were involved with your assistant."

"You know how these things are. It seemed…unprofessional, but you can't halt the course of true love." He'd already explained the same to three other would-be queens, so it rolled naturally off his tongue.

"Indeed." She cleared her throat. "Daddy accuses you of toying with my affections, but I assured him that I'm a big girl and that he should still fund the new industrial development."

These veiled threats were becoming familiar, too.

"I do hope he will. We look forward to entertaining you both at the palace again soon." He was smiling when he hung up the phone. Right now everything was going as smoothly as could be expected. He was now officially off the hook for choosing the next queen of Ruthenia. No one had actually pulled support from any key projects or threatened to fund a revolution. It was probably a plus that he hadn't offended one Ruthenian big shot by choosing the daughter of another. Selecting his American assistant as his bride had left all the local families equally offended—or mollified. And so far things were working out nicely.

He couldn't understand why he'd never plotted this tidy solution together with Andi, before she lost her memory. Choosing his wife now seemed like an agenda item he'd neatly checked off.

"Why don't you join me on the sofa?" Her come-hither stare and soft tones beckoned to him.

Blood rushed to his nether regions and he stiffened. Of course there were some aspects of their engagement that should remain off-limits until Andi's memory came back. It was one thing to pretend to love your assistant, it was quite another thing to actually make love to her.

"That dinner was delicious, but I find I'm still hungry." Andi's blue eyes sparkled. She curled her legs under her and stretched one arm sensually along the top of sofa.

Her voice called to a part of him that wasn't at all practical. Jake was struck by a cruel vision of the black lacy underwear beneath her jeans and T-shirt. *She'll be angry if you sleep with her under false pretenses.*

But were they really false? He did intend to marry her.

Which was funny, as he'd never planned to marry anyone. His parents' long and arduous union—all duty and no joy—had put him off the whole institution from an early age. They'd married because they were a "suitable" match, his father the son of the exiled monarch and his mother the daughter of a prominent noble, also in exile. They'd soon discovered they had nothing in common but blue Ruthenian blood, yet they'd held up the charade for five decades in the hope they'd one day inhabit this palace and put the Ruthenian crest on their stationery again.

They were both gone by the time the "new regime" crumbled and Ruthenia decided it wanted its monarchy back. Jake had assumed the mantle of political duty, but it didn't seem fair or reasonable to expect him to take it into his bedroom, as well.

He'd much rather take Andi into his bedroom. Her lips looked so inviting in that sensual half smile. And he could just imagine how those long legs would feel wrapped around his waist….

But that was a really bad idea. When she got her memory back she'd likely be pretty steamed about the whole scenario he'd cooked up. She'd be downright furious if he took advantage of her affections, as well. Much better if they kept their hands to themselves until they could talk things over sensibly.

"Do you want me to walk you back to your room?" His voice sounded tight.

"Why? I'm not going to sleep there, am I?" She raised a brow. She seemed far more relaxed, bolder, than he'd seen her so far. She was obviously feeling comfortable, even if her memory still showed no signs of returning.

"I think you should. It's a question of propriety."

She giggled. "You are joking."

"No." He felt a bit offended. "It's a royal thing."

"So, we've never…?" She rose from the sofa in an athletic leap and strode across the room. "I don't remember the details about my own life, but I remember general stuff and I'm pretty sure that it's totally normal for dating couples to…sleep together. So I don't believe that we've been dating for years and never done more than kiss."

Jake shrugged. She had a point. If only she knew he was trying to protect her. "Okay, I admit we may have been… intimate. But now that we're engaged and it's all official and formal, I think we should play by the rules."

"Whose rules?" She raised her hand and stroked his cheek with her fingers.

His groin tightened and he cleared his throat. "Those official, hundreds-of-years-old rules that the king should keep his hands off his future bride until after the wedding."

Her mouth lifted into a wicked smile. "These hands?" She picked up his hands and placed them squarely on her hips. Heat rose in his blood as he took in the curves beneath his palms. She wriggled her hips slightly, sending shock waves of desire pulsing through him.

I'm in full control of my hands and my mind. The thought did nothing to reassure him, especially when one of his hands started to wander toward her backside. Andi pressed her lips to his and her familiar scent filled his senses. Next thing he knew his hands were straying up and down her back, enjoying the soft curves under his palms.

His pants grew tight as Andi pressed her chest against his. He could just imagine what those deliciously firm breasts must look like in her lacy bra. If he coaxed her out of her T-shirt—which would not be difficult—he could find out right away.

But that might lead to other things.

In fact, he was one hundred percent sure that it would.

He pulled back from the kiss with considerable effort. "Don't you have some…embroidery to do or something?"

"Embroidery?" Laughter sparkled in her clear blue eyes. "Do I really embroider stuff?"

He chuckled. "Not that I know of, but does a man really know what his fiancée gets up to in the privacy of her room?"

"I guess that depends how much time he spends there." She raised a brow. "Maybe we should go to my room?"

Jake froze. That seemed like a really bad idea. Which underlined what a bad idea all this kissing and cuddling was. Much better to keep things professional, with just enough hint of romance to keep the people around them convinced. At least until Andi came back to her senses.

He flinched as Andi's fingers crept beneath the waistband of his pants. He'd grown rock hard and the thought of pushing her away was downright painful. Her soft cheek nuzzled against his and his fingers wandered into her hair. She looked so different with her hair loose, much less formal and more inviting.

Her cool fingers slid under his shirt and skated up his spine. Jake arched into the sensation, pulling her tighter into his embrace. Her breathing was faster and her pink lips flushed and parted. He couldn't resist sticking his tongue into her mouth and she responded in kind, until they were kissing hard and fast again.

"Still think I should go to my room?" She rasped the question when they came up for air.

"Definitely not." He had to take this woman to bed, whether it was a good idea or not.

He reached under her T-shirt and cupped her breast, enjoying the sensation of skin and scratchy lace under his fingers. He could feel her heartbeat pounding, like his own, as anticipation built toward boiling point.

"Let's go into the bedroom." He disentangled himself from her with some effort and led her into the other room. The plain white bedcovers looked like an enticing playground and he couldn't wait to spread her out on them and uncover her step by step.

He swept her off her feet—eliciting a shriek of delight—and laid her gently on the bed.

Suddenly horizontal, Andi looked up at Jake with alarm. Her entire body pulsed and tingled with sensation. About to reach for the buttons of his shirt, her fingers stopped in midair. Their eyes met, his dark with fierce desire that made her insides tremble.

Everything about this situation felt new and different.

Jake's hands showed no hesitation as he unzipped her jeans and slid them off. Heat snapped in her veins, deepening the sense of unease creeping over her.

"What's the matter?" Jake paused and studied her face.

"I don't know. It just feels strange."

"Go with it." He lifted the hem of her T-shirt and eased it off over her head. Her nipples stood to attention inside her lacy bra, which was now exposed to view along with its matching panties. Jake's devouring gaze raked her body and Andi felt both very desirable and very, very nervous.

Jake unbuttoned his own shirt and shrugged it off, revealing a thickly muscled chest with a line of dark hair running down to his belt buckle. His powerful biceps flexed as he undid the belt and the button of his pants.

Andi's hesitation flew away. "Wait, let me do that." She rose to the edge of the bed and unzipped his pants as excitement and arousal replaced her apprehension. She pushed them down to reveal dark boxers and powerful hair-roughened thighs.

Both in their underwear, they stretched out on the cool white sheets, skin to skin. She touched his chest with a tentative finger, enjoying the warmth of his body. She traced the curve of his pec and traveled lower, to where his arousal was dramatically evident against the dark fabric of his shorts.

Jake's taut belly contracted as she trailed over it then paused.

She looked up at his face. The naked desire in his eyes further unraveled her inhibitions. She let her hands roam lower, tugging at his boxers until they slid down and his erection sprang free. She gasped, and he chuckled. Then she pulled the soft fabric down over his strong legs until he was totally naked.

"You're gorgeous," she breathed. Then she blushed, realizing that must sound silly when she'd seen him naked many times before.

"You're far more gorgeous." His slightly callused fingers tickled her skin as he ran his hand along her side, from her bra to her panties.

"But you're not seeing me as if it was the first time."

"Yes, I am," he murmured. Then he looked up. "At least that's what it feels like." Excitement danced in his dark eyes. "I could never grow tired of looking at you."

Andi swallowed. If Jake's feelings for her were anything like the intense roar of passion pulsing in her veins right now, she could understand how this could feel new and fresh even after several years.

He slid his arm behind her back and tugged her closer. Her belly flipped as it touched his, and her breasts bumped against his chest.

"Time to unwrap this present," he breathed. He propped himself on one elbow and deftly undid the clasp on her bra, releasing her breasts. She felt his breathing quicken as he tugged the lacy fabric off over her arms and lowered his mouth to one tight pink nipple.

Andi arched her back and let out a little moan as Jake flicked his tongue over the delicate skin. The sound of her own voice in the still night air startled her, and quickened her pulse further. She pushed her fingers into his thick hair and enjoyed the silky sensations roaming through her body as he licked and sucked.

"Kiss me," she begged, when she couldn't take the almost painful pleasure anymore. He responded by pressing his lips to hers with passion and kissing the last of her breath away.

Arms wrapped around him, she held Jake close. His warm masculine scent filled her senses and the heat of his skin against hers only increased her desire. Fingers trembling with anticipation, she took hold of his erection. Jake released a low moan as she ran her fingers over the hard surface, then tightened them around the shaft, enjoying the throb of pleasure that issued through him.

Had she really done this before? She couldn't believe it. Again that odd sensation of unfamiliarity almost dampened her pleasure. Everything she did was like taking a step into the dark and hoping the floor would still be there under her foot when she put it down. Where would these strange and intense sensations and urges lead her?

Jake's mouth crushed over hers once more and her doubts crumbled beneath the fierce desire to feel him inside her.

Working together they eased off her panties and he climbed over her. The inviting weight of him pressed against her chest for a moment; then he lifted himself up with his powerful arms and entered her slowly.

Too slowly.

She found herself writhing and arching to encourage him deeper. Her insides ached to hold him and her whole body burned hot and anxious with an urgent need to join with him. Her fingers dug into his back as he finally sank all the way in and she released a deep moan of pleasure into his ear.

Jake layered hot kisses along her neck and cheek as he moved over her, drawing her deeper into the mysterious ocean of pleasure that felt so strange and so good at the same time. They rolled on the bed, exploring each other from different angles and deepening the connection between them. Her hands wandered over his body, enjoying the hard muscle, squeezing and stroking him as he moved inside her.

She loved riding on top of him, changing the rhythm from slow to fast and back again as the sensations inside her built toward a dangerous crescendo. Jake was over her again when she felt herself suddenly lose control of her muscles and even her mind as a huge wave of release swept her far out of herself. She drifted in limbo as pulses of sheer pleasure rose through her again and again. Then she seemed to wash back up in Jake's arms, exhausted and utterly at peace.

"That was..." She couldn't seem to find the words. Any words, really.

"Awesome."

Jake's unroyal response made her laugh. "Exactly." Then she frowned. "Is it always like this when we...make love?"

She could swear she felt him flinch slightly. "Yup. It is."

"I guess that's good." She smiled. She must be one of the luckiest people on earth, to have a loving relationship—with really hot sex—with this ridiculously handsome man who just happened to be a king.

She stretched, still feeling delicious pulses of pleasure tickling her insides. She couldn't help wondering how she'd arrived at this juncture. How did she find herself engaged to a gorgeous monarch? Maybe she was from some kind of upper-crust family herself. It was so odd not knowing anything about yourself. She opened her eyes and peered at Jake.

"Will you tell me some things about myself?"

His sleepy gaze grew wider and a smile tilted his mouth. "Like what?"

"My background, the kind of things I like to do, that sort of stuff."

He frowned, still smiling that half smile. "Hmm, it's hard to know where to start."

Adrenaline buzzed through her at the prospect of nailing down a few details. "How about at the beginning. Did I grow up in New York?"

"No. You moved there after college." He kissed her cheek softly. "You came to work for me right after you graduated."

"What did I study in college?"

"Hmm. I can't remember exactly. I think it was something to do with literature. Or maybe French. You spoke French fluently even though you'd never been to France. I remember that."

"Oh." It wasn't so odd that he didn't know what she'd majored in. That was before she met him. "Where did I go to college?"

Jake hesitated, and frowned. "Was it U Penn? Somewhere in Pennsylvania. I'm pretty sure of that."

"You don't remember where I went to college? You're almost as bad as I am. Where did I grow up?"

Jake licked his lips. His eyes showed a mild trace of alarm. "Pennsylvania, definitely. Philly, maybe. Or was it Pittsburgh?"

"We've never been there together?" An odd knot of tension was forming in her stomach. She propped herself up in bed on one elbow.

"No, our relationship has always been pretty under wraps. The whole professional thing."

"So you haven't met my family." Again, unease niggled somewhere deep inside her.

"No. You have parents and a sister somewhere, though. You get together with them for holidays."

"In Pennsylvania?"

"I think so. You usually took the train."

"Oh." How odd that she couldn't remember anything about them. Or Pennsylvania. And it was a little disturbing that Jake seemed to know so little about her. Did they never talk about her past? "What's my sister's name?"

Jake pursed his lips for a moment. "I don't know."

"I guess I didn't talk about her that much." Maybe she and her sister weren't close. What a shame. Maybe she'd try to improve their relationship once she got her memory back. "What about my parents? Do you know their names or where they live? We could get in touch with them and see if they could jog my memory back into existence."

Jake's brow had furrowed. "I suppose we should be able to find that information somewhere."

"It's probably on my computer if I could just figure out the password."

"We'll worry about that in the morning." Jake pulled her closer to him. "Right now let's just enjoy each other."

Andi let out a sigh and sank back into his arms. "You're right. Why get stressed out over something I can't control?"

But even in his soothing embrace, there wasn't a single second when she didn't ache to recover her memory—and her history. How could you really go forward, or even live in the moment, if you don't know who you are?

After breakfast, Jake left Andi in her office to look over her files. She seemed anxious that she wasn't able to do her job since she didn't remember the details of palace life, let alone any specific events. He mused that he should have been concerned, too, since a key purpose of this whole engagement was to keep her at his side running the show, but somehow the palace was managing to tick along. And he was enjoying her company far more than he'd imagined.

How could he have worked with her for six years and not even know where her family lived? As far as he knew she was born behind the desk in his Manhattan office. And he cringed at not knowing her sister's name. For all he could remember she just referred to her as "my sister."

He strode to his current office, intent on mining it for the information he should know simply on the basis of their long acquaintance. They spent all day together—did they usually talk about nothing but work?

Andi was always excellent about keeping them focused so no time was wasted. She managed their affairs with such efficiency that there was little downtime for chin-wagging, especially since they'd moved to Ruthenia and tackled challenges higher than the legendary Althaus mountains that loomed over the palace. He'd always appreciated her professional approach to her job and to life in general.

But now he was beginning to realize he'd missed out on enjoying her company all this time. She was much more complex than he'd realized, more vulnerable and intriguing—and not just because of her missing memory. He'd never seen her as a person with emotions, with needs, before, because she'd done such an excellent job hiding that aspect of herself.

And he'd never realized she was so tempting. She'd hidden that, too.

He closed his office door and walked through to the cabinets in the file room, where the personnel files from New York were stored. Thanks to Andi's relentless organization he quickly laid his hands on her file, and the résumé she'd submitted when she applied for the job as his admin back when he was simply a venture capitalist.

A quick scan revealed that she'd graduated from Drexel University in Pennsylvania—right state, at least—with a degree in business administration and a ridiculously long list of clubs and activities to her name. Apart from some temping in Manhattan, her first job was with him. She'd graduated from North Hills Senior High School in Pittsburgh—ha, right again, maybe he wasn't so bad after all. He had to congratulate himself on being able to pick such a promising employee despite her lack of relevant work experience.

But that didn't solve his current problem of finding out about her past and helping her recover her memory.

Wait. Did he even want her to recover her memory? If she did, she'd surely remember that their relationship had been strictly professional and the whole engagement his invention.

Discomfort rose in his chest, threatening to overwhelm the sense of satisfaction—of happiness, dammit—that had suffused his body and mind since their overnight encounter.

Andi was sensational between the sheets. He'd never have dreamed that his quiet, prim assistant hid so much passion and energy beneath her suited exterior. She even looked different, like she'd forgotten to put on the mask of no-nonsense propriety she usually painted on with makeup and pinned into place with a spritz of hair spray. The real Andi—the one without the mask—was soft and sexy and downright irresistible.

Desire stirred inside him again, tightening his muscles. Blood rushed to his groin as he thought about her in his arms that morning, scented with passion as well as her usual floral fragrance. He put the résumé back in its file.

Maybe her memory wouldn't come back and they could start over from the night he'd found her dancing outside, freed of the inhibitions and anxieties built by a lifetime of experience. He couldn't help believing that the woman who'd shared his bed was the real Andi, and that she'd been hiding inside all this time, waiting for a chance to be free.

Andi let out a cry of sheer joy. She'd finally cracked the password on her computer. A cryptic penciled list in the drawer seemed like a meaningless string of words—until she started typing them in one by one.

Queen had proved to be the key that unlocked her hard drive, and possibly her whole life. Funny! She must have picked it because she knew she soon would be queen.

That thought stopped her cold for a second. Queen Andi. Didn't quite sound right. Still, she'd get used to it. And maybe Andi was short for a more majestic name, like Andromeda or something.

Her heart raced as the computer opened her account and laid a screen full of icons out before her. Yikes. So many different files, some with the names of countries, some of companies. She didn't know where to start. A sound issued from the machine, and she noticed that the email icon announced the presence of fifty-three messages. She clicked on it with a growing sense of anticipation, and scrolled back to the last one she had opened. Eticket confirmation.

Frowning, she opened the email, which revealed an itinerary for Andi Louise Blake—apparently she wasn't really named Andromeda—to travel from Munich to New York. The date listed was…yesterday.

Her blood slowed in her veins and her breathing grew shallow.

Obviously she hadn't gone on the trip, and if it was a business-related one, surely Jake would have mentioned it.

Munich—the nearest international airport, perhaps?—to New York, where she used to live…

She had been planning to leave.

Head spinning, she sat back in her chair. Why would she leave, if she was in love and about to get engaged?

She should just ask Jake about this. Why get all worked up when it could be a business trip that just got canceled at the last moment, maybe due to her loss of memory, or their engagement?

Andi glanced down at her ring with a growing sense of unease. She never had figured out why her clothes were creased as if they'd been packed. She must have changed her mind and unpacked at some point, but when? And why did Jake not know about her plans to take off?

Had she issued an ultimatum and forced him into proposing to her?

She swallowed, then started to chew on a nail. Her stomach curled up into a tight ball. Maybe she should see what else was going on in her email before she spoke to Jake.

It was hard to read with so much nervous energy leaping through her system. Her eyes kept jumping around on the screen. Most of the emails were business related—responses to invitations, scheduling questions, orders for supplies and that kind of thing.

Then one titled What's going on? from a Lizzie Blake caught her eye. Blake—the same last name as her. What *was* going on? She clicked on it with her heart in her mouth.

Andi, I know you told me not to email personal stuff to this account, but I've tried calling you and you won't call back. We saw a news story on TV yesterday saying that you're going to marry Jake Mondragon, your boss. Is this true? How come you didn't tell us? I thought you were getting ready to quit from the way you've been talking lately. Mom is pretty upset that you'd keep something like this from us. I remember you saying years ago that your boss was hot, but you never mentioned dating him, let alone getting engaged. Anyway, get in touch ASAP and let me know if I need to find a dress for a royal wedding. XX Sis.

Andi sat back, blinking. She had a sister called Lizzie. Who knew absolutely nothing about her relationship to Jake. And who'd been calling her but not getting through. She *must* have another phone somewhere that she used for personal calls.

She scanned the rest of the emails, but nothing else looked truly personal.

Where would she keep another phone? Brain ticking fast, she hurried back to her bedroom, glad she didn't run into anyone in the hallway—especially Jake.

A pang of guilt and hurt stung her heart. She was avoiding him. Only this morning they'd lain in each others arms and she'd enjoyed such contentment and bliss that she hadn't even minded about her memory being gone.

Now she was racked with suspicion and doubt. She locked her bedroom door behind her and started to go through the closet and drawers again. Finally, in the pocket of a black pair of pants she found a small silver phone. The pants showed signs of being recently worn—slightly creased across the hips and behind the knees—so maybe she had them on just before she lost her memory.

She flipped the phone open and pulled up recent messages. There were three from Lizzie and one from her mom, who sounded noticeably upset. Her voice, with its hint of tears, struck a sharp and painful chord deep inside her. On instinct Andi hit the button to dial the number.

"Andi!"

"Mom?" Her voice shook slightly. "Is it really you?"

"Of course it's me. Who else would be answering my phone?" A bright laugh rang in her ear. "What the heck is going on over there?"

Andi drew in a steadying breath. "I don't really know, to be honest. I lost my memory."

"What?"

"Jake found me dancing around outside and I couldn't remember anything at all. I didn't even remember you or Lizzie until I saw her email and found the messages on my phone."

"Oh, my gosh, that sounds terrifying. Are you okay?"

"More or less. It's been strange and kind of scary, but I'm not sick or injured or anything."

"That's a blessing. Has your memory come back?"

Andi blinked. A blurry vision of a face—an energetic woman with short light brown hair and bright blue eyes filled her brain. "I think it's coming back right now. Do you have blue eyes?"

"Of course I do. That's where you got them from. You forgot my eye color?"

"I forgot you even existed. I didn't know my own name." Other images suddenly crowded her brain: a man with gray hair and a warm smile, a blonde with long curls and a loud laugh. "But it's coming back now that I hear your voice." Excitement crackled through her veins. Finally she had an identity, a past. The details crashed back into her brain one after the other—her childhood home, her school, her old dog Timmy…

"Are you really engaged to your boss?" Her mom's voice tugged her back to the present.

Andi froze. That part she didn't remember. "He says we got engaged right before I lost my memory. I don't remember it."

"Do you love him?" The voice on the phone was suddenly sharp.

"Oh, yes. I've always loved him." The conviction rang through her whole body. "I've loved him for years."

"You never said a thing. I had no idea you were even involved with him."

Andi blinked rapidly. The memories flooding her brain were curiously devoid of any romantic images of her and Jake. She had plenty of memories of working with him, but as she mentally flipped through them looking for signs of their relationship a strange and awful truth dawned on her. "That's because I wasn't involved with him."

Six

Her mom's confused and anxious reaction prompted Andi to make excuses and hang up the phone. She needed someone who could answer questions, not just ask them. Instinct told her to call her sister, Lizzie.

"Your Majesty!" Her sister's now-familiar voice made her jump.

"Lizzie, you wouldn't believe what's been going on."

"You're right. I don't, so you'll have to break it down into tiny pieces for me. Are you really marrying your boss?"

Andi bit her lip. "I don't know. It's the weirdest thing, I lost my memory and ever since then we've been engaged. But my memory's coming back now—since I found your phone messages and spoke to Mom—and I don't remember anything at all about being engaged to him."

"You never even told me you were dating him."

"I don't remember anything about that, either. I do recall being seriously attracted to him for, oh, years and years, but not that anything actually came of it. Now suddenly I seem to be engaged to him and I have no idea what's going on."

"How does he explain the situation?"

Andi blew out. "I don't know. I haven't spoken to him about it yet. My memory only just started coming back and he doesn't know yet."

"Do you remember him asking you to marry him?"

She thought for a second. "No. I don't remember everything, though. There's a gap." She raised a hand to her head where she could still feel a slight bump. "I must have fallen and banged my head, or something." She paused, remembering the etickets she'd seen on her computer. "Did I say anything about coming back to the States?"

"For Christmas, you mean?"

Andi wondered how much to reveal, then decided things were so complicated already that she might as well be truthful. "For good. I think I was planning to leave here. I had tickets back to New York."

"And you don't remember why?"

I do.

The realization was seeping back into her, almost like blood rushing to her brain. She had intended to leave. She wanted to go because she was tired of adoring Jake while he flirted with other women in the name of business.

Because she loved him and knew she could never have him.

A sharp pain rose in her middle around the area of her heart. How had six years of yearning turned—overnight—into a fantasy engagement?

It didn't add up. There was a missing piece to the puzzle and she had no idea what it was.

"So are you marrying him, or what?" Lizzie's amused voice roused her from her panicked thoughts.

Her eyes fell on the big ring, flashing in the afternoon

sunlight pouring through the large office window. "Yes." Then she frowned. "At least I think so."

"Well, I saw it in the *National Enquirer,* so it must be true, right?" Lizzie's voice was bright with laughter. "There's a picture of you with a rock on your finger the size of my Mini Cooper. Is that thing real?"

Andi stared at the glittering stones. She was pretty sure it was a real diamond, but was it a real engagement ring? "Sure. It's from a jeweler here in town. Jake bought it for me yesterday."

"Sounds pretty official to me. Is he good in bed?"

Andi's mouth fell open.

"Come on, I'd tell you. Or do royal romances not involve any sex?"

Her teasing voice brought a smile to Andi's lips. "He's amazing."

"Ha. I had a feeling. I've seen pictures of him and he's seriously handsome. I love the dark flashing eyes. Is he romantic?"

"Very." She could almost feel his arms around her right now, holding and steadying her. "He's been so sweet with me since I lost my memory. We've managed to keep it a secret so far. You and Mom and the doctor he called are the only other people who know."

"Why keep it a secret?"

"I guess because I felt so vulnerable. Like everyone around me knows more about me than I do. I didn't want anyone to know. It's all coming back now, though. Not all the tiny details yet, like work stuff I have to do, but the bigger things like who I know and where I'm from and…"

How much I've always loved Jake.

Were they really going to be married and live happily ever after? It seemed too much to hope for.

"So you're going to be a queen. Will I have to curtsy to you?"

"Gosh, I hope not." Andi laughed. "What a strange idea. I can't quite see myself with a crown on."

"You'd better get used to the idea. Can I be your maid of honor? Or maybe they don't have them in Ruthenia."

"I have no idea. I've never planned a wedding here and apparently I haven't paid close enough attention at the few I've attended." Images of Jake's other would-be brides crowded her mind. Alia and Maxi and Carlotta and Liesel… there were so many of them. Rich and beautiful and fawning all over him. Why, out of all the glamorous and powerful women available to him, had Jake chosen her?

It was time to track him down and ask some questions.

After promising to call Lizzie back and tell her the details, Andi went into the bathroom and looked in the mirror. Her cosmetics were strung out along a shelf, which was not how she used to keep them. She also remembered that she nearly always tied her rather wispy hair up in a bun and slicked it down with gel—she was always experimenting with different brands as the Ruthenian climate was surprisingly humid. Now her hair lay loose around her shoulders, and her face looked oddly colorless without the lipstick and blush she usually donned.

A glance in her closet reminded her she was a hard-core suit wearer. She felt it was important to project a professional image, and she liked bright colors as they seemed assertive and positive. Right now she had on a rather uncharacteristic pastel yellow blouse and a pair of slacks and her hair wafted around her shoulders. People must have noticed the difference.

Part of her felt embarrassed that she'd been walking around the palace looking like a paler, less polished version of herself. And part of her wondered whether Jake actually preferred the less made-up look. He'd chosen the super-casual jeans and T-shirt she'd worn all the previous day. She blushed as she remembered he'd also chosen the racy lingerie. A glance in her underwear drawer confirmed that cotton briefs and no-nonsense bras were more her style.

Still, if Jake liked lacy lingerie and jeans, she could adjust. She couldn't resist smoothing just a hint of blush on her cheeks. They were a bit pale with shock. But she used a clear gloss instead of lipstick and left her hair loose—maybe it didn't look so bad after all.

With a deep breath, she set off for his office. Her pulse rate roared like a runaway truck by the time she finally plucked up the courage to peek around the open door. Jake was in conversation with a man she instantly remembered as the minister of economics. Jake looked up when she entered the doorway, and an expression flickered across his face—shock?—almost as if he suddenly knew her memory was back.

Andi struggled not to fidget as the conversation continued for another couple of minutes—something urgent to do with trade tariffs. Her nerves were jumping and her palms sweating.

In his dark suit, with his usual air of unhurried calm, Jake seemed perfectly poised and in control of any situation. She, on the other hand, had no idea what their situation really was. She could remember nearly everything about her life—except a romance with Jake.

He finally closed the door behind the economics minister and turned to her. Again she could see in his face that he knew something was different.

"My memory is coming back." She floated the words out, as if on a string, wondering what his response would be. Would he take her in his arms with a cry of joy?

Jake didn't move an inch. "That's great." He seemed to be waiting for her to reveal more.

"It started when I saw an email from my sister. Then I phoned my mom. That jogged something in my brain and the memories started bubbling up."

"What a relief." His voice was oddly flat. He still made no move toward her.

Andi's eyes dropped to her ring, which seemed to sting the skin underneath it. "It's strange, I remember working with you for years, but I don't..." Her voice cracked as fear rose in her chest. "I don't remember anything about us." She faltered. "I mean us being...romantically involved."

Jake stepped up to her and took her hand. Her heart surged with relief and she was about to smile, but his deadly serious demeanor stopped her. "I'll be completely honest with you."

"About what?" Her pulse picked up and a sense of dread swelled inside her.

"We weren't involved. Our relationship was strictly professional until two days ago."

"We weren't dating? Not even in secret?" Her heart hammered against her ribs.

"No."

Andi swallowed hard and her rib cage tightened around her chest. The ostentatious ring suddenly seemed to weigh down her hand and drain her strength. "So, the engagement is fake?" Her voice came out as a rasping whisper, filled with every ounce of apprehension and terror she felt. "It was all pretend?"

Jake tilted his head. "No."

Andi wanted to shake him. "Could you be more explicit?"

He frowned. "It's hard to explain. You were going to leave, and I didn't want you to. I was under pressure to choose a bride, and then you lost your memory. Things fell into place and I realized you're the ideal woman to be my wife."

She blinked, trying to make sense of his words. "So we are engaged?"

"Absolutely." His dark eyes looked earnest.

Then a cold sensation crept over her. "But you're not in love with me."

He swallowed. "Love is something that grows over time. I'm confident that we'll enjoy a happy and successful marriage. The important thing is to provide stability for Ruthenia, and as a team we can do just that."

Andi struggled for breath. The man of her dreams, whom she'd fantasized about and mooned over for six long years, wanted to marry her.

Because she'd be a key member of his team.

A cold laugh flew from her lips. "Wouldn't it have been easier to just offer me a higher salary?"

He raised a brow. "I tried that."

"And I said no? Wait. Now I remember saying no. You were so sure you could talk me around, just like you always do." Her vision blurred as tears rose to her eyes. "And you really thought I'd go along with this crazy plan?"

"You're sensible and practical. I knew you'd see the sense in it."

"In spending my life with a husband who doesn't love me? You never even noticed I was female." A flashback to their lovemaking filled her brain. He'd noticed it then. But maybe he'd just pretended she was one of the glamorous socialites that usually buzzed around him. He'd had no shortage of girlfriends in the time she'd worked for him.

"My parents married because their families were both exiled Ruthenian nobles. They were married nearly fifty years."

His parents had died before she met him. She knew little about them except that they were part of New York society. "Were they happy?"

He hesitated. "Of course."

"You don't sound convinced. Did they love each other?"

"It was a successful marriage, and they achieved their lifelong goal of producing an heir who'd be ready to take the throne of Ruthenia when the time came."

"Lucky thing you were cooperative. It would be a shame to throw away fifty years of your life and have your son insist he was going to be a pro skateboarder. Did you really think I'd just go along with your plan?"

"Yes."

His calm expression exasperated her. He still thought she was going to go along with his scheme. He obviously didn't care about her feelings at all. "We slept together." Her body still sizzled and hummed with sensual energy from that amazing night.

The passion they'd shared might have been fake on his side, but on hers it was painfully real.

"I didn't intend for that to happen." His expression turned grim. "I understand that you must be furious with me for taking advantage of your situation."

"You're right. I am." Devastated would have been a better word. Their lovemaking wasn't the fruit of a long-term and loving romance, at least not for him. On her side she'd probably had enough romance in her head to last a lifetime.

He must have found it hilarious that she fell into his arms so easily. "Didn't you think it was wrong to sleep with an employee?"

His eyes narrowed. "Yes. I didn't intend to sleep with you until I'd explained the situation."

"Until you'd explained to me that you needed a wife and I was handy?" She still couldn't quite believe he took her so totally for granted.

Obviously he had no respect for her feelings and wishes. A chill swept through her and she hugged herself.

"You were confused after losing your memory. I didn't want to complicate matters when I knew you were in no state to make an important decision."

"So you just made it for me."

He drew in a breath. "You know me well enough to trust my judgment."

She struggled to check her anger. "I trust your judgment perfectly in matters of business, but not where my personal life is concerned. You already knew I intended to leave because I wasn't feeling fulfilled."

No need to say she couldn't stand to see him marry another woman. He'd assume she was thrilled that he'd made a coldhearted and clinical decision to marry her. "It's downright arrogant of you to assume I'd marry you."

"I know you're capable of rising to any challenge."

"But what if I don't want to?" Her voice rose a little and she struggled to check tears. A romance with Jake was such a heartfelt wish. Suddenly it had become a duty.

No doubt sex with her was supposed to seal the pact in some way.

What a shame she'd enjoyed it so much. Right now she wanted to chastise her body for still craving his touch. She should hate him for what he'd done when she needed his help the most.

Jake still stood there, calm and regal, chin lifted high.

A sinister thought crept over her. If he could plan something so outrageous as marriage to a woman who didn't know who she was, perhaps he contrived to put her in such a vulnerable position.

"Were you responsible for me losing my memory?" If he'd gone this far in his deception, who knew what he could be capable of?

"No." His answer was decisive.

She wanted to believe him—and hated herself for it.

"Then what did happen?" So many pieces were still missing.

"I don't know how you lost your memory. I found you outside dancing around on the grass in the moonlight."

Andi blushed. Had she done anything embarrassing? She couldn't remember a single thing about that night. Though now that he mentioned it, she did remember telling him she was going to leave. A cold sensation slithered through her. She was leaving to protect her heart.

Right now her heart was being flayed open. Jake's desire to keep her had nothing to do with him wanting her as his fiancée, or even his friend, and everything to do with keeping his office running smoothly.

And he'd seduced her into his bed on the pretext that they'd been dating for years.

Her insides still hummed with sense memories that would probably torment her forever. She'd thought they were making love—and her whole spirit had soared with the joy of it—but he was just cementing a deal.

On instinct she pulled the big ring from her finger. It wedged a bit over the knuckle, but she managed to get it off. "Take this back."

His eyes widened. "Oh, no. You must wear it."

"I don't have to do anything." She shoved it forward. "It's not real."

"I assure you those stones are genuine and worth a large sum of money."

Andi's mouth fell open, then closed shut. How could he not understand a word she was saying? She walked to his desk and put the ring down on the polished surface. It looked odd there, sparkling away amongst the piles of papers.

"I don't intend to wear or own any kind of engagement ring unless I'm actually engaged. And since we're not really engaged or even involved, I don't want anything to do with it." Tears threatened in her voice. She crossed her arms, and hoped it would hide the way her hands were shaking.

"But we are engaged." Jake's words, spoken softly, crept into her brain and heart. "I really do want to marry you."

Andi blinked, trying to catch her breath. How could a dream come true in such a horrible, distorted way?

The odd expression in his eyes almost made her consider it. There was something like…yearning in their dark depths.

Then again, she was obviously good at dreaming stuff up.

Now that her memory was back she knew—in the depths of her aching soul—that she'd loved Jake for years, pined for him and hoped that one day he'd see her as something other than an efficient assistant. She'd adored him in silence, occasionally allowing herself to fantasize that things might one day be different if she waited patiently for him to notice her. Their time as an engaged couple was the fulfillment of all secret hopes—and now she'd woken to find herself living a mockery of her cherished dreams.

Anger flared inside her, hot and ugly. "You honestly think I would continue with this charade that you sprung on me when I was at my most vulnerable? To let people think that we love each other when we're nothing more than boss and assistant, as always?"

"We'll be equals, of course, like any couple."

He said it simply, like he really believed it. But then Jake could convince anyone of anything. She'd watched him in action for too long. "I'm not sure that many couples are equals, especially royal ones." She'd be the official wife, sensibly dressed and courteous as always. The one who got left behind with her embroidery—not that she did embroidery—while he was out having affairs with other women.

"I need to leave, and right now." If she continued with this pretense for even another hour, she'd get sucked into hoping their official engagement might turn into true romance. Even with every shred of evidence pointing to that being impossible and hopeless, she'd already proven herself to be that kind of softheaded, dreaming fool.

"The story's gone around the world already."

She steadied herself with a breath. All her relatives knew, probably all her old friends. Everyone she'd ever known, maybe. "You'll just have to explain that it was all a big lie. Or a joke." Her voice cracked on the last word. It did feel like a cruel joke at her expense. She'd never experienced such feelings of happiness and contentment as during the last couple of days as Jake's fiancée. Their night of lovemaking had raised the bar of pure bliss so high that she'd likely never know anything like that again.

"I'm going to pack my bags." She turned for the door. Her whole body was shaking.

Jake caught hold of her arm and she tried to wrench it away, but his grip was too strong. "The people of Ruthenia are counting on you. I'm counting on you."

His words pierced her soul for a second, but she summoned her strength. "I'm sure the people of Ruthenia can find something else to count on. Television game shows, perhaps."

"We're going to be on television tonight. To talk about celebrating our engagement during the Independence Day celebrations."

Andi froze. "Independence Day. That's what this is all about, isn't it?" She turned and stared at his face. A memory of Jake's public promise to choose a wife formed in her mind. "You committed to picking a bride before Ruthenia's third Independence Day." She squinted at him, looking for signs of emotion in his face. "Your deadline had come right up on you and you had to pick someone or you'd be a liar. And there I was, clueless as a newborn babe and ripe for duping."

"Andi, we've been partners for years. It's not that big a leap."

"From the office to a lifetime commitment? I think that's a leap. You can't just get a plane ticket and leave a marriage." She lifted her chin as anger and hurt flashed over her. "Though apparently I can't just get a plane ticket and leave my job with you, either." Fury bubbled up inside her. "Do you think you can control everything and everyone?"

"I'm not trying to control you, just to make you see sense. We're a great team."

"I've never been into team sports. When I marry, it will be for love." Her heart ached at the thought that she'd loved Jake almost since the day she met him.

Though right now she hated him for tricking her into a relationship that meant nothing to him.

"Think it over, Andi. Be sensible."

"I am sensible. That's why I know this would never work."

Jake's expression grew impenetrable. "Stay until after Independence Day, at least."

"You think I'll change my mind? Or maybe you think I'll just be guilt-tripped into marrying you by seeing all those smiling Ruthenian faces. What if people don't like the idea of you marrying your lowly assistant? They'd probably rather see you marry some Ruthenian blue blood with twelve names."

"They'll all know I made the right choice."

His words hung in the air. *The right choice.*

Impossible.

Still, his quiet conviction both irked and intrigued her.

She stared hard at his chiseled face. "You really do want to marry me?"

He took her hands in his. Her skin tingled and sizzled, and she cursed the instant effect he always had on her. "I do want to marry you."

Those accursed hopes and dreams flared up inside her like embers under a breath.

He doesn't love you. Don't get carried away.

Still, maybe something could come of this crazy situation. Could she live with herself if she didn't at least try to make it work?

She inhaled a shaky breath. "If I agree to stay until Independence Day, then decide it won't work, you'll let me go?"

His expression clouded. "Yes."

She wasn't sure she believed him. Jake didn't often admit, or experience, defeat. But she could always sneak away this time.

Or stay here for the rest of her life.

Her heart thumped and her stomach felt queasy. "I can't really believe this is happening. We'll sleep in separate rooms?"

"If you prefer." His cool reply sounded like a challenge. He probably intended to seduce her again. She silently determined not to let him.

"Independence Day is three days away." Could she stand to be Jake's unloved but practical fiancée for seventy-two hours? She really didn't want to let everyone down and ruin the Independence Day celebrations. She could look at it as her job, as long as there was no kissing or sex involved.

And then there was that insane hope that they really could live happily ever after.

Jake picked up the ring from among the papers on his desk. "You'll need this."

Andi eyed it suspiciously. Putting the ring back on would mean agreeing to his terms. Clearly he expected her to, and why wouldn't he? She'd always done everything he asked in the past.

He picked up her hand without asking permission. Her skin heated instantly at his touch and she made the mistake of looking up into his face. His dark gaze dared her to refuse him—and she knew in that instant that she couldn't.

Why did he still have so much power over her?

She was disoriented right now. Confused. Her memory slipping and sliding back into her head while she tried to take in the strange new reality of Jake wanting to marry her.

Wanting to *marry* her.

It should be a dream come true—so why did it feel more like a waking nightmare?

Seven

The following afternoon, Andi adjusted the collar of her new and fabulously expensive dress. Fit for a queen. The rack of designer clothes had arrived with a coordinator from Ruthenia's most snooty bespoke tailor to help her choose the right look and make any necessary alterations.

She'd tried not to tremble when the seamstress stuck pins in around her waist and bust. Now the freshly sewn green fabric draped over her like a second skin of luxurious silk.

But did she look like a future queen? She'd be paraded on TV as one tonight. RTV was setting up cameras in the ballroom to interview her and Jake. She'd tried to beg off and delay any public appearances until after she'd made her decision, but endless calls from the television station had hounded her into it and at this point she'd appear snooty and uncooperative if she said no again.

"Earrings." A representative from the jeweler where

they'd bought the ring opened a case filled with sparkly gems. Andi hadn't even noticed her come in, but then people were coming and going in a constant scurry, preparing for the evening shoot. The earrings blurred into a big shiny mass.

"You choose." Andi didn't even want to look at them. Better to let these professionals decide whether she looked like a future queen or not.

She certainly didn't feel like one.

Was it her job to act this part? It felt more like her patriotic duty. Which was silly since she was American, not Ruthenian. At least until she married Jake.

If she married Jake.

She tried to keep her breathing steady as the girl clipped big emeralds to her ears and murmured, "Perfect." The seamstress nodded her approval and beckoned across the room.

A middle-aged woman with a blond pompadour and a rat-tail comb approached with a gleam in her eye. She picked up a strand of Andi's limp hair between her thumb and finger and winced slightly. "Don't worry. We can fix it."

Thirty minutes later her hair hung around her shoulders in plump curls that everyone assured her looked "lovely." The woman staring back at her from the mirror, wide-eyed and pale beneath her carefully applied makeup, didn't even look like her. She'd barely managed to remember who she was, and now she was being turned into someone else.

"Andi, can you come in for a moment? They want to check the lighting."

She steadied herself and walked—slowly in her long, rather heavy dress—toward the formal library where the cameras were set up.

Jake was nowhere to be seen.

It's your job, she told herself. Just be professional. Being a monarch's fiancée definitely felt more like a career assignment than a romantic dream come true.

Strangers' hands shuffled her into place under blistering hot lights that made her blink. More powder was dotted on her nose and fingers fluffed her curls. Out of the corner of her eye she could see the local news anchor going over some notes with a producer. What kind of questions would they ask?

I won't lie.

She promised herself that. This whole situation was so confusing already; she had no intention of making it worse by having to keep track of stories. She'd try to be tactful and diplomatic, of course.

Just part of the job.

A sudden hush fell over the room and all eyes turned to the door. His majesty. Jake strode in, a calm smile on his face. Andi's heartbeat quickened under her designer gown. Fear as well as the familiar desire. Would she manage to act the role of fiancée well enough to please him?

She cursed herself for wanting to make him happy. He hadn't given her feelings any thought when he'd tricked her into wearing his ring.

Their eyes met and a jolt of energy surged through her. *I really do want to marry you.* His words echoed in her brain, tormenting and enticing. How could she not at least give it a shot?

A producer settled them both on the ornate gilt-edged sofa under the lights, in full view of three cameras. Andi felt Jake's hand close around hers, his skin warm. She almost wished he wouldn't touch her, as she didn't want him to know she was shaking and that her palms were sweating.

No aspect of her job had ever made her so terrified. She'd greeted foreign dignitaries and handled major international incidents without so much as a raised pulse. Why did every move she made now feel like a matter of life and death?

Silence descended as the interviewer moved toward them, microphone clipped to her blue suit. Andi's heart pounded.

I won't lie.

But Jake didn't have to know that.

"Your Majesty, thank you so much for agreeing to this interview." Jake murmured an assent. "And for allowing us to meet your fiancée." The journalist smiled at Andi.

She tried not to shrink into the sofa. Yesterday morning she'd been totally comfortable and happy as Jake's fiancée. It had felt as natural as breathing. But now everything was different and she'd been dropped into the middle of a movie set—with no script.

The reporter turned her lipsticked smile to Andi. "You're living every young girl's dream."

"Yes," she stammered. *Except in the dream the prince actually loves you.* "I still can't believe it."

No lies told so far.

"Was the proposal very romantic?"

Andi grew hyperconscious of Jake's hand wrapped around hers. She drew in a breath. "I was so stunned I don't remember a word of it."

The reporter laughed, and so did Jake. Andi managed a smile.

"I guess the important part is that you said yes." The reporter turned to Jake. "Perhaps you could tell us about the moment."

Andi stared at Jake. Would he make something up? He'd lied to her when he'd told her they were engaged. Unless a king could become engaged simply by an act of will.

"It was a private moment between myself and Andi." He

turned to look at her. Then continued in a low voice. "I'm very happy that she's agreed to be my wife."

Until Independence Day. He was obviously confident he'd convince her to stay after that, but as she sat here under the lights with people staring at her and analyzing every move she made, she became increasingly sure she'd couldn't handle this.

It would have been different if Jake wanted to marry her for the right reasons and she could look forward to true intimacy and companionship, at least when they were alone together.

But she'd never been enough for him before, and she was painfully sure that she wouldn't be enough for him now—ring or no ring.

"What a lovely ring." Andi's hand flinched slightly under the reporter's gaze. "A fitting symbol for a royal romance."

Yes. All flash and pomp. "Thanks. We bought it right here in town. The local village has such skilled craftspeople."

"I think it's charming that you chose the work of a Ruthenian artisan, when you could so easily have bought something from New York or Paris."

"Both Andi and I are proud of Ruthenia's fine old-world craftsmanship. It's one of the few places where attention to detail is more important than turning a quick profit. Some people might see our steady and deliberate approach to things as a hindrance in the modern world of business, but I see them as strengths that will secure our future."

Andi maintained a tight smile. He was turning their engagement interview into a promotional video for Ruthenia. Something she would have heartily approved of only a few days ago, but now made her heart contract with pain.

With his "steady and deliberate" approach to marriage,

he expected her to devote her life to Ruthenia and fulfill the role of royal wife, whether he loved her or not.

Andi startled when she realized the reporter was staring right at her. She'd obviously just asked a question, but Andi was so caught up in her depressing ruminations that she hadn't even heard it. Jake squeezed her hand and jumped in. "Andi will be making all the wedding arrangements. In our years of working together she's proved that she can pull off the most elaborate and complicated occasions."

He went on to talk about Ruthenian wedding traditions and how they'd be sure to observe and celebrate them.

What about my family traditions? Andi remembered her cousin Lu's wedding two summers ago. A big, fat Greek wedding in every sense of the word. What if she wanted to celebrate her mom's Greek heritage as well as Jake's Ruthenian roots?

Not a chance. Just one more example of how her life would slide into a faded shadow of Jake's.

But only if she let it.

Resolve kicked through her on a surge of adrenaline. She didn't have to do anything she didn't want to. "Of course, we'll also honor our American roots and bring those into our planning. I have ancestors from several different countries and we'll enjoy bringing aspects of that heritage into our wedding."

The reporter's eyes widened. Jake was so big on being all Ruthenian all the time, trying to prove that despite his New York upbringing, every cell in his blue blood was Ruthenian to the nucleus. Right now she couldn't resist knocking that. If he wanted a Ruthenian bride there was no shortage of volunteers.

But he'd chosen an American one. She smiled up at him sweetly. His dark eyes flashed with surprise. "Of course. Andi's right. Our American background and experience have enriched our lives and we'll certainly be welcoming many American friends to the wedding."

Andi felt his arm slide around her shoulders. She tried not to shiver at the feel of his thick muscle through her dress. "And now, if you don't mind, we have a lot to do to prepare for the Independence Day celebrations this week. Our third Independence Day marks a turning point for our nation, with our gross national product up and unemployment now at a fifty-year low. We hope everyone will join us in a toast to Ruthenia's future."

He circled his arm around her back, a gesture both protective and possessive. Andi cursed the way it stirred sensation in her belly and emotion in her heart. The reporter frowned slightly at being summarily dismissed, but made some polite goodbye noises and shook their hands.

Andi let out a long, audible sigh once the cameras finally turned off.

Jake escorted her from the room, and it wasn't until they were in the corridor outside that he loosened his grip on her arm slightly. "Nice point about our American heritage."

She wasn't sure if he was kidding or not. "I thought so." She smiled. "I'm kind of surprised you decided to pick an American wife. I was sure you'd marry a Ruthenian so you could have some ultra-Ruthenian heirs."

An odd expression crossed his face for a second. Had he forgotten about the whole royal heir thing? This engagement scenario seemed rather by-the-seat-of-the-pants; maybe he didn't think it through enough. Did he really want a Heinz 57 American girl from Pittsburgh to be the mother of Ruthenia's future king?

"Being Ruthenian is more a state of mind than a DNA trait." He kept his arm around her shoulders as they marched along the hall.

"Kind of like being king?" She arched a brow. "Though I

suppose that does require the right DNA or there'd be other claimants. The only way most Ruthenians can claim the throne is by marrying you. I guess I should be honored."

Jake turned to stare at her. She never usually talked back to him. Of course she didn't—he was her boss. Maybe once he discovered the real, off-hours Andi had a bit more spunk to her he'd lose all interest in hoisting her up onto his royal pedestal.

"I don't expect you to be honored." Humor sparkled in Jake's dark eyes. Did nothing rile him? "Just to think about the advantages of the situation."

"The glorious future of Ruthenia," she quipped.

"Exactly."

"What if I miss Philly cheesesteak?"

"The cook can prepare some."

"No way. She's from San Francisco. She'd put bean sprouts in it."

"We'll import it."

"It'd go cold on the plane."

"We'll fly there to get some."

"Is that fiscally responsible?"

He laughed. "See? You're a woman after my own heart."

"Cold and calculating?" She raised a brow.

"I prefer to think of it as shrewd and pragmatic." He pulled his arm from around her to reach into his pocket and she noticed they were at the door to his suite. She stiffened. She did not want to go in there and wind up in his bed again. Especially if it was the result of some shrewd and pragmatic seduction on his part.

The intimacy they'd shared left her feeling tender and raw. Probably because she'd always loved him and the act of making love only intensified everything she'd already felt. Now that she knew he didn't love her—that it was a mechanical act for him—she couldn't bear to be that close to him again.

"I guess I'll head for my room." She glanced down at her ridiculously over-the-top interview dress. "Am I supposed to give this dress to someone?"

"You're supposed to wear it to the state dinner tonight."

State dinner? She didn't remember planning any dinner. In fact she remembered deliberately not planning anything for the first few days after she intended to leave. "Maybe my memory isn't fully back yet, but I..." It was embarrassing to admit she still wasn't in full control of her faculties.

"Don't worry, you had nothing to do with it. I pulled the whole thing together to butter up all the people cheesed off by our engagement."

"That's a daring use of dairy metaphors."

Jake grinned. "Thanks. I'm a man of many talents."

If only I weren't so vividly aware of that. She sure as heck wished she'd never slept with him. That was going to be very hard to forget.

"So let me guess, all your recently jilted admirers, and their rich and influential daddies, will be gathered around the table in the grand dining room to whisper rude remarks about me." Her stomach clenched at the prospect.

"They'll do no such thing." Jake had entered the suite and obviously expected her to follow. He'd totally ignored her comment about heading for her room. "They wouldn't dare."

That's what you think. Powerful people could afford to be blissfully ignorant about what others thought, since no one would dare say anything to their face. She, on the other hand, was more likely to get a realistic picture of their true feelings since people didn't bother to try to impress a mere assistant.

But would they act differently now they thought she was engaged to Jake?

She glanced down at her perfectly tailored dress. It might be interesting to see how they behaved now the tables were turned and she was the one about to marry a king.

And it would certainly be educational to see how Jake behaved in their midst now that he was officially engaged to her.

"You look stunning." Jake's low voice jolted her from her anxious thoughts. His gaze heated her skin right through the green silk as it raked over her from head to toe, lingering for just a split second longer where the bodice cupped her breasts.

"Thanks. I guess almost anyone can look good when they have a crowd of professionals available to take charge."

"You're very beautiful." His dark eyes met hers. "Without any help from anyone."

Her face heated and she hoped they'd put on enough powder to hide it. Did he mean it or was he just saying that to mollify her? She didn't really believe anything he said anymore.

On the other hand, maybe he'd come to see her in a new light since he started considering her as wife material. She did feel pretty gorgeous under his smoldering stare.

"Flattery will get you everywhere." A sudden vision of herself in his bed—which was less than forty feet away—filled her mind. "Okay, maybe not everywhere. How long do we have until dinner?" She wasn't sure hanging around in his suite was a good idea. It might be better to spend time in more neutral territory.

"About half an hour."

"And who arranged this dinner if I didn't?" Curiosity goaded her to ask the question. The palace seemed to be running pretty well without her input, which should make her feel less guilty about leaving, but it irked her somewhat, too.

"Livia. She's been really helpful the last few days. Really stepped into your shoes."

"Oh." Andi stiffened. Why did it bother her that Livia might be after her job? She was planning to leave it, after all. Still, now that she remembered more of her past, she knew Livia had always felt somewhat competitive toward her, and resentful that Andi was hand in glove with Jake while she did the more routine work like ordering supplies and writing place cards.

She couldn't help wondering if Livia might now be resentful that Jake planned to marry her—talk about the ultimate promotion.

If you were into that sort of thing.

"Champagne?" Jake gestured to a bottle chilling in a silver bucket of ice. He must have had it brought here during the interview.

"No thanks." Better to keep her head. She had a feeling she'd need it. "But you go ahead."

"I couldn't possibly drink alone. And it's a 1907 Heidiseck."

"Are you sure it's not past its sell-by date?"

He chuckled. "It was recovered from a ship that was wrecked on its way to deliver champagne to the Russian Imperial family. It's been brought up from the bottom of the sea and tastes sublime even after decades of being lost."

"Very appropriate, considering the history of Ruthenia."

"That's what the friend who gave it to me thought. Won't you join me in a toast to our future?" His flirtatious glance tickled her insides.

She took a deep breath and tried to remain calm. "Not until I've figured out whether I want us to have a future."

Jake tilted his head. "You're very stubborn all of a sudden."

"That's because we're discussing the rest of my life, not just some seating placements or even a corporate merger."

"I like that about you. A lot of women would jump at the chance to marry me just to be queen."

Or just because you're embarrassingly attractive and shockingly wealthy. She tried to ignore those enticements herself.

Jake lifted a brow. "That doesn't mean much to you, does it?"

"I've never had the slightest desire to be called Your Majesty."

"Me, either." He grinned. "But if I can learn to put up with it, I'm sure you could handle it, too."

"Did you always know you'd be king one day?" She'd wondered this, but never dared ask him.

"My parents talked about it, but I thought they were nuts. I planned to be a king of Wall Street instead."

"And now you're doing both. I bet your parents would be very proud. It's a shame they weren't alive to see you take the throne." She knew they'd died in a small plane accident.

"If they were alive they'd be ruling here themselves, which would have been just fine with me."

"You don't like being king?" She couldn't resist asking.

"I like it fine, but it's a job for life. There's no getting bored and quitting. Sometimes I wonder what I would have done if I'd had more freedom."

"You were brave to take on the responsibility. Not everyone would have, especially with the state Ruthenia was in when you first arrived."

"I do feel a real sense of duty toward Ruthenia. I always

have, it was spooned into me along with my baby food. I couldn't turn my back on Ruthenia for anything."

She didn't feel the same way. In fact she could leave and never look back—couldn't she? She hadn't been raised to smile and wave at people or wear an ermine robe, but she had always felt a strong sense of commitment to her job—and her boss.

Who stood in front of her tall and proud, handsome features picked out by the light of a wall sconce. She admired him for stepping up to the responsibilities of getting Ruthenia back on its feet, and committing himself to help the country and its people for the rest of his life.

She should be touched and honored that he wanted her help in that enterprise, regardless of whether he loved her.

Still, she wasn't made of stone. Something she became vividly aware of when Jake reached for her hand and drew it to his lips. Her skin heated under his mouth and she struggled to keep her breathing steady.

He's just trying to seduce you into going along with his plan. It doesn't mean he really loves you—or even desires you.

Her body responded to him like a flipped switch, but then it always had, even back when he saw her as nothing more than an efficient employee. Heat flared in her belly and her fingertips itched to reach out and touch his skin.

But she'd resisted six long years and she could do it now.

She pulled her hand back with some difficulty. Her skin hummed where his lips had just touched it. A quick glance up was a mistake—his dark eyes fixed on hers with a smoldering expression that took her breath away.

But she knew he was an accomplished actor. You had to be to pull off international diplomacy, especially when it involved placating all the outrageous characters he dealt with in Ruthenia.

"You're very suspicious." His eyes twinkled.

"Of course I am. I woke up from amnesia to find myself engaged to my boss. That kind of thing makes a girl wary."

"You know you can trust me." His steady gaze showed total confidence.

"I thought I could trust you." She raised a brow. "Over the last day I've learned I can't trust you. You used me to your advantage, without consulting me."

His expression darkened. "I couldn't consult with you because you didn't know who you were."

"You could have waited until my memory came back and we could discuss it calmly." *Instead you decided to convince me between the sheets.* He'd undermined all her inhibitions and drawn her into the most intense and powerful intimacy.

Too bad it had worked so well.

"Time was of the essence. Independence Day is coming right up."

"And you couldn't disappoint the people of Ruthenia."

"Exactly. I knew you'd understand."

She did. The people of Ruthenia and his own reputation were far more important than her feelings.

Did he even know she had feelings?

She had three days to put him to the test.

Eight

Andi would have liked to sweep into the dining room and smile confidently at the gathered Ruthenian dignitaries and their snooty daughters, then take her place at the head of the table.

But it didn't work like that.

The toe of her pointed shoe caught in the hem of her dress on her way into the anteroom and she pitched through the doorway headfirst. Jake, walking behind her, flung his arms around her waist and pulled her back onto her feet before she fell on her face into the Aubusson carpet. It was not an auspicious entrance into high society.

Her face heated, especially when she saw the looks of undisguised glee on Maxi's and Alia's faces.

Jake laughed it off and used the occasion to steal a kiss in front of the gathered audience. She was too flustered to attempt resistance, which would have looked rude and strange anyway, since as far as everyone knew they were madly in love.

The kiss only deepened her blush and stirred the mix of arousal and anguish roiling in her gut.

"Congratulations!" A portly older man with medals on his jacket stepped forward and bowed low to Andi. She swallowed. This was the Grand Duke of Machen. He didn't have any marriageable daughters left, so he was one of the few non-hostile entities in the room. He turned to Jake. "We're all thrilled that you've finally chosen a bride to continue the royal line."

The royal line? Andi's muscles tightened. As Jake's wife she'd be expected to produce the future king or queen. Which meant that even if it were a marriage of convenience, there would be some sex involved. She'd already learned that making love with Jake touched something powerful and tender deep inside her. Not something she could do as a matter of routine. Could he really expect that of her? It was different with men. They could turn off their emotions and just enjoy the pure physical sensations.

If only she could do that.

A glance around the room revealed that not everyone was as thrilled as the grand duke. Maxi's father Anton Rivenshnell looked grim—salt-and-pepper brows lowered threateningly over his beady gray eyes. Maxi herself had abandoned her usual winning smile in favor of a less-flattering pout.

"I suppose an American bride seemed a natural choice when you spent your entire life in America," growled Rivenshnell, his dark suit stretched across an ample belly. "Though this is naturally a disappointment for the women of Ruthenia."

Jake seemed to grow about a foot taller, which, considering his already impressive height of six-one, made him a little scary. "Andi has demonstrated her commitment to Ruthenia over the last three years, living and working by my side. She is one of the women of Ruthenia."

Ha. Andi couldn't help loving his spirited defense of her. "I've never been so happy as I am here." The honest truth. She wasn't going to lie. "I've spent every day enjoying the people and the beautiful countryside, and I've come to love Ruthenia as my home."

"And you fell in love with your boss, too." The grand duke's laugh bellowed across the room.

"Yes." She managed a shaky smile. Again, it was the truth—but no need for Jake to know that. As far as he was concerned she was just fulfilling her part of the arrangement.

Andi felt very self-conscious as they were ushered into the dining room by a rather smug Livia. This was the first time she'd attended one of these affairs as a guest, not one of the staff members hovering along the walls ready to serve the diners and tend to Jake's needs. Livia shot her at least three meaningful glances, though she couldn't actually tell what they meant.

At least she managed not to fall on her face on her way to the end of the table, where she was seated far, far away from Jake, probably in between two daddies of rejected girls.

Jake was seated between Alia and Maxi, just as she'd sat him before she lost her memory. Then she'd done it as a joke, to torment him with his two most ardent admirers and hopefully put him off both of them. Now he must have planned it himself, for reasons she could only guess at.

Did he intend to have affairs with each of them now that he was no longer on the hook to make one his queen? Surely quiet little Andi wouldn't object.

The very thought made her seethe. Still, she didn't

remember Jake ever cheating on one of his many girlfriends. On the other hand, he rarely dated the same one for long enough to get the chance. As soon as a girl showed signs of getting serious, he brought an abrupt end to things.

Andi had rather liked that about him. He never continued with a relationship just because it was there. He was often blunt and funny about the reasons he no longer saw a future with a particular girl. And it always gave her fresh hope that one day he'd be hers.

And now he was. At least in theory.

Irritation flickered through her at the sight of Alia brushing his hand with her long, manicured fingers. Jake smiled at the elegant blonde and spoke softly to her before turning to Maxi. The sultry brunette immediately lit up and eased her impressive cleavage toward him. Jealousy raged in Andi's gut and she cursed herself for caring.

"Your parents must be delighted." The gruff voice startled Andi, who realized she was staring.

"Oh, yes." She tried to smile at the white-haired man by her side. Up close she could see he was probably too old to have a jilted daughter, so that was a plus.

Her parents would be happy if she married Jake. At least she imagined so. How would they feel if she refused to marry him?

"Have they visited Ruthenia before?"

"Not yet. But I'm sure they'll love it here."

"I imagine they'll move here." His blue eyes twinkled with…was it warmth or malice?

"They have their own lives back in Pittsburgh, so I don't think they'll be leaving."

"But they must! Their daughter is to be the queen. It would be tragic for a family to endure such separation."

"It's quite common in the U.S. for families to live hundreds or even thousands of miles apart."

"In Ruthenia that would be unthinkable."

"I know." She shrugged. Was he also implying that having such a coldhearted and independent American as their queen was unthinkable? "But they have jobs they enjoy and friends where they live. I'm sure they'll come visit often."

"They've *never* visited you here? How long have you been here?"

"Three years, but it's an expensive trip and…" He was making her feel bad, and she had a feeling that's exactly what he intended. "Have you ever visited the States?" She smiled brightly. Every time she looked up, someone was peeking at her out of the corner of their eye. Including Livia. She was beginning to feel under siege.

Jake shot her a warm glance from the far end of the table. Even from that distance he could make her heart beat faster. He looked totally in his element, relaxed, jovial and quite at home in the lap of luxury, surrounded by Ruthenian nobles.

Whereas she felt like a scullery maid who'd wandered into the ballroom—which wasn't a million miles from the truth. In all her dreams of herself and Jake living happily ever after, they lived happily in a fantasy world of her own creation. While life in the Ruthenian royal palace was definitely someone's fantasy world, it wasn't hers, and Jake was clearly making a terrible mistake if he thought this could work.

Jake beamed with satisfaction as staff poured the coffee. Andi looked radiant at the far end of the table, resplendent in her regal gown and with her hair arranged in shiny curls that fell about her shoulders. Ruthenia's haughty beauties disappeared into the drapery with her around. He'd tried to reassure them that his marriage was a love match and not a deliberate insult to them and their families. He couldn't afford to lose the support of Ruthenia's most powerful businessmen. Noses were definitely bent out of shape, but no one had declared war—yet.

A love match. He'd used the term several times now, though never within earshot of Andi. He couldn't say something so blatantly untrue right in front of her—at least not now that she had her memory back. He knew nothing of love. Raised by a succession of nannies while his parents traveled, he'd been groomed for duty and honor and not for family life and intimate relationships. Love seemed like something that happened in poems but not in real life, and he didn't want to promise anything to Andi that he couldn't deliver.

He was hotly attracted to her and admired all her fine qualities, and that was almost as good. Many people married for love and ended up divorced or miserable. It was much more sensible to go into a lifetime commitment with a clear head and a solid strategy.

Andi seemed concerned about the lack of love between them once her memory returned and she knew they hadn't been involved. His most important task over the next two days was to convince her they were meant to be together, and surely the best way to do that was to woo her back into his bed. The warm affection they'd shared stirred something in his chest. Maybe it wasn't the kind of love that inspired songs and sonnets, but he ached to enjoy it again.

It took some time for the guests to filter out the front door, and he kept half an eye on Andi the whole time in case she should decide to slip away. She looked tense, keeping up her end of every conversation but looking around often as if checking for escape routes. He'd been so busy rebuilding the relationships he'd worked hard to cement in the past three years by dancing with different girls that he hadn't danced with Andi. There was plenty of time for him to catch up with her after the guests left.

He kissed Alia on the cheek and ignored the subtle squeeze she gave his arm. He slapped her father on the back and promised to call him to go over some business details. So far, so good. Now where was Andi? She'd managed to slip away as the Kronstadts made their exit.

Irritation and worry stirred in his gut along with a powerful desire to see her right now. He strode up the stairs from the foyer and intercepted her in the hallway outside her room.

He slid his arms around her waist from behind—just as he'd done when she dove unceremoniously into their company earlier. A smile spread across his mouth at the feel of her soft warm body in his arms, and he couldn't wait to spend the night together.

But she stiffened. "I'm tired, Jake."

"Me, too." He squeezed her gently. "We can sleep in each other's arms."

"I don't think that's a good idea." She unlocked her door and he followed her in, arms still wrapped around her. Her delicious scent filled his senses. He twirled her around until they were face-to-face—and noticed her face looked sad.

"What's going on, Andi? You did a fantastic job this evening."

Her mouth flattened. "We should close the door, for privacy."

"Sure." That was a promising start. He turned and pushed it shut. "Why do you look unhappy?"

"Because I can't do this. I don't fit in here. I feel like an intruder."

"That's ridiculous. You fit in here as well as I do."

"I don't. I felt out of place and people kept going on about me being American. They obviously don't like the idea of you marrying a foreigner."

"Monarchs nearly always marry foreigners. That's how the British royal family ended up being German." He grinned. "They used to import brides from whichever country they needed to curry diplomatic favor with. It's a time-honored tradition."

"I don't think marrying me will get you too far with the White House."

"Oh, I disagree." He stroked her soft cheek with his thumb. "I'm sure any sensible administration would admire you as much as I do."

Her eyes softened for a moment and a tiny flush rose to her pale cheeks. But she wouldn't meet his gaze.

He placed his hands on either side of her waist. She had a lovely figure, a slender hourglass that the dress emphasized in a way her stiff suits never could. The tailored bodice presented her cleavage in a dangerously enticing way, and a single diamond sparkled on a fine chain between her small, plump breasts.

A flame of desire licked through him. "You were the loveliest woman in that room tonight."

"You're sweet." There was no hint of sparkle or a smile in her eyes. She didn't seem to believe him.

"You know I'm not sweet." He lifted a brow. "So you'd better believe me. Every minute I danced with those other girls, I wished I was dancing with you."

But you weren't.

He'd danced with those women because it was good for the nation's economy to keep their families on his side. Maybe he'd desired them, too, but that wasn't why he twirled them around the floor. Andi knew that business would always come first with Jake. She's always known that, and admired it. But now that she contemplated the prospect of spending the rest of her life with a man who didn't love her, it seemed like a mistake.

Mostly because she loved him so much.

The press of his strong fingers around her waist was a cruel torment. Her nipples had thickened against the silk of her bodice, aching for his touch. The skin of her cheek still hummed where he'd brushed his thumb over it.

She even loved him for the fact that he'd marry a woman he didn't love just for the sake of his country. That kind of commitment was impressive.

Unless you were the woman he didn't love, and had to watch from the sidelines, or even under the spotlight, while he gave his heart and soul to Ruthenia and its people.

His presence dominated her room, with its neat, impersonal decor. He was larger than life, bolder, better-looking and more engaging than any man she'd ever met. Wasn't it enough that he wanted to marry her?

Why did she think she was so special she deserved more than he offered? Maybe it was the independent-minded American in her who wanted everything. It wasn't enough to be queen and have a handsome and hardworking husband—she had to have the fairy-tale romance, as well.

Jake leaned in and kissed her softly on the mouth. Her breath caught at the bottom of her lungs as his warm, masculine scent—soap and rich fabrics with a hint of male musk—tormented her senses. Her lips stung with arousal as he pulled back a few inches and hovered there, his dark gaze fixed to hers.

Her fingers wanted to roam under his jacket and explore the muscles of his back and she struggled to keep them still at her sides. If she let him seduce her she was saying "yes" to everything he offered.

Including sex without love.

Yes, they'd had sex once already, but at the time she'd been under the delusion that he loved her and had proposed to her out of genuine emotion. Which was very different from the business arrangement he'd presented to her earlier.

His lips lowered over hers again, but she pulled back, heart thumping. "Stop, Jake. I'm not ready."

His eyes darkened. "Why not?"

"It's all happening too fast. I still barely know who I am. I can't think straight with you kissing me."

"Maybe I don't want you to think straight." A gleam shone in his seductive dark eyes.

"That's what I'm worried about." She tugged herself from his embrace, and almost to her surprise, he let her go. "I don't want to rush into this and realize a year or so from now that it was a huge mistake."

"I'll make sure you never regret it."

"I think that's quite arrogant of you." She tilted her chin. She'd never spoken to him like this before and it scared her a little. How would he react? "You seem to think you know exactly what I feel, and how I'll react."

"I know you very well after six years together." His warm gaze and proud, handsome face were dangerous—both familiar and alluring.

"But those were six years together in a professional relationship, not a marriage." For a start, he'd never barged into her room with his arms wrapped around her waist.

"I don't really see the difference." He looked down at her, slightly supercilious.

Indignation surged inside her, battling with the infuriating desire to kiss his sensual mouth. "That's the problem. It is different. As your assistant I have to follow certain rules of behavior, to always be polite and not express my opinion unless it's directly relevant to our work. To be on my best behavior and keep my emotions to myself. Maybe I'm not really the person you think I am at all." Her voice rose and she sounded a little hysterical.

Which was probably good, since he seemed to think she was some kind of well-mannered automaton who could easily approach the rest of her life as a kind of well-paid job with excellent benefits and perks.

"So the real Andi is very different from the one I know?"

She let out a long sigh. "Yes." She frowned. Who was the real Andi and what did she want? For so long she'd wanted Jake—while knowing in her heart that he would never be hers—that it was hard to think straight. "I don't know. But that's why we need to take it slow. You don't want to marry me and then find out I'm not the faithful and loyal helpmeet you imagine."

"I'd love to get to know your wild side." His eyes narrowed and a half smile tilted his mouth.

"I'm not sure I have one."

"You do." His smile widened, showing a hint of white teeth. "I've seen it."

Her face heated. "I still can't believe you slept with me under false pretenses." Her body stirred just at the memory of being stretched against him, skin to skin.

"They weren't false. We really are engaged."

She crossed her arms over her chest, and tried to ignore the tingling in her nipples. "I beg to differ. You hadn't asked the real me to marry you. You just assumed that I would. Not the same thing at all."

"But you seemed so happy about it." His expression was sweetly boyish for a moment, which tugged at a place deep inside her. "I thought you truly wanted us to be together."

I did.

She blinked, trying to make sense of it all. Jake's sturdy masculine presence wasn't helping one bit. She was painfully aware of the thickly muscled body under his elegant evening suit and how good it would feel pressed against hers.

He picked up her hand and kissed it. A knightly gesture no doubt intended to steal her heart. She shivered slightly as his lips pressed against the back of her hand, soft yet insistent.

During the nightmare of not knowing who she was, the one source of relief and happiness was Jake. He'd been the rock she could lean on and draw strength from while everything else around her was confusing and mysterious. She had been happy then, at least during the moments that the rest of the world fell away and they were alone together, lost in each other.

Could that happen again?

"I think we should spend some time together away from the palace." Getting out of their everyday work environment would be an interesting test of their relationship. They really hadn't spent leisure time together. Of course Jake didn't exactly have free time, unless you counted junkets with investors and state dinners. She didn't either, since she'd always devoted every minute to her job. She never went on the staff trips to the local nightclub or their weekend jaunts to Munich or Salzburg. As Jake's assistant she'd always felt herself too needed—or so she'd told herself—to disappear for more than an hour or two.

Jake stroked her hand, now held between both of his. She struggled to keep herself steady and not sink into his arms. "Is there someplace near here that you've always wanted to go?"

He tilted his head and his gaze grew distant. "The mountains."

"The ones you can see out the window?"

"Yes. I've always wanted to climb up and look down on the town and the palace." He shrugged. "There's never time."

"There isn't time right now, either." She sighed. "I don't suppose you really can get away from the palace right before Independence Day." Her request for time alone seemed silly and petty now that she thought about it. He had a lot of work to do and people would be arriving from all over the world in the run-up to the celebrations.

"Then we'll have to make time." He squeezed her hand.

An odd sensation filled her chest. He was willing to drop everything on a whim to get away with her? "But who will greet the arriving guests? We'd be gone for hours." There was a large group of Ruthenian expats arriving from Chicago, including three prominent businessmen and their families who had been invited to stay at the palace.

"I'm sure the staff can manage. Livia's proving very capable."

A slight frisson of anxiety trickled through her. Why did the idea of Livia quietly taking over her job make her so uncomfortable? Surely it was ideal.

"And how would we get there?"

"My car." Amusement twinkled in his eyes. "I can still drive, you know, even though I rarely get the chance."

"No driver or attendant?"

"Not even a footman. And we'll leave our PDAs behind, too. No sense being halfway up a mountain texting people about trade tariffs."

Andi laughed. He really was prepared to drop everything just to make her happy. Selfish of her to want that, but it felt really good. And the mountains had always called to her. Right now the slopes below the snow-covered peaks were lush with grass and wildflowers. "We'd better bring a picnic."

"Of course. Let the kitchen know what you want and tell them to pack it in something we can carry easily."

Andi blinked. This would be a test for her of how she could handle the transformation from staff to employer.

Or as Jake's wife was she just a high-level member of staff? The situation was confusing.

She pulled her hand gently from his grasp. "When should we go?"

"Tomorrow morning. I've learned to seize the moment around here. If we wait any longer we'll get sucked into the Independence Day activities."

"I guess we should call it an early night." She hoped he'd take a hint and leave.

"But the morning is still so far off." A mischievous twinkle lit Jake's eyes.

"It's after midnight."

"One of my favorite times of day. Maybe we should go dance around on the lawn outside." His gaze swept over her elegant dress—and sent heat sizzling through the defenseless body underneath it. "You're dressed for it."

"I don't think so. I might lose my memory again." *Or just my heart.*

She did not want anything sensual to happen between them until she'd had a chance to wrap her mind around the whole situation and make some tough decisions. Jake's touch had a very dangerous effect on her common sense, and this was the rest of her life at stake here.

"Just a stroll in the moonlight?" He took a step toward her. Her nipples thickened under her bodice and heat curled low in her belly.

"No." She'd better get him out of here and away from her while she still could. It wasn't easy saying no to something you'd dreamed of for six long years. "We'll be doing plenty of walking tomorrow. Conserve your energy."

"What makes you think I need to?" He lifted a brow. Humor sparkled in his eyes.

Andi's insides wobbled. Was he really so attracted to her? It was hard to believe that he'd gone from not noticing her at all, to trying every trick in the book to lure her into his bed.

Then again, he was known for his ability to close a deal by any means necessary.

It was more important right now to learn whether he could respect her wishes, or not. This was a crucial test.

"Goodnight, Jake." She walked to the door and opened it. "I'll see you in the morning." Her pulse quickened, wondering if he'd protest and refuse to leave.

"Goodnight, Andi." He strolled to the doorway and brushed a soft kiss across her lips. No hands, thank goodness, though her body craved his touch. He pulled back and stepped into the hallway.

Her relief was mingled with odd regret that she wouldn't be spending the night in his strong arms.

He'd passed her test.

Then he turned to face her. "I have a bet for you."

"A bet? I'm not the gambling type."

"I didn't think you were." His mouth tilted into a wry smile. "But I bet you that tomorrow night you'll sleep in my bed—with me."

Her belly quivered under the force of his intense gaze, but she held herself steady. "What are the odds, I wonder?"

"I wouldn't advise betting against me." He crossed his arms over his powerful chest.

"Normally, neither would I." She couldn't help smiling.

His confidence was rather adorable. "But I think it's important to keep a clear head in this situation."

"I completely agree." He flashed his infuriating pearly grin.

His arrogance alone made her determined to resist. Apparently she'd be the one with a test to pass tomorrow.

Nine

Andi watched as two footmen loaded their picnic lunch—impractically packed in two large baskets—into the trunk of Jake's black BMW sedan. The cook had acted as if Andi was already mistress of the house. No questioning of her ideas or complaining that they were low on certain ingredients, as she usually did.

Livia managed to pass on a couple of comments from the staff gossip—including that everyone knew Jake had slept alone the previous night. Andi blushed. Of course everyone knew everything in the palace, especially the maids. Livia obviously wasn't intimidated by Andi's new status and she made it clear that Jake would have had company in bed if she were in Andi's shoes.

In the old days it would be expected for her to wait until the wedding night. Now it was quite the opposite. People would wonder what was wrong if she persisted in sleeping alone.

She'd dressed in those jeans Jake liked and a pale pink shirt she'd bought on a whim, then decided it wasn't professional enough. Her hair was in a ponytail—not as formal as the bun—and she'd forgone all makeup except blush and lip gloss.

Apparently she wanted him to find her attractive.

This whole situation was very confusing. She wanted him to want her—but only for the right reasons.

Jake strode down the steps, talking on his phone. He'd abandoned his usual tailored suit for a pair of dark jeans and a white shirt, sleeves rolled up over tanned arms. He smiled when he saw her, and her stomach gave a little dip.

Pulling the phone from his ear he switched it off and handed it to one of the footmen. "Kirk, please hold this hostage until I get back. I don't want any interruptions." He turned to Andi. "Did you leave yours behind, too?"

"It's on my desk. I can handle the challenge of being incommunicado all afternoon."

"What if you need to call for help?" asked Kirk.

"We're quite capable of helping ourselves." Jake held the passenger door open for Andi. She climbed in, anticipation jangling her nerves. She couldn't remember being anywhere all alone with Jake. She felt safe with him though. He'd be a match for any wolves or bears or whatever mythical creatures stalked the mountains of Ruthenia.

He climbed in and closed the door. In the close quarters of the car he seemed bigger than usual, and his enticing male scent stirred her senses. His big hand on the stick shift made her belly shimmy a little. "How do you get so tanned?"

"Tennis. We should play it sometime."

Of course. He played with any guests who showed an interest, and invariably won. He was far too naturally competitive to be diplomatic while playing a sport.

"I haven't played since college."

"I bet you were good." He shot her a glance.

"I wasn't too bad." Her nerves tingled with excitement at the prospect of playing with him. There was something they had in common. Of course he'd beat her, but she'd enjoy the challenge of taking even a single point off him. "We'll have to give it a try."

If I stay.

They pulled out of the large wrought-iron gates at the end of the palace driveway and past the old stone gatehouse. Andi waved to the guards, who nodded and smiled. Somehow living here as Jake's…partner didn't feel all that odd right now.

It felt downright possible.

"Do you know which roads to take to get to the foot of the mountain?"

"I know which roads to take to get halfway up the mountain, and that's where we're headed."

"Don't like climbing?"

"I love it, but why not climb the high part?"

Andi laughed. "That sounds like a good approach to life in general."

"I think so."

They drove through the ancient village, where some of the buildings must be a thousand years old, with their sloping tile roofs and festoons of chimneys. The road widened as they left the village and headed through a swathe of meadows filled with grazing cows. The sun was rising into the middle of an almost cloudless sky and the whole landscape looked like a 1950s Technicolor movie. She almost expected Julie Andrews to come running down a hillside and burst into song.

"What would you have done if you were born to be king of somewhere really awful?"

Jake laughed. "Everywhere has its merits."

"Antarctica."

"Too many emperors there already—the kind with flippers. But I see your point. Still, a lot of people said Ruthenia was too badly broken to be fixed. Years of decline during and after the fall of communism, no work ethic, low morale and motivation. And it's turned on its head in three short years since independence. You just have to believe."

"And work hard."

"No denying that. But when you have concrete goals and a good road map, almost anything is doable."

The sunlight pouring through the windshield played off his chiseled features. His bone structure alone contained enough determination for a small, landlocked nation.

He'd been totally up-front about his goals and road map where she was concerned. The goal was obviously a long and successful marriage that would help him as a monarch, and the road map apparently included seducing her into his bed tonight.

She was not going to let him do that. Her judgment was already clouded enough by his sturdy, masculine presence in the car next to her.

The car started to climb steadily, as the road wound around the base of the mountain. It looked much bigger from here, the snow-capped peak now invisible above a band of conifers that ringed the mountain's middle like a vast green belt. The road petered out into a steep farm track past a group of cottages, then finally ended at a field gate about a mile farther on.

"We're on our own from here." Jake climbed out and popped the trunk. "And since we don't have sherpas, we'd better eat lunch close by. These baskets look like they were designed for royal picnics in the nineteenth century."

"They probably were." Andi touched the soft leather

buckles on the big, wicker rectangles. She and Jake carried one together through the gate and into the field. Distant sheep ignored them as they spread their blanket under a tree and unpacked the feast.

Jake took the lid off the first dish. “Cabbage rolls, very traditional.” He grinned. She had a feeling he’d appreciate her picking a Ruthenian dish. The spicy meat wrapped in soft boiled cabbage was as Ruthenian as you could get, and there was a jar of the hot dipping pickle and onion sauce served with it at Ruthenian inns. Jake picked up a perfectly wrapped cabbage roll and took a bite. “Ah. New Yorkers have no idea what they’re missing out on. We really should market this for the States.”

“Do you ever stop thinking about business?” She raised a brow.

“Truthfully? No. But then you know that already.” His eyes twinkled as he took another bite.

At least he was honest. Andi reached into another dish and pulled out one of the tiny phyllo pastry wraps filled with soft, fresh goat cheese. This one came with a dish of tangy beetroot sauce. She spooned the sauce onto her pastry and took a bite. Like many things in Ruthenia it was surprising and wonderful. “These would definitely be a big hit. Perhaps a Ruthenian restaurant in Midtown.”

“To give the Russian Tea Room a run for its money?” Jake nodded and took a phyllo wrap. “I like the way you think. You can’t deny that we’re a good team.”

Her heart contracted a little. “Yes.” A good team. They were that. But was that enough? She wanted more. She wanted…magic.

The midday sun sparkled on the roofs of the town far below them. “Why didn’t they build the castle up here? It would have been easier to defend.”

"It would also have been really hard getting a cartloads of supplies up and down that steep track."

"I guess the peasants would have had to carry everything."

"And maybe they would have staged a revolt." Jake grinned, and reached for a spicy Ruthenian meatball. "Easier to build on the flat and put a town nearby."

"As an imported peasant I have to agree."

Jake laughed. "You're the king's fiancée. That hardly makes you a peasant."

"Don't think I'll forget my humble peasant origins." She teased and sipped some of the sweet bottled cider they'd bought. "I'm the first person in my family to go to college, after all."

"Are you really? What do your parents do?"

Andi swallowed. So odd that they hadn't talked about her past or her family before now. Jake had never been interested. "My dad works at a tire dealership and my mom runs the cafeteria at a local elementary school."

Jake nodded and sipped his cider. Was he shocked? Maybe he'd assumed her dad was a lawyer and her mom a socialite. Discomfort prickled inside her. "Your ancestors would probably be scandalized that you're even thinking of marrying someone like me."

"I bet the old Ruthenian kings married the miller's daughter or a pretty shepherd girl from time to time."

"Maybe if they could spin straw into gold," Andi teased. "Otherwise they probably just had affairs with them and married girls who came with large estates and strategically located castles."

He laughed. "You're probably right. But you can spin straw into gold, can't you?"

"I find that spinning straw into freshly minted Euros is more practical these days." She bit off a crunchy mouthful of freshly baked Ruthenian pretzel, fragrant with poppy seeds. "Gold makes people suspicious."

Jake smiled. Andi really did make gold, at least in his life. "If only people knew that you're the dark secret behind the salvation of the Ruthenian economy. Sitting up there in your office at your spinning wheel."

"They probably figure I must have mysterious powers. Otherwise why wouldn't you marry a Ruthenian glamour girl?"

"Those Ruthenian ladies are all a handful. None of them grew up in Ruthenia, either. I'd like to know what they're doing in those Swiss finishing schools to produce such a bunch of spoiled, self-indulgent princesses. They're far too much like hard work, and you'd certainly never catch them doing any real work." And none of them had Andi's cute, slightly freckled nose.

She looked pleased. "They can't all be like that."

"The ones who aren't are off pursuing careers somewhere—probably in the U.S.—and aren't hanging around the palace trying to curry favor with me."

"You could have staged a campaign to invite all Ruthenian expats to come back and compete for your hand."

Jake shuddered at the thought. "Why would I want to do that when you're right here?" He took a bite of a pretzel. "You've already passed every possible kind of test life in Ruthenia has thrown at you and proved yourself a star."

She blushed slightly. "I wouldn't say that."

"I would." His chest filled with pride that Andi had managed the big shift in lifestyle with such grace and ease. She'd eased the transition for him in so many ways that he'd probably never even know. No one could deny they were a powerful team. "Let's drink to us."

She took a glass with a slightly shaky hand. "To us."

"And the future of Ruthenia." Which would be a very bright one, at least for him, with the lovely Andi at his side. He'd seen another side of her since her memory came back—a feistier, more independent Andi than the one who'd worked so tirelessly as his assistant. He liked her all the more for being strong enough to stand up to him.

And the chemistry between them…if that's what it was. He couldn't put it into words, but the very air now seemed to crackle with energy when they got a little too close. He hoped she felt it, too—and suspected she did. Her cheeks colored sometimes just when he looked at her, and there was a new sparkle in her lovely blue eyes—or maybe it had always been there and he'd just never noticed it before?

Obviously he'd been walking through life with blinkers on where Andi was concerned. Thank heavens he'd finally realized what he'd been missing out on all these years.

After they'd finished eating they packed the baskets back in the car and set off up the grassy slopes on foot. The meadows grew steeper as they climbed, and the view more magnificent. They could see over the ancient forest on the far side of the town, and to the hills beyond, with villages scattered in the valleys, church steeples rising up from their midst. Jake's heart swelled at the sight of his beautiful country, so resilient and hopeful.

"Thank you for bringing us up here." He wanted to touch her, to hold her and kiss her and share the joy that pulsed through him, but Andi managed to remain out of reach.

After about an hour of steady climbing, they reached a small round tower, almost hidden in a grove of trees.

"Yikes. I wonder if the witch still has Rapunzel imprisoned in there." Andi peered up at the gray stones, mottled with moss and lichens.

"It's a lookout post," he replied. "I've seen it on the old

maps. They would watch for soldiers approaching in the distance, then signal down to the palace—which was a fortified castle back then—with a flag that let them know what was happening. Let's go inside."

He strode ahead into the arched doorway. Andi followed, rather more hesitant.

"There was probably a door, but it's gone," she said as she peered up into the tower. Any ceiling or upper floors were also gone, and the stone walls circled a perfect patch of blue sky. "It would make a great play fort for kids."

"We'll have to refurbish it for ours." Jake smiled. He'd never given much thought to having children, but the prospect of sharing family life with Andi stirred something unexpected and warm inside him.

Andi's eyes widened.

"Have I shocked you?"

"Maybe. It's all just a bit…sudden."

Jake shrugged. His changed relationship with Andi felt surprisingly natural, as if it had been in the cards the whole time without him knowing it, almost in the same way he was destined to return to Ruthenia.

But one thing still pricked at him. She'd been planning to take off—to abandon him and Ruthenia in search of… what? "Why were you going to leave?"

She startled slightly. "I already told you. I didn't see any future in my job and I felt it was time to move on."

He frowned. He couldn't help but feel there was more to it than that. "What were you going to do, back in the States?" He walked toward her. Sunlight pouring through the open roof illuminated her hair with a golden halo and cast sunbeams over her slender form.

"Um, I was thinking of starting my own business."

Shock and hurt surprised him. Her leaving still felt like

a personal betrayal. "Intriguing. What kind of business?" She could start her business here.

"Event planning. I intended to find a job at an event-planning company, then gradually branch out on my own."

"You've certainly got the experience for it."

"I know." She lifted her chin. "I must have planned hundreds of events over the last six years."

She wanted to be independent, in charge of her own destiny. He admired that. "As queen you'll have significant responsibilities. You'll be an important person in your own right. People will request your presence for events I can't attend." He knew she'd find it fulfilling.

"It's hardly the same." She lifted her chin. "I'd still be working for you."

"Working *with* me." He took a step toward her. "As equals." Another step. She hadn't moved. He reached out and took her hand. His skin hummed as their fingers met.

"You shouldn't," she breathed, tensing at his touch. "I really was planning to leave, and I still might."

His chest tightened, though he didn't really believe her. "You'll have a wonderful life here. You already know that. You'll never be bored and you can run all the businesses you want, as well as being queen." He stroked her hand with his thumb. Her skin was so soft.

"I still don't believe that staying is the right thing to do."

"I'll convince you." Pride mingled with emotion coursed through him as he raised her hand to his mouth and pressed his lips to her palm.

She gasped slightly and tried to pull her hand back, but he held it fast.

Her lips quivered slightly as his moved closer. Her delicious scent tormented his senses. He eased toward her until their chests were almost touching. She still hadn't moved. He could see in her darkening gaze that she felt the same fierce attraction he did. She wanted him every bit as much as he wanted her, despite her foolish worries and reservations. He'd just have to prove to her that her future should be right here, with him.

His lips closed over hers in a single swipe that drew them together. She arched into him, and he felt her nipples tighten inside her blouse as her fingertips clutched at his crisp shirt. She kissed him back hard, running her fingers into his hair and down his collar.

Jake sighed, reveling in the glorious sensation of holding Andi tight in his arms and kissing her doubts away.

She shuddered as his hand slid over her backside and down her thigh. Her knees buckled slightly as he touched her breast with his other hand, squeezing gently through her soft blouse.

No denying the energy between them. It had a life force of its own and drew them closer and bound them more tightly together every time they touched.

She shivered as his hand roamed under her blouse and his fingers brushed her taut nipple through her bra. At the same time his tongue flicked hers in a way that made her gasp.

Jake grimaced. He'd grown painfully hard. The sheer pleasure of kissing Andi was rather undermined by the powerful urge to strip off her clothes and make mad, passionate love to her right here, right now.

But he didn't want to drive her away. He'd already pushed too far too fast and he needed to let her come to him—to leave her wanting more.

He eased his mouth from hers and left her blinking in the half light of the tower as he pulled back. "Let's not get carried away. It's not too comfortable in here."

When he took things further, he needed to be sure she'd say yes. It was a delicate dance and he didn't entirely want her to know how much power she had over him. She could use it against him. The last nights alone had been painful and he had no intention of prolonging the torment by coming on too strong. He couldn't risk losing her now.

They walked a little higher up the mountain, then decided they'd scaled lofty enough heights for one day and turned for home. A bit out of character for him. Normally if he started something he had to take it as far as it could go.

In the car on the way back he realized he was going to forfeit his bet. Yes, he could seduce her on a whim—her reaction in the tower proved that. But he no longer wanted to. He wanted her heart and mind entwined with his, not just her body, so winning a bet seemed meaningless in the grand scheme of things.

It was a sign of maturity to forfeit a battle in order to win the war. He kissed her good-night with chaste tenderness, and watched her walk away to her own room with regret and desire singing in his blood.

Andi couldn't help a tiny twinge of guilt when she awoke in the morning and remembered that she'd made him lose his bet.

The kiss in the tower had shocked and scared her. How easily she fell into his arms, panting and moaning and letting him know just how easily her control evaporated around him. If he hadn't broken off the kiss she'd probably have made love to him right there on the moss-covered stones.

All that talk about their children and her future as queen had mingled with his powerful touch to throw her into a swoon of excitement, and at that point she might have agreed to anything just to feel his body against hers.

Not good.

She needed to think with her head, and not with her heart. Or any other parts of her body. Jake was still Jake—all business, all about Ruthenia, practical and not personal. He'd never for one instant hinted that he loved her. He was too much of a gentleman to lie about something like that.

She shivered, despite the morning sun. Why did she have to be so crazy about him?

It was the last day before the Independence Day celebrations turned Ruthenia into a countrywide party. She knew they'd both be flat-out busy today making last-minute plans and it should be easy to avoid him.

At least until tonight.

A tiny ray of pride shone through her anxiety. She'd managed to resist him after all, which meant she could still be clearheaded about her choice to stay or go. After the kiss in the tower she hadn't been so sure.

She showered and dressed, hoping she could manage not to be alone with him too much today. Her schedule—so recently abandoned—was packed with things to organize for the festivities. Plans made long before his crazy idea of marrying her, and which she couldn't really trust to anyone else.

Or that she didn't want to.

"Hey, Andi." A voice through the door made her jump. Not Jake's voice. Livia's. "Want me to take over for you so you can spend the day with His Majesty?"

"Not at all. I have everything covered." She hurried to the door and pulled it open, glad she'd painted on her usual business face. "I'll run through the guest list and make sure plans are in place to receive all the dignitaries arriving today. If you could check the menus and make any adjustments based on availability, I'd appreciate that."

A smile pulled at Livia's mouth. "You don't have to do all this stuff anymore, you know."

"This is the biggest occasion in Ruthenia's history—since independence, anyway, and I intend to pull my weight." And keep as busy and as far away from Jake as possible.

"I can handle it." Livia crossed her arms.

"I'm sure you have plenty of other things to handle." Would Livia offer to handle Jake, as well? Andi felt sure she'd be happy to take charge of his very personal needs, if requested. A twinge of jealousy tweaked her. "I have some phone calls to make."

She spent the day running from her office to the various meeting rooms and dining rooms, making last-minute changes to travel schedules and setting up tours of the local area for the visitors. Around lunchtime, visitors started to trickle in, arriving in their diplomatic cars and in hired limos, and she welcomed them to the palace.

Of course she welcomed them as Jake's fiancée, and the congratulations rang painfully in her ears as guest after guest remarked on how happy they were for the royal couple.

Jake looked rather pleased and proud, but then maybe he always looked like that. Twice he managed to slide his arm around her in situations where it would have been embarrassing to resist. Once in front of the French ambassador, and another time while greeting the Taiwanese cultural attaché. She cursed the way her skin hummed and sizzled under his touch, even through her tailored suit.

The big ring glittered on her finger, like a sign saying, Property of the Palace.

But Jake didn't own her. She hadn't agreed to marry him, simply to stay until after the celebrations.

At least that's what she tried to tell herself.

Feelings of foreboding and guilt, that she'd let down the

entire country as well as Jake, gathered in her chest like a storm. Could she really leave?

If it meant escaping a lifetime of heartache, yes.

Ten

This was it, his last chance. Jake eyed Andi from the far end of the long table, over the sparkling crystal and polished plates of the state dinner. Tomorrow was Independence Day and he could feel in his gut that he still hadn't convinced her to stay.

Why was she so stubborn?

She knew how many women would give a limb to be in her position, but she didn't seem to value the role of queen at all. Andi wasn't interested in wearing inherited diamonds or dressing up in silk and lace. She didn't care about dining with international luminaries or being called Your Majesty. She cared about people, regardless of whether they were important or not.

All of which only made him like her more.

And then there was that face. Curious and intelligent, with that active mouth and slightly upturned nose. Those sharp blue eyes that never missed anything.

And her slim but strong body, which beckoned him from beneath her fitted golden dress. Tonight he would claim her and sleep with her in his arms, assured that she'd never leave him.

He danced with her three times—heat crackling through his veins—while the jazz quartet played in the ballroom. In between, while dancing with other women, he barely took his eyes off her.

"I'm afraid Andi and I must retire," he announced, after the shortest decent amount of time. He didn't want to give her a chance to escape. "We've got a big day tomorrow, so I'm sure you'll excuse us."

He strode toward her and took her arm, then swept her out of the ballroom. She stiffened once they exited the soft lighting and sensual music, and entered the gilt-trimmed hallway.

"I'm exhausted," she murmured, avoiding his gaze.

"No, you're not." Not yet. He slid his hand along her back and saw the way her nipples peaked under the fine silk of her gown. A flush spread from her cheeks to her neck.

Desire flashed through him at this fresh confirmation that she wanted him as badly as he wanted her.

And he was going to make sure neither of them was disappointed.

"You're coming with me." He tightened his arm around her waist and marched her along the hallway.

"You can't make me." She whispered while her flushed cheeks and dark, dilated pupils argued with her words.

"I'm not going to make you do anything." Her hand felt hot in his, and desire whipped around them, distinct and intoxicating. It had been building all day. All week. For the past six years—though he'd been too wrapped up in business to notice it until now.

He opened the door to his suite and tugged her inside.

Then closed and locked it. Her mouth opened in protest, lips red, and he kissed her words away.

She struggled slightly—a token resistance he'd expected—before she softened and her arms closed around him as he knew they would. Once again he felt her fingertips press into the muscle of his back—claiming him—and he grew hard as steel against her.

Andi's soft body felt like a balm to his aching soul. Her mouth tasted like honey and sunshine, and her skin was warm and soothing. His fingers roamed into the silk of her hair and down over her gentle curves.

She writhed, and a gentle sigh slid from her lips as he cupped her breast. He could feel the connection between them, invisible and powerful, and he knew she could feel it, too, when she let down her resistance.

Her dress came off easily, via a simple zipper concealed behind a row of false buttons. Pleasure rippled through his muscles as the luxurious fabric pulled away, revealing soft lace and even softer skin.

Groaning, he settled her onto the bed and pressed a line of kisses over her chin and neck, then down between her breasts and over her belly, which twitched as he roamed lower, burying his face in the lace of her panties.

He felt her fingertips in his hair and heard her low moan as he sucked her through the delicate fabric and enjoyed the heat of her arousal. Her legs wrapped around his shoulders, pulling him closer into her and he licked her to a state of silky wetness before slipping the delicate lingerie down over her smooth thighs.

"You're so beautiful." He murmured the words as his eyes feasted on her lush nakedness. All wide, blue-eyed innocence, her gaze met his for a second before she reached for him and pulled him over her, kissing him with ferocity that snatched his breath and tightened his muscles.

Struggling together they removed his formal suit, baring his hot skin. Aroused almost to the point of insanity after these past days of torture, he couldn't wait to be inside her.

And the feeling was mutual. Andi raised her hips, welcoming him as she breathed hot kisses over his face and neck. Sinking into her again was the best feeling he'd ever had. He guided them into a shared rhythm that made Andi gasp and moan with pleasure.

He wanted Andi at his side—and in his bed—for the rest of his life. She was perfect for him in every way. Brilliant, beautiful, sensual and loyal.

He eased them into another position that deepened the connection between them and made beads of delicious perspiration break out on Andi's brow. Her breathing was ragged and her lips formed an ecstatic smile. Pleasure swelled in both of them, thickening and deepening and growing into something new—their future together—as they moved together, clinging to each other with fevered desperation.

Jake held his climax off for as long as he could, until Andi's cries reached a pitch of pleasured anguish that sent him over the edge. They collapsed onto the bed together, panting and laughing, then relaxed into a sleepy embrace.

A sense of deep contentment settled over him, along with the languid desire unfurled in his limbs. Emotions he couldn't name flickered through him and illuminated his visions of the happy future they'd share, as he drifted off to a peaceful sleep.

Andi watched Jake's chest rise and fall, while silver beams of moonlight caressed his skin through a crack in the curtains. Her heart swelled with painful sensation.

It had been so easy. She'd told him she was tired and that

she wanted to go to bed. Did he care? No. He had his own agenda and her needs were irrelevant.

He also knew she never had a prayer of resisting him. How could one person have so much power over her? He'd ruled her life for six years. Six years during which the joy of being with Jake was mingled readily with the sorrow of knowing their relationship was strictly business.

Now he'd followed through on his promise to seduce her into his bed. He'd driven her half mad with sensation—just because he could—and now he slept like a newborn, without an ounce of recrimination.

If only life could be that simple for her.

He didn't care if she loved him or not. That didn't matter to him one bit. He needed a wife and she was a promising candidate with a good résumé. Tried and tested, even, in more ways than one.

Jake probably didn't want to love anyone. Emotions were complicated and messy, and he wouldn't like anyone else having that kind of power over him. No doubt he preferred to keep things clearheaded and businesslike.

At least for one more day, she could manage to do the same. She couldn't bear to think ahead any further than that right now.

The next morning, Andi helped Jake host a palace breakfast for nearly fifty guests. Then they rode through the town in an open carriage with a procession of schoolchildren in front and the town's marching band behind them. Flags waved from windows and hands and the whole country seemed alive with enthusiasm and energy.

At one point Jake slid his hand into hers and warmth flared in Andi's chest at the affectionate gesture. But she turned to look at him and he was waving out the window with the other hand. No doubt the romantic gesture was just intended to look picturesque to the gathered crowds.

Her heart ached that she wanted so much more than a relationship put on for show.

Back at the palace a feast filled long tables on the patio outside the ballroom. She had her work cut out for her chatting with female guests—each of whom congratulated her on her engagement and wished her every happiness.

Are you happy? she wanted to ask each of them. Did these elegant women in their designer clothes enjoy close and loving relationships with their important husbands? Or were they content to follow along and smile, enjoying the gourmet food and expensive shoes that came with the job?

She envied the few women who were there in their own right as ambassadors or dignitaries of sorts. In charge of their own destinys and not dependent on anyone.

Whenever she glimpsed Jake, he looked right at home amidst the glamorous crowd, smiling and talking and laughing—in his element.

By midafternoon Andi felt exhausted. Last night's late-night shenanigans hadn't helped. As servants cleared the coffee cups and the guests wandered out onto the lawn, she slipped back into the palace for a moment's breather.

"Hey, Your Majesty." Livia's voice startled her as she hurried along the corridor. "Playing hooky?"

"Getting something from my room." She just wanted to be alone.

"Don't you have servants for that?" Livia's brown eyes twinkled with mischief as she caught up with Andi and followed close by her.

"I'm used to doing things for myself."

"It must be hard to make the leap from PA to princess. Though I think I could manage it." She crossed her arms.

"Shame Jake didn't notice me first. Still, maybe it's not too late." She raised a brow. "I don't imagine kings usually stick to one woman for the rest of their lives."

"Have you lost your mind?" Andi's temper finally snapped. She ran up the stairs, hoping Livia would not follow.

Livia laughed, climbing right behind her. "Oh, dear. We have turned into a princess, haven't we? I'm just saying what I've observed. It must be difficult watching your fiancé dance with other women almost every night. It takes a special person to put up with that, I'd imagine."

"It's just part of his job."

"And I suppose that putting up with it is part of yours." Livia followed her down the hallway to her own door. "Oh, dear, will I get fired for speaking my mind?"

Her voice grated on Andi's nerves. "Quite possibly."

"You must feel pretty powerful right now."

Not in the least. She wanted to cry. If she was just Jake's assistant she'd have had no difficulty issuing Livia some task, then talking later to Jake about how she wasn't working out. Now, somehow, everything seemed more loaded.

More personal.

"Don't you have a job to do?" Andi turned to her. "There's a big event going on and you should be running it."

"You should be attending it, so I guess we're both skiving off. I'm leaving anyway. Off to New York." She grinned and crossed her arms.

Curiosity goaded Andi. "You have a job there?"

"You'd know all about it. It's the one I told you about that you tried to steal from me. I guess it's lucky for both of us that I tripped you on those stairs in your silly dress."

"What?" Shock washed over her. "Is that when I hit my head?"

"Oh, did I just say that out loud?" She shook her head, making her red curls dance. "Must be loopy from packing. Certainly was lucky, though! I'd have said 'have a nice trip' if I'd known I was sending you into King Jake's affectionate arms. I saw you dancing around like a loon and him coming to your rescue."

Andi stared at her. "I think you should leave right this minute before I tell someone you tried to hurt me."

Livia just laughed. "I couldn't agree more. I'm looking forward to leaving this sleepy backwater and getting back to the big city. Ah, freedom!"

Anger flashed through Andi as Livia waltzed away. None of this would have happened if it wasn't for her interfering jealousy!

She couldn't help being jealous of Livia, now. If Andi married Jake she'd never get to live in New York again. Never be mistress of her own destiny again, with plans and hopes and dreams that could change on a whim.

She'd have duties. Responsibilities. She'd have to be loyal and faithful, serving Ruthenia and Jake until the end of her days.

While Jake danced and flirted and chatted with other women, day after day, night after night.

At least Livia wouldn't be around to taunt her anymore.

In the bathroom she splashed water on her face. She looked pale and haunted, so she slapped on a bit of her familiar blush. But even that couldn't pick up her spirits right now, though. She'd been in the public eye all day, and even though Jake was right there at her side for much of the time, it felt as if they were a thousand miles apart—her craving affection and love, and him needing a royal spouse to put on for ceremonial occasions, much like his sash and scepter.

Last night's intimacy didn't make things better. The closeness they'd shared for those brief hours seemed so distant now, like it wasn't real at all. The memory of his embrace still made her heart beat faster, which only made it hurt more that he didn't love her.

Were her suitcases still here under the bed? Sudden curiosity prompted her to look. They were. She'd only committed to stay through the end of today. After that she could pack her things—again—and get back on the track she'd planned before Jake derailed her for his own professional needs.

A wife by Independence Day. That's all he'd needed. If she wasn't around, he might well have asked Livia. It probably didn't matter all that much to him as long as she did her job.

Still, she did have a job to do for today. She dabbed on a little of her favorite scent, hoping it would lift her spirits. Didn't work.

Lying in his arms last night had been so bittersweet. A dream come true, but with the knowledge that it was just a dream. He'd slept with her to win her over to his side, much as he'd done while her memory was gone.

Any pleasure she'd enjoyed withered away when she remembered that.

She dabbed a bit of powder on her nose—it suddenly looked red—and steeled herself to go back downstairs again. She'd pushed herself through enough long and tiring events over the past six years; she could manage one more, even if her heart was breaking.

"Where's your fiancée?" Maxi sidled up to Jake as a waiter refilled his champagne glass.

"Andi's around somewhere. It's a big crowd." Where was she? He'd been so wrapped up in their guests he'd only glimpsed her a couple of times through the crowd. Still, they'd spent a full hour together this morning being dragged through the town in the ceremonial carriage. Andi had been quiet, which was fine with him. He liked that she didn't have to chatter on all the time like some women. He hadn't stopped thinking about her all day, wanting to see her smile, her frown, hear her laugh and even her scolding. She was becoming an obsession.

"Daddy has a proposition for you."

"Oh?" Jake sipped his freshly filled glass.

Maxi nattered on about some proposed factory project in the eastern hills. He was used to listening with one side of his brain and making the right noises, while using the other side of his brain to plan ahead.

Tonight he needed to let Andi know how much she meant to him. He'd told her with his body, but Andi was a pragmatist and he knew she'd want to hear it in words.

I love you.

The truth rang through him like the old church bell tolling in the distance. Maybe he'd known it all along but not realized it until right now. The reality of it left him stunned and filled with a powerful sense of joy.

He loved her and he had to let her know that.

"What?"

He didn't realize he'd said the words aloud until he looked into Maxi's startled face. Her lipstick-painted mouth stretched into a wide smirk. "Thank you, Jake, I'm touched."

He schooled his face into a neutral expression. "Don't take it personally." He raised a brow. "I'm talking about the development project." He must be losing it. Andi had cracked open some tender new part of him that didn't quite know how to act. He was so used to being all business all the time that it was hard to switch off that part of him and just be.

Andi certainly didn't have trouble reining her emotions in. She acted as if she was trying to decide whether to accept a promotion or not. It stung that she had no personal feelings for him at all. He could be alarmed that one slender woman had such a strong hold over him—instead he just wanted to kiss her again.

Andi stood there for a moment, incredulous. A cold, empty space opened up inside her. If Jake loved Maxi, why didn't he just marry her?

She stepped backward, shrinking back into the crowd before Maxi noticed her. Jake couldn't love Maxi, could he? She was insufferably arrogant and annoying—he'd said so himself. Unless he was just trying to throw her off the scent.

Maybe he didn't really love Maxi but just said that to her to keep her favor now that he intended to marry someone else. Maybe he was going around telling every girl in Ruthenia that he loved them and if only he didn't need a wife who can type and file efficiently…

Her mind boggled.

Jake was a master manipulator; that was how he accomplished so much and managed to get so many people on his side. Now he was masterminding his marriage, and his relationships with every beauty in the nation, with the easy grace she'd always admired.

Except that now she was its victim. So easy to seduce. Such a quiet and willing accomplice. Ready to sacrifice her life in his service.

Except that she had no intention of making that sacrifice.

She'd tell him why she was leaving, and give him a chance to reply, but nothing he said could now change her decision to get away before she signed up for a lifetime of heartache.

She made it through the grand afternoon tea and an enormous dinner. She barely saw Jake at all, so the hardest part was accepting the continued stream of congratulations on her engagement. She wanted to tell them, "I'm not marrying him!" but she didn't. Too well trained in royal decorum for that.

No. She waited until the last guests had left or gone to bed and she was alone with Jake. She let him lead her to his suite, steeling herself against the false reassurance of his hand around hers or his warm smiles.

Once inside she closed the door. "Independence Day is over, and I'm leaving."

Jake's expression turned dark. "You can't be serious."

"I am, and I'll tell you why." She straightened her shoulders and dared herself to look him right in the eye. He might have power over her, but she was stronger. "You don't love me."

"I do. I love you. I've been meaning to tell you." His expression was the same as always, bright and good-humored. Like none of this really mattered.

"But you forgot?" She forced a laugh, though inside she was crumbling to pieces. "You have been busy, of course. I overheard you telling Maxi you loved her. Perhaps you got us confused for a moment."

Jake smiled. "That's exactly what happened. I said it to you in my mind and it came out of my mouth in front of Maxi."

"You must really think I'm a total idiot." Anger snapped through her at his ludicrous response. "I know I've been pretty gullible, believing that we're engaged when we're not, and going along with your oh-so-convenient plan to get engaged in time for the big day, but it's all stopping right here."

"Andi, be sensible. It's been a long day."

"I'm tired of being sensible. I've been sensible to the point of madness lately, smiling at strangers while they congratulate me on an engagement I fully intend to break off. It's enough to drive almost anyone stark mad."

"I do love you." Jake's dark eyes fixed on hers and the intense look in them almost made her weaken.

Almost, but not quite.

"No you don't!" Her voice rose. "I don't think you even know what love is. All your relationships are carefully orchestrated for maximum effect. You stage manage us just like the seating plans at your dinners, swapping and changing people to curry favor when needed."

"I'm not trying to curry favor with you."

"Obviously not. I was seated as far as possible from you all day." She enjoyed the retort. "Maybe royal couples are supposed to be kept apart so they don't get tired of each other."

"You know that's just convention. You and I already have a close, intimate relationship."

"No, we don't." She cursed the way his words made her chest swell. "Just because you've seduced me into bed does not mean we're intimate. You think you can fix everything with sex. If you pleasure me in bed then somehow it will turn into a love that isn't there. It doesn't work like that. True intimacy is based on trust, and I don't trust you."

He stared at her, the good humor draining from his face. "I know I broke your trust. I promise you I'll never do anything to lose it again."

"Once lost, trust cannot be regained. Whether you love Maxi or not, I really don't care, but either way, I can't trust you and I won't live my life with someone when I don't know if I can believe what they say. It's too late."

Just the fact that she could even suspect him of carrying on with another woman made marriage to him a recipe for disaster.

"I want a normal life that isn't under any spotlights. I'd like to marry an ordinary man who doesn't have glamorous women kissing up to him all day." Did she? She couldn't imagine being involved with anyone after having her heart pummeled by this whole experience. She needed to get out of here before she burst into embarrassing tears.

"I've told you I love you." His features hardened and his eyes narrowed. Silence hung in the room for an agonizing moment. "I've given you ample proof that I care about you and think you're the perfect wife, yet you persist in wanting to leave. Leave then." His gaze pierced right through her. "I won't hold you here."

Andi swallowed. Now he was dismissing her.

Isn't that what she wanted? She'd already told him there was no chance. "I can't be the perfect wife for a man who really just wants a permanent assistant."

"Naturally." He seemed to look down on her along the length of his aristocratic nose. His eyes flashed dark fire. "I don't want you to marry me against your will."

"Good, because I don't think that would be right for either of us." Was she trying to convince him, or herself? "It's important to marry someone you care about. Someone you love." Her voice cracked on the word love.

Once she'd have thought she had enough love in her for Jake to sustain both of them, but lately she'd learned different. She couldn't stand by as the faithful wife while he continued to flirt with and cajole other women, even if it was just for "business" reasons. Not if she didn't know that alone, in bed, he was all hers, heart and soul.

She needed a man she'd believe when he said, "I love you."

"Goodbye, Jake." Her whispered words hovered in the night air of his dimly lit room. She pulled the big engagement ring from her finger and left it on the table.

He didn't respond. Obviously she was worth nothing to him now that she'd scuppered his neat plans. No more protestations of love, or even of how useful their union would be to Ruthenia.

Nothing but his icy glare.

Andi let herself out of the room and hurried along the corridor, grim sensations of regret trickling over her like cold water. She half hoped—and feared—that she'd hear the door open and sense Jake's powerful stride covering the carpet after her.

But nothing disturbed the small, nighttime noises of the palace.

She had to leave right now, even though there were no trains until morning. She didn't want to see him ever again.

Tears streamed down her face as she shoved her clothes back into her two suitcases for the second time in a week. How had she let herself get sucked into such an insane situation? Something about Jake Mondragon undermined all her good sense and left her gasping and starry-eyed. She'd already spent years hoping he'd suddenly fall madly in love with her, which was no doubt why his ridiculous and unsuitable engagement idea had been so easy to put over on her.

Her face heated at the thought of how happy she'd been back when she had no idea that their whole engagement wasn't genuine. He'd smiled at her and kissed her and held her like they were madly in love, knowing all along that the whole thing was a lie.

How humiliating.

She threw her hairbrush into her suitcase with a pleasant thud. Almost done with the packing. Her clothes would be really crumpled now after being shoved in so haphazardly, but she could iron them out again.

Shame she couldn't do that with her heart. She suspected it would be crushed and creased for a long time. Possibly forever.

There was still one thing hanging in the closet. The long, floaty pale dress she'd been wearing the night she lost her memory. She let out a long breath as she remembered why she had it on. She'd brought it with her to Ruthenia thinking she'd need something smart and beautiful to wear at parties now that her boss was a king. She'd chosen it after much giggling deliberation with a girlfriend, because it made her feel like Cinderella at the ball.

She'd never worn it before that night. Since she was staff, she didn't actually attend the parties. A crisp black suit had proved to be the most suitable evening attire as she hovered around the edges of the festivities, making sure everything was running smoothly and attending to Jake's every need. Her Cinderella fantasies had remained locked in the closet, just like the dress.

She'd taken it out that one night, just to see what it would feel like to wear it. The whole palace was wrapped up in the party happening in the dining room and ballroom, so no one noticed when she walked down the stairs, tiptoeing carefully in the silver sandals she'd bought to match the dress and never worn before.

She'd walked to one of the narrow casement windows and looked out. Pale moonlight glanced off the mountains in the distance and bathed the green valley in its soft glow. She'd grown to love the rugged countryside and its fiercely independent and engaging people. The palace and its nearby town were her home now, after three years. Leaving felt like stepping out of her own life and into a big, scary unknown.

Inspired by her pretty dress, she'd wanted to take one last walk around the grounds in the moonlight, just to let her imagination run free and think about what might have been before she left for the last time. The weather was surprisingly warm for so early in the spring and the soft grass, silver with dew, begged her to walk across it.

She'd crossed the wide terrace and taken off her sandals, not wanting to get the soft leather wet or have the heels sink into the lawn. Had Livia really tripped her? That's when her memory stopped. Sometimes the steps were slippery, the stone worn smooth by the passage of feet over two hundred or more years since they were built. She could see them from her window right now.

But she would never walk down them again. No detours this time. She had to get out of here and away from Jake.

She'd since worn far more fabulous and expensive dresses, tailored right on her body by Ruthenia's finest seamstresses, and she knew that they felt like the world's stiffest armor as she moved through her ceremonial duties next to a man who didn't love her.

She turned and scanned the room to see if she'd missed anything.

Her belongings had fit so neatly into her two bags, almost as if they'd just been waiting to pack up and go. Her heart sank at the sight of her empty dressing table, the gaping closet with its almost vacant hangers. Soon someone else would live in the room, and she'd never see it again.

Now all she had to do was get out of here without being seen. She couldn't bear to explain the situation to anyone. They'd be so shocked and disappointed. Disgusted even, at how she wouldn't slot into Jake's plans for the good of the nation.

Guilt snaked through her heart, or maybe it was just grief at what she was leaving behind. The memory of Jake's face—hard and angry—would stay with her forever. She shivered and turned to pick up her bags.

Even though it was well after midnight, she'd need to sneak down the back stairs. The cleaners sometimes worked late into the night, especially after a major event. If she could make her way to the rear entrance without being seen, she could cut across the gardens to the old barnyard and take one of the runabout cars kept near the old stables for staff to share on errands.

She grabbed the handle of each bag and set off, pulse pounding. No looking back this time. The pretty dress could stay right there in the closet, along with all her romantic fantasies. They'd caused her nothing but pain.

From magical fairy-tale engagement to shocking scandal overnight. She'd have to keep her head down for, oh, the rest of her life.

She let herself into the old staircase, dimly lit by aging sconces, and hurried down the steep, winding steps, bags thumping unsteadily behind her like chasing ogres no matter how high she tried to life them.

She held her breath as she opened the heavy wood door at the bottom. It led out into the back kitchen, which was rarely used, only if they were catering a truly enormous feast—like the one today. Freshly scrubbed pots and baking trays covered the sideboard and big bowls of fruit stood on the scrubbed table ready to be sliced for breakfast, but the lights were low and she couldn't see anyone about.

Lowering her bags onto their wheels, she crept across the flagstone floor.

One the far side of the old kitchen, she could see the

door that led directly out into the kitchen garden. Before she took a step into the room, a burst of laughter made her jump. She froze, heart pounding, peering into the shadows. Voices reached her from the next room, the passage to the modern kitchen. She didn't recognize them, but the palace often hired extra caterers for big events. Were they already up, making breakfast?

She shrank back into the stairwell, but after an anxious minute, no one had appeared, so they obviously hadn't heard her. Bags lifted by her straining biceps, she crept across the floor. She lowered her bags for a moment and tried the handle—old, but well-oiled, the door slid quietly open, and cool night air rushed in.

She drew in a breath, then stepped out and closed the door quietly behind her. The click of the latch struck an ominous chord in her chest. She'd left the palace forever. She should feel happy that she'd escaped the building without being seen. Instead, she felt like a thief, leaving with stolen goods.

Which was ridiculous. She'd given years of her life to this place. Was that why it hurt so much to leave? And she wasn't gone yet. She still had to get across the grounds and past the sentries at the gatehouse.

She scanned the walled garden—a gloomy well of shadows in the cloudy moonlight—then hefted her bags past the menacing dark rectangles of the large herb beds. An arched doorway on the far side led to the stable yard, where the staff cars were parked. The ancient door creaked on its hinges as she pulled it open, and she shot a glance behind her. A lightbulb flicked on in one of the upper windows, and she held her breath for a moment. Was it Jake's window? Would he come look for her?

She cursed herself when she realized that it was on the upper, staff-only floor. Why would Jake come looking for her? He'd told her to get lost. Which was exactly what she'd wanted.

Wasn't it?

Heaviness lodged in her chest as she crept across the paved stable yard. She retrieved a key from the combination-locked box in the wall—they'd be sure to change the code tomorrow—climbed into the nearest car and started the engine.

Andi glanced up at the house to see if anyone would look outside, but no one did. Cars did come and go at all hours when the house was full of guests and there were meals to prepare. She didn't turn the lights on right away.

A sharp pang of regret shot through her as she pulled onto the wide gravel drive for the last time. A ribbon of silver in the moonlight, it led through an allée of tall trees. It was hard to believe she'd never see this beautiful place again. She certainly wouldn't be welcome back for return visits.

And she'd never see Jake again. She should be happy about that, considering what he'd done, but all the years they'd spent working side by side—and that she'd spent mooning over him and hoping for more—weighed on her mind. He was a good man at heart and she didn't wish him ill.

Don't think about him.

There was still one more gauntlet to run—the gatehouse. The guards didn't usually pay too much attention to cars leaving the palace, especially familiar staff cars, so she hoped they'd simply wave her through. She cringed, though, when she saw a uniformed figure emerge from the stone gatehouse and approach.

She cleared her throat and rolled down the window. "Hi, Eli, it's only me. Picking up a friend." The lie was the first thing that sprang to mind.

Eli simply smiled and gave her a little salute. She raised her window and drove out the palace gates for the last time, blinking back tears. In the morning, Eli and everyone else would know she'd run off into the night.

The town was deserted as she drove through it. She parked on a quiet street so she could walk the last stretch to the station. No need to advertise where she'd gone, since it would probably be hours until the first train of the morning. The staff cars were all identical Mercedes wagons and easily recognizable, and she didn't want to be too easy to find.

Not that anyone would come looking for her. She left the keys in the glove compartment. Petty crime was almost nonexistent in the town as everyone knew each other too well.

She groped in her bag for dark sunglasses. No need for strangers to see her red and puffy eyes. She wrapped a blue scarf around her head and neck. It wasn't cold but she didn't want anyone to recognize her if she could help it.

All she had to do was wait for the early-morning train to Munich, then book a flight to New York.

Her original plan had been to head to Manhattan and stay at the 92nd Street Y and temp until she could find an apartment and a job. She'd even had that promising interview set up. So, there'd been a hitch in her plans, involving all her lifelong dreams coming true and then turning into a nightmare, but she'd just have to get back on track and start rebuilding her life.

She glanced up and down the dark empty street before hurrying past the old stone buildings toward the ornate nineteenth-century train station at the edge of town.

She'd intended to leave Jake behind, and now she was doing it.

So why did it still hurt so much?

Eleven

Jake paced back and forth in his bedroom, anger and pain firing his muscles into action. His wounded pride sparked fury inside him. He'd been mad enough to lose his heart to a woman, and now she flung it back in his face.

No one had ever treated him so coldly. He'd offered her his life and she'd turned him down. He should despise her for being so heartless and cruel.

So why did the thought of facing even one day without her make his whole body ache?

He'd have to announce to the whole country—to the world—that their engagement was over. People would wonder why she left and gossip would echo around the villages for months.

But he didn't care about any of that. It was the prospect of nights without Andi's soft body in his bed. Of days lacking her bright smile. Long evenings without her thoughtful conversation.

He couldn't force her to marry him against her will. Lord knows he'd come close enough by thrusting this whole engagement on her when she was indisposed by her lack of memory.

Shame trickled over him that he'd taken advantage of her so readily. She'd been so willing—in her lack of knowledge about their true past—and it had been so wonderful. A natural extension of their happy working relationship.

Idiot. Having sex with your assistant had nothing to do with work. Why had he tried to convince himself it was okay? If he really wanted to marry her he should have waited until she got her memory back, courted her like a gentleman—or at least a conventional boyfriend—then proposed to her.

Maybe he thought that as a king he was so special he didn't have to follow any of the conventions of romantic love? He certainly put a lot of energy into following other conventions, so why had he veered so badly off course with Andi?

He halted his pacing at the window. He'd been keeping an eye out for lights from a car traveling up the driveway, but had seen none. She was probably still here in the palace.

But she'd already rejected him and it was too late to change her mind. She needed a man she could trust, and in taking advantage of her amnesia, he'd given her good reason to never trust him again.

He'd given up a lot to take on his role as king of Ruthenia. Now he'd just have to learn how to live without Andi, as well.

Andi flinched as the ticket agent looked at her. She'd removed her dark glasses because, well, it was still dark outside. But there was no flicker of recognition in his eyes.

Without extravagant jewels and fancy dresses she just slipped right back into the regular population.

As the platform filled with people waiting for the first train, she shrank inside her raincoat, raising the collar. The occasional stare made her want to hide behind a column. Soon enough they'd all know who she was and what she was doing.

She climbed onto the train without incident. Had she thought Jake would send the cavalry after her? The Ruthenian hills were notably free of galloping horsemen and the roads almost empty of cars as the train pulled away from the town at 7:43 a.m.

Perhaps he was secretly relieved to see her go. He could blame her for breaking off the engagement and carry on with his merry life as an eligible royal bachelor, with gorgeous women kissing up to him at every opportunity.

Her heart still ached with jealousy at the thought of Jake with another woman. Which was totally ridiculous since she'd just rejected him.

The train picked up speed outside the town and flew through the open fields and villages with their tall steeples, clustered at the foot of the proud mountains. She'd never even heard of Ruthenia until she met Jake, but it had come to feel like home and she was going to miss it.

She pulled a book from her bag, but the words blurred before her eyes and she couldn't concentrate. Tears threatened and she pushed them back. Was she making a terrible mistake? Would Jake have grown to love her?

She'd never know now, but it was too late to turn back.

It was midmorning by the time she reached the border crossing between Ruthenia and Austria. She held her breath while the border guards walked through the train checking passports.

The young, clear-faced guard looked at her passport, then pulled out his phone. He spoke rapidly in German and made a sign to another guard on the platform. The two elderly ladies seated on the bench opposite her glanced at each other. Andi felt her heart rate rise.

"I don't have anything to declare." She gestured to her two suitcases. "You can look through them.

"Will we be moving soon?" Her voice sounded shaky. Sitting here made her feel anxious, like she wanted to get up and run. Was Jake behind this? She cursed the pinch of hope that jangled her nerves.

Unlikely. She'd never seen him look so furious as he did last night. If only she could make that memory go away.

Jake's car swerved on a gravel patch in the road and he righted it quickly, coming around another of those hairpin turns on the mountainside. He probably should have taken the train, like Andi. It was the most direct route as it cut right through one of the larger mountains.

But he didn't want anything to hold him up. He also didn't want other people around. This was between him and Andi.

His pride still hurt at her forthright rejection, but something inside him couldn't let her leave like this. She'd said she didn't trust him, and that hurt more than anything. He'd broken her trust. He'd tried to keep her at his side using seduction and bargaining.

When he told her he loved her, she simply didn't believe him.

She thought his declaration was just more words. She didn't understand that his feelings for her had transformed him.

Swinging around another tight corner, he felt a twinge of guilt about using the border guards to hold the train.

Another aspect of royal privilege he'd abused. Still, it was an emergency situation. Once she got back to the U.S., she'd be gone from his world, and he knew in his heart that he'd never get her back.

Then he'd spend the rest of his life missing her and kicking himself for losing the only woman he wanted.

He drove through the Dark Forest at warp speed, adrenaline crackling through his muscles, and emerged into the open plain on the other side just before noon. He'd had to stop on the way for one simple, but important, errand. This time he intended to get everything right.

He spotted the long train at the border crossing from quite a distance away. Luckily the road ran almost directly across the tracks near the village, so he pulled onto the verge and jumped out. Bright morning sun shone off the dark blue-and-gold surface of the cars and turned each window into a mirror. Which car was Andi in? And would she even talk to him after how he'd behaved at their last meeting? Every cell in his body, every nerve pulsed with the desperate need to see her and make things right.

The train was an old one, with individual compartments seating about six people each. The first three he peered into contained no familiar face, but in the fourth, opposite two older women in wool berets, sat a pale-faced and anxious-looking Andi.

He grasped the cool handle and inhaled. She looked up as he pushed the door open and he heard her gasp.

"I can't live without you, Andi."

He hadn't planned what to say. He'd done too much planning lately. "I really do love you." He prayed that the truth would ring through in words that now sounded hollow from overuse. "I didn't realize it myself. I've never known love before. I was raised to think with my head and not my heart. I spent so much time convincing myself I wanted to marry you because it was a sensible decision, because our marriage would be good for Ruthenia. The truth is that now my desire to keep you has nothing to do with Ruthenia. I want you for myself and I can't imagine spending the rest of my life without you."

Tears welled in her eyes for a moment and his heart clutched.

The two women opposite her suddenly rose, grabbing their carryalls, and hurried toward the door where he stood. "Please excuse us," one puttered in Ruthenian. He'd forgotten they were there. He stood aside to let them pass, eyes fixed on Andi.

She hadn't moved an inch, but color rose to her pale cheeks.

Hope flared in his chest. "I admit that our engagement began for the wrong reasons. I'm ashamed about that." Guilt stung him. "All I knew was that I enjoyed your company, and that once I kissed you…" He blew out a breath. "Once I kissed you, nothing was ever the same again."

He saw her swallow, fighting back tears that made her blue eyes glisten.

He ached to take her in his arms and kiss away her tears. The few inches between them seemed an agonizing gulf. "I need you, Andi."

Her lips didn't flinch. Her silence hurt him, but she hadn't told him to go. There was still hope.

He reached into his pocket and drew out the item he'd picked up on the way here. The simple ring, the one she'd chosen in the shop that morning.

He knelt on the floor of the train car and pulled the ring from the box. "Andi, I know this is the ring you wanted. I made you get the other one because it was showier. I realize I was making decisions for you and trying to turn you into someone you don't want to be. I'd like to go right back to the beginning and start over."

She hesitated for a moment, eyes fixed on the ring.

His heart clenched. She'd already told him that she didn't want to be his wife. She didn't want a life of royal duty and an existence in the public eye. But that wasn't all he offered. How could he make her see that despite all the trappings of royalty, he was just a man? A man who loved and needed her with every fiber of his being.

"Andi, right now I wish I wasn't a king." It took effort to stop his hands from reaching out to her. "That I could promise you an ordinary life, in a comfortable house in some American suburb, where our children could attend the local school and play in Little League. The truth is I can't. I'm already married to Ruthenia and that's my destiny. I can't turn away from it any more than I could turn back the river flowing through the mountains."

He saw her throat move as she swallowed. Her hands shifted slightly, clutching at each other through her black gloves. How he longed to take them in his own hands.

"But I need you, too, Andi. Not because you can help me run the country or the palace, but because you're the woman I want to share my life with. That I need to share my life with."

Emotion flickered across her lovely face and made hope spark inside him. "I do love you, Andi. I love you with all my heart and soul, with parts of me that I never knew existed. I tried to ignore the new tender feelings starting inside me because they scared me. It was easier to talk myself into using practical reasons to keep you. To convince myself I was still in full control of my emotions, that I didn't truly need you, or anyone else." He drew in a ragged breath. "But I do need you."

He paused, emotions streaming through his brain and

mind. How hard it was to put into words things that he could only understand at gut level. "I didn't know until now that I've been living a half life, devoid of emotion and even of true joy. In your arms I've found happiness I never knew existed."

He blinked, embarrassed by his frank confession. "I know you no longer believe me when I tell you I love you." He shook his head. "I don't blame you. Those words have lost their power. They've been used too many times. I don't know how to express what I truly feel except to say that my life is empty and hollow without you. Please don't leave me, Andi."

Andi blinked, eyelashes thick with tears. The raw emotion in his voice stunned her. He was always so calm, so controlled, so in charge of every situation. Right now she could sense that every word he said was true.

No guile, no charm, no winning ways—just a heartfelt plea that shook her to her core.

She hadn't dared to utter a single word until now, and when she opened her mouth, the painful truth emerged. "I love you, Jake. I've always loved you." Why hide anything now? "I've loved you almost since the first day I came to work for you. You're kind and fair and thoughtful, and tough and strong when you need to be. I've admired you every day and dreamed about you every night."

Putting her thoughts into words took effort, but it was a relief to finally get them off her chest. "So you see, when my memories—and the resulting inhibitions—were erased, I fell so easily into the kind of relationship I've always dreamed of. I'm sure it was frightening to know that someone you've worked so closely with for years had those kind of feelings."

She shivered slightly. "I didn't want you to ever find out.

That's one of the main reasons I wanted to leave. It was all wrong from the start."

"But it's not wrong." Jake kept his gaze fixed on hers. "I was wrong to take advantage of you, but we're meant to be together. I don't want a ceremonial wife *or* an assistant. I want someone who'll remind me I've never been up the mountain, and who'll take me there. I don't want someone who'll take good minutes on my life, I want someone to live it with me and make it fuller and richer than I ever imagined."

Unable to hold still any longer, Andi reached out to him and clasped his hands. He was still holding the ring, the pretty, simple diamond she'd liked, and the fact that he'd brought it touched her deeply. "I was already cursing myself for leaving you—and Ruthenia. I felt like I was leaving a big chunk of my heart behind." She hesitated and drew in a breath. "I don't want to leave you behind."

"Then don't. I'll come with you. Ruthenia can get along without me for a while." He rose from the floor and sat on the seat beside her. "We should visit your parents. It seems only right that I should ask them for your hand in marriage." A twinkle of humor brightened his eyes. "And maybe I'll have better luck with them."

He held up the ring between finger and thumb. "Though it would be nice to put this ring somewhere safe, like your finger, so it doesn't get lost while we're traveling."

The ring blurred as Andi's eyes filled with tears. She pulled off her gloves and held out her bare hands, which trembled. "I will marry you, Jake." Her voice cracked and a violent shudder rocked her as the cool metal slid over her finger. The act felt far more powerful and meaningful than the first time, when she didn't even know who she was. "I do want to spend the rest of my life with you."

Now that Jake had poured out his feelings, everything

felt different. She no longer had any doubt that he loved her as much as she loved him. Sun poured in through the large railcar window, and the world outside seemed bright with promise. "I love the idea of going to see my family. They'll be thrilled to meet you. If this train ever gets moving again, that is."

Jake grinned. "Let's see what we can do about that. But, first things first." He slid his arm around her back and pulled her close. Andi's eyes slid shut as their lips met and she kissed him with all the pent-up passion and emotion she'd planned to lock away for the rest of her life. Relief and joy flooded through her and her heart exploded with happiness at the feel of his strong arms around her. When they finally pulled apart, blinking in the sun, she had a strange sensation of her life starting afresh from this moment.

"I love you, Jake." At last she could say it out loud without a hint of embarrassment or doubt. She'd waited years for this moment and it was sweeter than she'd ever dreamed.

"Not as much as I love you." Jake's eyes sparkled.

"You're so competitive."

"So are you." He grinned. "One more reason why we're perfect for each other." Then he pulled out his phone. "Now, let's see if we can get this train moving."

Epilogue

"Of course you need an assistant." Jake leaned in and kissed Andi's neck.

Piles of envelopes and résumés covered her desk. The prospect of going through them seemed more than daunting. "But we already have a full staff. And three nannies."

"You need someone just for you." He eased his thumbs down her spine. "So you can come up with a crazy plan for the weekend, and put her to work making it happen while you and I go for a stroll on the mountain."

"That's too decadent."

"It's an important part of any monarch's job to be decadent."

Andi laughed. "Says who?"

"The paparazzi. They don't want to cover a bunch of dull worker bees."

"True." She giggled. "They did have fun taking those ridiculous shots of me sailing when I was eight months pregnant."

"See? You're helping people earn their livelihood. And what about the tourists? They want glamour and excitement, romance and majesty, not a queen who licks her own envelopes."

"I can think of better things to lick." She raised a brow.

"Now that you put it that way, I think I'll cancel this afternoon's meeting on foreign policy."

"Don't you dare." She shot him a fierce glare. "Just save your energy for later." She stroked a finger over his strong hand, where it rested on her desk.

"Have I ever run out of energy?" He growled the question in her ear.

"Never. Now I know where our son gets it from." Little Lucas was a tireless eighteen-month-old bundle of energy. They'd managed with just two nannies until he learned to walk; after that, three—plus Andi—were required to keep up with him.

A joyful shriek outside the door alerted her that his morning nap must be over. Jake dodged to the side as little Lucas barreled into the room, blond curls bouncing. "Mama, read me a story!"

"Of course, sweetie."

"See? You need an assistant so you have someone to read through all these résumés for you while you read Lucas a story." Jake chuckled.

"You're hired." She winked and gathered Lucas into her arms. "Lucas and I have an appointment with Thomas the Tank Engine."

"And James the Red Engine." Lucas's serious face reminded her so much of Jake's sometimes, despite the pudgy dimpled cheeks.

"This sounds like a very important meeting. Perhaps I should attend, too."

"Most definitely. Foreign policy can wait. Tell them

Ruthenia just wants to be friends with everyone." Andi swept Lucas up in her arms as she stood.

"A very sensible approach. We'll just have a big party with cupcakes and tell everyone to play nicely." Jake squeezed Lucas's little hand.

"Chocolate cupcakes, 'kay, Daddy?"

"Hmm. Not sure. We might have to put a committee together to discuss the finer details."

"How 'bout rainbow sprinkles?" Lucas's bright blue eyes stared at his dad.

"If rainbow sprinkles are involved I'll just have to issue an executive order."

Lucas clapped his chubby hands together.

Andi shrugged. "I do like to be surrounded by men who can make important decisions without a lot of fuss. Really takes the pressure off. Where's the book?"

Lucas pointed at his nanny Claire, who stood in the doorway with a stack of paperbacks and a freshly made snack on a plate.

"Let's head for the garden." Andi moved to the door. "Claire, can you call ahead and have some blankets spread on the lawn? And maybe bring out Lucas's trike and stick horse." She tickled under his chin and he giggled. Then she glanced up at Jake. "See? I am getting better at not doing everything myself."

"Your efforts are admirable. And much needed since you'll soon be in the third trimester and Lucas isn't getting lighter." He picked his son up and held him in his arms. Lucas clapped both chubby palms against his cheeks and laughed aloud. "What if his sister has as much energy as he does?"

"Then we'll need six nannies. If we keep having kids there will be zero unemployment in Ruthenia."

Lucas arched his back, signaling his desire to be free on

his fast-moving feet. Jake put him gently down and they both watched as Lucas tore off down the corridor with Claire running after him. "How do people manage a toddler without a nanny while they're pregnant?" Already she could get a little short of breath climbing stairs without carrying anyone.

"I don't know. I always had a nanny." He winked.

"It's amazingly easy to get used to being spoiled rotten. Where's my dish of peeled grapes?"

They both laughed. They knew they worked hard, for much longer hours than most people. Andi had come to enjoy the routine round of entertaining. It felt good to bring people into their home and make them feel welcome. As the host she took special pleasure in making sure everyone had a good time, quite different than when she simply had to make sure the events ran smoothly.

Her parents had fallen in love with both Ruthenia and Jake. With her father newly retired and her mom only working during the school year, they'd allowed Jake and Andi to give them a quaint house right in the town as a "vacation home," insisting they wanted to visit regularly without being on top of the couple.

Andi's sister and her husband flew in for the wedding, and their little daughter was a flower girl in the majestic old town church where they said their vows. They now also came to visit regularly, and the sound of little Lucy's childish laughter bouncing off the palace walls had urged Andi and Jake into parenthood.

Since Lucas was born the palace no longer felt like a place of business where people slept, but was fully a family home, where people also worked.

The difference was subtle, but transformative. Jake slid his arms around her waist. "Would you like me to carry you downstairs, Your Majesty?"

"That won't be necessary." She wriggled against him, enjoying the flash of heat that always sparked between them when they touched. "But you can kiss me."

His lips met hers and her eyes slid closed. She could always lose herself in his kiss. She'd dreamed of it so long and come so close to never tasting him again. Her fingers played over the muscle of his chest through his tailored shirt.

She pulled back, lips humming with desire. "Hold that thought. I have a story to read and you have to bring about peace in our time. I'll see you tonight."

"And every night." His soft glance was loaded with suggestion.

She glanced down at her hand, where the simple diamond ring she'd first chosen sparkled behind her engraved wedding band. A smile crept over her mouth. "For the rest of our lives."

* * * * *

She [illegible] another [illegible] Suddenly [illegible] in his [illegible] and [illegible] her.

* * *

THE PRINCESS AND THE OUTLAW

LEANNE BANKS

This is dedicated to the family members and friends who hang in there for the long haul when a loved one is terminally ill. May the special people in your life who have passed on continue to inspire you, make you laugh, make you wise and make you love forever…

Prologue

"What is *he* doing here?"

Phillipa was wondering the same thing. At her sister Bridget's gasp, her other sister, Tina, leaned toward Bridget. "Zach says he's a huge contributor here. Everyone loves him," Tina said distastefully.

"They clearly don't know him," Bridget said and nudged Phillipa. "Why can't we escape him?" she whispered. "Maybe it's because he's the devil and that means he can be everywhere at once."

At that moment, Phillipa almost agreed with Bridget. Nic certainly seemed to have some kind of dark power over her.

Phillipa had tried to slow things down with Nic Lafitte, but persuading the man to move at anything other than warp speed had proven impossible. He was a force of nature with a will that rivaled every kind of powerful destructive weather. Typhoons and tornadoes had nothing on him. She'd successfully avoided him for the past three weeks and she had been certain that fleeing her home country of Chantaine to visit her sisters in Texas would buy her even more time.

Who would have ever thought she would be caught staring at him at a charity social ball in Texas as he accepted an award for philanthropy? Phillipa knew that Nic had ties to Texas, but with his extensive business dealings, he had ties to many places.

The ballroom suddenly felt as if it was shrinking. Panic squeezed her chest. She had to get out. She had to catch her breath. Feeling her sister's curious gaze, she swallowed hard over the lump in her throat. "I'm not feeling well," she said. "Please excuse me."

When Bridget offered to come with her, Phillipa had to remain firm. "I'll be back in a little bit."

Sticking to the perimeter of the room as she fled, she kept her head down, hoping she wasn't drawing attention to herself. If she could just get out of this room, she would be fine, she told herself. Out of the room and away from Nic. Away from how he affected her.

She stepped out of the ballroom and held the door so it would catch softly as it closed, then took a few more steps away and leaned against the wall, which felt cool against her skin. Her sisters hadn't been exaggerating when they'd told her Texas summers were hell.

Phillipa took several deep breaths, willing her heart and mind to calm. How had she gotten herself into this? Why? Among her siblings, she'd done her best to maintain a low profile. As number five out of six strong personalities, it hadn't been that difficult. Her oldest brother, Stefan, had been born and bred to rule—everyone except his siblings anyway. Phillipa had found refuge in academia. It was much easier pleasing a few professors than being a princess and constantly making public appearances and dealing with the media. By nature, she'd always been an introvert. She'd never enjoyed crowded gatherings, hated posing for photographs and had little patience for all the effort it seemed to take to make her presentable.

When her first two sisters began to focus on their new husbands instead of royal duties, Phillipa had plunged herself into graduate studies to avoid being in the public eye. Her sister Bridget had seen through her plan and it had clearly irritated her, although Bridget had bucked up and done a fantastic job. The trouble now was that Bridget was determined to get a break and she had earned it. Phillipa cringed at the prospect of all the public appearances she would be forced to make.

"I'll be damned," a familiar male voice said, making her eyes pop open. "If it isn't the missing Her Highness Phillipa of Chantaine."

Phillipa stared into the dark gaze of Nic Lafitte and her lungs seemed to completely shut down. "I didn't know you would be here."

His mouth twisted in a half smile. "Why doesn't that surprise me?" he asked and slipped his hand around her arm. "Lucky for both of us that I am. We have unfinished business. You're coming with me. I can have my car delivered in seconds."

Her heart pounded. "I can't. My sisters expect me back for the rest of the event. They'll call the authorities if I go missing," she said.

"It wouldn't be the first time your family has tried

to get me in trouble with the law." He glanced around and tugged her down the hallway. "If you won't leave with me, then I'll take my moment somewhere else."

"Where are you taking me?" she asked. "This is crazy. I need to go back to my table. I need—" She broke off as he pushed open the door to a room marked Coat Closet and dragged her inside.

He pulled her to the back of the small room and gently, but firmly gripped her shoulders. "Tell me what you really need, Pippa. What do you really want?" he asked her in that dark, sexy voice that made her feel as if she were turning upside down.

A half-dozen images from the stolen moments they'd shared shot through her brain. The time they'd gone swimming at night. The afternoon she'd spent on his yacht. The walk they'd taken on the opposite side of the island when she'd learned so much about him and he'd made it so easy for her to talk about herself. Despite the bad blood between her family and his, Phillipa had never felt so drawn to another man in her life.

He lowered his head, holding her gaze until his mouth took hers. His kiss set off a riot of reaction and emotion inside her. He made her feel alive and out of control. She pulled back and whispered. "This is insane. It will never work. That's what I tried to tell you before."

"Why not?" he challenged her. Nic was always challenging her. Sometimes gently, sometimes with more strength. "If I want you and you want me, what is most important?"

Pippa bit her lip and struggled to remain rational. Members of her family had caused a lot of trouble by giving in to their emotions. She didn't want the same kind of trouble. "Want is a temporary emotion. There are more important things than temporary emotions."

"If that's true, why did you kiss me back? Why are you here with me right now?"

Pippa heard a gasp from the doorway and terror rushed through her. "Someone is here," she said. "We've got to get out of here," she said, stumbling toward the door. Nic helped to steady her as they stepped outside the closet.

Her sisters Bridget and Tina greeted them with furious disapproval stamped on their faces. Pippa inwardly cringed.

"Get away from my sister," Bridget said.

"That's for her to say, not you," Nic said.

"You're just using her," Tina said. "You only want her because she can redeem your terrible family name."

"Not everyone finds my family name reprehensible. Some even respect it," he said.

"That's respect you've bought with money," Tina said. "Leave Phillipa alone. You can never be good enough for her. If you have any compassion, you'll at least protect her reputation by leaving now."

Nic tightened his jaw. "I'll leave, but Phillipa will make the ultimate decision about the future of our relationship." He glanced behind him and met Phillipa's shocked, pale face. "*Ciao,* darling. Call me when you get some courage. Some things are meant to be," he said and strode away.

Chapter One

Seven Months Later

She'd started running for exercise. That was what Pippa told her security detail anyway. She knew the truth. She was running from memories. Memories and the possibility that there was only one man for her and he was the one man she couldn't have.

"Stop it," she told herself, staring at the empty beach in front of her. Azure waves dappled onto white sands. By noon, there would be quite a few more bodies enjoying the beach. At six in the morning, however, she was the only one around. She debated turning on some music via her smartphone. She usually welcomed the noise, hoping it would drown out some of her thoughts. Today, she was searching for a little peace. Maybe the sound of the waves would help, she thought, and started out.

One foot in front of the other, she ran for two minutes, then walked for three. It was called interval training and the different paces suited her. Pippa had never been athletic. From the time she'd learned to read, she'd always been happiest with her nose stuck in a book. Her nanny had been relieved because her brothers and most of her sisters had been more demanding in one way or another.

Running again, she inhaled the scent of the salt air. The humidity was low today and she could feel the moisture on her skin begin to evaporate. Slowing after three minutes of running, she took a swig of her water and trudged onward.

Along the shore, in the distance, she spotted a long figure walking. She would wave and be friendly. Pippa was a royal and Chantaine royals were not allowed to be snooty. Other runners might be able to put their blinders and zip past everyone in their path, but not a Devereaux.

As she drew closer, she saw that the figure was that of a woman. Short white hair crowned her head, and a sundress that resembled a nightgown covered her petite frame.

Pippa nodded. "Good morning," she said.

The woman looked away and stumbled.

Curious, Pippa vacillated as to whether to approach her. Perhaps she was longing for solitude just as Pippa was. The woman stumbled again and Pippa felt a twist of concern. She walked toward the woman. "Pardon me, may I help you?"

The woman shook her head. "No, no. I'm fine. It's so beautiful here," she said in a lilting voice that contrasted with the lines on her face and the frailness of her frame.

Something about her seemed familiar, but Pippa

couldn't quite identify it. The woman stumbled again, and Pippa's concern grew. Was she ill?

"Yes, the beach is lovely. Are you sure I can't help you? I could walk you back to where you started," she said. "Or perhaps you would like some water."

The woman's face crumpled. "No, no. Please don't make me go back. Please don't—" She broke off and collapsed right in front of Pippa.

Alarm shot through her. "Oh, my God!" she exclaimed and bent over the woman. This was *one* time when she would have loved to have had her security detail close by. Pippa put her arms around the woman and lifted her, surprised by her light weight. Glancing around, she pulled her toward a small stand of palm trees.

Frantic, she held the woman and gently shook her. "Please. Miss. Please." She spilled water from her bottle onto one of her hands and gently patted the woman's face. "Please wake up. Please."

Terrified that the woman was dying, she reached for her cell phone. The woman clearly needed emergency medical attention. Just as she put her finger over the speed dial for her security, the woman blinked her eyes. Huge and full of emotion, her eyes captivated Pippa.

She held her breath. "Are you all right? Please take a few sips of my water. It's clearly too hot out here for you. I'll call for help and—"

"No," the woman said with a strength that surprised Pippa. "Please don't do that." Then the woman closed her amazing, mesermizing eyes and began to sob.

The sound wrenched at Pippa. "You must let me help you."

"There's only one thing I want," she said and met Pippa's gaze again. "I just want to die in Chantaine."

Pippa gasped. Then a lightning flash of realization rocked through her. She looked at the woman and saw the resemblance of Nic in her eyes. His bone structure was a stronger, more masculine version, but his eyes were all Amelie. "Amelie," she whispered. "You're Amelie Lafitte."

The woman reluctantly nodded. "How do you know?"

"I know your son Nic." Pippa also knew that Amelie was in the final stages of cancer. Her time was drawing painfully close.

Amelie looked away. "I just wanted a little walk on the beach. I bet he's quite peeved that I left the yacht."

Peeved wasn't the word that came to Pippa's mind. "I'll call him for you," she said.

"Then all my fun will be over," she said with a cute pout. "He's such a worrywart."

Stunned at how quickly Amelie's spirit had returned, she hesitated a half beat, then dialed his cell. Despite the fact that she'd deleted it from her phone records months ago, every digit was engraved on her brain.

Five minutes later, a black Mercedes came to screeching halt on the curb of the road above the beach. Pippa immediately identified the dark figure exiting the driver's side of the vehicle. Nic. As he strode swiftly toward her and Amelie, she could see the tension in his frame. Seeing him after all these months set off a visceral response inside her. Her stomach clenched. Her heart beat unevenly.

"Hi, darling," Amelie said, remaining seated on the sand under the tree as she sipped Pippa's water. Pippa was still surprised at how quickly the woman had recovered after fainting. "Sorry to be a bother, but I woke up early and I just couldn't resist the chance to go for a walk on the beach."

"I would have been happy to walk with you," Nic said and turned to Pippa. What she wouldn't give to get a peek behind his dark sunglasses. "Thank you for calling me. I'll take her back to the yacht now and you can continue your run. I didn't know you were a runner."

She felt her face heat with self-consciousness. "I'm more of a combination walker and runner."

He nodded and glanced back at his mother. "Dad's beside himself with worry. It was all I could do to keep him from tearing after you."

"Paul can't hobble with crutches let alone tear after me with that broken foot of his. The doctor said it will be ten more weeks before he can put any weight on it at all," she said, then turned her head thoughtfully to the side. "You know what I'm in the mood for? Crepes. There used to be a wonderful café on the edge of town. They made the most delicious crepes."

"Bebe's on Oleander," Pippa said. "It's still there, and Bebe's granddaughter helps makes the crepes."

"Oh," Amelie said, clasping her hands together. "It's still there. We must go. And we can bring one back for Paul." She turned to Pippa. "You must come, too."

Pippa blinked at the invitation and slid a quick helpless glance at Nic.

"Mother, do you know who Pippa is?" he asked as he extended his hand to help her rise to her feet.

Amelie studied her for a long moment and frowned. "She looks a bit familiar. I can't quite." Her eyes widened. "Oh, dear. You're a Devereaux. I can see it in your eyes and your chin. Oh, dear. This could get a bit messy."

"Just a little," Nic said in a wry tone. "But let's give her the choice. Would you like to join us for crepes, Your Highness?"

Pippa heard the hint of goading challenge in Nic's voice. She'd heard it before, but it seemed to hold more of an edge than ever. The truth was she didn't want her photo taken with Nic and his mother. To say it could cause problems was a huge understatement.

"That's okay," he said before she could respond. "Thanks again for looking out for my mother. Ci—"

"I'm coming," Pippa said impulsively. "Unless you're rescinding the invitation," she tossed back at him in her own challenging voice.

He paused a half beat and tilted his head as if she'd taken him off guard. The possibility thrilled her. "Not at all. Would you like to ride with us in my vehicle?"

"Thank you, but no. I'll drive myself and meet you in about fifteen minutes," Pippa said and turned her gaze to Amelie. "I'll see you soon. Please drink some more fluids."

"Thank you, darling. Isn't she delightful?" she said to Nic. "She fusses just like you do."

"Yes," he said in a dry tone. "Delightful."

Fifteen minutes later as Pippa put a ball cap on her head and adjusted her large pair of sunglasses, she wondered if she'd lost her mind agreeing to join Nic and his mother, the notorious Amelie, for crepes. Glancing in the rearview mirror, she could easily imagine the horror on the face of the royal advisers. Running on the beach at 6:00 a.m. in her current state was one thing, but walking into a public place of business was quite another. She thought of Nic's goading attitude and made a face at the mirror. Well, she couldn't back down now. Stepping from her car, she could only hope she wouldn't be recognized.

Because she'd spent far less time in the public eye than her siblings, that was on her side. Her hair, however, was very distinctive and not in a good way. Wavy and brown with a tendency to frizz, she hoped she'd concealed it adequately by pulling it back in a ponytail and covering it with a cap.

She walked into the old but elegant eating establishment that featured every kind of crepe one could imagine. As soon as she stepped inside, she spotted Amelie, who also saw her and lifted her hand in a wave. Nic, sitting opposite Amelia, turned his head around to look at her and also waved. His gaze said he was surprised she'd shown up, which irritated Pippa.

She walked to the booth where Amelia and Nic sat and sank onto the red vinyl seat.

"Lovely that you joined us," Amelie said and smiled as she lifted a menu. "How shall I choose? I want one of everything."

Enchanted, Pippa picked up the menu. The array of choices was vast and mind-boggling. "What are you in the mood for?"

"Something sweet," Amelie said. "Sweet, fruity. Oh, no, chocolate, too." She shrugged helplessly.

The waitress approached. "*Bonjour.* How can I help you? Coffee?"

"Yes," Amelie said. "Café au lait."

"Tea," Pippa said.

"Coffee, black," Nic said. "Ladies, any idea what you want to order?"

"Apricot crepes. Strawberries and cream. Chocolate hazelnut. Banana cream." Amelie paused.

Wondering how the woman could possibly consume that many crepes, she exchanged a quick glance with Nic, who shook his head and rubbed his jaw. She glanced back at Amelie. "Do you want anything with protein?"

"Not particularly," Nic's mother said.

"And you?" Pippa asked Nic.

He shrugged. "I'm here for the ride."

"Can you please also bring us the crepe suzette and some carryout boxes?" Pippa asked the server.

"No problem, ma'am," she said and stared at Pippa for a long moment. "Pardon me, you look familiar."

Pippa fought a sliver of panic and held her breath. *Please don't recognize me.*

"Are you a newscaster?"

Relief rushed through her, making her almost giddy. She shook her head and smiled. "Nope, I'm just a university student. Thanks for the compliment, though."

The server's face was sheepish. "No trouble. I'll have your order up as soon as possible."

"Thank you so very much," Pippa said and after the server left, she felt the gazes of both Nic and Amelie.

Amelie sighed, lifting her shoulders and smiling with a charm that lit up the room and Pippa suddenly realized who the woman resembled. Gamin with super-expressive eyes, Amelie could have been a white-haired twin of Audrey Hepburn. “It’s so wonderful to be here again. Magic. The smell is divine. I should have come back sooner, so I’ll just make up for it today.”

“You don’t want to make yourself sick,” Nic said.

“Of course not. I’ll just take a bite of each, and we can take the rest back to Paul.” Amelie’s smile fell and she made a tsking sound. “Poor Paul. He’s in such pain with his foot.”

She said it as if she suffered no pain herself, but Pippa knew she did. She took a quick glance at Nic and caught the tightening of his jaw. She was struck by Amelie’s determination to grab at every experience in life and Nic’s struggle to hide a myriad of the emotions he was experiencing.

“I’ve heard the recovery from a broken foot can be a bear,” Pippa said.

“Oh, and trust me, Paul is a being a complete bear,” Amelie said. “He doesn’t like being restrained. Never has.” Amelie glanced at Nic. “It runs in the family.” She turned back to Pippa with an expressive, interested gaze. “But enough about us. Tell me about you, your interests, your life. Over the years, I’ve read a few stories in the news about the Devereauxs, and I must confess I wondered about Edward’s children. I’m sure he must have been proud of all of you.”

Pippa paused. The truth was her father hadn’t been very involved with any of his children. He’d given the most attention to her brother Stefan because he would be the heir, but her father was mostly pleased that he had enough children to do the work, so he could spend more time playing on his yacht. Often with women other than his wife.

"I've always been a bit of a bookworm. I'm working on my doctorate in genealogy with a specialization on the medical impact on the citizens of Chantaine. My brother Stefan is determined to improve the health care of our people, so he has approved my path of studies."

"That's fascinating," Amelie said. "What have you learned so far?"

"Like many countries, our people are more susceptible to some diseases and conditions than others. These can be traced back hundreds of years to the introduction of different immigrants, new foods and changes in our environment. The neurological disease that struck down my father can be traced back to his great-great-grandmother's family. There are also certain cancers that became more common such as when Chantaine experienced a large immigration from Iceland."

Amelie gave a slow nod. "I wonder if—" She glanced up and broke off with a smile. "The crepes are here."

Just as she'd said, Amelie only took a bite of each crepe. She savored each bite, closing her eyes and making a *mmm* sound. "I'm tempted to eat more, but I know it would be a mistake." She leaned toward Pippa and extended her hand. "Dear, I must tell you that even though I couldn't marry your father all those years ago, I wished him only the very best after we parted. I hope he was happy."

Pippa tried to think of how to respond to Amelie's words. The story about Edward and Amelie's courtship was the stuff of tabloids. Before he'd taken the throne, Prince Edward had fallen for Amelie and Amelie had been entranced by him for a short while. When she'd met Paul Lafitte, from the States, however, she'd fallen for the tall, dark Texan hook, line and sinker. The Lafittes descended from pirates and even Pippa had to agree the Lafitte men held a dark, irresistible charm.

When Amelie tried to break off her engagement, Prince Edward had refused. Paul had intervened on her behalf and there'd been a terrible brawl. Her father the prince had been humiliated and Pippa wasn't certain he'd ever truly given his heart away again.

"I think he enjoyed his life," Pippa finally said. "He loved his yacht and the sea and we always felt glad that he was able to indulge his passion."

Amelie patted Pippa's hand. "You're a lovely girl. As they say in Texas, you do him proud. Now, if you'll both excuse me while I powder my nose," she said and stood.

Nic also stood. "Need an escort?" he asked.

"Not this time, darling. Maybe you can talk Pippa into nibbling on some of those crepes," she said and walked away.

"Is she okay?" Pippa asked when he sat down.

He shrugged. "For the moment. The next moment could bring something totally different. She knows her time is short and she's decided to make the most of it. The only problem is she's turned into an eight-year-old. Impulsive, runs off without thinking. With my father down due to his broken foot, I've become her keeper."

Pippa swallowed over the knot of emotion in her throat and began to put the crepes in the carryout boxes. "I'm sure it's difficult. On the one hand, you want to give her everything she wants. On the other, you want to keep her safe. It's an impossible situation. She told me," she said, biting her lip, "that she wants to die in Chantaine."

His gaze narrowed. "That's going to be a tough wish to fulfill given the fact that my father isn't allowed to set foot on Chantaine."

Cold realization rushed through her. "I forgot all about that. I can't believe that would be enforced after all these years."

He gave a rough chuckle. "After all these years, your family still hates me. I can't take the chance that your family would lock him up in prison."

"It wouldn't be my family. It's a silly law," she said.

"Same result. It sucks, but Amelie can't have every wish on her bucket list. I'll do my damn best to make sure she gets as many as I can," he said and stood as his mother arrived at the table.

Amelie met his gaze and sighed. "We should leave, shouldn't we?"

He nodded and placed the boxes in a bag.

"Let me look around just one more moment," she said, surveying the room as if she wanted to savor each detail, the same way she'd savored each bite of the crepes. "I've already spoken to Bebe. She's lovely as is her granddaughter. *Ciao,*" she whispered and picked up the bag, then led the way to the door.

A terrible helplessness tore at Pippa as she followed Amelie out the door. She felt Nic's presence behind her and tried to tamp down the painful knot in her chest. Seeing him again had been like ripping off a bandage before the wound was healed. She'd thought the longing she'd felt for him before was awful, but now it was even worse. Knowing that he was facing some of his darkest days and that she shouldn't, couldn't, help him, was untenable. Meeting his magical mother face-to-face and seeing her courage and joy made her feel like a wimp. Her biggest challenge to date was writing her dissertation.

Amelie stopped beside Nic's Mercedes and turned to Pippa. "I hope we meet again, Your Highness. You're the nicest princess I've ever met. I'm sorry I frightened you with my annoying fainting spell. But then you gave me water and helped me remember Bebe's. I certainly came out the winner in this situation."

"I beg to differ," Pippa said. "It was my great pleasure to meet you."

"*Ciao,* darling princess," she said and Nic opened the door for her.

Pippa should have turned away, but she couldn't resist one more look at his face. It was the worst kind of craving imaginable.

He turned and met her gaze for a heart-stopping moment that took her breath away. "*Ciao,* Princess."

Still distracted by her encounter with Nic and his mother after she'd returned to the palace, Pippa started down the hallway to her living quarters. She would need to set the Lafittes' situation aside if she was going to make any progress on her research today, and heaven knows, progress had been very slow coming since she'd made the insane mistake of getting involved with Nic. The problem was that even after she'd broken off with him, he still haunted her so much that she struggled to get her work done.

Just as she turned the corner toward her quarters,

she heard a shrill scream from the other wing. *Tyler,* she thought, easily identifying one her sister's toddler stepsons. He was going through a screaming stage.

"Tyler, darling, you're not dressed," her sister Bridget called, her voice echoing down the marble hallways. "Don't—"

Pippa heard Tyler cackle with glee. She also heard the sound of her sister's heels as she ran after him. Chuckling to herself, she wondered when Bridget would learn that toddlers and high heels didn't go together. She rushed down the hall and turned another corner, spotting Tyler running toward her in all his naked glory. Bridget followed with Travis in her arms.

"Oh, Pippa, you saved my life. Can you grab him? The little beast thinks it's funny to run all over the palace bloody naked."

Tyler shrieked when he saw Pippa and skidded to a stop. Glancing over his shoulder at Bridget bearing down on him, he knew he was caught. Pippa scooped him up in her arms before he had a chance to get away.

"What are you doing? Did you just get a bath?" Pippa asked and buried her nose in his shoulder, making him laugh. "You smell like a deliciously clean little boy."

"Thank you so much," Bridget said breathlessly. "At least I got a diaper on Travis."

As soon as she stepped within touching distance, Tyler flung himself at her. "Mumma," he said and pressed an open mouth kiss against Bridget's cheek.

Bridget squeezed him against her and shifted Travis on her hip. "Now, you get all lovey-dovey," she said and gave him a kiss in return.

"Where are the nannies?" Pippa asked and held out

her hands to Travis. He fell into her arms, then stuck his thumb in his mouth.

"I gave Claire the morning off and Maria had to take care of an emergency with her mother," she said. "I had planned to check on the ranch Ryder and I are having built." Bridget rolled her eyes and laughed. "I never dreamed Stefan would permit a ranch to be built on Chantaine."

"I never would have dreamed you would live on a ranch with twin stepchildren."

"They're not steppies to me," Bridget said. "Ryder and I are in the process of making it all legal. The little perfect, gorgeous beasties will be mine just as much as they are his."

"Would you like me to watch the boys while you go check on the new house?" Pippa offered. Because Chantaine was an island, new construction was a long process and she knew both Bridget and Ryder were eager for their own place.

"I feel like I take advantage of you far too often. I know I'm not helping you get caught up on your studies...."

Pippa felt a sinking sensation in her stomach. Bridget and the boys weren't the real reason she'd had a difficult time focusing on her studies. "It's not as if you'll be gone all day," she said.

"True," Bridget said. "Only an hour or two. You're the perfect sister," Bridget said, leaning forward to give Pippa a kiss on the cheek. "Let's go back to my quarters so I can at least get my little nudist dressed before I leave."

Pippa smiled as she followed Bridget down the hall

and into her family's suite of rooms. "I think it's your outlook that has changed. Since you got married to Ryder, everything's close to perfection."

"That just goes to show the power of having a good man in your life," Bridget said. "As soon as I have more than half a moment, I must get to work on finding one for you."

Alarm shot through Pippa. "Oh, so not necessary. I still have to finish my work for my PhD."

"That won't be forever," Bridget said as she dressed wiggly Tyler.

"I can only hope," Pippa muttered.

"It won't be," Bridget said emphatically. "Besides, you can't wait forever to move on, romantically speaking. I can help with that."

"You seem to forget that our family is dreadful when it comes to matchmaking," Pippa said. "How much did you enjoy Stefan's attempts at matchmaking?"

Bridget waved her hand in a dismissive gesture. "That's different. I won't be trying to match you up with someone who can contribute to Chantaine. I'll find someone hot and entertaining."

"Lovely intentions," Pippa said. "Don't strain yourself. The boys and I will have some fun in the playroom."

"Perfect. If I'm late they can have lunch in an hour."

"Will do," Pippa said. "Are you truly going to have cattle at this ranch?"

"If Ryder has his way," Bridget said with a sigh. "If we have to take the man out of Texas, we'll just bring Texas to him. *Ciao.* I'll be back soon," she said and kissed both of the boys.

As soon as Bridget left, the twin toddlers looked at her with pouty faces. Travis's lower lip protruded and he began to whimper. Tyler joined in.

"Absolutely none of that. She'll be back before you know it." Bridget set both of them on their feet and took them by the hand. "To the playroom," she said and marched them into the small backroom. If there was one thing she'd learned about caring for toddlers, it was that it helped to be willing to make a bloody fool of herself. She immediately turned on the animal sounds CD and followed the instructions to make honking sounds. The boys dried up and joined her.

Just over an hour later, Bridget returned and Pippa could no longer escape her studies. She retreated to her room with a half sandwich for lunch. She thought of the crepes and her stomach clenched. Her mind kept wandering to the time she'd spent with Nic and his mother.

She told herself not to think about it. It wasn't her responsibility. These genealogy charts required her complete and immediate attention. She'd used every possible device to procrastinate doing her work entirely too long. Inputting her second cousin's name to the chart, she forced herself to focus. Whenever she conducted her research on people whom she knew, she often thought about their personal stories. Her second cousin Harold had moved to Tibet and his sister, Georgina, had married a man from England and was raising her children in the countryside. Pippa had always liked Georgina because she'd been such a down-to-earth sort of woman. It was a shame she didn't see her more often.

Harold and Georgina's deceased parents had owned a lovely cottage on the other side of Chantaine that was now left vacant because neither Harold nor Georgina visited Chantaine very often. Why, in fact, Pippa was certain it had been nearly eight years since either of her second cousins had set foot on Chantaine.

Pippa stopped dead, staring at the cursor on her laptop. *Vacant lovely cottage. Nic's parents.*

"Stop it," she hissed to herself. It would be incredibly disloyal. If her brother Stefan ever found out, he would never forgive her. And there was no way he wouldn't find out. Not with her security haunting her. She was lucky she'd escaped discovery today.

Back to work, she told herself sternly and worked past midnight. She finally crawled into bed, hopeful she would fall into deep sleep. Thank goodness, she did. Sometime during the night, she sank into a dream where a black limo crawled through a beautiful cemetery. Cars and people dressed in black but carrying flowers followed the limo. Everything inside her clinched with pain. A white butterfly fluttered over the black limo, capturing her attention. It could have been the spirit of…

Pippa suddenly awakened, disoriented, the images of the limo and the butterfly mingling in her mind. She sat up in bed, her heart slamming into her chest. Images of her brother Stefan, Nic, his mother, Amelie.

This wasn't her business, she told herself. Her heart ached for Nic and his mother, but she couldn't go against her family to make his mother's dream come true. She just couldn't. It wouldn't be right. It would be a terrible betrayal.

She tried to catch her breath and closed her eyes.

She tried to make her brain stop spinning. How could she possibly deceive her family for Nic? For Amelie?

But how could she not?

Chapter Two

It took most of the rest of the day to catch up with her cousin to get permission to use the cottage. Georgina was so gracious that it made Pippa feel guilty. Oh, well, if she was going to go through with providing the cottage for Nic's mother and father, then her web of deception was just getting started. The choice to deceive her family was unforgivable, but the choice to turn her back on Amelie was more unacceptable. Her stomach churned because she wasn't a dishonest person. The prospect of all the lies she would have to tell put a bad taste in her mouth.

She would normally try to reason with Stefan, but Pippa knew her entire family was unreasonable about the Lafitte matter. She would have to learn to push aside her slimy feelings about this and press on. The first task was to call Nic.

* * *

Nic studied the recent reports from his and his father's business on his tablet PC while he drank a glass of Scotch. He took a deep breath of the Mediterranean night air as he sat on the deck of his yacht anchored close enough to shore for his mother to catch a glimpse of her precious Chantaine whenever she liked. He just hoped she didn't do anything impulsive like jump overboard and swim to shore. Rubbing his chin, he shuddered at what a nightmare that would be. He couldn't put it past her, though, especially after she'd sneaked off the other morning.

Nic was caught somewhere between genie and parent, and he wasn't equipped to be either. The reports on both his father's businesses and his own looked okay for the moment, but he knew he would have to go back to the States soon for his father's company. With Amelie's illness, Paul Lafitte had understandably been distracted. Despite the fact that they'd separated on two different occasions, Amelie was the light of Paul's life and Nic wasn't sure how his father would survive after his mother… Nic didn't even want to think the word, let alone say it, even though he knew the time was coming.

Sighing, he took another sip of his Scotch and heard the vibrating buzz of his cell phone. The number on the caller ID surprised him. After his surprise meeting with Princess Pippa the other morning, he figured he'd never see her again except for public affairs.

He picked up the phone and punched the call button. "Nic Lafitte. Your Highness, what a surprise," he said, unable to keep the bite from his voice. Pippa had turned out to be the tease of his life.

"Hello. I hope I'm not interrupting anything," she said, her voice tense with nerves, which made him curious.

"Just a perfect glass of Scotch and rare solitude," he said.

A short silence followed. "Well, pardon the interruption, but I have some news that may be of interest to you."

"You called to tell me you missed me," he said, unable to resist the urge to bother her. During and after their little interlude last year, the woman had bothered the hell out of him.

He heard her sharp intake of breath and realized he'd scored. "I called about your mother."

His pleasure immediately diminished. "What about her? Have you discussed the situation with your family, and now they won't even allow her and my father in the harbor?"

"No, of course not," Pippa said. "If you would just let me finish—"

"Go ahead," he said, the semi-peacefulness of the evening now ruined.

"I found a cottage for your parents where they can stay," she said.

Nic blinked in sudden, silent surprise.

"Nic, did you hear me?"

"Yes. Repeat that please."

"I found a cottage for your parents on Chantaine," she said.

"Why?" he demanded.

Another gap of silence followed. "Um, well, I have these cousins Georgina and Harry and neither of them live in Chantaine anymore. They haven't even visited in years, and they inherited a cottage from their parents. It's been vacant, again for years, so I thought, why not?"

"Exactly," Nic said. "Why not? Except for the fact that my father has been banned from setting foot on Chantaine. I don't suppose your brother experienced a sudden wave of compassion, or just a rational moment and has decided to pardon Paul Lafitte."

"You don't need to insult Stefan," she said. "My brother is just defending my father's honor."

"Even though Stefan wouldn't have been born if your father had married Amelie," Nic said.

"Yes, I know it's not particularly logical, but the point is I have found this house. Your mother wants more time in Chantaine. Staying there can make it happen."

"You still haven't addressed the issue about my father," Nic said.

"Well, I thought we could work around that. Your mother mentioned that he broke his foot, so it's not as if he'll be able to tour much. When he does, perhaps he could wear a hat and glasses."

"And a fake mustache?" he added, rolling his eyes. It was a ludicrous plan.

"I know it's not perfect," she said.

"Far from it," he said.

"But it's better than nothing."

"I can't take the chance that my father will end up in jail."

"Perhaps that's not your decision to make," she countered, surprising him.

"What do you mean by that?"

"I mean shouldn't he be given the choice?" she asked. "Besides, your father's presence may never be discovered. It's not as if there are copies of his photo posted everywhere the way you do in the States."

"It's called a Wanted Poster, and they're mostly just displayed in post offices and convenience stores these days. We've progressed since the Wild West days," he said.

"Exactly," she said. "And so have we. No one has been beheaded in over one hundred and fifty years, and we haven't used the dungeon as a prison for nearly a hundred."

"Why don't I feel better? I know that Chantaine doesn't operate under the policy of innocent until proven guilty. Your judicial system, and I use the term loosely, moves slower than the process of turning coal into diamonds."

"I didn't call to debate my country's judicial system. I called to offer a place to stay for your mother and father. If you want it, I shall arrange to have it cleaned and prepared for them. Otherwise…" She paused and he heard her take a breath.

"Otherwise?" he prompted.

"Otherwise, *ciao,*" she said and hung up on him.

Nic blinked again. Princess Pippa wasn't the rollover he'd thought she was. He downed the rest of his exquisite Scotch, barely tasting it. What the hell. She had surprised him. Now he had to make a decision. Although his father had caused trouble for the entire family, Nic felt protective of him, especially in his father's current state with his broken foot and his grief over Amelie.

Nic closed his eyes and swore under his breath. He

already knew how his father would respond if given the choice of risking prosecution in Chantaine. Paul Lafitte was a blustering bear and bull. He would love the challenge…even if he was in traction and confined to the house.

Raking his hand through his hair, he knew what he had to do. He walked inside to the stateroom lounge where his father dozed in front of the television. A baseball game was playing and his father was propped in an easy chair snoring.

Maybe he should wait until tomorrow, Nic thought and turned off the television.

His father gave a loud snort and his eyes snapped open. "What happened? Who's ahead?"

"Rangers," Nic lied. The Rangers were having a terrible season.

"Yeah, and I'm the Easter bunny," his father said.

Nic gave a dry laugh. His father was selective with the use of denial, and apparently he wasn't going to exercise that muscle with the Rangers tonight. "Good luck hopping," he said. "You need anything to drink?"

"Nah. Take a seat. What's on your mind? I can tell something's going on," he said, waving his hand as if the yacht belonged to him instead of Nic.

Nic sank onto the sofa next to his father. "I got an interesting call tonight."

"Must have been a woman. Was she pregnant?" his father asked.

Nic gave a short laugh. "Nothing like that. I've been offered a cottage where you and Mom can stay. On Chantaine."

His dad gave a low whistle. "How did you manage that?"

Nic shrugged. "Lucky, I guess. The problem is you still have legal issues in Chantaine."

His dad smiled and rubbed his mouth. "So I do, and punching Prince Edward in the face after he insulted your mother was worth it ten times over."

"Easy to say, but if you stay in Chantaine, there's a possibility that you could get caught." Nic shook his head. "Dad, with their legal system, you could be stuck in jail for a while."

"So?" he asked.

"So, it's a risk. You're not the young buck you once were. You could end up stuck there while Mom is…" He didn't want to say the rest.

His father narrowed his eyes. It was an expression Nic had seen several times on his father's face. The dare a pirate couldn't deny. He descended from wily pirates. His father was no different, although his father had gotten caught a few times. "Your mother wants to rest in Chantaine. We'll accept the kind offer of your friend. To hell with the Devereauxs."

"Might not want to go that far," Nic said, thinking another glass of Scotch was in order. "A Devereaux is giving you the cottage."

"Well, now that sounds like quite the story," his father said, his shaggy eyebrows lifted high on his forehead.

"Another time," Nic said. "You need to rest up for your next voyage."

His father gave a mysterious smile. "If my great-

great-grandfather escaped the authorities on a peg leg, I can do it with a cast."

Nic groaned. "No need to push it, Dad."

The next morning, he dialed the princess.

"Hello," she said in a sleep-sexy voice that did weird things to his gut.

"This is Nic. We'll accept your kind offer. Meet me at the cottage and I'll clean it. The less people involved, the better."

Silence followed. "I didn't think of that," she confessed. "I'm accustomed to staff taking oaths of silence."

He smiled at her naïveté. "This is a different game. Too many people need to be protected. You, my mother and father. We need to keep this as quiet and low-profile as possible."

"Okay. I'll meet you at the cottage mid-morning," she said.

"What about your security?" he asked.

"I'll tell them I'm going to the library," she said.

"Won't they follow you?"

"I'll go to the library first. They'll get bored. They always do."

"Who are these idiots on your security detail?" he asked.

"Are you complaining?"

"No," he said. "And yes."

She laughed, and the breathless sound made his chest expand. He suddenly felt lighter. "How do you end up with the light end of the security detail?"

"I'm boring. I don't go clubbing. I've never been on

drugs. I babysit my nieces and nephews. I study genealogy, for bloody's sake."

He nodded, approving her M.O. "Well done, but does that fence ever feel a little too tall for you? Ever want to climb out?"

"I climb out when I want," she said in a cool voice. "I'll see you this afternoon around 1:00 p.m. The address is 307 Sea Breeze. *Ciao,*" she said and hung up before he could reply.

Nic pulled the phone away from his ear and stared at it. He was unaccustomed to having anyone hang up on him, let alone a woman. He must have really gotten under Pippa's skin to affect her manners that way. The possibility brought him pleasure. Again, he liked the idea of *bothering* her.

Just before one, he pulled past the overgrown hedges of the driveway leading to an expansive bungalow. Looked like there was a separate guest bedroom. Dibs, he thought. He could sleep there and keep track of his parents while keeping on top of the businesses.

He stopped his car behind another—Pippa's. He recognized it from the other day. Curious, he stepped from his vehicle and walked to the front door and knocked. He waited. No answer. He knocked again.

No answer again, so he looked at the doorknob and picked the lock. Pirates had their skills. He opened the door and was shocked speechless at the sight in front of him. Pippa, dressed in shorts and a T-shirt with her wild hair pulled back in a ponytail, was vacuuming the den.

The princess had a very nice backside, which he enjoyed watching for a full moment…okay, two.

Pippa turned and spotted him, screaming and dropping the vacuum handle. She clutched her throat with her hands. The appliance made a loud groan of protest.

"Did you consider knocking?" she demanded.

He lifted two fingers, then pulled up the vacuum cleaner handle and turned it off. "Twice. You didn't answer. I would have never dreamed you could be a cleaning fairy. This is a stretch."

"I spent a couple summers in a rustic camp in Norway. Cleaning was compulsory. We also cleaned the homes of several of the camp leaders."

"You didn't mention this to your parents?" he asked.

She laughed. "I didn't speak to my parents very often. I mentioned something about it to my nanny after the second summer and was never sent back after that. The cleaning wasn't that bad. The camp had a fabulous library and no one edited my reading choices. Heaven for me," she said.

"Will clean for books?" he said.

She smiled and met his gaze. "Something like that."

He held her gaze for a long moment and saw the second that her awareness of him hit her. Breaking the visual connection, she cleared her throat. "Well, I should get back to work."

"Anything special you want me to do?"

"Mop the floors if you don't mind. I've already dusted the entire house, but haven't touched the guest quarters outside. I think it would also be a good idea for you to assess the arrangement of the furniture throughout the house for any special needs your parents may have, such as your father's foot problem. We don't want him tripping and prolonging his recovery."

"I don't know. It might be a good thing if my father is immobile. He could cause trouble when he's full strength," Nic said. "He's always been a rebellious, impulsive man. I hate to say it, but he might just take a trip out of the house so he can feel like he's flying in the face of your family."

Pippa winced. "He wouldn't admit his name, would he?"

"I hope not. That's part of the reason I wasn't sure this was a good idea," he said.

"What made you change your mind?"

"You did. My father will be okay if he's reminded that his responsibility is to make this time for my mother as trouble-free as possible. I'll make sure he gets that message in multiple modalities every day."

"Thank you very much," she said.

"If you're so terrified that your family will find out, why did you take this risk for yourself? Your relationship with your brothers and sisters will never be the same if they know you did this."

She took a deep breath and closed her eyes for a half beat as if to bolster her determination. "I hate the idea of disappointing my brothers and sisters. I hate it more than you can imagine, but I wouldn't be able to live with myself if I could help your mother with this one wish if I had the ability. And I have the ability."

"I'll do what I can to make sure the rest of the Devereauxs don't find out. I haven't told my mother yet about the cottage. She's going to be very excited."

Pippa smiled. "I hope so."

"Thanks," he said. "I'll go check out the bedrooms."

An hour later, after Pippa finished vacuuming and tackled the kitchen, she found Nic cleaning the hall bathroom. It was an ironic sight. Hot six-foot-four international businessman scrubbing the tub. Just as he wouldn't expect to find her turn into a cleaning machine, she wouldn't expect the same of him, either. She couldn't help admiring the way his broad shoulders followed the shape of a V to his waist. Even in a T-shirt, the man looked great from behind. Bloody shame for her. *Get your mind out of the gutter.*

He turned around before she had a chance to clear her throat or utter a syllable. She stared at him speechless for a second, fearing he could read her mind. *Not possible,* she told herself as she felt her cheeks heat with embarrassment.

"Can I help you?" he asked.

In too many ways, she thought, but refused to dwell on them. "I'm almost finished with the kitchen, and it occurred to me that it might be a good idea to arrange for some groceries to be picked up for your parents before they arrive."

"Groceries?" he echoed.

"Yes, I was hoping you could help with a list."

He made a face. "I don't do a lot of grocery shopping. My housekeeper takes care of that."

"I have less experience with grocery shopping that I do with cleaning. That's why I thought we could send someone."

"Who can we trust?" he asked.

She winced. "Excellent point."

"After we move them in, I'll just arrange for a member of my staff from the yacht to take care of house and shopping duties," he said. "But unless we want to delay their move-in, it looks like we'll need to do the initial run ourselves."

"We?" she squeaked.

"I didn't think it would be nice to ask you to do it by yourself," he said.

But it had clearly crossed his mind. She frowned.

"Will that put you a little close for comfort to the plebeians?"

"No," she told him, detesting the superior challenging expression on his face. "I was just trying to remember if I'd left my cap in my vehicle."

"I have an extra," he said. "I'll take you in my car."

"What about the list?"

"We'll wing it," he said.

Moments later, she grabbed her cap from her car and perched her oversize sunglasses on her nose. She didn't bother to look at her reflection. After spending the afternoon cleaning, she knew she didn't look like anyone's idea of a princess. Nic opened the passenger door for her and she slid into his car.

After he climbed into the driver's side, the space inside his Mercedes seemed to shrink. She inhaled to compensate for the way her lungs seemed to narrow at Nic's proximity, but only succeeded in drawing in a draft of the combination of his masculine scent and subtle but sexy cologne. He pulled out of the driveway.

"Which way to the nearest market?" he asked.

Pippa blinked. She had no idea.

"Here," he said, handing her his phone. "Find one on my smartphone."

It took a couple moments, and Nic had to backtrack, but they were moving in the right direction.

"I'm thinking eggs, milk, bread and perhaps some fruit," she said, associating each item with one of her fingers. It was a memory trick she'd taught herself when she was young. The only problem was when she ran out of fingers.

"Chocolate, cookies and wine," Nic added. "A bakery cake if we can find it. My mother's priority for eating healthy went down the tubes after her last appointment with the doctor. My dad will want booze and carbs. His idea of health food is a pork roast with a loaded baked potato."

"Oh, my," she said, trying to wrap her head around Nic's list versus hers. "I hope we can find—"

"They'll be happy with whatever we get for the first twenty-four hours," Nic said as he pulled into the parking lot. "Let's just do this fast," he added and pulled on a ball cap of his own. "The faster we move, the less chance you have of being discovered."

"I think I'm well-disguised," she said as he opened the door and helped her out of the car.

"Until you open your mouth," he said.

"What do you mean by that?"

He led her toward the door of the market. "I mean you have a refined, distinctive voice, PD. A combination of husky sweet and so proper you could have been in Regency England."

"PD," she echoed, then realized PD stood for Pippa Devereaux. "Well, at least I *look* ordinary," she huffed.

He stopped beside her. "And I don't," he said, tugging on his ball cap.

She allowed herself a forbidden moment of looking at him from head to toe. He could have been dressed in rags and he would be sexy. She swallowed an oath. "You don't know the meaning of ordinary," she said and walked in front of him.

Hearing Nic grab a cart behind her, she moved toward the produce. "Surely, they'd enjoy some fruit. Your mother seemed to favor fruit crepes the other day."

"They were wrapped in sugar," he said as she picked up a bunch of bananas and studied them. "In the basket," he instructed. "We have a need for speed, PD."

"I'm not sure I like being called PD," she said, fighting a scowl as she put the bananas in the cart.

He pressed his mouth against her ear. "Would you prefer PP instead? For Princess Pippa?"

A shiver of awareness raced through her and she quickly stepped away. "Not at all," she said and picked up an apricot. "Does this look ripe?"

"It's perfect," he said, swiping it from her hand and added two more to the cart. "Now, move along."

She shot him an affronted look but began to walk. "No one except my brothers or sisters would dream of speaking to me that way."

"One of my many charms, PD," he said and tossed a loaf of bread into the cart.

Moments later, after throwing several items into the cart, they arrived at the register. Pippa picked up a bag of marshmallows.

"Good job," he said.

"I thought they could make that camping dessert you Americans eat," Pippa said. She'd read about it in a book.

"Camping treat?" he echoed.

"Some More of something," she said.

His eyes widened. "S'mores," he said. "We need chocolate bars and graham crackers. Get him to hold you," he said and strode away.

"Hold me?" she said at the unfamiliar expression and caught the cashier studying her. He was several years younger than she was with rings and piercing in places that made her think *ouch.*

He leaned toward her. "If you need holding, I can help you after I finish my shift," he said in a low voice.

Embarrassment flooded through her. She was rarely in a position for a man to flirt with her. Her brother usually set her up with men at least twenty years older, who wouldn't dare make an improper advance, so she wasn't experienced with giving a proper response. "The grocery order," she finally managed. "I was repeating what my, uh, friend said. He misspoke, as he often does. The grocery order need holding."

The cashier looked disappointed. "The customer behind you is ready."

Pippa considered pulling royal rank, but knew it would only hurt her in the end, so she stepped aside and allowed the person behind her with a mammoth order go first.

Less than a moment later, Nic appeared with chocolate bars and graham crackers. He glanced at the person in front of her and frowned. "How did that happen? I told you to hold the cashier."

"There was a mix-up and he thought I wanted, uh, him for reasons other than his professional duties. When I refused his kind invitation, he felt spurned and allowed the customer behind me to proceed." She sighed. "Do all men have such delicate egos?"

Nic lifted a dark brow before he pulled his sunglasses over his eyes. “Depends on how many mixed messages we get. Poor guy.”

Chapter Three

"Are you sure you want to read to Stephenia tonight?" Eve Jackson Devereaux, the wife to the crown prince of Chantaine, asked in her Texas twang as she walked with Pippa to her stepdaughter's room inside the royal master suite. "You look a little tired."

"I wouldn't dream of missing it. You and Stefan enjoy a few extra moments this evening. You deserve it."

"You are a dream sister," Eve said.

Pippa felt her heart squeeze at how Eve left off at the in-law. "As are you," she said and studied her sister-in-law. "You look like you could use a long night's rest yourself."

Eve frowned and pressed her hands to her cheeks. "Oh, no. Maybe I need one of those spa boosts Bridget is always talking about."

"Or just rest," Pippa said. "You may be Texan, but you're not superhuman."

Eve laughed. "If you say so. I didn't want to ask, but I have a routine medical appointment tomorrow. Can you backup for the nanny?"

It wasn't convenient, but Eve so rarely asked that she couldn't refuse. "No problem. You're sure it's just routine?" she asked.

Eve smiled. "Nothing else. Thank you. I knew I could count on you. But Stefan and I were talking the other night and we both realized how much you do for all the nieces and nephews. You're due some happy times of your own and we're going to work on that."

"Work?" Pippa echoed, fighting a sliver of panic. She definitely did not want to become the object of her family's attention. Especially now. "How?"

Eve shot her a sly look that frightened her. "You'll find out soon enough."

"There's no need to work that hard," Pippa said. "I'm busy with my dissertation and—"

"Don't worry. Just enjoy," Eve said.

"Right," Pippa said nervously. "Don't work too hard."

Eve opened the door to Stephenia's room where the three-year-old sat playing with her toys. "Steffie, I thought you wanted Pippa to read to you tonight. You're not in bed."

Stephenia immediately crawled into bed with an innocent expression on her face, her ringlet curls bouncing against her flushed cheeks. "I'm in bed," she said in her tiny voice, which never failed to make Pippa's heart twist.

Eve tossed a sideways glance at Pippa and whispered, "She's such a heart stealer. We're so screwed."

Pippa laughed under her breath. "Thank goodness Stefan has you. I'm lucky. She'll fall asleep by the time I finish the second book."

"Or first," Eve said in a low voice. "She's been a Tazmanian devil today. I have to believe she's spent some of her energy."

Stephenia lifted her arms. "Mamaeve."

Pippa knew Eve had felt reluctant to take on the name of Stephenia's mother even though the woman had perished in a boating accident. Out of respect, Eve had taught the child *Mamaeve.* Eve rushed toward the child and enveloped her in a loving hug.

"Daddy?" Stephenia asked.

"In the shower," Eve said. "He'll kiss you good-night, but you may already be asleep."

Steffie sighed and gave Eve an extra hug. The sight was heartwarming to Pippa because she'd mostly been raised by hired nannies. She knew it could have been much worse, but it gave her such relief to know that her nieces and nephews would have such a different life than she'd experienced.

"Pippa," Stephenia said, extending her arms, and it occurred to Pippa that she would fight an army to get to her niece.

"I'll let you two go to *Where the Wild Things Are,*" Eve said, backing toward the door and giving a little wave. "Sweet dreams."

"Good night," Pippa said.

"'Night Mamaeve."

Eve smiled and left the room closing the door behind her.

Pippa sank onto Stephenia's twin bed and pulled the child against her. *Where the Wild Things Are* was especially appropriate for Stephenia because the child had been such a bloody screamer when she'd first arrived at the palace. Stephenia was the product of a relationship between her brother Stefan and a model who'd never bothered to tell Stefan about his child. He'd only learned about Stephenia after the mother's death. It had been a shock to the family and the country of Chantaine, but everyone had taken Stephenia into their hearts. How could they not? She had Stefan's eyes and spirit and she was beautiful.

Pippa began to read the book and before she was halfway through, Stephenia was slumped against her, sleeping. She felt the warmth of sleepy drool on her shirt underneath the child's face. Pippa chuckled to herself and carefully situated Stephenia onto the bed. She brushed a kiss onto her niece's head and slid out of the bed, leaving the book on the nightstand. Pippa turned off the light and kissed Stephenia once more, then quietly left the room.

As she walked down the hall, she wondered, not for the first time, if or when she would have children of her own. Pippa knew she'd been shielded from normal relationships with the opposite sex. Every date, and there'd been few, had to be vetted by Stefan, the advisers and of course, security. The only relationship she'd had that approached normality had been her brief *thing* with Nic. She supposed she couldn't really call it an affair because they hadn't done the deed, but Nic hadn't bowed to her unless he'd been joking. He'd treated her like a desirable woman. Pippa couldn't remember another time when she'd felt genuinely desirable.

She rolled her eyes at herself as she entered her small suite. She had far more important things to do than worry about feeling desirable. Thinking back to what Eve had said about how she and Stefan were planning to work on her happiness, she cringed. This was *not* the time.

Nic moved his parents into the cottage. The activity exhausted both of them, so they were taking naps, his mom using her oxygen. She'd begun to use it every night. Nic had adjusted the bed so that her head would be elevated. Many days his mother hid her illness well, but lately he could tell she'd had a harder time of it. She resisted taking too much pain medication, complaining that it made her sleepy. Amelie was determined to get every drop of life she could, and she was giving Nic a few lessons he hadn't expected along the way.

He'd brought over a few members of his crew to clean the pool and jacuzzi and get them operational as soon as possible. He dug into the labor with his men, hoping that expending physical energy would help relieve some of his frustration. Even though he mentally knew that he couldn't make his mother well, he had a bunch of crazy feelings that he spent a lot of effort denying. It was important that he continue that denial because his parents sure as hell had enough on their own plates without his crap.

As he cleaned the side of the pool wall with a brush, he spotted Pippa coming through the gate carrying a bag. She was wearing a skirt that fluttered around her knees and a lacy cotton blouse. As usual, her wild hair was pulled into a topknot. He'd always thought her hair was a sign that she wasn't nearly as proper as she seemed. He knew she considered herself the plainest of the Devereaux sisters, but during that brief period they'd spent time together, he sure had enjoyed making her fair skin blush with embarrassment or pleasure. She was the most sincere and sweetest woman he'd ever met.

Appearing intent on her plan, whatever that was, she walked right past him as if she didn't see him. Just as she lifted her hand to the door to knock, he gave a loud wolf whistle.

His men stopped their work and gaped at him. Pippa stood stock-still, then lifted her hand again to knock.

"Hey, PD," he called, climbing out of the pool. "What's the rush?"

Hearing his voice, she whirled around to look at him. "I didn't see you." She glanced at the pool. "You were working?" she said as if such a thought was impossible.

"Yes, I pitch in with manual labor every now and then. It's good for the soul, if I have one, and it usually helps me get a good night's sleep." He liked the way her gaze skimmed over his shoulders and chest, then as if she realized, she was looking where she shouldn't, her gaze fastened on his nose. "My parents are both taking naps. They're worn out from the move."

"It's already done," she said. "You move quickly."

"When it's necessary," he said, thinking perhaps he'd given Pippa too much wiggle room all those months ago.

The door suddenly opened and his mother, wiping

sleep from her eyes, blinked at the sunlight. "What—" She broke off when she saw Pippa and her lips lifted in a smile. "Well, hello, fairy princess," she said.

"Mom," Nic said. "Don't use the P word. Remember this is all on the down low."

"Oh, sorry," she said with a delicate wince. "I'm just so grateful and you made it happen with the snap of your fingers."

"My cousins made it easy," Pippa said.

"But you made the call," Nic's mother said. "I must leave them something in my will."

Pippa bit her lip.

"TMI, Mom," Nic said. "What's in the bag?" he asked Pippa.

"Gelato," she said. "I know we got ice cream yesterday, but this is from one of our favorite gelaterias."

"Let me think of the name," his mother said. "It's on the tip of my tongue."

Pippa opened her mouth, then closed it.

His mother's eyes widened. "Henri's."

"Yes," Pippa said, clearly thrilled. "You have a great memory."

"Bet you brought hazelnut chocolate," his mother said.

"Yes, and a new flavor from the States. Rocky Road. It has marshmallows, chocolate and nuts. Worth a try," Pippa said with a shrug.

"I'll say," his mom said. "Let's taste it now or I'll have to fight the mister for that one."

Nic chuckled at the interchange between his mother and Pippa.

"What are you laughing at?" his mother asked. "Be careful or you'll get no gelato."

"No gelato for me. Water now and beer later," he said.

"Spoil sport," his mother said and he guided Pippa and his mother inside the house.

"I didn't know you were going to fill the pool," his mother said. "Could be a waste," she warned.

"If you enjoy it once, it won't be," he said, heading toward the kitchen. "If you enjoy thinking about taking a dip in the pool or Jacuzzi, then that's enough, Mom," he called over his shoulder as he went to the kitchen and grabbed a bottle of water.

"You're such a good son," she said.

"Does that mean I get some of that gelato?" he asked as he reentered the room.

"And you are the very devil," she said. "Just like your father."

He glanced at both his mother and Pippa. "And you know I'm not anyone but me," he reminded her.

"True," she said. "But he is a scoundrel," she said to Pippa.

"I agree," Pippa said, her eyes swimming with emotions that reflected the drama of the moment. "Well, I can't stay, and I must confess I thought you might not even move in until tomorrow, but I clearly underestimated your son."

"It's not the first time I've been underestimated," he said, meeting Pippa's gaze.

She gnawed on her lower lip and he felt a tug toward her. He'd made a mistake with that before, but something about her got under his skin. He'd known a few women. Some as beautiful as beauty queens and world-class models. Why did she affect him this way?

"I'll try not to do the same thing again," she said.

He shrugged. "We'll see."

"I want gelato," his mother said.

"Then you shall have gelato," Nic said.

Pippa met his gaze, then looked away and walked to the kitchen. "Let me scoop it for you, Mrs. Lafitte. I hope I didn't overdo the chocolate."

"Call me Amelie," she said as she followed Pippa into the kitchen. "And you can never overdo chocolate."

"That's good to know," Pippa said and searched through several drawers for a scoop. "There we go," she said and dipped a scoop of both flavors into a bowl. "Enjoy," she said with a smile on her face.

She shot an uncertain glance at Nic. "Would you like some?"

"I'll wait until later," he said, noting the way Pippa pressed her lips together.

She nodded. "I should go," Pippa said.

"Oh, no," his mother said. "You just arrived."

"You need to rest. You've had a busy day," Pippa said.

His mother frowned. "Promise you'll return."

"Of course I will," Pippa said. "Don't let your gelato melt."

"You're so right," his mother said and dipped her spoon into the treat.

"I'll walk you to your car," Nic said.

"I can do that myself," she said.

"No," he said and escorted her to the driveway. "You need to know," he told her. "It's going to go down from here. She was good just now, but she's struggling and it's just going to get worse. A lot of people wouldn't be able to handle it…."

She stopped and turned, looking offended. "I'm not a lot of people. I'm not the type of person to abandon someone when—" She broke off and realization crossed her face. "You said that because I broke off our relationship."

He shrugged. "If the shoe fits."

"That was a totally different situation," she said. "It was a temporary flirtation. You and I are not at all well-suited."

"Because your family hates mine," Nic said, feeling a twist of impatience.

"That's part of it. There's no good reason for us to continue a relationship when we know there's no future. It was sheer craziness on my part."

He laughed. "Good to know. You're saying you weren't really attracted to me. You were just temporarily insane."

"I—I didn't say that," she said.

Nic watched the color bloom in her cheeks with entirely too much pleasure.

"And what if my last name was not Lafitte?" he had to ask because the question had dug at him at odd moments.

Her expression changed and a hint of vulnerability deepened her eyes. She opened her mouth, then closed it and looked away. "I can't let my mind consider that because you are who you are. I am who I am." She shook her head and turned toward her vehicle. "I need to leave. I'll check on your mother la—"

Nic saw her foot catch on a tree root and instinctively caught her as she tripped. He pulled her against him and inhaled her soft, feminine scent and felt her body cling to him. For about three seconds. Then she pushed at his arm and moved away from him.

"I should have been watching. Sorry," she said and met his gaze.

"No big deal. You're okay. That's what matters," he said.

In that moment, in her gaze, he saw the same tug and pull of feelings that he had inside him about her, about them. There was so much she wasn't saying that she looked as if she could nearly pop from it. "Thank you," she finally said.

"Ciao," he said and watched her as she got into her car and drove away. There was unfinished business here for both of them, he thought. He'd tried to leave Pippa behind, but something about her nagged at him like a fly in the room he couldn't catch. He needed to find a way to get her out of his system.

That night Pippa dressed for the family dinner her brother Stefan had called. With her youngest brother playing soccer in Spain, and her oldest two sisters and their families out of the country, that left Bridget, her husband, Ryder, the twins and Stefan and Eve and Stephenia. She was extremely bothered from her visit with Nic and his mother this afternoon. Amazing how such a brief time in the man's presence could disrupt her so much. She'd suspected he would get over her in no time. He was far more experienced than she was. There must have been a dozen women ready and willing to soothe his ego.

Yet, he acted as if he was still irritated by the fact that she'd ended things. It wasn't as if she'd truly dumped him. They had never had a public relationship, just a few furtive meetings. She couldn't deny he'd made her knees melt with the way he'd looked at her, and the connection she'd felt with him had made her breathless. She also couldn't deny that he'd acted as if he were attracted to her, as if she meant something to him.

The truth was part of the reason she'd refused to see him again was because her out-of-control feelings frightened her. If ever a man was unsafe, it was Nic Lafitte. Yet she'd found him irresistible which only proved that she must have some sort of self-destructive tendency inside her that she hadn't known existed. Now that she knew she had this tendency, she had to beware of it and fight it if it ever reared its head again.

Pippa looked into the mirror and adjusted her topknot of out-of-control hair. She called it her curse. Every once in a while, the humidity lowered and her hair was almost controllable. Not today, though. Putting on a little lip gloss, she dismissed it and her other thoughts and headed toward the royal dining room.

Stefan had instigated the "family dinners" a couple years ago. Ever since Bridget had gotten married, she'd felt the odd man out at the dinners. She'd worked around those feelings by focusing on her nephews and niece. But still…

Entering the dining room, she spotted Bridget and Ryder holding the twins while Eve chased Stephenia.

With the three high chairs, the palace looked far different from last year.

"Stefan will be here any minute. No need to put the darlings in the high chairs until then. How was your day?" Eve asked Pippa.

"Good," Pippa lied. "Made a little progress on my research."

"Good," Ryder said as he held Tyler and shifted from foot to foot. "Your genealogy studies could really help me with medical plans for Chantaine. I'm working on health prevention at the moment, and I'd like to see a better developed hospice plan in space."

Pippa's stomach clenched at the mention of hospice, although she wished Amelie could have access to such a program. "Both of those are vital. We're very fortunate Bridget brought you to us."

Bridget held Travis and smiled up at Ryder. "I can't agree with you more," she said as she jiggled the boy. "I hope Stefan doesn't take much longer or this family dinner is going to turn into a family scream-in."

Eve winced. "He said it would be just a moment."

"Yes, but we all know it's tough being crown prince and we're glad he's doing it and not us."

Seconds later, Stefan entered the small room with a broad smile. "You're all here. And healthy. This is good."

"And rare," Bridget added. "Given the twins' on-and-off sniffles. We'd better get on with the family dinner. I can't promise how long they'll last."

"No problem," Stefan said. "Sit down and relax. The food will arrive immediately. My assistant advised the chef."

The small group situated the children and sank into their chairs as staff poured water and wine for the adults and juice for the young ones. Before too much fussing, a server brought Cheerios for the babies.

"Takes them longer to pick up," Eve said with a smile.

"Well done," Bridget said.

"The main course will arrive in just a moment. I'd like to take this moment to share some good news. Eve and I are expecting our first child."

"Second, including Stephenia," Eve added.

"Oh, how wonderful. Another baby," Bridget crowed. "Takes the pressure off me."

Pippa laughed at her sister's reaction. "And me."

Bridget and Eve gasped at the same time. "You wouldn't dare. You're the good sister."

"Oh, no," Bridget corrected herself. "That's what we said about Valentina and she got pregnant before she was married."

"I was just joking," Pippa said.

"Thank you," Stefan said as he lifted his glass of wine and took a hefty sip. "One heart attack at a time, please."

"Besides," Bridget said as the staff served filet of sole. "We have plans for you."

Pippa felt a sliver of nervousness and took a sip of her own wine. "You and Eve keep talking about plans. You're making me uneasy."

"They're good plans," Bridget said as she set a plate of cheese, chicken and vegetables on Tyler's tray.

"We know you've been cooped up working on your degree," Eve added.

"Chantaine has several celebratory events scheduled during the next few weeks," Stefan said.

Pippa took a bite of the perfectly prepared fish.

"And we're going to set you up with some of the most eligible bachelors on the planet," Bridget said gleefully. "How exciting is that?"

Pippa's bite of fish stuck in her throat. "What?"

"It will be fun," Bridget said.

"No pressure," Eve said. "We just want you to enjoy yourself. You work hard with your nephews and niece and your studies."

"It's occurred to me," Stefan said, "that you haven't had many opportunities to form relationships with men. You've been protected. Perhaps overprotected."

Pippa's stomach tightened. "How lovely of you all to decide it's time for me to have a relationship. Without consulting me, of course."

Silence descended over the room. Even the children were silent as they munched on their food.

"We thought this would make you happy," Bridget said. "You work so hard. We wanted you to have some fun."

"Would you want your sisters and brother to make decisions about men you would date?" Pippa challenged.

Bridget winced. "When you put it that way..." she said.

"I am," Pippa said. "I don't need or want you to find dates for me. It's embarrassing," she said, her appetite completely gone.

"We don't intend it to be embarrassing," Stefan said. "Your position in the royal family makes it difficult for you to socialize with men. We'd like to make that easier."

"The same way the advisers tried to make it easy for you," Pippa said, setting down her fork.

"There's no call for that," Stefan said.

"And there's no call for matchmaking for me," Pippa said.

"Pippa, you haven't been the same since the incident with—" Bridget cleared her throat and lowered her voice. "That horrible Nic Lafitte. We just want to help you get over it."

"I'm completely over it. I know he was only interested in me to make a point with his ego." Even as she said the words she knew her family wanted to hear, she felt as if she were stabbing herself. "I may be naive, but I'm not a complete fool." She debated leaving the table, but knew her family would only worry more about her. She lifted her drink. "We have more important things to celebrate. Cheers to Stefan and Eve's new baby. May your pregnancy be smooth and may your child sparkle with the best of both of you."

Ryder lifted his glass. "Here, here."

"Here, here," Bridget said.

Tyler let out a blood-curdling scream, and the tension was broken. Soon enough, Travis joined. Stephenia followed.

Most important the focus was no longer on Pippa. She took another big sip of wine and knew she wouldn't be able to eat one more bite of food. With the children providing a welcome distraction, she gave a discreet signal to one of the servers, who immediately removed her plate. As she looked at each face of her family, she felt a combination of love and sheer and total frustration. She wished she could scream just like Tyler did.

Chapter Four

Two days later, Pippa mustered the time and courage to visit the Lafittes. The name Lafitte was like pyrotechnics as far as her family was concerned. Perhaps she should mentally give them another name so her stomach didn't clench every time she even thought it. Instead of Lafitte, she could think of them as the LaLas. Much less threatening. No unnecessary baggage with LaLa.

The idea appealed to her and Pippa smiled to herself when she thought about it, which was entirely too often. It was difficult not to become impatient with her sisters and brothers over the feud with the Lafittes. After all, the Lafittes were human, too. Look at their current situation with Amelie trying to make it through her dying days and poor Paul with his broken foot. And poor Nic trying to manage all of it.

Sighing, she pulled into the driveway and stopped the car. She glanced over her shoulder even though she was certain her security guy had been dozing when she'd left. That was Pippa. She knew well how to bore a man to sleep. She glanced in the mirror and bared her teeth at herself.

Grabbing the flowers from the passenger seat, she got out of the car and braced herself for the possibility of seeing Nic in workman mode in a tight T-shirt and slim-fitting jeans. Walking into the courtyard, however, she saw no workers around and the pool and Jacuzzi were full of fresh clean water. The sunlight glinting on the water made it all the more enticing, but she suspected the water was frigid.

The house was so quiet and peaceful she wondered if Amelie and Paul might be napping again. She hesitated as she stood in front of the door, not wanting to disturb their rest.

"Hey."

Pippa turned at the sound of Nic's voice as he walked from the guest quarters closer to the driveway. "Hello," she said. "I was afraid to interrupt. It's so quiet."

"I heard your car in the driveway," he said. "Last I checked both my parents are napping again, although I think my mom is getting restless. She'll need a field trip soon. Nice flowers. Come on inside," he said and opened the door to the cottage. He paused, cocking his head to one side. "I'll check to see if the bedroom door is still closed. Just a minute."

She watched him walk down the hallway. Seconds later, he returned, his face creased with concern. "She's gone."

Pippa bit her lip, feeling a quick spurt of apprehension. She couldn't help remembering how Amelie had fainted the last time she'd gone out on her own. "Are you sure she's not somewhere else in the house? Taking a nice long bath. Maybe she's in the kitchen."

He shook his head as he walked toward the kitchen. "I could see the open door of the bathroom." He glanced in the kitchen. "Not there. This isn't good."

"Maybe she went for a little walk in the neighborhood," Pippa suggested hopefully.

"The problem with my mother is that she doesn't take little walks. She probably escaped when I was working and the new house staff went to the market. I thought she was sleeping," he said and swore under his breath. "I have to go look for her."

"But where?" Pippa asked, watching his muscles bunched with tension even as he rolled his shoulders.

"I don't know, but I can't sit here waiting. I'll leave a note for Dad and Goldie. He'll be helping out here at the cottage for the time being."

Wanting to help, she impulsively offered, "I'll go with you." She suspected she surprised herself as much as she'd surprised him.

He gave the offer a flicker of consideration, then shook his head. "There's nothing you can do. I'll call or text you when I find out anything."

His easy dismissal of her irritated her. "I do know Chantaine better than you do."

"What's to know? The island isn't that big," he said.

"Did you know about Bebe's Crepes?" she asked.

"No, but—" He broke off and raked his hand through his dark hair. "Okay. But my first priority is finding my mother. If you're afraid someone may be able to identify you, you'll just have to duck behind the seat."

"Yes. Just let me put the flowers in water and grab my baseball cap," she said.

"I'll go ahead and call Goldie and ask him to come back now. I don't want my dad freaking out here by himself."

Pippa quickly placed the flowers in a pitcher she filled with water because she couldn't find a vase. Hearing Nic's low voice in the background gave her a sense of urgency. She raced to her car to grab the baseball cap. She'd put her hair in a topknot again, refusing to fight with it this morning. Pulling it down, she looked for an elastic band so she could put it in a ponytail and slip it through the back of the cap.

Hearing Nic's feet on the gravel of the driveway, she glanced up and pushed her fingers through her hair self-consciously.

"You should wear it down more often," he said.

"Oh, so I can look like I put my finger in an electrical socket?" No one had ever pretended to like her hair. She'd heard of a treatment that might tame it, but the idea of the hours it would take to accomplish it put her off.

"I like it," he said with a slow grin. "It's kinda wild. Makes me wonder if you have a wild streak underneath."

"I don't," she assured him and stuffed the unruly mass through the back of the ball cap as best as she could. "Shall we go?"

"I'm ready," he said and tucked her into the passenger side of his Mercedes.

"Has your mother mentioned any particular places in

Chantaine that she wanted to visit?" she asked as soon as Nic pulled out of the driveway.

"Since she moved into the cottage, she's just talked about how happy she is to be here, how beautiful it is."

"Hmm. Where are we headed first?" she asked.

"The beach," he said.

"That's a bit to cover. I don't supposed you've heard her talk about any specific beaches," she said.

"I've heard her talk about Chantaine a lot," he said, narrowing his eyes in deep thought. "She used to tell us bedtime stories about Chantaine before we went to sleep at night when my father was gone."

"Gone?" she asked.

"In prison," he said. "His conviction was overturned on a technicality. For a while there, she wouldn't let him come back."

Shocked by his revelation, she blinked. "I'm sorry. I didn't know. That must have been difficult."

"It was the gift that keeps on giving. My older brothers never forgave him. My younger brother just withdrew."

"But they've been in touch with your mother since she's been ill," she said.

"They won't talk to her if there's any chance they have to speak to my father," he said.

"Oh, my goodness, they're as bad as my family," she blurted. "If not worse."

He shot her a sideways glance, but kept his focus on the road. "Yeah."

"I'm sorry, but I'm just shocked. You never told me about all of this. Of course, I'd heard things about your father from my family, but you just said his conviction was overturned."

"Yeah, well, everyone's got a few skeletons in their closet. Even Stefan with his surprise daughter," he said.

Pippa bit her lip. It had been both scandalous and traumatic for the entire family and country for Stefan to learn he'd fathered a child fifteen months after the fact. "As soon as he'd learned about her, he'd done his fatherly duty. He's been a wonderful improvement over the example he had, let me tell you."

"Does that say more about your father or Stefan?" he challenged.

"My father wasn't involved with us. He procreated so that there would be children to carry on the work of the Devereauxs. The more he procreated, the more he could stay on his yacht and the less he would have to do." Her heart was slamming against her rib cage. She'd thought she'd settled all this as a child. Heaven knew, it was old news. "Stefan *reads* to his daughter most nights."

"Okay, okay," he said. "No need to yell."

"I wasn't yelling," she said, then reviewed her words and felt a slap of embarrassment. "Was I?"

"Just a little, but I probably deserved it," he said and pulled the car alongside the beach. "Let's check here." He opened the door for her and they scanned the beach from each direction.

"Did she mention this as one of her favorite beaches?" she asked, staring past rows of hot bodies.

"No. It's just the closest to the cottage. Why do you ask?"

"Well, Chantaine's beaches may share sand and

water, but they each have their own personalities," she said.

"Such as?"

"This is more of a singles scene, a pickup beach. As you can see from the demographics, a younger crowd frequents this beach. Farther north near the resorts, you'll find the celebrities and international visitors. Even farther north, there's a family beach where you'll see more children."

His hair whipping in the wind, he narrowed his eyes. "What's the name of the family beach?"

"St. Cristophe," she said.

"It was on the tip of my tongue," he said. "Let's go there. She went there often as a child before her parents died. She talked about eating fruit, cheese and crackers at the beach. I just hope she didn't decide to go into the water."

They both got into the car, traveling in silence up the coast. Pippa could sense Nic's tension. "If you could just persuade her to leave a message before she leaves..."

"Tell me something new. Maybe she'll listen to you if you say something to her," he said.

"Me? Why would she listen to me?" she asked, surprised at the suggestion. Amelie had only just met her.

"She's grateful to you for the use of the cottage and you're female. She thinks I'm just being overbearing and protective," he said.

"I'll give it a try," she said, full of doubt. "Maybe we could get a list of things she wants to do."

"Like a bucket list?"

She cringed. "That's morbid."

"But part of the program at this point," he said, clenching his jaw.

Pippa's heart twisted. She hated it for all of them, but Nic was only speaking the truth. "St. Cristophe Beach is just a few more kilometers north. We should be there soon."

As soon as the sign for the beach greeted them, Nic again pulled onto the side of the road and helped her from the car. Pippa scanned the beach. "Do you see her?"

He shook his head. "Let's split up. I'll go south. You go north. Call my cell if you find her and I'll do the same. Okay?"

She nodded in agreement and walked northward. The breeze was picking up and the clouds were rolling in, bringing the air temperature down. With Amelie's slight frame, Pippa feared the woman could become easily chilled even though it was summer.

Walking along the beach, she looked from one side to the other. Chantaine's beaches had their share of rocks and trees. Going barefoot could lead to serious discomfort. One more thing to worry about if Amelie had impulsively removed her shoes.

"Look! Isn't that Princess Phillipa?" a woman's voice called.

Pippa froze. Bloody hell, now what could she do.

A woman and several children raced toward her. Oh great, her security detail was going to kill her.

"Your Highness," the woman said, making an awkward curtsy. "Boys, take a bow. Girls, curtsy."

Pippa couldn't help smiling at the woman's delight and friendliness. "It's not necessary. I was here just taking a little walk. St. Cristophe is such a lovely beach. Are you enjoying your day?"

"Very much," the woman said.

The children echoed, "Yes, ma'am."

"Even more so seeing you here," the woman said. "Is there any chance you would give me an autograph? It would be a dream come true."

Seeing a small crowd forming, Pippa knew she'd better make the best of it. "Now, I didn't want to make a big production of this, so you're going to keep my little escape to the beach a secret. Won't you?" Fat chance with Facebook and Twitter alive and well.

She began to shake hands, sign autographs and make pleasant conversation. It really wasn't that difficult. The people were so lovely and kind. Her cell phone rang in the small purse she carried. "Excuse me for just a moment," she said and drew back slightly from the crowd.

"I found her," Nic said. "She was sitting beside a tree sleeping."

"I'm so relieved for you," she said. "But I've been discovered. Go ahead and take her home."

"How will you get back?" he asked.

"I'll figure out something. Or someone will alert security and it won't be necessary. I just wish my car wasn't in your driveway."

"I'll have Goldie take care of it. Where do you want it?"

"Close by, but he doesn't have the key."

"Goldie won't need it," he said. "I'll text you when he's close. He'll grab a cab ride back. *Ciao.*"

Pippa opened her mouth to protest, but she knew Nic had hung up, so she turned back to the crowd and continued to chat, sign autographs and even pose for a few photographs. Yes, there was going to be an inquisition in her very near future. Several moments later, her cell signaled a text. Certain it was from Nic, she didn't bother to look and began to say her goodbyes.

"It was lovely meeting all of you," she said. "But I really must go. *Ciao*."

She climbed the sandy hill to the road and after walking south a short distance, she spotted her vehicle. Unfortunately she also spotted the vehicle belonging to her security man Giles. Dread tightening her stomach, she walked toward the man. She really didn't want to lose Giles as her personal security guard. He was, after all, the oldest security member on the force. With the exception of her secret meetings with Nic nearly a year ago, he regarded her as a sweet but boring student who posed very little security threat. Plus he was given to taking nice long naps in the afternoon.

"Your Highness," he said wearing an extremely displeased expression. "You didn't inform me of your plans to visit the beach today."

"I know," she said. "I'm terribly sorry. It was an impulse after lunch. I mentioned my plans to pop into a café for lunch, didn't I?"

Giles shook his head. "No, ma'am, you didn't."

"Oh, it must have slipped my mind. You know I usually pack a lunch, but I forgot this morning. My recent studies have been a bit depressing, detailing the causes of deaths of all our ancestors. I just felt a walk on a family beach would clear my head," she said, hoping she was boring the bloody stuffing out of him.

"But you usually prefer the more isolated Previn Beach," he said.

"I know. I guess I just wanted to see happy families playing on the beach. I do apologize. I would never want to trouble you."

"I know you wouldn't," he said. "But you must apprise someone of your whereabouts. If something happened to you, I would never forgive myself."

"You are absolutely correct and I'll never do it again," she lied and felt guilty, but she couldn't change the course she'd started and she wouldn't if she could.

"But you should have informed your Giles or someone," Frank, the head of security said to her. Because one interrogation wasn't enough.

"I know," Pippa said. "But I also know that Stefan has said that he wants us to make more impromptu public appearances."

"Impromptu to the public, not to security."

"So sorry," she said, and tried to conceal her insincerity. It seemed to be growing easier. She hoped she wasn't becoming a lying wench.

Frank sighed and began to pace across her public den. "Your Highness, except for your lapse with *Mr. Lafitte,* you have been an easy royal to protect. Since then, your studies and family have dominated your life. We don't wish to intrude, but if you continue to be unpredictable, then we will need to provide further security."

"I apologize again for not giving you more information today. I will do my best to be as predictable as possible in the future," she said.

Frank gave a sideways tilt of his head. “Perhaps I wasn’t clear. We need you to be transparent.”

Pippa gave a slow nod. The last thing she wanted to be was transparent. “Of course. And that’s exactly what I shall be. Transparent. Predictable,” she quickly added.

“Thank you very much, Your Highness,” Frank said. “It is only our desire to protect you.”

“I know,” Pippa said. “And I’m very grateful,” she added, exaggerating.

Frank smiled and nodded. “Thank you, Your Highness. I knew we could count on you.”

Pippa lifted her lips in a smile as he left her suite. She’d just bought herself a couple more days of freedom. She hoped.

The following day, Pippa skipped visiting the Lafittes and even texting Nic. She felt as if she needed to stick to being predictable and transparent for at least one full day. That next night, however, she tossed and turned as she tried to sleep. She couldn’t be what she needed to be for her family. She couldn’t be what she wanted to be for the Lafittes.

She finally fell into a fitful sleep full of images of Nic and Amelie. Strong, strong Nic who would never admit pain or vulnerability, yet his dark eyes said something far different. Unable to sleep, she paced her bedroom and tried to work. She finally gave in and sent a text to Nic. I’m going to need a different disguise.

When a civilized time of day finally arrived, Pippa took a shower and got ready to go to the library. She sat down to work, and even though she had the concentration of a water newt, she forced herself to focus. Some time later, a package was placed beside her.

Glancing up, Pippa caught sight of a big bald man walking away from her. She lifted her hand. "Sir?"

The man didn't turn around. Pippa frowned, staring at the package. She glanced around her, then turned it over. The package bore the initials PD. Curious, she eyed the package with a sideways glance and slid it onto the chair beside her. Nic Lafitte was crazy. Who knew what scheme he had in his wicked mind?

She glanced back at her own laptop and with her heart racing, she tried to stare at the screen. Forget concentration. She would just like to be able to *read* the words on her screen. After seven tries, she gave up, grabbed the package and walked to the ladies' room. She went into a stall, ripped open the package and pulled out a gray-haired wig. Pippa couldn't help snickering. Her curiosity shooting upward, she pulled out the rest of the contents of the package. A hat, an ugly gray dress, tennis shoes and a key to a car.

She fished out a scrawled note at the bottom of the package. "The car is old, gray and rusty. In America, we call it a POS mobile. More later."

POS mobile? She couldn't wait to hear his explanation, she thought as she changed into the ugly gray dress. After she finished dressing, she carefully folded her other clothing and placed it into the package. Walking out of the restroom, she looked into the mirror and gaped. She looked at least thirty years older if not more. Pippa snickered again. *Well done, Nic.*

Following her instincts, she walked out the back door of the library and looked around for an old gray, rusty car. She immediately spotted it. The car was the most hideous vehicle she'd ever seen. Pippa walked to it, unlocked the door and got inside.

She turned the key and pressed the accelerator. The engine coughed to life. The summer heat combined with her wig and droopy dress made her feel as if she were suffocating. Pippa pushed the button for the air-conditioning, but only hot air blew from the vents.

"Bloody hell," she muttered and drove out of the parking lot.

Nic heard the sound of an engine backfiring outside his window. Glancing away from his tablet computer, he saw a gray-haired woman in a black dress exit the car and felt a ripple of pleasure. She'd come. He hadn't been sure she would. Pippa was an odd mix, and he'd already learned the hard way her first loyalty was to her family. She'd probably endured some pressure from her security guy and maybe even her family if they knew about it.

He was surprised she continued to visit. After all, her conscience should be clear. She'd made a dying woman's wish come true. Heading for the door of the guesthouse, he wondered why Pippa clearly felt the need to do more.

He stepped outside and caught sight of her walking toward the back door. "May I help you, miss?" he called, relishing the opportunity to tease her.

Whirling around with her hands on her hips, she stared at him, the gray curls of the wig so stiff they didn't move. "Very funny," she said. "As if you didn't handpick this lovely disguise."

"It worked, didn't it?" he asked as he strolled toward her.

She gave a reluctant nod. "Yes, but the car is another matter."

"I'll get Goldie to do something about the engine backfiring. We wouldn't want to call attention to you."

"The car may be a little over the top," she said. "It's distinctive and there's no air-conditioning."

"That must be hard on a woman your age," he said and bit back a grin. Lord, he felt like someone had turned on the light for the first time in two days. His mother had been alternately ill and sleeping. "I wasn't sure you'd come."

Her expression of contempt waned slightly. "You made it easy." She sighed. "How is she?"

He shook his head. "Not good. Sick or sleeping for close to thirty-six hours. It seems she gets a burst of energy and uses up all of it, then she can barely lift her head for days. I never know when one of these dips is the beginning of the—" He broke off. "Something bad."

"I'm sorry," she whispered. "I'm really sorry."

Feeling as if he'd revealed too much, he looked away from her and shrugged. "Part of the program. I'll deal with it. Good thing I've got Goldie. He's a licensed practical nurse, too."

Pippa blinked. "Goldie appears to be a man of many skills. Where on earth did you find him?"

"He and my father were in prison together. Goldie's record wasn't expunged, but he was a good guy. I hired him and he developed a hobby of educating himself. I paid for all the courses, but they've ended up benefiting me."

He felt her gaze on her for a long moment.

"I would like to meet him, please," Pippa said. "So far, I've only caught glimpses of his talents and abilities."

His gut tightened with something strange he almost couldn't identify. It took several seconds. Jealousy? He racked his brain to remember when he had felt this way before and couldn't. He led the way to the house. "Sure, I'll introduce you to Goldie. He's in the main house probably putting together a gourmet meal for dinner."

"He's a chef, too?" she asked.

"Oh, yeah, that was another one of his certificates. It's paid off in spades."

"The palace would *love* to have someone like him…."

"Don't even think about it. But if you do, he'll turn you down flat. He's the most loyal ex-con ever," Nic said.

"That remains to be seen," Pippa said. "The Devereauxs have seduced more than a few of the best of the best."

He stopped at the front door and turned around to meet her gaze. "I know that better than most."

Her cheeks heated and her eyes darkened. She cleared her throat. "Um…"

"Yeah, um," he echoed, saving her a response and opened the front door. "Let's go inside."

He guided her past the foyer into the kitchen. "Goldie," he said in a low voice.

The multitalented man appeared within two seconds, wearing an apron around his waist. "Yes, sir."

Goldie was sixty, but looked fifty because he worked

out. He was bald, muscular, with a gold hoop in his right ear. He usually wore a black T-shirt and black pants. He looked intimidating, but Nic knew he had a heart softer than that of a teddy bear. "Her Royal Highness, Princess Pippa Devereaux, this is Gordon Goldwyn."

Goldie gave a solemn bow. "Your Highness, my pleasure," he said.

Pippa smiled. "My pleasure," she said. "You're a man of many talents. Thank you for delivering my car to me at the beach and also leaving the envelope and car for me."

"I'm honored to serve," Goldie said respectfully.

"How is it that you are talented in so many areas?" she asked.

"I'm a lifelong student. Some things I learned got me into trouble. I'm fortunate that Mr. Lafitte encouraged me to explore my interests. Would you care for a drink or something to eat?"

"I'm fine. Thank you very much."

Goldie nodded, then turned to Nic. "Can I get something for you, sir?"

Nic waved his hand. "No, thanks. Any sign of my mother?"

"No, but your father is getting restless watching her," Goldie said.

"You're saying he could use some TV time. Sports Central," Nic said.

Goldie nodded. "A game would be even better."

"I got a million on DVD," he said.

"Then you've got what he needs," Goldie said.

At that moment, his mother walked into the room, looking gray and gaunt. "I'm thirsty," she said.

Nic rushed to her side. "What are you doing?"

She leaned against him. "I'm Lazarus rising from the dead. Hopefully, I'll do it a few more times," she said and stared at Pippa. "You look familiar. Are you someone who went to school with me?"

"Not quite," Pippa said with a smile. "But I would have loved that."

His mother frowned. "Were you in the orphanage with me?"

Pippa shook her head. "No, but you and I went to Bebe's Crepes together."

His mother stared at her for a moment, then smiled. "Princess Pippa," she crowed. "I love the look," she said, stretching out her hands. "You're my old best friend Rosie."

Pippa nodded and he saw that she was holding back her laughter. "Thank you so much. I'm sure Rosie is a most excellent person."

His mother nodded. "She is, but you are, too." Her eyebrows furrowed. "May we please have some refreshments?" she asked.

"What would you like, ma'am?" Goldie asked.

"Something fruity," she said. "Orange juice or lemonade."

"I'll bring both," he said. "Please take a seat in the den."

Nic assisted his mother to sit on the sofa. "There's no need to treat me like an invalid," she complained.

Nic gritted his teeth. Every other day, if not more often, his mother *was* almost an invalid. Yes, he was happy as hell that she didn't want to be treated like one. In his mind, that meant she might be around a little longer.

Pippa put her hand over his and met his gaze as if she knew everything he was feeling. Still dressed as a gray-haired lady wearing a baggy dress, she looked like an angel to him. An angel he wanted more than he'd ever wanted anyone else.

Chapter Five

Pippa concealed her alarm at how weak Amelie appeared. Just two days ago, she'd seemed an entirely different woman, going off by herself for a jaunt to the beach.

"I want to go on another adventure soon," Amelie announced as she sipped lemonade. "I'd like to go today, but I'm too bloody tired. Tomorrow will be a different story."

Pippa caught sight of Nic rubbing his forehead and face. She could see his shoulders bunch with tension. "Just let someone go with you so we don't have to call out a search team."

"A search team isn't necessary," Amelie said with a stubborn tilt of her chin. "I was fine."

"You were asleep on a public beach. You overestimate your energy level," he said.

She waved her hand in a dismissing gesture. "Plenty

of people doze on the beach. It's one of the pleasures of life. You wouldn't understand because you don't know how to relax."

"If you would agree to a GPS monitoring anklet…"

Amelie's eyes widened in indignation. "I'm not on house arrest. I refuse to be treated like a prisoner during my last days."

"It's just for tracking. Safety. It would give me some peace of mind," Nic added.

"Well, it wouldn't give me peace of mind walking around in public with an anklet designed for criminals."

Nic sighed. "I'm worried about you. What if you collapse and there's no one there to help you? Is that really the way you want to go?"

Pippa cringed at his bluntness, but she could tell he was feeling pressed. She honestly wouldn't like to be in his situation.

Amelie lifted her chin. "I don't get to choose the way I want to go. If it were up to me, I'd transform into a butterfly and float away, but the doctor says that's not possible."

A tense silence followed. Pippa felt it inside her and took a deep breath to ease it. "Well, I can see that the genes for independence and outspokenness are quite strong in both of you. I'm sure both of you enjoy those qualities in each other."

Nic glared at her, but Pippa forced herself to smile. "Mrs. Lafitte, perhaps you and I could go on an outing tomorrow or the next day, depending on how you're feeling. With my new disguise, I believe I'm safe to go anywhere."

Amelie smiled in delight. "Call me Amelie. And you

don't look a thing like yourself. That wig is so horrible, I think you may look even older than I am."

"Thank you," she said and shot Nic a wry look.

"I've been thinking I'd like to learn a new hobby. Years and years ago, I learned to knit, but I've forgotten everything. Do you know of any knitting shops on Chantaine?"

Ignoring Nic's astonished expression, she nodded. "I know of one downtown. If you feel like it, we could also have lunch."

Amelie seemed to brighten at the suggestion. "Lovely. This will be wonderful. I like having something to look forward to." She paused and glanced at Nic. "Have you heard anything from your brothers?"

"No," he said, and Pippa noticed the slight clench of his jaw. "You should let me call them again."

She shook her head. "You did that last year when I had my last treatments and they all visited then. It was a disaster with your father. I was just hoping things could be different now." She sighed. "There are some things we can't change. Best not to focus on them. I'll look forward to my outing with you tomorrow," she said to Pippa. "I think I'll sit outside by the pool with a book and this lovely lemonade."

"It's a beautiful day," Pippa said. "I think you'll enjoy it."

Goldie appeared in the doorway. "Can I get you something to eat?" he asked.

Amelie made a slight face. "If I tell you I'm not hungry, you'll tell me I need to eat something to keep up my strength. Crackers," she said.

Goldie's face fell. He'd clearly hoped her appetite had improved. "Yes, ma'am."

"Are you sure I can't join you outside?" Pippa asked.

"No, thank you, darling. I just want a little Chantaine sunshine," Amelie said and carefully rose from the sofa.

As soon as Amelie left, Pippa turned to Nic. "What is wrong with your brothers? Even my terribly dysfunctional family came together at the end of my parents' lives. Surely your brothers could do the same. It's the only humane, compassionate choice. You must make them come here at once."

Nic leaned toward her and gave a short laugh. "Here's a news flash, Princess. There's no royal decree available for the Lafittes. Besides, we don't respond well to attempted force or manipulation. My older brothers are holding on to a mile-wide grudge against my father. My youngest brother makes sure he's too busy to be contacted."

"But you must have some influence with them," she said, appalled at the situation.

"My oldest brothers would make the trip if they didn't have to face my father," Nic said. "My mother won't allow that. She refuses to turn her back on my dad even though she's earned the right more than once."

Frowning, Pippa rose and paced across the lush burgundy carpet placed on top of the ceramic tile floor. "There's got to be a way. Perhaps Goldie or I could take your father for a drive—"

Nic shook his head. "Not gonna happen. My mother wouldn't allow it."

"Well, we will just have to figure out another way," she said.

"We?" he echoed, rising to walk toward her.

Her stomach dipped as he moved closer. She kept trying to forget his effect on her, but every time she felt she was successful in staying focused on Amelie, Nic did something to upset her equilibrium. Unfortunately, it took very little. Seeing him stand and breathe was apparently problematic for her.

"I'm still not sure why you feel my mother's problems have anything to do with you," he said, looking down at her and resting his hands on his hips.

"Technically, I suppose they don't, but I would think any compassionate person would want to help," she said.

"Including Stefan?"

She bit her lip. "If Eve had anything to say about it, yes, he would help. I know you believe Stefan is a monster, but he's not. Just as he believes you are the very devil, and you're not."

"Good to know you don't think I'm the devil," he said.

She opened her mouth to retract her statement, then decided against it. "I will try to come up with a solution for your mother and your brothers. In the meantime, I can take Amelie shopping tomorrow, but I'll be busy the day after. I'm supposed to escort some soccer player around the island, then accompany him to a charity fundraiser that evening."

He lifted an eyebrow and his eyes glittered with something that gave her pause. "Is that so? Is the fundraiser at the St. Thomas Hall?"

"Yes, as a matter of fact, it is."

"This should be—" His lips twitched. "Fun. I'm invited to the same fundraiser."

"Oh," she said, her stomach taking a downward plunge. "You probably weren't planning to attend, were you?"

"I hadn't decided, but I could use some entertainment. May as well."

"But what about your mother?"

"It will just be for the evening," he said. "Goldie can call me. I'm not glued to Chantaine. I'll have to leave for business commitments within the next couple of weeks." He paused. "I'm at peace with my mother, and she's at peace with me. We have no unfinished business."

Pippa felt the oddest sense of calm and excitement from Nic. She'd never, ever felt that combination before. She took a deep breath and pushed past her feelings of panic about her feelings. That peace Nic had just mentioned, that was what was important. She felt it and knew it deep inside her. "I'm so glad that you have a good relationship with your mother. It will help you after—" She broke off, not wanting to say the words.

"After she's gone," he said.

Pippa nodded slowly.

"Because you didn't have the best relationship with your mother," he said.

"It wasn't horrible," she said quickly. "It was just distant. Our family was different. We weren't raised the way most other children are raised."

"It's different being royal," he said.

She nodded.

He reached out to take her hand in his. His fingers felt strong and sure wrapped around hers. "Most people don't have perfect childhoods. You take the good and screw the bad stuff."

His simple words gave her the biggest rush. They reverberated inside her. She wanted to be that person who could *take the good and screw the bad.* Every once in a while, though, she felt caught between herself as the chubby preteen who didn't feel worthy of her parents' attention and a grown woman who was on her way to earning her doctorate. The touch of his hand just made her want more… At that moment, Nic made her feel she was capable of anything she wanted to do and be.

A loud cough sounded. Mr. Lafitte stood on crutches at the entrance of the room. "Where's Amelie?" he asked, looking more than a little rough around the edges. His hair stuck up in a wild Mohawk and his jaw was heavily whiskered. "Is she okay?"

Pippa automatically pulled her hand from Nic's while Nic turned to his father. "She's fine. Outside by the pool."

Mr. Lafitte slumped forward slightly. "Good. As long as she's not swimming."

Nic winced. "Good point. Goldie," he called, "can you see my mother?"

"She's in a lawn chair, sir."

"Good." Nic took a quick breath. "Can I walk you to your car, Great-Auntie Matilde?"

Pippa felt a flash of realization. She'd forgotten she looked thirty years older. She smothered a laugh at herself. She'd been concerned that she was giving Nic mixed signals.

Well, she would have if she didn't look like his grandmother. Walking out of the cottage, she waved at

Amelie and strode the rest of the way to the horrid vehicle she would drive to the library, where she would change out of her outfit and return to her identity as Princess Pippa.

Nic opened the door for her.

"I hope it's cooler now. I burned up on the drive over here," she said.

"Goldie did a little magic. You should be more comfortable now."

"Thank you," she said.

"Thank you." He leaned toward her slowly and pressed his mouth just next to hers. It could have been a kiss on her cheek, but it just missed the mark. It could have been her mouth, but it wasn't. He almost made her forget that she was dressed like his grandmother.

Nic watched Pippa putter away in the POS mobile. She continued to make him admire her. He tried to name a woman who would be willing to disguise herself as a woman thirty years older and drive a wreck of an automobile just to check on a dying woman who was not related to her. Pippa was different. He'd known that from the beginning.

He returned to the front door.

"Nic, darling, come sit with me for a moment, please," his mother called. "Ask Goldie to bring you a Scotch. Or whatever it is that you drink."

"No need," he said. "It's early for that."

His mother glanced up from her wide-brimmed hat. "Haven't you heard? It's five o'clock somewhere." She rang the little bell Goldie had given her, insisting that she ring it anytime she wanted anything.

Goldie immediately appeared. "Yes, Miss Amelie."

"Please fix a drink for Nic. His usual," she said.

Nic sank into the chair beside her. "How's the book?"

"I fell asleep, so I don't know," she said. "But I'm loving the sunshine. You will have many stars in your crown for bringing me to Chantaine."

"That was Pippa's doing," he said.

"And you're quite taken with her," his mother said and sipped her lemonade.

"I wouldn't say that," he said, irritated at her suggestion.

"No, but I'm dying, so I can speak the truth," she said and shot him a knowing glance from the top of her sunglasses. "I would never ever suggest going after a royal especially because Paul and I made a bit of a mess with the Devereauxs back in the day. That said, I can tell the princess is also taken with you."

Goldie delivered his Scotch and Nic took a long drink. "Yes, that's why she dumped me like garbage several months ago."

His mother waved her hand dismissively. "Family's a tricky thing. You ought to know. I'm quite impressed that she's made such an effort to please a dying woman. Especially when her family wouldn't approve. I can't help believing some part of her is trying to help you."

"If so, then that part is buried very deep," Nic said dryly.

"You have to find your own way. I'll just tell you that some people are worth fighting for. Some people are your destiny," she said.

"You're speaking of Dad," he said, always stunned by the fervency of her devotion to his father.

"I am. He would steal for me. He would die for me. He would go to prison for me. He would do anything for me. I hope you'll know that kind of love," she said and leaned back against the chaise longue.

After a lovely lunch and bit of shopping spent with Nic's mother, Pippa prepared herself for her afternoon and evening scheduled with Robert Speight, the world-famous soccer player from England.

"Aren't you excited?" Bridget asked as she *helped* Pippa get ready for an afternoon outing. "He's so hot. Stefan protested. He wanted to put you with a count from Italy, but I insisted. You deserve a treat after all the academic work you've been doing along with being such a good auntie. Good Lord, don't you ever go shopping?" Bridget continued. "All I see are long skirts and blouses."

"I haven't had a lot of time for shopping," Pippa said, wishing she didn't feel such a strong sense of dread about the setup with the soccer player. She feared he was going to be quite disappointed and bored.

"Well, there's always catalogs and online shopping. For that matter, the palace stylist would be happy—" She broke off as she whisked through the hangers of clothing in Pippa's closet. "Don't you even own a cute little pair of shorts?"

"I'm sure there are some in there somewhere. I just prefer skirts. They're more comfortable," Pippa said and reached for a beige linen skirt that flowed to her calves.

"Absolutely not," Bridget said, scooping the skirt back from her. "If you insist on wearing a skirt," she muttered, pushing through a few more hangers. "Ah," she said, pulling out one of Bridget's few above-the-knee skirts. "Here, this one will work."

"I'm not sure it fits anymore," Pippa murmured, holding the pink skirt against her. "And I think I may have stained the blouse that goes with it."

Bridget pulled out a white scoop-neck cotton blouse. "There. It will be perfect with sandals. Why did you cancel the salon appointment I made for you yesterday? I told you about the new treatment. Smooth, shiny hair and because you're Miss Practical, you won't have to spend so much of your time styling it every day."

"I don't spend that much time, now," Pippa said. "I either pull it back or put it on top of my head."

"Hmm," Bridget said and studied Pippa for a long uncomfortable moment. Bridget took her hand and led her to the sitting area of Pippa's suite. "I'm not sensing a lot of enthusiasm about your outing with the soccer player." She sighed. "Please tell me you're not still pining for that terrible Nic Lafitte."

Pippa looked away. "Of course I'm not pining for him. But I'm not pining for a setup, either. Think about it. Did you like it when Stefan set you up with men hoping for a romance or marriage?"

"I hated it," Bridget said. "Fought it with every bit of my strength, but most of those men were at least ten years older than me. Robert is your age. And he's regarded as one of the most eligible bachelors in the world. I'm not trying to arrange a marriage. I just want you to have a little fun. You're due."

Pippa gave a slow nod. "I appreciate the sentiment. You're sweet to want me to have some fun."

Bridget met her gaze and groaned. "But you're not

at all interested. Well, at least give the poor man a try. Trust me when I say I didn't have to do any coaxing to make this happen. He was more than happy to spend the day and evening with you. And who knows? You may have a fabulous time. Promise me you'll *try* to have fun."

"I'll do my best and I'll also try to make sure that Mr. Speight is entertained," Pippa said.

Pippa treated the date as if it were a project. She planned to take the soccer player on a tour of the island, stopping at a few of the famous beaches. If time permitted, she'd arranged for a brief turn on the royal yacht.

Robert Speight was an impressive specimen. He stood over six feet tall with a well-muscled body. His hair was red and skin extremely fair. The exact opposite of Nic, she thought, and immediately wished she hadn't made the comparison. Their date started out well enough with Pippa giving a running commentary on the history of Chantaine as she showed him points of interest. It was only when she saw his head rolling back against the headrest, his eyes closed and his mouth open that she got her first clue that she'd begun to bore the poor man.

Thank goodness she'd arranged for a picnic lunch at a private beach. She and Robert sat on a large blanket and ate food from a gourmet basket prepared by the palace chef. Robert asked for photos, but kept fighting the yawns.

"Sorry," he said sheepishly. "Late night last night partying," he said waggling his bushy red eyebrows suggestively. "If you know what I mean."

She didn't, so she just made a vague little sound. "I

thought it was very generous of you to lend your name to the charity fundraiser this evening. So many people are looking forward to meeting you."

He shrugged. "I have to do a few of these every now and then for the sake of my image. It helps me get other endorsements. This one included exotic beaches and a date with a princess. What's not to like?" He leaned toward her and placed his hand over hers. "I've heard Chantaine has some nude beaches. You want to take me there?"

Pippa blinked at the proposal and tried not to laugh. She'd spent a lifetime trying not to be photographed in a bathing suit. A nude beach was totally out of the question. "I'm not really permitted on the nude beach," she whispered. "Photographs live forever. If you have time tomorrow, I can arrange for a driver to take you."

"But it would be much more enjoyable with you," he said.

"I'm so sorry," she said and took back her hand. She was going to have a chat with Bridget tomorrow, she promised herself.

Later that afternoon, Pippa received a visit from the palace stylist, Peter, to make sure she was properly dressed and coiffed. Dressed in a designer gown that reminded her of a pink cocktail napkin, she bit her teeth. Peter applied more makeup than she wore in a year. He sighed and swore over her hair. "A keratin treatment would change your life."

"It takes too long," she said.

"It's not as if you would have to sit in a salon like the rest of the world. We would bring the cosmetologist to the palace. Your hair would be straight for three to four months after one treatment."

Pippa stared into the mirror at herself and made a face. "I don't know if I want it straight."

Peter lifted one eyebrow. "As you wish, Your Highness."

"Your way of saying I'm crazy," she said.

Both of Peter's eyebrows flew upward, which was quite an accomplishment given the Botox he regularly had injected into his forehead. "Pardon me, Your Highness if I offended you."

"It's true. You think I should get the treatment and have straight hair. Straight hair is more fashionable than crazy, wavy hair."

Peter seemed to work on his restrained. "It's my job to keep the royal family informed of current fashion. Your hair…" He began and moved his hands, but couldn't seem to find the words.

"I hate my hair and love my hair because it's different," she told him. "You have to admit, it's not like anyone else's hair in the family."

Peter tilted his head to one side. "You make an excellent point, Your Highness. We shall begin to capitalize on your hair," he said. "We shall make your hair a new trend. We can name it the Princess Pippa hairstyle. Perfect."

Alarm shot through her. "No need to go that far," she said.

He lifted his hands. "I can see it now. Magazine shoots, commercials. It will be fantastic publicity for the royal family."

"Not in my lifetime," she said quietly.

He sighed. "Begging your pardon, ma'am, you give this impression of being a people pleaser, yet you somehow stop me in my tracks when I try to expand you."

"And you like me for that, don't you, Peter?" she said more than asked, unable to hold back a grin.

Peter shook his head but smiled. "I do. Let me spray you one more time," he said lifting a can of hair spray.

She lifted both her hands to block him. "I'll die if you do."

"An exaggeration," he said.

"You would know because you're the master of exaggeration," she retorted, her hands still braced to shield herself from the hair spray.

Peter groaned. "You make this difficult for me, ma'am. What if this man is your future husband?"

"No worries," she said, adapting a phrase she'd learned from Bridget. "He pushed hard for me to take him to a nude beach."

Peter frowned. "A cad. In that case, perhaps I should give you sea salt spray. It will take your curls to a new level."

Pippa laughed. "No need. Thanks for your help tonight."

"Someday, a man will sweep you off your feet."

Pippa laughed again, and her mind automatically turned to thoughts of Nic. She clamped down her thoughts and feelings. "I prefer my feet on the ground."

Thirty minutes later, she joined Robert Speight in a limo headed for the charity event. "Nice dress," Robert said, staring at her cleavage. "Are you sure I can't talk you into a trip to one of your nude beaches tomorrow?"

Pippa refused to honor the subject, let alone the question. "Did you know that I'm working on a doctorate in genealogical studies? I had some extra time this afternoon while I was waiting on alterations for my gown. Did you know that you may be distantly related to Attila the Hun?" The truth was just about anyone could be distantly related to Attila.

Robert shot her a blank look. "Attila the Hun?" he echoed.

"Yes, he's quite famous."

"I'm drawing a blank," Robert said. "Can you refresh my memory?"

"He was a ferocious warrior. The Romans were terrified of him. He was excellent with a bow and an amazing horseman. Quite the sportsman," she said.

Robert stuck out his chest with pride and smiled. "Like me."

"Exactly. He was known as a conqueror." *And barbarian.*

"I've got to make a little speech tonight. Maybe I could mention him," he said. "Maybe spice things up for people interested in history."

She opened her mouth to correct him, but couldn't quite make herself do it. "Just as long as you understand that I said that you *may* be related to Attila. I would need to do an in-depth study to verify the possibility."

"Hey, it's a good story. That's all that counts to me," he said, leaning toward her as if he were going to kiss her. "You're cute. Let's make some private plans after the event."

"Oh, I—" The limousine pulled to a stop. She glanced out the window, thankful for the interruption. "We're here."

"Yeah," Robert said as the driver opened the door. "First time with a princess. In more ways than one," he added against her ear as he folded his hand around her waist.

Pippa's stomach rolled.

She stepped out of the car and felt a thousand camera flashes as she strode toward the entrance of the building. Robert grabbed her hand and she struggled to free it. She pointed at a camera and she took advantage when he loosened his grip. Clasping her hands firmly together, she walked inside and smiled at the crowd that applauded.

"Pippa, Pippa!"

She was surprised to hear so many call her name. She'd always thought of herself as the anonymous Devereaux.

Robert put his arm around her and whispered in her ear, "Give me a kiss. They'll love it."

She bit her lip and turned her head. "I see some of your fans," she said.

"Where?" he asked.

Moments later, they entered the ballroom and Pippa waved to the crowd. There, several people screamed out loud. "Rob, Rob!"

"There you go," she said, but she needn't have. Robert was fixated on the crowd, waving and throwing kisses.

They were led to the head table and Pippa took her seat. The rest of the guests took their seats. Instinctively, she glanced around and her gaze landed on a man with broad shoulders, dark eyes and dark hair. Tonight he wore that Stetson as if to proclaim to all of Chantaine and her family that he didn't give a damn.

She liked him even more for that.

"This is fun," Robert said. "Just tell me it's not another rubber chicken dinner," he said.

"Lobster," she said and barely managed not to roll her eyes.

She felt Nic's gaze on her. He was silently laughing.

"So that guy's name is Atowla?"

"Attila," she said. "Attila the Hun." She was caught between a barbarian and a pirate. She wasn't sure which was worse.

Chapter Six

A server discreetly handed Pippa a piece of paper with her sorbet. Putting it in her lap, she opened it and glanced at it. *Meet me on the second floor in 5. N.* Pippa took a quick sip of water and briefly met Nic's gaze. She shook her head.

Her so-called date whispered in her ear. “It's time for more pictures,” he said. “Stand up and I'll give you a passionate kiss. The press will love it.”

Pippa nearly choked. “I was just going to tell you that I need to, uh, powder my nose. I'll be back shortly.”

Robert's face fell. “Well, damn.”

“I won't be long,” she said and stood. She gave her security man a wave of dismissal and quickly walked to the hall outside the ballroom. Restroom was to the right, she remembered. Pippa had attended several events at this venue. The second floor offered a lovely view of the beach. Her stomach took a dip. Nic clearly remembered that fact, too.

She headed toward the restroom.

"Pippa."

She automatically paused, her heart leaping at the sound of Nic's voice. Pippa sucked in a quick, sharp breath and forced herself not to turn around. She didn't need to because Nic was at her side in seconds. "This is not a good idea. Go away," she whispered.

"Your Highness," a woman called. "Princess Philipa."

Pippa frowned and turned at the distress in the woman's voice. She stared into the lovely heart-shaped face of a very young-looking woman. She was dressed in a miniskirt and tank top.

"You can't have him. I'm having his baby."

Pippa dropped her jaw. "Pardon me?"

"You can't have Robert. He belongs to me. He's all excited about being with a princess, but it will pass. He'll come back to me. He has to," she said and began to sob.

Pippa instinctively gathered the girl into her arms and glanced searchingly at Nic. "You're getting too upset," she said.

"He belongs to me. I'm having his baby," the young woman continued to sob. "He belongs to me."

"Darling, I wouldn't dream of taking Robert from you. This was just a charity appearance for both of us."

The girl pulled back, her baby blues filled with tears. "But he was so excited about being with a princess. He told me he couldn't make a commitment. Big things were coming in his future," she said, her voice fading to another sob. The woman buried her face in Pippa's shoulder again.

She met Nic's gaze again. "Please ask a server to give Robert a note. Robert's friend and I will be upstairs. He should join us immediately."

Nic lifted a dark eyebrow and dipped his head. "As you wish, Your Highness."

As soon as he turned away, she felt a rush of relief. "Let's go upstairs," she said. "I didn't hear your name."

"Chloe," she said and sniffed and swiped at her cheeks as Pippa led the way upstairs. "You're much nicer than I thought you would be. I was sure you would steal Robert from me."

"Oh, Chloe, I wouldn't dream of that," she said with complete and total honesty. She wouldn't take Robert if he was handed to her on a silver platter. She guided Chloe into a room and propped open the door.

Just a couple moments later, she heard voices coming from the hall. Nic's and Robert's. The door swung open and Nic and Robert stepped inside.

Robert's eyes widened. "Chloe, what are you doing here?"

Chloe bit her lip. "How could you leave me, Robert?"

Looking incredibly awkward, Robert shrugged his wide shoulders. "It was just temporary." He shot a quick glance at Pippa. "The princess required my presence for the charity event."

"I did not," Pippa said, unable to contain herself. She wanted to punch the scoundrel. She clenched her fists.

"Okay, well, I had to show for the charity event. The princess was just a bonus," he amended.

Nic cleared his throat. "I think Chloe has some important news to share."

Chloe gulped and appeared to force a smile. "I'm having your baby," she said.

Pippa looked at Robert and saw the tall, strong athlete turn as pale as ghost. "Baby?" he echoed.

"Yes, I'm having your baby," Chloe said and walked toward him.

Robert fainted backward. Nic caught him just before he would have hit the floor.

Pippa sighed, crossing her arms over her chest. "Are we going to have to call the medics, too?"

"Let's try something a little more basic," Nic said. "Can you get a glass of water?"

She glanced around the room and saw a stack of paper cups and pointed at them. "There's a water fountain in the hall."

"I'll take care of it," Chloe said.

"Get two cups," Nic said and gently lowered Robert's head to the carpeted floor.

Chloe ran out of the room. Seconds later, she returned.

"I think you should have the honors," he said to Chloe.

"What do you mean?" she asked, clearly confused.

"Throw the water in his face," he said.

Chloe's eyes widened in alarm. "In his face."

"It's the best thing for him," he said.

"Are you sure?"

"Couldn't be more sure," he said. "If you don't do it, then I will."

Chloe took a deep breath and threw a cup in Robert's face.

The athlete blinked and shook his head.

"It worked," Chloe said with a delighted smile. "You were right."

Nic nodded and extended his hand. "Can you give me the second cup?"

"Of course," she said and gave it to him.

"You coming around, Speight?" Nic said as the man lifted his head.

"Yeah," he said, rubbing his hand over his face. "Why am I wet?"

"So many reasons," Nic said. "You okay? Are you conscious?"

Robert lifted himself up on his elbows. "Yeah, I'm good."

Nic nodded and dumped the second cup of water on Robert's head.

Robert scowled and swore. "Why the hell did you do that?"

"In Texas we would say you need a good scrubbin'," he said in his Texas drawl. "I just thought I'd get you started. Pops."

After Robert pulled himself back together and dried himself with some paper towels, he returned to the ballroom and Nic arranged for a car to take Chloe back to her hotel.

Pippa felt the pressure of passing time. She knew her absence would be noted if she didn't return soon, but she wanted to thank Nic for his help. After stepping just outside the door, he returned and strode toward her.

"You okay?" he asked, his dark gaze intent on her.

She laughed. "Of course I'm fine, thank you. I wasn't the least bit enamored of Robert from the beginning."

Nic walked closer. "Are you sure about that?"

Pippa frowned. "Of course I'm sure. Do you really think I could be so easily won over by a man just because he's a world-famous soccer player?"

"You fell for me pretty quickly in the beginning," he said, lowering his mouth to half a breath away from hers.

Her heart skipped. "I was young and foolish."

He laughed, and the deep, hearty sound echoed inside her, making her feel alive. "It was six months ago."

"Eight months," she corrected.

He lifted a brow. "I didn't know you were counting."

She opened her mouth, but at the moment, she couldn't deny… Anything.

His mouth brushed hers, and the sensation made her felt as if she were melting and blooming at the same time. His mouth searched, plundered and empowered hers. She felt sensual, womanly, and it sounded crazy, but she felt as if she could fly. It was such an amazing, euphoric sensation that she didn't want it to ever end. During a moment that felt like centuries or seconds, she slid her arms around Nic and reveled in the strength of his body. It seemed to flow into hers.

She craved more of the feeling. There was more, she thought. More…

Nic pulled back slightly. "Let me take you away," he whispered. "For just a while."

Every fiber of her wanted to say yes, but her duty and obligation screamed no. "I want—" She took a breath and tried to clear her head. "They're expecting me for the end of the dinner. After twelve minutes, people start to notice when a royal is gone." She swallowed over the craziness rolling through her, but she fought the drowning sensation she felt when she stared into his eyes. "They actually notice before that, but if there's a distraction such as a famous soccer player, we get a bit more time."

"After the dinner, then," he said.

Her stomach dipped as if her amusement park ride had abruptly plunged and risen and plunged again. "Oh," she said. "Uh, I—" She broke off and shook her head. "This is crazy. We tried it before. It didn't work out."

"Why?" he asked, his gaze wrapping around hers and holding it.

She opened her mouth to answer, but the words stopped in her throat.

"What's the problem, Princess Pippa? Cat got your tongue?" he asked and kissed her again.

Pippa melted again, feeling as if she were having an out-of-body experience. His arms felt better than chocolate, his mouth, the same. She felt as powerful as the ocean. She clung to him, but duty tugged at her. It was so ingrained that she couldn't quite forget it.

Pippa pulled back. "I have to go."

"Chicken," he said.

Something inside her wanted to prove him wrong. "Blast you," she whispered, and wiped her mouth as she ran from the room.

Although she was bloody distracted, Pippa finished the interminable evening. With photos, but no passionate kisses. She took a separate limo to return to the palace, all the while consumed with thoughts of Nic. What if she could have met him? Where? She felt a terrible aching need to be with him, but she knew she couldn't. For a thousand reasons. She arrived to find Bridget waiting in her quarters, bouncing with excitement.

"Tell me all about it," Bridget said. "How hot was he?"

"Too hot for me, given the fact that a, he pushed to go to a nude beach."

Bridget's jaw dropped.

"B, he wanted to French kiss me in public for the sake of getting photographs with a princess."

"Oh, my—"

"And c, congratulations are in order. The very young mother of his baby showed up at the charity event."

"He has a child?" Bridget asked, her eyes wide with horror and shock.

"He is a father-to-be. I believe the popular term is baby daddy."

Bridget gave an expression of pure disgust. "Oh, how horrible. I don't know what to say."

"Just say you won't set me up again," Pippa said. "Please."

Bridget winced. "I'm so sorry." She lifted her hands. "I just wanted you to have a little fun."

"I know your intentions were good," Pippa said. "They always are. You have a good heart and you love me. I know you love me. I just need to find my own way in this area." She decided to make a bigger push. It was her moment. "As you know, my birthday is right around the corner. Everyone is pushing for the palace to make budget cuts. I've decided I want a little more control over where I go. I'm going to request more limited security."

Bridget shook her head, fear filling her eyes. "Oh, no, you can't do that. Not after what almost happened to me. Not after what happened to Eve."

"If you recall, you actually had security when you were leaving that charity event when you were almost stampeded by that gang. I think it makes sense to follow what other royal families are doing. I'm *way* down the list to take the throne and heaven knows I have no interest. Current practices suggest I be given security for official events with a panic button for my use at all times. Do you know how much the head of security grilled me because I took a walk on a family beach last week?"

"It's the social media," Bridget said. "People with camera phones are everywhere, tweeting, taking photos. You can't possibly expect anonymity or privacy, Phillipa."

"It doesn't help to have security nipping at my heels every minute," Pippa said.

"I thought you had a soft spot for your security man. You seemed to have an easy enough relationship with Giles before, well—" Bridget broke off. "Before the Lafitte incident."

Pippa felt her irritation grow. In the past, she would have just sighed and fallen silent. "All of you made entirely too much of a fuss. Can you honestly say you never dated someone Stefan would have considered inappropriate?"

"Stefan considers any man he doesn't choose to be inappropriate," Bridget scoffed and began to pace.

"He almost didn't approve of Ryder until he figured out Ryder could be the new health minister. But Lafitte was different. His family—" Bridget shook her head. "There's just too much bad history between his family and ours. Plus his father had to have been a terrible influence on him."

"Some people might say the same about the influence our father had on us," Pippa muttered.

Bridget shot her a sharp look. "What are you saying?"

"I'm saying I want my personal business to be my business. I'm saying I want to make my own decisions about security and dating."

"We just all adore you and we don't want you to be hurt," Bridget said.

"I realize that, but I'm not four years old. I'm a grown woman. I may be the youngest daughter, but I don't need all of you looking after everything in my life. I want you, Tina and Stefan to stop it. Now." She barely kept herself from stomping her foot for emphasis.

Bridget blinked, then sighed. "You may be able to persuade Tina and me, but good luck with Stefan."

It was a good thing she didn't care what the tabloids said about her, because she would have become extremely depressed the following day. Princess Phillipa Dumped by Soccer Player the headline read with photos from the charity event and her impromptu visit last week on the beach. Not cover-girl shots. Pippa had always shrunk from any potential emphasis of her image. She was no fashion leader, that was certain. Her sisters Fredericka and Bridget had seemed to do enough of that for everyone, thank goodness. It had taken the focus off her. Her other sister, Valentina, had been a bit less fashionable, more normal in her figure and ultimately more concerned with relationships than her image.

That was probably the reason the weight of royal appearances had worn heavy on Tina's shoulders and she'd become the wife of a Texas businessman rancher. Tina made occasional appearances for the family and attended to a few royal duties, but her focus was happily fixed on her marriage and young daughter. Over the years, Pippa had filled in the gaps on the schedule or substituted when one of her siblings couldn't make an event.

She hadn't spent a lot of time thinking about what she truly wanted for herself because she'd been so busy finding ways to avoid causing trouble or being in the spotlight. Ever since she'd gotten involved with Nic all those months ago, she found herself fighting a restlessness that seemed to grow worse every day. She wished it would go away. She'd thought once she'd broken off with Nic that she could go back to normal, but normal didn't fit anymore. Sipping a cup of tea and sitting inside the small suite where she'd lived since she was a teen, she stared outside her window to one of the palace courtyards and felt like a caged bird. She didn't like the feeling at all.

Taking a deep breath, she prepared herself for her meeting with her brother Stefan. He'd requested the meeting first thing this morning. She suspected he had something on his mind and she intended to do what she'd heard Eve say on more than one occasion. Pippa was going to give her brother, the crown prince of Chantaine, a piece of *her* mind.

She walked down the long hallway to the opposite wing of the palace, then up the stairs to the office where her brother worked. On rare occasions, her father had also worked here.

Her brother was a working prince and he'd spent most of his adult life living down their father's yachting playboy prince image. All the Devereaux children had been raised to understand that duty was first and foremost. Some had accepted the duty more easily than others.

Pippa lifted her hand to knock on the door.

Stefan's assistant immediately responded with a slight bow. "Good morning, Your Highness. His Highness is ready for you."

"Thank you," she said and walked through the outer office into Stefan's office.

Stefan stood and smiled. "Thank you for coming on such short notice," he said and moved from behind his desk to embrace her.

Pippa hugged him in return, noting he wore a suit, signaling he had other official meetings today. "As if you would let me refuse you," Pippa gently teased him, taking in the office. The decor combined the history of the Devereauxs with Stefan's interests in horses, his studies in leadership and economics and a few of Eve's homey touches from Texas.

She also noticed a wooden toy on the corner of his desk and pointed at it. "For Stephenia?" she asked, smiling as she thought of his toddler daughter.

"Eve and the nanny bring her to visit. I like to have

at least a couple things in the room that she's allowed to touch. I don't want her to remember my office as the no-no room," he said.

"I like that," Pippa said. "It's a lot different than the way we were raised."

Stefan nodded. "That's the plan. Please have a seat."

Pippa sat on the edge of one of the leather chairs. She would have preferred to remain standing. Standing somehow made her feel stronger. "How is Eve?" she asked.

His eyes lit at the mention of his wife's name. "A bit of nausea and I think she's more tired than usual, but she's trying not to let me see it. I've asked her assistant to limit the number of invitations she accepts. We'll see how long that works. She can be as stubborn as—" He broke off. "As I am."

Pippa laughed. "One of the many things we love about her."

Stefan nodded, then turned serious and she could tell he was going to start discussing the reason he'd invited her to his office. "I'd like to go first, please," she said breathlessly.

His eyes flickered in surprise and he paused a half beat, then gave a slow nod. "All right. Go ahead."

Pippa took a teeny, tiny breath and clenched her hands together. "My birthday is next week," she said.

Stefan smiled. "I know. That was part of the reason I asked you here."

"Really," she said. "Well, I've been thinking about this a lot and I believe I'm ready to drop my security back to official events only."

Stefan stared, again in surprise.

"It's really the current trend among royals and I know you're trying to keep us up-to-date. All of our expenses are being scrutinized by the government and the press, and I think it would be an excellent way to show that we can be economical."

Pippa sat back and waited for Stefan to respond.

"I'll take it under advisement. However, my first response is no. With the brawl Bridget and Eve faced last year, we've learned that we can't count on all our citizens behaving in a welcoming or even civil manner."

"If you'll recall, that was an official event and security was present."

His eyes narrowed with irritation and dark memories. Pippa understood the dark memories. Stefan had been falling in love with Eve when she'd been injured. "I said I would take it under advisement, but you must understand that I regard your protection as a very serious responsibility."

"I appreciate that very much," she said. "But I'm insisting."

He tilted his head to one side in shock. "Pardon me?"

Pippa's stomach clenched. She knew that expression. He'd used it far more often with Bridget because her older sister had felt perfectly free to argue with Stefan. Pippa, on the other hand, avoided arguments like the plague. Except this time.

"I said I'm insisting. I don't do a lot of insisting, but I am this time. And I think you should also know I'm considering moving out of the palace."

Another shocked silence stretched between her and her brother.

"And how do you plan to pay for this apartment?" he challenged.

"I earn a small stipend with the research I do, and I have a savings account. It's true most of my clothes have been provided by the palace, but I don't need a different dress every day. It's not as if everyone is watching every move I make."

"You underestimate how interested our people are in you," he said. "As evidenced by the crowd you drew during your impulsive walk on the beach last week."

Pippa winced. She wondered who had ratted on her. It wasn't as if Stefan spent a lot of time on internet social sites. "Yes, and everyone was perfectly polite."

"You'll be entirely too vulnerable if you were to move away from the palace," he said.

"Entirely too vulnerable to what? I would still have a panic button and I could have alarms set up in an apartment. Admit it. Jacques will be of age soon enough and you would allow him to live away from the palace."

"That's different," Stefan said. "He'll be a young man and would feel trapped here."

"The same way I feel trapped," Pippa said.

Stefan looked as if he'd been slapped and she felt a stab of regret. "I thought you liked having access to the family, the twins and Stephenia, the family dinners."

"I do," she said. "I love my nieces and nephews. I love my family. There's no reason I still can't babysit and attend family dinners. I just need some space."

Stefan sighed, then straightened his shoulders. "Perhaps you just need a break. When I tell you what I have planned for you, I know you'll be pleased."

Pippa felt her stomach twist with dread. There was

always a catch involved when Stefan had a *plan*. "No, really," she began.

He held up his hand. "You've had your turn. Now it's mine. I've arranged for you to take a holiday to the coast of Italy for your birthday."

Pippa immediately thought of Amelie and shook her head. "That's a lovely thought, but this isn't a good time for me to take a holiday. Due to my studies," she added.

"It's only for a few days and the break will be good for you. You'll have only two appearances to make during your trip. One celebrating the anniversary of a museum and the other will be a christening ceremony for a new cruise ship that will be making stops in Chantaine. I've arranged for an escort for you. Count Salvatore Bianchi. He's a bit older than you, but his family is considering opening several wineshops here, so we'd like to further that relationship. And who knows? Perhaps the two of you will hit it off," Stefan said, wearing his most charming smile.

Pippa felt a twist of suspicion. "Just how much older is Count Bianchi?"

Stefan shrugged. "I'm not sure. He's a widow with children. I believe one of them goes to school with Jacques." Jacques, her nineteen-year-old brother.

"So what you're saying is he could be my father," Pippa said.

"Age is just a number, Pippa. I assure you that you'll have more in common with the count than the soccer player Bridget arranged as your escort. My assistant will give you your itinerary later today and the palace stylist will help you with your attire for the trip."

"And if I don't want to go?" Pippa said.

"The arrangements have been made. People will be expecting you. Besides, I can tell by our discussion today that you need this holiday. You *will* enjoy it," he said and stood.

"Because His Royal Highness decreed it," she muttered and also rose.

A flicker of irritation passed over Stefan's face. "I've always counted on you for your sweetness."

She felt a quick surge of pain at the prospect of disappointing Stefan. "I'm sorry. I'll go on the trip, but Stefan you need to understand that it won't change my intentions regarding my security and moving out."

"We'll see," he said.

Chapter Seven

Two days later, Pippa managed to make her way to the Lafittes' temporary cottage. She drove the rickety car from the library wearing the terrible disguise over her clothes and pulled off the wig as soon as she pulled into the cottage driveway. Unbuttoning the too-large matronly blouse, she stepped out of the car and pushed down the hideous skirt.

She heard a wolf whistle and glanced up to see Nic smiling at her as he leaned against the guest quarters door wearing jeans and a black T-shirt that outlined his broad shoulders and muscular arms. "Don't stop now," he said, referring to her awkward striptease.

She bundled up the disguise in her arms and rolled her eyes as she walked toward him. "I despise this outfit."

"But it gets the job done," he said.

Unable to argue his point, she pushed open the gate. "How is your mother?" she asked.

"Restless. She may need an outing," he said. "A short one. Any ideas?"

"I'll think of something. Have you made any headway with your brothers?"

"Heard from one and I'm hounding the others. I may have to resort to unconventional methods of getting their attention."

She shot a sharp glance at him and he shook his head. "You don't want to know."

"Actually, I do," she said. "I may need to use subversive tactics with my own family at some point."

She felt his glance at her, but didn't meet his gaze. "Okay. I'll send a fake officer to stop them on their way to work. This officer will deliver a message."

She met his gaze. "That's drastic."

Nic shrugged. "Drastic times…"

She couldn't help smiling at his creativity. "Well done."

He shot her a half grin. "It's only the first step. I have others planned if this doesn't work."

She nodded. "What are we doing with Amelie this afternoon?"

"I don't know. Depends on her mood."

"How is her appetite?"

"Temperamental at best," he said.

"Maybe she'll take a few bites of gelato."

"You'll have to put on your disguise again," he reminded her.

"I know. I want to cool off until then."

Nic opened the door for her and she stepped inside

the cool foyer. Pippa walked toward the den and saw Amelie and Paul cuddling on the sofa and watching television. She hesitated to interrupt, but Paul glanced up at her.

"Hey, y'all come on in," he said.

Amelie glanced up at her. "It's Pippa!"

The delight in Amelie's voice grabbed at her heart. "Yes, I'm here for just a while."

"We should have another adventure," Amelie said.

Nic gave a low groan from behind her.

Pippa smothered a smile. "We should plan something."

"I want to do something now," Amelie said. "Paul is feeling better tonight."

Pippa remembered her earlier suggestion. "Would you like some gelato?"

Amelie's face lit up. "Perfect." She turned to Paul. "Do you think you can manage a ride in the car?"

"I can do anything for you," Paul said. "And gelato sounds good, too," he said with a rough chuckle.

Pippa's heart twisted at the obvious love that flowed between the two of them. Reluctantly, she put on her costume again. The four of them got into Goldie's SUV and drove to Chantaine's best gelato shop. They ordered ten flavors. Amelie took a teeny bite of each of them. When they returned, both Amelie and Paul were worn out.

Pippa stripped off her disguise again. "I hate this disguise," she muttered to Nic as they sat by the pool. "I think I hated it from the beginning," she said. "Do you think your mother enjoyed the outing?"

He nodded. “My father did, too. They won’t admit it, but it helps if the trip is a short one.”

“How do you think your father is dealing with your mother’s illness?” she asked.

“Depends on the day. Sometimes he’s in denial. Other days he’s trying to grab the moment. He’s definitely not fit for making business decisions.”

“So you’re doing that for him?” she asked.

He nodded, his head still resting against the chair, his eyes closed.

“He’s lucky to have you stepping in for him,” she said.

“Someone has to,” Nic said.

She stared at Nic as he sat in the chair, in his jeans and T-shirt, his head tilted back. “But why you?” she asked.

He cracked open an eyelid. “Because no one else would.”

“Does that mean you would have preferred to let one of your brothers take on this challenge?”

“I would have preferred to have just about anyone take on the challenge, but I knew no one would. My father is an ex-con. Trust in his business is precarious at best. I have to both check behind him and authenticate his company to his customers.”

“If his business is so precarious, how are your mother and he surviving so well?”

Silence settled between them, making Pippa wonder about the mysteries of Nic’s family. Suddenly, it dawned on her. “You’re taking care of them, aren’t you?”

Nic sighed. “His business has huge potential, but with the economy and his reputation, it’s a struggle.”

Pippa thought about all Nic was trying to do for his parents and felt an overwhelming sense of admiration and something deeper, something she couldn't quite name, for Nic. "You're quite the amazing son."

"You would do the same in my circumstance," he said.

Pippa shook her head. "I wouldn't know how to do everything you're doing," she protested. "Plus my relationship with my parents wasn't half what yours is."

Nic pulled his head from the back of the chair and met her gaze. "But you were there at the end."

Pippa took a deep breath, remembering both of her parents' deaths, and nodded. "Most of us were. Stefan and Valentina pulled us together. It wasn't easy. I think they suffered because of it."

Nic nodded. "It's a tough time. If there are more people, there's a bigger cushion."

"But you have none," she said.

He shrugged and cracked a grin. "I'm from tough stock. We've had to scrabble for everything. No royalty in my blood."

"Hmm," she said. "Bet there is. Just about everyone has a bit of royalty in their background."

He chuckled. "You would know. Your Highness genealogist. Bet you can get me that information by next week."

Pippa's feeling of lightness sank. "Not next week now that Stefan is sending me on a trip," she said glumly.

"Where?"

"The place isn't the bad part. It's my escort."

Stefan's eyes widened. "Another escort?"

"Yes, that's what I said. I also told him I want to

ditch my security and move into an apartment away from the palace."

"Bet that went over well," Nic said in a dry tone.

She laughed. "Not at all. He ignored me."

Nic nodded. "You may have to go ahead and make your move before he has approved. And be prepared to be have your title taken away. Stefan is known for his priority on loyalty."

Her heart twisted at his words. He'd described Stefan perfectly. "I hate the idea of disappointing him. He's always counted on me not to cause any trouble."

"Sometimes you have to cause trouble if you're going to be who you're meant to be," Nic said.

His words vibrated through her. "When did you learn that?"

"When I was about eight years old," he said.

She smiled. "Wise words."

"Children are wiser more often than not. Where are you headed and when?"

"Capri, Italy, in three days. This is supposed to be a birthday gift, but I have to make two appearances and I have an escort who has a child as old as my youngest brother."

"Stefan's idea?" he said more than asked.

"Yes, they're trying to make a match. Bridget was trying to give me a hot, young sports guy. Stefan is always about the man who can bring added value to Chantaine. Ultimately, he was thrilled that Bridget fell for a doctor who became our medical director."

"But you have to live with the choices," Nic said.

She nodded. "I do."

"My mother will be crushed if we don't get a chance to celebrate your birthday," he said.

Pippa racked her brain for a time she could break away. "Friday afternoon."

"Night," he said.

She blinked at him. "Night?" she echoed. "How am I supposed to do that?" she asked.

"Creativity, ingenuity," he said. "You're a Devereaux," he said in a slightly mocking voice. "You can do it."

Pippa sighed. "I'll try to figure it out," she said. "I need to put on my disguise so I can return to the library."

"Unless you want to stay here," he said, his tone seductive.

Pippa wanted to stay far more than she should admit to anyone, including herself.

Nic told his mother about Pippa's birthday and she immediately asked Goldie to make a cake and instructed him to get ice cream and noise-making toys. At seven o'clock on Friday, Pippa arrived in a rush, wearing her horrid costume, and he'd never seen a more welcome sight. Greeting her at the gate, he helped her disassemble her disguise.

"You have no idea what I had to do to make this happen," she said, ripping off her wig and raking her fingers through her hair. She pulled a band from her wrist and pulled her hair up into a ponytail.

"We'll make it worth it," he said and led her toward the front door of the cottage. He knocked first.

She frowned at him. "Why are you knocking?" she asked.

"Don't discourage me. I'm being polite."

"Oh," she said, realization crossing over her face.

"Come in," a female voice called.

"Amelie is awake," she said.

Nic opened the door and Pippa walked inside.

"Surprise!" the small group cried. Streamers filled the air.

Pippa gaped. "Oh, my goodness." She clasped one of the streamers in her hand. She clearly couldn't help grinning. "How cool is this. You shouldn't have done it. I didn't expect it."

"We wanted to celebrate," Amelie said. "You deserved a party. Bring the cake, Goldie."

Seconds later, Goldie carried in a birthday cake with lit candles.

"Is that a fire hazard?" Nic joked.

Pippa frowned at him, then returned her gaze to the cake. "Oh, wow," she whispered.

Nic felt a ripple of pleasure at her obvious delight. "Ready to blow out those candles, Princess? Make a wish," he coached next to her ear.

"Just one?" she asked.

He chuckled. "As many wishes as you can fit in while you're putting out the candles."

"Okay," she said and bit her lip. She inhaled deeply and blew out the candles. Milliseconds after they were snuffed out, she looked at him and smiled. "I did it."

"So you did," he said.

"Time to cut the cake, eat the gelato, open gifts," Amelie said.

"Gifts," Pippa echoed. "There weren't supposed to be any gifts."

"Why not?" Amelie asked. "If there are birthday parties, there should be gifts."

Goldie served the cake and gelato, along with champagne. Mr. Lafitte then presented Pippa with a wrapped box.

"It's from me," Paul said.

"Really?" Pippa said and unwrapped the gift which held a box of chocolates and a bottle of champagne, along with a gift certificate to one of her favorite local shops.

"You did too much," she said, clearly surprised and delighted. "I didn't expect this."

"We Lafittes like the element of surprise. Don't forget that," he said with a broad wink.

"Thank you, Mr. Lafitte," she said and brushed a kiss over his cheek.

"Call me Paul, sweetheart," he said.

"Thank you, Paul," she said and another gift was given to her. She opened it to find a long knitted scarf.

Her eyes filled with tears, Pippa looked at Amelie. "Oh, no, you didn't."

"I fear I did," Amelie said with a laugh in her voice. "I realize it's not the best handiwork, but hopefully my effort will warm your heart."

"I will treasure it," Pippa said through a tight throat. She tried to remember when she'd had a birthday that had made her feel more special. She couldn't. For various reasons, her birthday had often been overlooked. There had been conflicting schedules. Her brothers and sisters had been busy. There were always more pressing obligations.

Tonight, however, she was the most important part of the Lafittes' evening. "I don't know what to say. You are—" Her voice broke and she swallowed hard over the lump of emotion lodging in her throat. "You have no idea how special this is for me."

"Bet you had gourmet cakes and birthday balls," Paul said.

"I had birthday cakes and birthday balls, but only a couple of times. My parents were rarely around for my birthdays. It was also sporadic for my brothers and sisters. Everyone was so busy," she said and shrugged, fearing she'd revealed too much. She bit her lip and smiled. "But this is fabulous. You've made me feel so special."

"That's because you *are* special," Amelie said and reached to embrace her.

Pippa hugged the woman and Amelie's gaunt frame frightened her. She was so thin. She felt so fragile. At the same time, Pippa had learned that Amelie was a strong, strong woman.

Goldie poured her another glass of champagne, but Pippa asked for water. She had to drive back to the palace.

"This has been delightful," Amelie said. "But I'm pooped. Tomorrow I'll be stronger, though, I promise," she said, wagging her finger.

"Of course you will," Pippa said. "I would expect nothing less. I have to go away for a few days, though, so I'll check in when I return."

Amelie frowned. "Away? We'll miss you."

"I'll miss you, too," Pippa said, hating the prospect of leaving the Lafittes behind. With Amelie in such fragile health, Pippa wondered if something would happen to her when she was gone on the Italian holiday.

"Good night, darling. Happy birthday," Amelie said. Paul followed, giving her a kiss on her cheek.

After they left, Pippa turned to Nic. "I should probably go."

"You didn't finish your cake," he said.

How could she? she wondered. She could barely breathe, let alone swallow Goldie's cake.

"You're gonna hurt Goldie's feelings," Nic added.

She winced. "I can't eat that entire cake," she whispered.

"Let's take part of it to the guest quarters. That should help," he said. "Bring your champagne."

She shook her head. "I have to drive back to the palace," she said.

"I'll handle that," he said.

"How?" she asked.

He shrugged. "Trust me."

Pippa decided, for once, to trust him. Heaven knew, she'd seen an entirely different side of him with the way he was dealing with his mother's illness. "Lead me on," she said, lifting her glass of champagne.

She followed him out the door and he led her into the guest bungalow. A breeze flowed through the window, more delicious than any central air-conditioning could ever be. "This feels nice in here. Have you had a hard time adjusting to the small quarters?"

"There are interruptions from my parents when I'm

working sometimes, but for the most part, I've liked it. I don't need that much space," he said.

She laughed. "I'm thinking of your yacht. It's huge."

"That's different," he said.

"And your ranch in Texas?" she asked. "Your big, big ranch? Is that different, too?"

"And your big, big palace?" he returned.

"I live in a small suite in the big, big palace," she said. "And I'm prepared to live in a small apartment."

"Why are you making the big move now?"

She shrugged and moved around the small den of the bungalow. "It's overdue. It just took me a while to see that."

"Have a seat," Nic said from behind her.

Too aware of his presence, she felt a dozen butterflies dancing in her stomach. She sank down onto the sofa and took a sip of her second glass of champagne. Nic sat beside her holding the plate with her piece of cake and soft gelato.

"It was better a few minutes ago," he said, scooping up a bite with a spoon and lifting it to her mouth.

She opened her mouth and swallowed the sweet treat. "It really is delicious. Goldie could be a bakery chef."

"Goldie is a lot of things," Nic said. "Bodyguard, medic, mechanic, cook. Hell, he would make a great nanny."

She smiled. "He's so big and brawny. That's a funny image." She took another bite of cake.

"All packed for your holiday?"

The cake stuck in her throat and she coughed. Nic handed her the glass of champagne. She took a quick sip, then shook her head. "No, I've procrastinated. The palace stylist chose some things for me, so I'll take them. I hate to admit it, but I'm dreading it, which is ridiculous. Who wouldn't be happy with a trip to Capri?" She made a face. "But with those appearances and the fact that I'm supposed to spend time with the count, it doesn't feel like a holiday. It feels like an assignment."

"Do you have any free time?"

"The last day," she said.

"I could meet you," he said.

Her heart stopped, then started at his suggestion. "Oh, that would be—" *Fantastic,* she thought before she stifled herself. "We shouldn't. I'm sure my bodyguard will be there."

He shrugged. "We could get around him," he said. "But if you'd rather not—"

"Are you sure you can leave Amelie?" she asked.

He nodded. "She's been fairly stable. It would be just a day or two. To be honest, I have business with a colleague in Rome. I've been putting it off. I could take care of business, then meet you in Capri."

Although she knew it was insanity to even consider a secret rendezvous, Pippa could not make herself say no. She opened her mouth to try to form the word and her lips refused. Her whole body and being wanted to be with Nic and she was bloody tired of denying herself. "Yes," she finally said and closed her eyes. "But this could be messy. You know that, don't you?"

Nic laughed. "I've been dealing with messes since I was six years old."

She wondered what it was about Nic that made her feel stronger. When she was with him, she felt as if she could do almost anything.

He met her gaze and he must have read her feelings in her eyes. Pulling her slowly toward him, he gave her a dozen chances to turn away, but she didn't. She couldn't. But she couldn't help wondering why he continued to pursue her. He was experienced. He could have any woman he wanted.

"Do you want me just because you can't have me?" she whispered, the fear squeezing out of her throat.

"No," he said. "Besides, we both know I can and will have you. The question is when," he said and lowered his mouth to hers.

Pippa melted into him. She was afraid to trust him, afraid to trust her feelings because she never really had before, but her fear of missing him was bigger than her fear of trusting him.

She kissed him back with all the passion in her heart and felt his surprise and pleasure ripple through her. He paused just a half beat before he kissed her more thoroughly.

She slid her fingers through his hair, craving the sensation of being as close to him as possible. He leaned back on the sofa and pulled her on top of him. She felt his arousal, swollen against her, and the knowledge made her even more crazy. She squeezed his shoulders and biceps and shuddered against him as he took her mouth in yet another kiss that took her upside down.

Pippa couldn't remember feeling this way. Even though she and Nic had been involved before, they'd never gone all the way. Now she wondered how she could possibly fight how much she wanted him.

She felt his hand tenderly rub her back. "Hey, you

know where this is headed, don't you?" he asked against her mouth.

Pippa moved her mouth from his and buried her head in his shoulder, taking desperate breaths.

"Pippa, are you sure you're ready?" he asked.

He wasn't going to make it easy for her. He was going to make her choose. And maybe that was part of the reason she wanted him so much. It was time.

She lifted her head to meet his gaze. "Yes, I am."

He sucked in a quick, sharp breath and chuckled. "I'm ready, too, but I want you to think about it a little longer."

Pippa blinked. "Pardon me, are you refusing to be with me?"

He rose to a sitting position with his arms still around her. "I don't want you to do something impulsive and regret it."

Anger flickered through her and she narrowed her eyes. "You sound like my family. You sound like you don't trust me to make my own decisions."

"It's not that. I'm protecting you," he said.

"That's what they say, too," she said. "No one trusts me to make my own decisions. No one," she said and pushed away from him.

"I'm going home," she said.

"I have to drive you," he said. "You've had too much champagne."

Pippa stood, wrapping her arms around her waist, feeling humiliated. "Goldie can take me."

"I will take you," Nic said, rising.

Pippa bit her lip, feeling rejected and vulnerable. She wanted to hide.

"Pippa, you know I want you," he said and cupped her chin with his hand. "How much of a demonstration do you need?"

She swallowed over the desire pulsing through her. "It seems so easy for you to turn it off," she whispered.

He took her hand and placed it over his chest where his heart thundered against her palm. "Does that feel easy? I can show you more," he said as he moved her hand to his hard abdomen.

"S'okay," she said breathlessly.

"What do you want?" he asked.

"You've confused me," she said, clinging to him.

"Well, damn," he said. "Why would I do that?"

She looked up, studying his face. "I thought you would be the ruthless type when it comes to sex."

He held her against him for a long moment. "I am, but for some reason just not with you," he said.

Confusion and a half dozen other feelings swarmed through her like bees. The part of her that knew she was no beauty queen stabbed her with self-doubt. Pippa had made it a practice not to think about image, but all the criticism she'd received from the press over the years suddenly bombarded her. Maybe she wasn't sexy enough. Even though he'd been aroused, he'd been able to stop without a great deal of effort. At the same time, she'd lost all sense of time and place and could have gone much further without a second thought.

Self-conscious, she pulled away. "I really should get back to the palace," she said.

"Pippa—"

"I don't want to talk right now, if that's okay. I have

so much I need to do in a short amount of time to get ready for this trip."

With Goldie following in another vehicle, Nic drove her to the palace, and the silence between them was so uncomfortable that Pippa could barely stand it. Yes, she knew she'd told him she didn't want to talk, but now she would be leaving for her holiday, and she would just be full of doubts. Maybe it was for the best. Maybe this had been a close call and she could get her head back on straight with this trip.

He stopped a block away from the palace. "Can you make it the rest of the way?"

"Of course," she said. Overwhelmed by all the feelings tugging her in different directions, Pippa bit her lip. "Thank you for the birthday celebration and the ride to the palace. Listen, there's no need for you to make a special trip to Capri. I'll be there only a day and—"

"Are you saying you don't want me to come?" he asked, his gaze dark and penetrating.

She took a deep breath. "I'm saying you know my situation. I may not be able to spend time with you. The decision is completely up to you. *Ciao,*" she said and got out of the passenger side of the car.

Chapter Eight

Pippa arrived in Italy the next day. Count Bianchi greeted her at the airport. He was nearly bald with a paunch, but she tried very hard not to compare him to Nic. It was difficult because she had begun to compare every man to Nic.

"A pleasure to meet you, Your Highness," he said.

"And you, Count Bianchi," she said.

"Please call me Sal," he said. "You're such a lovely young woman. I'm pleased to have you by my side."

"Thank you very much, Sal," she said. "Tell me about your children."

During the ride, to Sal's chateau, she learned that Sal's oldest child was, in fact, older than her by five years. Sal also had several grandchildren. He showed her several photos and mentioned his wish to marry again.

Pippa rode the fence by praising his children but not

encouraging any discussion of her interest in him. After a quick respite in her room, she shared dinner with him in his formal dining room. Finally, they made the trip to the museum where Pippa made a brief speech encouraging historical and genealogical research.

Pippa begged off when Sal invited her to join him for a nightcap.

The following day, she geared up for a ride on a yacht, complete with photos. Afterward, she helped christen a new cruise ship with the count by her side. Every second, she damned Stefan for arranging this. Someone had clearly given the count entirely too much hope and she had to find a way to let him down easy. A chauffeur drove them back to his estate after the event.

"Have you enjoyed yourself?" the count asked, leaning toward her.

Pippa discreetly scooted away. "It's certainly been a long day. I'm more than ready for a good night of sleep."

"I understand you'll be in my country tomorrow night," the count said. "I would love to show you Capri. I know several restaurants and beaches that might please you."

"I couldn't trouble you," she said. "You've already done too much for me."

The count sighed.

"Sal, may I ask you? How long has it been since your wife passed away?" she asked.

He looked at her in surprise. "Ten months and three days."

She smiled and took his hand. "You're still counting days," she said gently. "I don't want to be presumptuous, but I don't think you're ready for a new wife. I know you're lonely, but I encourage you to take your time. You're a good man. You deserve a good woman."

He inhaled and smiled at her. "I'm an old fool to think I could attract a young princess like you."

She shook her head. "It's not that," she rushed to assure him. "I can tell that you're still not over your wife. I'm sorry for your pain, but at the same time, I know you're fortunate to have experienced that kind of love."

"Yes, I am," he said and began to talk about his former wife. Nearly an hour later, they arrived at his home. He appeared startled by the passage of time.

"I'm sorry if I've bored you," he said, clearly chagrined.

"No apologies necessary. I treasure a good love story, and that is what you and your wife had," she said.

"You're such a warm, lovely person. I wish I were at a different place in my mourning," he said.

"The right time will come," she said and pressed a kiss against his cheek. "The right woman will come."

He gave a soft chuckle. "Funny how the young can teach us so much," he said and helped her out of the limousine. "If I can ever do anything for you, it would be my pleasure," he said and kissed her hand.

"Thank you, Count Sal. My biggest wish for you is someone who will provide comfort to your heart. In the meantime, enjoy those grandchildren."

Sal gave a light laugh. "I'll take your advice."

The following morning, Pippa left the count's estate. After her last meeting with Nic, she wasn't sure he would meet her. She'd been so temperamental. He'd been so calm. His calmness infuriated her. She felt as if she couldn't control her passion. She didn't want to feel alone in her feelings and wanted to know that he felt the same way.

As she walked into her room with a lovely view of the ocean, Pippa stood in front of the open windows and inhaled the sea air. Her resort was located just outside the busy section of the beach, so she was able to enjoy the view without the crowds thronging to the pebbled beaches. Although Chantaine had its share of rocky beaches, Pippa had to confess Capri offered breath-taking vistas of steep cliffs, narrow gorges and lime-stone formations.

The sight was so beautiful she thought it might just clear her mind, and that was exactly what she needed. She refused to wonder if Nic would show or not. She had one day to truly relax and enjoy herself and that was what she intended to do. Pulling on the bathing suit the palace stylist had purchased for her, she glanced in the mirror and shrugged. Not too bad, she thought, then slathered herself with sunscreen from head to toe and grabbed her cover-up.

Situated on a hill, the hotel offered several decks with lounge chairs for sunning and enjoying the gor-geous views. Pippa accepted the assistance of staff to position an umbrella over her as she reclined in a chaise longue. She stared at the rocky coastline, willing it to clear her head. It occurred to her that Amelie would have loved this. The thought made her unbearably rest-less. Perhaps a magazine or book, she thought, rum-maging through her bag. She pulled out the book on French history she'd been reading just before bedtime during the past month.

A shadow fell over her. Another waiter, she thought. Pippa had never been one to overindulge, especially when it wasn't even lunch yet. But perhaps a mimosa… She glanced up to see Nic standing over her.

Her heart lurched and the rush of pleasure she felt was so powerful that she couldn't squeak out a sound, let alone a word of greeting. He was dressed in jeans, a shirt and a ball cap, and his expression was gently mocking.

"Still pissed?" he asked.

She could argue that he was the basis for her *irritation* and confusion, but she was so bloody glad to see him that she knew it would be a waste. "Not too much."

"That's good. You want to chill here on the deck or are you in the mood for a little adventure?"

"Adventure," she said without waiting half a beat. "I'll tell my security I'm taking a tour."

Within a half hour, she was riding on the back of a motorcycle, clinging to Nic for her very life as he zigged and zagged around the curvy streets. If Stefan or Giles knew, they would have her head. Nic took another curve and she burst out laughing at the thrill.

"What's so funny?" he yelled at her.

"I'm terrified. I've either got to scream or laugh," she yelled back.

He nodded in approval. "We're just getting started."

After a lovely but terrifying ride, Nic pulled into the driveway of a chateau with stairs descending to a dock where several boats were moored. "What now?" she asked.

"We're going for another ride, this one on the ocean. You don't get seasick, do you?" he said, taking her hand.

She shook her head. "I'm a Devereaux. It's not allowed. My father never would have permitted it," she said as she walked down the steps with him.

"What trait would he have chosen over seasickness in his children?"

"Oh, I don't know. Two heads," she joked.

He stopped and looked at her and laughed. "You ought to get out more. I think it's good for you."

"And you?" she asked.

"Haven't had a lot of time for that lately," he said, his smile fading for a second. "But we've got today and a boat at our disposal."

"How did you arrange it?" she asked.

"My friend owns this chateau. He's out of town and he said I could use the house, the boat and the pool. I have access to a ski lodge in Switzerland he has used, so it all evens out." They walked across the dock and he helped her into a boat.

"Where are we going?" she asked.

He shot her a mysterious smile. "Places you can reach only by boat."

Joining him on the motorboat, Pippa reveled in the wind in her face. Nic didn't coddle her with a slow speed or by taking it easy on the curves. The wake made the ride bumpy enough that she had to sit down a few times.

"You're a fast pilot," she shouted to him. "Have you ever raced?"

He nodded. "But now we need to get to a special place."

"What special place?" she asked.

"You'll see soon enough," he said. He glanced over

his shoulder toward her. "Come here," he said extending his hand. "Wanna drive?"

Surprised by the offer, accepted his hand and he pulled her onto the seat next to him. "We have to slow down just a bit," she said.

He lowered the speed and she took the wheel. It was her first time because heaven knew her brother wouldn't have ever permitted it, let alone security. She gripped the steering wheel with her hands and turned it away from a huge yacht headed for the port side of their craft. The wake of the yacht created ripples, making the boat bounce against the waves.

Pippa laughed at the bumpiness but held tight.

"Doing good," Nic said, placing his hand at her back. It was a steadying sensation. Supportive, but not controlling. "Head this way," he said, pointing left.

She drove several more moments, then turned the wheel over to him. "Thank you. That was glorious," she said, unable to wipe her smile from her face.

"Glad you enjoyed it," he said, then revved up the speed again. "Hold on, Your Highness."

After several minutes, Nic slowed as they drew close to a series of rocks jutting from the ocean. "Where are we going?"

"Guess," he said, slowing the speed even more.

In the distance, she saw a rowing boat. Realization hit her. "The Blue Grotto," she said, so excited she could hardly stand it. "I know it's supposed to be a huge tourist spot, but I've always wanted to see it."

"I was hoping," he said.

"But it's supposed to be incredibly crowded." She glanced at Nic. "Why is it deserted? Is there a problem?"

"I bought an hour for us. No other boats during that time," he said.

She blinked. "That would be obscenely expensive," she said. "Stefan would throw a fit if he knew."

"He doesn't have to know," Nic said with a smile. He pulled closer to the rowboat and dropped anchor. The guide from the rowboat pulled right up next to their motorboat. Nic and the guide assisted her onto the rowboat.

"Buongiorno," the man said. "I'm Roberto. I will be your guide."

"*Buongiorno* and *grazie,* Roberto. I'm very excited to see the Blue Grotto," she said.

Nic hopped aboard. "Just tell me you've got a great singing voice," he said and shook Roberto's hand.

Roberto's mouth lifted in a wide grin. "The best. When I tell you, you must lie down in the boat." He turned to Nic. "Hold on to your sweetheart."

Pippa sank to a sitting position. Nic sat behind her and wrapped his arms around her. "Just following orders," he said.

She laughed, feeling the same terror and exultation she'd felt on the motorcycle and the speedboat. As they drew closer to the famous cave, she and Nic reclined in the boat.

"Prepare to enter the Blue Grotto, a spectacle providing thrills since the Roman times. Statues of pagan gods rest on the floor of the grotto. Once inside, you will see a surreal view that will make you feel as if you are floating through a clear sky. The reflection of the sunlight produces a unique transparency. There is no bluer blue," Roberto said. "Stay low, then you may sit up for a few minutes."

Sitting cradled in Nic's arms, Pippa stared in wonder at the blue universe on which they floated. They could have been riding on the sky if not for the lapping sound of the ocean against the cave walls.

"Put your hands in the water," Roberto said.

Both Nic and Pippa dipped their fingers into the cool water.

"It's so beautiful," she said.

"As are you, *signorina,*" he said, and began to sing *"Bella Notte."* The acoustics were amazing. She almost didn't want to breathe because she didn't want to miss a nuance of the experience. Surrounded by Nic's strength and the wonder of the Blue Grotto, Pippa wanted to absorb everything. This was the kind of magic she wanted to store up inside her for sad, bad days.

When Roberto sang the last note, she glanced up at Nic. "This was amazing," she said.

"Quite a show," he said and took her mouth in a kiss.

After they boarded the motorboat, Nic took them back to the chateau. "Are you starving?" he asked. "My friend offered me anything in his pantry and refrigerator, but I thought we'd order takeout. The view is great and I thought you'd just as soon skip a public restaurant."

"That sounds perfect," she said and joined him as they climbed the steps to the chateau. Chugging her water, she sank onto a chair on the patio which overlooked the sea and sighed in contentment as she heard Nic call in an order to a restaurant.

Nic sat down across from her, lifting a bottle of beer to his lips. "You like Capri?"

"How could I not?" she said and shook her head. "I've never had a day like this."

"It was pretty good, wasn't it?"

"That's an understatement, and you know it," she said.

He chuckled at her response.

"Perhaps you do these kinds of things on a far more regular basis," she said.

"I've had some thrills, but the person you share it with can make a big difference," he said. "You need to make any calls to your security guy?"

She made a face at the reminder. "He said for me to call him when I returned to my room." She drummed her fingers on the table. "I suppose I could tell him I've returned and I'm safe and sound."

"Your choice," he said and took another drink from his beer.

Her stomach dancing with a combination of anticipation and apprehension, she placed the call. Her security man seemed satisfied. "I'd like to freshen up," she said and Nic pointed her to the toilet.

When she looked in the mirror, she nearly didn't recognize herself. Her cheeks and lips were flushed a deep pink. Her eyes looked so blue against the contrast of her skin and her hair was wilder than she'd ever seen it. Pippa chuckled and shook her head. It was hopeless. There was no use trying to tame it.

Dinner arrived and she and Nic enjoyed a meal of pasta, seafood and wine. Pippa knew Nic joked to diffuse tensions and cover his feelings, but she knew underneath it all, he had his share of stress. She'd never seen him this relaxed since she'd met him.

"You enjoy the sea. It's therapeutic for you," she said, touching his arm.

"It can be. It's not always." He shrugged. "What about you? Do you enjoy boating?"

She shrugged. "I haven't always. When I was a child, my father was known for spending as much time on his yacht as possible. He missed birthdays, appointments so he could escape on his yacht. In retrospect, he must not have been a very happy man."

"Tough being crown prince," Nic said with a wry grin.

"Perhaps. Some are better suited for the job than others. Stefan takes it very seriously, sometimes too seriously in my opinion. He's very controlling. I remember once when I was a teenager, we were on a family outing on the yacht and I asked if I could take the wheel just for a moment."

"Let me guess," Nic said. "He refused. There are plenty of men who can't give up the wheel."

"Why did you let me?" she asked. "For all you knew, I could have wrecked the boat."

"You're excessively responsible, Pippa. If you'd been concerned, you would have asked for my help. Plus, you underrate your abilities," he said in a matter-of-fact voice as he took another sip of red wine.

"You can't know that. I could be a total klutz," she said. "For all you know, we could be in a hospital from my flipping that boat."

He shot her a sideways glance full of humor. "I have excellent instincts."

She sighed and took a sip of her own wine. "Well, I can't argue with that."

"Anything else you want to argue about?" he asked, swirling his wine in his glass.

She couldn't help chuckling. She had been a bit contrary. "No."

"Good," he said. "Want to go for a swim in the pool? We can turn out the lights."

Pippa was still wearing her swimsuit under her clothes. The invitation for an evening swim was irresistible. She stood. "I'm ready."

He chuckled at her immediate reaction. "I should have asked earlier. I'll grab some towels. Let's go."

Cutting the lights, Nic grabbed some towels and led her down to the pool with a flashlight. Pippa tripped on a step, but he caught her against him. "Okay?" he asked.

"Yes. It's so dark," she said, laughing nervously.

"That's the idea," Nic said and led her the rest of the way to the pool. Clouds cast a filmy cover over the moon, but there was some light reflected against the water of the pool.

"It's beautiful," she said.

Nic jumped into the pool, the splash spraying over her legs. "It is," he said, with a wicked smile on his gorgeous wet face. "Come on in."

She paused half a second and jumped in. Two seconds later, she felt Nic's arms around her. "It's a little chilly."

"You'll warm up in a minute. Trust me," he said, pulling her against him.

She looked up into his face, feeling a crazy joy at the sight of the droplets on his face. "You're not warm," she said. "You're hot."

"I'm that way every time I get around you," he said and dipped his mouth to hers for a quick kiss.

The brief touch of his mouth on hers made her sizzle and burn deep inside.

She instinctively wrapped her legs around his waist.

"I like that," he said, pressing his hand at the back of her waist.

Everything that had been brewing between them for months tightened so much that she could hardly breathe. "Whew," she breathed.

"Take it easy," he said. "You okay?"

"Yeah," she breathed.

"You look like you need another kiss," he said with a half grin and lowered his mouth.

She sank into his mouth, feeling him, inhaling him. She couldn't get enough. His tongue slid past her lips and she savored the taste of him, the feel of him wrapped around her. The buoyancy of the water only added to the sensuality of the experience.

Nic slid his hands over her thighs and cupped her hips as he gave her a French kiss that made her feel as if she were turning upside down. She felt the same excitement race through her that she'd experienced earlier today when she'd driven the boat.

He squeezed her against himself. "I love your laugh," he muttered against her mouth.

"Good thing," she said. "I can't remember laughing more than I do with you."

"Hold your breath." He kissed her again, twirled her around again and sank, inch by inch underwater. It was a crazy, sexy, amazing experience kissing Nic that way. Seconds later, he rose, bringing her to the surface. She sucked in a quick breath of air, staring into his face. His strong, sexy face was covered with droplets of water. His eyes bored into hers.

The electricity between them sizzled and burned. She lifted her hands to cradle his face. "You're quite an amazing man."

He stopped dead. "That's quite the compliment," he said.

"I'm just telling the truth," she said.

"Good to know," he said and untied the top of her bathing suit. His hands slid over her breasts.

She inhaled quickly.

"You want me to stop?" he asked.

She hesitated a half beat. "No," she whispered.

He leaned his forehead against hers. "Pippa, I'm not gonna wanna stop," he said.

Her heart slamming against her ribs, she bit her lip. "Neither am I."

They played and frolicked in the pool. He kissed and caressed her, coaxing her out of the bottom of her bathing suit so that she swam nude with him. They got each other so worked up that he almost took her in the pool. Instead, he dragged her from the pool, wrapped a towel around her, another around him and half carried her up the stairs to the house.

Carrying her to the master bed and following her down, he seemed to devour her. And Pippa wanted him to consume her.

"Are you sure you're okay with this?" he asked, clearly reining himself under control.

"Yes," she said and stretched her arms out to him.

Nic slid his hand between her thighs, testing her

readiness. He rubbed and caressed her, making her wet with wanting. Sliding his finger inside her, he drove her even further. He made her want deep inside her.

"Nic," she said, squeezing his arms.

"You want me?" he asked, his voice raspy with his own desire.

"Yes," she said, close to pleading.

He slid his lips down to her breast, taking one of her nipples in his mouth. The sensation electrified her. She felt the instant connection between her breast and lower, deeper inside her.

"I want you inside me," she said. "In me."

In some corner of her mind, she knew he was putting on protection. Seconds later, he pushed her thighs apart. He thrust inside her and she felt a rush of shock and burning pain at the invasion. "Oh," she said.

Nic stopped, staring at her in surprise. He swore under his breath. "You should have told me."

"I wasn't thinking about it," she said. "My mind was on—" She wiggled as she grew more accustomed to him. "Being with you," she said and wiggled again.

His gaze darkened and he fastened his hands around her hips. "You're gonna make this tough on me," he said in a rough voice.

"Hopefully, it won't be all bad."

Nic groaned and began to move in a slow, delicious rhythm. Pippa felt the beginning of exquisite sensations sliding throughout her.

"You okay?" he asked in a low, uneven voice.

"Yessss," she said. "This is sooo—" The twist of tension growing inside her took her breath.

The pulsing rhythm continued, and she clung to him,

staring into his dark gaze, taking and feeling taken. His jaw tightened with restraint, he reached down between her legs and sought her sweet spot, sending electrical impulses through her. The combination of his possession and his caresses were too much.

She jerked and rippled in response. Suddenly, her body clenched in indescribable pleasure and she arched toward him. "Nic," she called, feeling as if her voice were separated from her body.

He held her tight and she felt and heard his own climax ripple through her.

It was the most profound experience of her life and she knew she would never, ever be the same.

Their harsh breaths mingled in the air. The sound was as primitive as what she'd just experienced. At this moment, she felt Nic inside her body, her mind, her blood. She wondered if she would ever breathe without being aware of him again.

Chapter Nine

Nic lay on his side and pulled Pippa against him. She was half asleep. He tried to take in the impact of what they'd done. Nic had known it was inevitable. He had known they would make love. He had known she would be his.

He just hadn't known how much it would affect him. Months ago, when he'd first met Pippa, he'd wanted her, reluctantly felt a need for her. Something primal had driven him toward her. He'd hoped it had all been about sex, but now he knew he'd been wrong.

Something in his psyche was tangled with this woman, and he wasn't sure how in hell he could untangle himself from her. Aside from the fact that she felt so soft and right nestled against him, he felt himself wanting more. Wanting something he hadn't known was possible.

It didn't make sense. Other women had made themselves available to him. Sometimes he'd accepted their overtures. Sometimes he'd refused. Now, he felt himself falling deeper than he'd ever expected.

He frowned as he luxuriated in her naked body against his. He'd thought that once he took her, he would be okay. He would be rid of the itch that plagued him day and night for her. But it hadn't worked. Now that he'd taken her, it was almost as if he was more committed. He wanted her more.

That was strange as hell.

He slid his hand over her crazy, curly hair. She sighed and the sound did something crazy to his gut. He felt incredibly protective of her. More so now. He knew she was mostly asleep, but her hand closed over his, as if she were protecting him. The notion was amusing, but the gesture stole his heart.

The rude ping of his cell phone awakened Nic. It took a few pings, but he finally recognized the sound. Grabbing his cell phone from the bedside table, he pulled it up to his ear. "Yes," he said.

"Nic," his father said. "Your mother's in trouble. She needs help. The regular doctor can't be reached."

Nic sat up straight in bed. "What's wrong?"

"Her belly's distended. She's in pain," his father said.

"I'll take care of it," Nic said. "I'll be there soon."

Pippa opened her gloriously blue, groggy eyes. "What's wrong?"

"Amelie is having problems. Her belly's distended."

Pippa frowned, rising in the bed. "Oh, no. Your doctor isn't available?"

Nic scowled. "He should have been. She may need

to have some sort of draining from fluid buildup. I may have to find another doctor."

Pippa blinked, then frowned again. "If it takes too long, maybe I can find another doctor."

"Who?" he asked.

"My brother-in-law, Ryder McCall," she said.

"Won't that cause problems for you?" he asked.

"What's more important?" she asked. "My problems, or your mother's?"

Two hours later, they were on a plane, in different rows, to Chantaine. Even though she wasn't sitting next to him, Pippa could feel Nic's tension reverberating throughout the jet. She wished she could help him, but ultimately, she knew she couldn't. Ultimately, she knew Amelie would die. And she would die soon. The question was how could they make Amelie's passing easy. The jet landed in Chantaine and she exited the plane ahead of Nic.

Needing to get away from the watchful eye of Giles, her security man, she made a quick trip to the ladies' room.

Nic called her on her cell. "I can take her to a clinic, but that won't guarantee her privacy. The news could get out that she's here."

"Wait," she said. "Let me see what I can do."

She took several deep breaths, then dialed the number for her brother-in-law, Ryder. He immediately answered.

"Ryder McCall," he said.

"This is Pippa," she said. "Don't reveal who you're speaking to. It's an emergency."

He paused a half beat. "How can I help you?"

"There's a cancer patient who needs some kind of draining. I'm hoping you can help."

He paused again. "Where can I meet you?"

Pippa gave him the address. An hour later, she arrived at the cottage and met with Nic. "Ryder is coming."

"Can he help?" he asked as they stood in the den. Amelie was in the bedroom, bloated and suffering.

Paul banged his crutch on the floor. "She's in pain. What's taking so damn long?" he demanded.

"Ryder will be here any moment," Pippa tried to reassure him.

"Ryder?" Paul echoed. "Who the hell is Ryder? What kind of doctor is named Ryder?"

Seconds later, Pippa's brother-in-law strode into the house. He met Pippa's gaze. "How sick is she?" he asked.

"She's terminal," she said in a low voice. "We want to keep her as comfortable as possible," she said.

Ryder met her gaze. "You should share this with your family," he said.

"My family wouldn't understand," she said. "You know how much they hate the Lafittes."

"I don't understand the grudge," Ryder muttered.

"I need your help and your confidence," she said.

"The first is easy. The second is not. Soon, you must tell your family about this," he said.

Pippa felt her stomach twist. "There's enough trouble today," she said. "Please help Amelie."

Moments later, Goldie drove Amelie to a local clinic

where Ryder performed the procedure that would bring her relief.

Just a few hours passed and Amelie was brought home.

"Thank you," Nic said, clearly weary from the whole experience. "How much trouble will this cause you?"

Pippa shrugged. "Ryder will give me some time. It's more important that Amelie is okay."

Nic's gaze grew shuttered. "You know it's only a matter of time for her," he said.

"I know that," she said. "But I want her to be as comfortable as possible."

He took her hand and clasped it for a long moment. "How did I get so damn lucky to know you?"

She smiled. "That's an excellent question. I feel the same way about you."

In the middle of the night, Pippa returned to the palace. Happily enough, she didn't have to endure a screening from her security detail. Unfortunately that didn't extend to Bridget. Her sister could out-snoop any P.I., and Pippa was doomed to face her questions.

"How was the count? Was he a prick? Was he determined to get into your pants?" she asked as Pippa gulped down her first coffee of the day.

"He was lovely. Just older. We both realized that he was still in love with his wife and he should take his time before getting involved with anyone else even though he was lonely."

Bridget blinked. "Really?"

Pippa nodded. "Really."

"So what did you do for the rest of your trip in Capri?"

"I took a tour," Pippa said.

"A tour?" Bridget echoed, chagrined. "The least the count could have done was to give you a proper tour of Capri."

"I didn't want him to do it," Pippa said. "He was a sweet man, but I used up all my patience during the two days I spent with him. I just needed to take a break after that."

"I suppose I can understand that. I feel bad that you've experienced such bad matchups from Stefan and me," Bridget said.

"There are worse things," Pippa said.

"True," Bridget said. "Ryder went out last night to help a terminal cancer patient."

Pippa's stomach clenched. "How terrible."

Bridget shook her head. "He has a difficult job."

Pippa nodded. "Yes, he does," she murmured.

Bridget shrugged. "Well, did you enjoy Capri? I hate to think the whole trip was a waste."

Pippa nodded again. "Yes, I got to see the Blue Grotto. It was amazing."

"Did you really take a tour?" Bridget asked.

"Yes," Pippa said. "The sight of it was amazing. Worth the crowd."

Bridget shook her head. "Better you than me. I would love to see it, but I couldn't stand the crowds."

"It wasn't that crowded when I was there," Pippa said. "I guess I got lucky."

"Did the guides sing for you?" Bridget asked.

"'*Bella Notte,*'" she said with a smile.

"How romantic," Bridget said. "A shame you didn't have a handsome man accompanying you."

"It was beautiful," Pippa said.

Bridget sighed. "You're a saint. You know how to make the best of everything."

"I would never call myself a saint," Pippa said.

"That's because you don't know what demons the rest of us are," Bridget said with a dirty giggle.

"You overstate your evil," Pippa said. "Most of us just do the best we can."

"That attitude is what makes you a saint," Bridget told her.

Guilt stabbing at her. She was lying to her family. "Please don't call me a saint. I'm not worthy of that," Pippa said.

Bridget tilted her head, studying Pippa's face. "If you insist," she said. "But if anyone ever deserved sainthood—"

"It wouldn't be me," Pippa said in a flat voice.

Stefan wouldn't meet with her the following day. His assistant said he was too busy. After soldiering through her brother's romantic aspirations for her with the count, Pippa was more than peeved, so she took a rare move. She sent him an email and text. In general, the family was instructed not to bother Stefan with personal texts. She usually respected the instruction. After all, she knew he had a terribly demanding schedule and she didn't want to add to his burden. Today, her patience wore thin.

Happy birthday to me. I'm moving out and ditching my security. Cheers, Pippa.

Seconds later, she received a text from Stefan. I order you not to make any changes before you and I have an opportunity to talk.

She sent a return text. Apologies. You used up your orders when you tried to match me up with a man nearly the age of our father. *Ciao.*

Then she turned off her phone. Pippa felt a rush of adrenaline race through her. Her heart hammered against her rib cage. She was so rarely defiant. She exulted in the feeling. For a moment. Then she realized she needed to find a place to live. Immediately.

She spent the morning making calls to apartments, eliminating those without a security gate. By afternoon, she had a list of properties and made visits. At five-thirty, she signed a lease for a one-bedroom apartment. It cost a little more than she'd hoped, but the situation was perfect for her. Now if she could just ditch her security detail.

Pippa finally turned on her phone again, dreading the incoming voice mails and messages. She was immediately deluged by messages from Stefan, some of which had been written in all capital letters. She deleted them without reading and sent one last message regarding her security and the fact that she was ready to make a press release regarding her status change in security.

A half beat later, her phone rang, and her stomach immediately tightened. Pippa saw that it was Stefan and considered pushing the ignore button. *Coward.* Scowling at the truth in the accusation, she picked up the call. "Good evening, Your Royal Highness," she said.

"What in bloody hell has gotten into you?" Stefan demanded. "I realize getting you together with the count was a stretch, but your overreaction is totally unnecessary."

"It's not an overreaction. I just turned twenty-five," she said.

"But you've never complained before," Stefan said. "I can't allow you to move out and dismiss your security. Are you sure you're not having some sort of women's issue?"

If his pompous attitude weren't so offensive, she would have laughed. "Pretend I'm male and this will all seem overdue," she said.

"But you're not. You're my youngest sister and it's my duty to protect you."

Her heart softened. "That's so sweet, Stefan, and I do appreciate it, but I will die of suffocation if I stay at the palace. It's time for me to go."

"I don't understand this. You've always been so reasonable," he said.

"Acquiescent," she corrected. "I feel like Rapunzel, but with bad hair."

Stefan sighed. "At least continue your security."

"No. My security is a leash. It's unnecessary except when I make appearances assigned by the palace. Trust me, the citizens of Chantaine will cheer when they see another expense deducted by the palace."

"They won't know about it until after the fact," Stefan said and swore. "Promise you'll still attend family dinners," he added.

"I will," she said, her heart softening again. "You're so busy you won't notice that I'm gone."

"I already notice," he said.

Pippa felt her eyes burn with tears. Her emotions

caught her off guard, but she refused to give in to them. "I promise to babysit your new child," she said. "None of the new generation of Devereauxs will escape my terrible singing voice."

Stefan laughed. "I love you, Pippa."

Pippa's heart caught. For her hardnosed brother to admit such feelings aloud was monumental. It was all she could do to choke the words through her throat. "And I love you."

They hung up, and Pippa began to weep.

The following day, she enlisted the help of security to help her move into her apartment. She was able to make her move under the radar of Bridget because her sister was busy with the construction of the new so-called ranch. Pippa didn't want her security man to get a hernia, so she insisted he get help.

By noon, she was moved into her apartment. Surprisingly enough, she had more room in her new quarters than her previous suite at the palace. She felt a strange combination of relief and anxiety.

Sinking down onto the antique sofa that seemed so out of place in her new surroundings, she took a deep breath. She was free. That was what she'd wanted. Right?

A knock on the door startled her. She rose, looked through the peephole and saw Nic standing outside her door. She whipped the door open. "How did you find me? And how did you get through security?"

"Goldie," he said with a shrug. "You gonna invite me in?"

Fighting a sudden, strange awkwardness, she nodded. "Of course."

He stepped inside and glanced around. "Downsizing?" he asked.

"Actually the apartment is larger than my quarters at the palace," she said, folding her arms over her chest.

"Really," he said more than asked as he glanced around the apartment. "Did they put you in the palace dungeon or something?"

She laughed. "No, but I had no children, so I didn't need a larger suite. How did Goldie find out about my move?"

Nic shrugged. "Goldie has his ways. I don't question him. He just gets the job done. Why didn't you tell me about your plans for the big move?"

"Besides the fact that I didn't know if it would all work out, I don't owe anyone an explanation about my plans," she said.

He gave a low whistle and dipped his head. "As you say, Your Highness."

She wrinkled her nose at his response. "Truthfully, would you feel the need to make explanations about your own living arrangements?"

He met her gaze and gave another shrug. "Touché. I'm just curious what inspired all this."

"It's been a long time coming," she said, walking toward the balcony window. "Stefan fought it every inch of the way. I know he means well, but it will take him a long time to understand what I said about feeling like Rapunzel with very bad hair."

"I like your hair," Nic said.

She laughed, her heart warming at his comment. "That's not the point. I must confess I'm a bit worried that it was so easy for Goldie to find me. If he can get through the security, others could, too."

"Not likely," Nic said. "Many foreign nations could learn a lot from Goldie."

"But how did you get through?" she asked.

"I'm interested in buying the entire complex," he said.

Pippa blinked. "Pardon me?"

"It's just a story, but you never know," he said. "Have you ordered pizza?"

"What do you mean?"

"It's a tradition. Whenever you move, you order pizza for dinner because you're too tired for anything else," he said.

"I hadn't thought of it, but—"

"It's on me," he said with a sexy smile. "Because I didn't get here fast enough to help you move in."

Her heart softened. "That's very nice," she said.

"I have ulterior motives," he confessed. "I want you to share it with me."

"I can do that," she said.

Forty-five minutes later they sat with their feet propped on the boxes, munching on a loaded pizza. "I would have chosen vegetarian," Pippa said, but took a bite of her second slice anyway.

Nic shook his head. "No. Moving day turns everyone into a carnivore."

"If you say so," she said, smiling at him. "What made you put Goldie on me?"

"When I didn't hear from you, I got worried. I didn't know how hard your family would be on you once they learned about your relationship with the Lafittes."

"They still don't know," she said, taking a long draw from her glass of water.

He shot her a look of disbelief. "You sure?"

"Reasonably sure. I can't believe neither Stefan nor Bridget would be able to hold back their opinions if they knew. They're both extremely outspoken," she said.

"Bet Stefan hated that you moved out. I don't think he thought you would go through with it," he said.

"Hate is a mild term for it," she said, smiling at him. "And you're right. He didn't believe I would go through with it even though I'd warned him."

He grinned at her in return. "I'm surprised the palace didn't disintegrate from his temper tantrum."

"The palace has endured temper tantrums over the course of several centuries," she said. "I must confess I wonder if Stefan has cracked a few walls."

"Well, he's turning the tide. He's no playboy prince," Nic said. "That kind of will is going to shake some foundations."

Pippa nodded. "That's a good way of saying it. Stefan has fought to overcome my father's reputation."

"I'd say he's doing a pretty damn good job."

"He is. I've tried to support him, but I had to move away from the palace. I couldn't stand the restraints anymore."

"The timing's interesting. Did the Lafittes have anything to do with your decision?"

"Perhaps," she said. "You're all such independent sorts, even Amelie. You made me aware of how trapped I feel."

"And how do you feel now?" he asked.

"Great," she said, reluctant to reveal even her tiniest regret.

"And a little scared," he said.

"I didn't say that," she said.

"Your mouth didn't, but your eyes did," he said and cupped her chin. "You're gonna be okay, Pippa. You're stronger than anyone thinks."

"What makes you so sure?" she asked.

He gave a dry chuckle. "You've already proven yourself ten times over."

The strength in his gaze both empowered and aroused her. The combination of feelings was strange but undeniable. She leaned toward him and he took her mouth. The room began to spin.

The kiss turned into another and another. Soon enough, he'd removed her blouse and skirt. She pushed away his shirt and jeans, and he was inside her. This time, slowly.

"Okay?" he asked, his restraint vibrating from his body.

"Yes," she said, drawing him into her.

The rhythm began. She took him and he filled her. More than ever, they had more in common. She was a rebel just like him, and their joining was more powerful with the knowledge of it.

The next morning, Nic awakened before dawn on the mattress on which they'd collapsed on the floor. Pippa breathed in a deep, even sleep. She'd been exhausted and he could still feel her tiredness against him. But Nic had tasks calling him, even at this time of day. His businesses, his father's business, his mother's illness.

He tried to make himself slow down and relax for just a few moments.

"You're awake," Pippa whispered and turned her face into his throat.

His heart stuttered. "How did you know?"

"Your whole body is tense. I can almost feel your mind clicking a million kilometers an hour," she said.

He felt the slightest easing inside him. "I thought you were asleep."

She gave a soft chuckle that tickled his throat. "Not."

He tugged her fabulous, curly hair with one hand and slid his hand low between her legs. "As long as you're awake."

She gave a soft intake of breath. "Oh, my."

"Oh, yeah," he said and began to make love to her.

An hour later, they took a shower together and had to hunt for towels. They dried off with blankets instead which provided even more of a distraction.

Nic dressed in the clothes he'd worn the day before. Pippa stood before him with a damp blanket wrapped around her.

"Will you be okay?" he asked.

"Of course," she said. "I have a dozen boxes to unpack. My biggest fear of the day is a visit from Bridget or a call from Tina."

He rubbed her shoulders. "You can handle them."

"Yes, it just won't be fun," she said and made a face.

"Call me if you need me to break any legs," he said.

She laughed. "Now that would go over well."

"I'll check in on you later, but seriously, call me if you need me," he said.

"I will," she said. "And I may take a break from unpacking to visit your mother."

"She would like that," he said. "She did okay physically after the procedure to drain extra fluid, but I can tell it bothered her to need it."

She sighed. "I wish I could change this for her."

"You already have," he said.

"Have you been able to reach your brothers?" she asked.

"Two down, one to go," he said. "They said no the first three times I talked to them. I've got them up to a maybe."

"You're amazing and they're stupid," she said.

"It's complicated with my dad," he said. "If I hadn't been successful on my own so young, I may have shared their attitude. The weird thing about that success is that it freed me to forgive him."

Pippa loved him even more for his ability to express how he'd grown. Not every man could do that. She reached for his hand. "You're a good man."

His hand enclosed hers. "Careful. Never forget that I come from pirates."

Chapter Ten

Nic chewed through another two antacids as he stared at his electronic tablet and tried to figure out when he could break away for a two-day business trip. His mother had seemed more tired than usual lately, sleeping more during the day. He didn't know what in hell to do. If he left and she passed, he would never forgive himself.

He had thought that spending the day and night with Pippa in Capri would rid him of the increasing edginess he'd felt 24/7. Being with Pippa calmed a part of him, and he'd thought just a little time away with her would give him the break he'd never admit to needing.

He'd known going into this that it would be no picnic, but he would never have predicted the effect the situation would have on his body. He had begun to feel like a caged animal, rarely sleeping longer than three hours at night. The knowledge of his mother's impending death seemed to squeeze his throat tighter and tighter every day. He was always running out of antacids. He'd been determined to keep his emotions under strict control, but his frustration at his inability to change his mother's pain and the ugly progress of her disease wore him down.

He heard the sound of his mother singing outside his window and immediately glanced outside. He stared in disbelief at the sight of her as she approached the pool. It was 1:00 a.m.

Alarmed, Nic raced out the door. "Mother, what in hell are you doing?"

Amelie glanced over her shoulder. "Oh, hello, darling. What are you doing up so late?"

Nic felt a sliver of relief. At least she was lucid. He let out a half breath. "Finishing up some work," he said, moving toward her. Although she was still eating, she looked thinner.

Amelie tilted her head, sympathy creasing her brows. "You're not sleeping well, are you?" she said more than asked. "Come here and sit with me for a few minutes. I was going to go for a swim, but it can wait," she said as she sank into a chair.

Nic shook his head, but joined her. "You can't go swimming. Dr. McCall said you have to wait for five days after the procedure to swim or take a tub bath."

She frowned. "I could have sworn it's already been five days." She waved her hand. "My memory's not the best lately. The pain meds help the pain, but they make me sleepy. Makes for a difficult choice." She sighed. "But enough about me. I'm sick of it all being about me. How are you and Pippa?"

"What do you mean me and Pippa?" he asked, rubbing his jaw.

"Well, there's obviously something between you. It's a wonder the sparks don't burn down the cottage. What are you going to do about it?"

"It's complicated," he said.

She laughed. "You think I don't understand complications?"

"She's very devoted to her family. They hate me. It's an impossible situation for her. I can't ask her to give up her family," he said.

"Pippa is a very strong woman. You're a strong man. The two of you together, you may be able to achieve something that seems impossible," she said.

Nic couldn't see it. He couldn't see asking such a thing of Pippa after all she'd already done for him and his mother.

"You have no faith," she said. "You'll have to find your way. But remember what I said."

"I will," he said.

"And I wish you wouldn't suffer so much about the fact that I'm dying. I'm going to be fine. I'm a bit worried about your father, but I think if you get him a dog, it will help."

Nic blinked. "A dog?"

His mother nodded. "He'll need the blind adoration and companionship. Trust me on this."

His stomach knotted at the direction of their conversation. "We don't have to talk about this."

"Yes, we do," she said and put her hand over his. "I'm worried about you."

He clenched his jaw. “You don’t need to worry about me. You raised me to be strong.”

“Yes, but you don’t have superpowers. Deep inside, you think you should be able to save me, and the fact that you can’t is ripping you apart. If I’d known it would be this hard for you, I would have stayed in the States and worked with hospice. This has been too much of a burden on you.”

“I wouldn’t have it any other way,” he said. “Except for you not to die,” he said, his eyes stinging with emotion.

“Oh, darling, you will always have me with you,” she said. “I promise. And I believe you’ll feel it. It will hurt terribly in the beginning, but I’ll always be with you. You’re doomed. You have my genetic material and that won’t go away.”

He laughed at her words, struggling with a dozen emotions, most of them sad and wrenching. “Is there anything else I can do for you?”

“You’ve already done it. You’ve given me this wonderful gift of time in Chantaine. Now live your life,” she said. “If you need to take care of business, do it. But don’t forget your heart. Never ever forget to have fun and to have heart. Promise?” she asked.

He took a deep breath. “I promise.”

She looked wistfully at the pool. “Are you sure you won’t let me cheat and take a quick dip?”

“One more day, and you can be a dolphin. But not until.”

“You’re such a tyrant,” Amelie said. “But I’m tired again anyway. Good night, darling. Try to get some rest. You know how cranky you get when you don't get your beauty sleep."

He rolled his eyes. "I'll try," he said and helped her to her feet and walked her to the front door. At that moment, he knew what he had to do. She hadn't asked for it, but there was one more thing his mother wanted and he was damn well going to do it for her.

The next day, Pippa came to visit. She began pulling off her disguise the second she climbed out of the car. "Hate this," she muttered. "Completely and totally hate this."

Even her griping made Nic feel a little lighter. He stepped outside his door and grabbed her from behind. She gave a squeal.

"It's me," he assured. "The gray wig brings out my primal urges," he said.

She laughed breathlessly and turned toward him. "You're insane."

"I do my best," he said. "It's damn good to see you." He took her mouth in a long kiss that made him want far more than a kiss.

"I've been unpacking," she said. "I didn't think I had that much, but I clearly underestimated. Plus, I had nothing in my refrigerator and couldn't ring the chef for breakfast or dinner."

"Oooh, tough break, Your Highness. Sure you don't want to move back into the palace?" he asked. "I know Stefan would take you back."

She shook her head. "There will be adjustments. That's expected. Nothing a toaster and microwave won't cure. Plus I'm told my security detail is retiring at the end of this week. The true beginning of my new life will start then."

"Yeah, just be careful," he said. As much as Pippa's security had been a pain in his backside, the fact that she'd had it had given him a measure of relief.

"Oh dear, you're sounding just a bit like Stefan," she said.

"Cut me some slack. I can be protective, too," he said.

She nodded. "I know. It's not totally bad when not taken to extremes," she said. "How are your mother and father?"

"Dad is getting stronger. Mom is getting weaker. It's going to be tricky keeping my dad occupied," he said.

She frowned. "Do I need to take him on an outing?"

Nic chuckled at the image of Pippa taking his dad to the knitting store or brunch. "Nah, I'll just get Goldie to wear him out with some extra workouts."

She nodded. "And what about you?" she asked and he felt as if she were turning a searchlight on his insides.

"I'm good," he said with a shrug.

"You lie, but I understand," she said and squeezed his arm. "I'm sorry this is so hard for you, but you wouldn't be the man I—" She broke off. "You wouldn't be the man I admire you if it weren't hard for you."

"Yeah, well," he said and picked her up off her feet.

Her eyes widened. "What are you doing?"

"Just checking your weight. Making sure you're not wasting away without a chef."

She laughed. "I'm not suffering that much," she said.

He pulled her against him and slid her down the

front of him. "I'm headed out of town tomorrow. Can you come over tonight?"

She nodded.

He felt a rush of relief. "I'll send Goldie to pick you up. Wear this and you'll be fine."

Pippa groaned. "As soon as my security guy retires, I'm burning the wig."

"Don't rush it. You never know when you'll need it."

"Where are you headed?"

"Back to the States for business and one personal mission. Let's go see my mom. She'll fuss if she knows I kept you from going inside," he said.

Pippa saw the weariness stamped on Amelie's face. Nic's mother tried to hide it, but it was unmistakable. Still, Amelie seemed happy to see her and Pippa promised to visit with her the following day. Not wanting to tire her further, Pippa gave the woman a hug and left. Nic walked her to the dreadful machine that was her covert car.

"I'll see you later," he said, pulling her against him. His strength tugged at her. She didn't know how he kept everything together. She just longed to help him as much as she could.

"Later," she promised and kissed him, then drove away.

Hours later, she ate a frozen dinner and tried to play catch-up with her academic work. First, she waited for her security detail to leave for the evening, then she waited for Goldie's call. Her stomach danced with nerves on her way to see Nic.

The more time she spent with Nic, the more she felt

as if she were making a commitment toward him. With the way her family felt about the Lafittes, she just didn't see how anything between her and Nic could end well. Pippa closed her eyes against the thoughts. She couldn't think past tonight. There was too much to work out and she knew she couldn't do it all at once.

But she could be with Nic tonight, hold him and treasure the way she felt when she was with him, the way she felt in his arms.

When Goldie pulled into the driveway, he immediately got out and opened the door for her. "Your Highness," he said with a dip of his head.

"Thank you, Goldie," she said. "But I already told you to call me Pippa."

"Yes, you're welcome, Your—" The big man broke off and smiled. "Your Pippa," he said.

She smiled. He was such a gentle giant.

"I'll take you home whenever you like," he said. "Enjoy your evening."

Pippa walked the few steps to the guest suite and lifted her hand to knock on the door, but it opened before she had a chance.

Nic caught her hand and pulled her inside. "What took you so long?"

"I waited for my security detail to go home," she said.

"Good for you," he said. "Have you had dinner?"

She nodded. "As a matter of fact, I have."

"Are you going to tell me what you ate?"

She shook her head. "No."

He chuckled. "That tells me enough. Goldie put together some appetizers and he baked a pie."

"A pie?" she echoed. "Is there anything he can't do?"

"Not much," he said. "Have a seat. I'll get you a glass of wine."

They shared easy conversation while they ate the appetizers. Pippa was almost too full for pie.

"The proper way to eat this apricot pie is with ice cream," Nic said.

"À la mode," she said. "But I can't imagine eating a full slice."

"Then we can share," he said and scooped up a bite for her. The gesture was both generous and sensual.

"Delicious again," she said. "What time do you leave tomorrow?"

"We're not going to talk about tomorrow, but I'm leaving around 5:00 a.m."

Pippa gasped. "You should go to bed and I should leave. You need to get your rest."

"I can sleep on the flight, but I like your idea of going to bed," he said, his dark gaze wrapping around hers and holding tight.

She took a last sip of her wine and met his challenge. "Then what are you waiting for?"

He immediately took her hand and led her to the bed. He skimmed his hand over her crazy, curly hair. "I didn't expect to want you this much after the first time we were together," he said, kissing her. "How can I want you more?"

Her heart hammered in her chest. "I hope I'm not the only one who feels this way," she whispered. "It's almost too much."

"I know," he said. "I've never felt this way before."

"That's a relief," she said and tugged at his shirt.

"Maybe for you. It's hell for me," he said, and began to undress her.

They kissed and caressed each other into a frenzy. He made her breathless and she did the same to him. Finally he filled her and they stared into each other's eyes.

Pippa wasn't sure if it took seconds or moments later. She only knew she felt taken all the way to her soul.

"I want you," he muttered. "I need you. I—"

He didn't finish, but she craved the words, the emotion, everything that he was. Her heart and stomach clenched, and she arched toward him as he thrust deeply inside her.

Her climax sent her soaring.

"It's never enough," he said. "I can't get enough of you."

Thank goodness, she thought and wrapped herself around him from head to toe. She clung to him with every fiber of her being, wanting him to draw her strength into him.

"I want you with me," he said next to her ear. "All the time."

Love me, she thought. *Love me just for me, that's all I want.* She wished he would say, *I'll take care of you forever.* The thought took her by surprise. Pippa didn't want to be the one taken care of. She wanted to be the woman strong enough to stand up and take care of her man and give him anything he needed from her.

"I want to be with you anytime," Pippa whispered. "Every time."

They made love again and afterward, Pippa realized that Nic needed rest. He might deny it, but the truth was he needed rest. She knew he needed far more rest than he could possibly get tonight.

Relaxed against him, Pippa fought sleep. "I need to go back to my apartment."

Nic swore. "I wanted to talk you into staying here all night."

"It will be easier for you to rest tonight, then wake up to leave tomorrow without me here," she said.

"Says who?" he said.

"Says me," she said and lifted her hand to stroke his forehead. "You have a tough trip ahead of you. Business and something else you're not telling me."

He leaned his head back and narrowed his eyes. "How do you know?" he challenged.

"I just do," she said. "Besides, you said you had a personal mission, too."

He scowled at her, then chuckled. "I'm going to bring my brothers back. Even if I have to kidnap them."

Pippa gasped, then bit her lip. "Well, bloody hell, if anyone can do it, you can."

He laughed louder this time and put his hands on either side of her hand as if she were the most precious thing in the universe.

"If you get arrested," she began.

"Would you pay my bail?" he asked.

"Oh, yes," she said without a second thought. She squeezed his hands. "Call me anytime," she told Nic.

"I will, unless a police officer does…asking you to make bail," he said and gave a dry chuckle.

"You're a bad, bad boy with an amazing heart," she said.

"That's why you fell for me from the beginning," he said.

She bit her lip. "Yeah, maybe. Just promise me you'll take care of you," she said.

"I will. Spend some time with my mother," he said. "She's on the edge and I have a feeling you could bring her away from it."

Surprised at his belief in her ability, she shook her head. "I'll visit her tomorrow, but you know I can't control her future."

"Yeah," he said. "I think being with you makes things better for her."

"I'll do my best," she promised. "My very best."

Pippa reluctantly dragged herself from Nic's bed and washed her face and pulled on her clothes. Stepping out of the bathroom, she felt Nic step behind her and wrap his arms around her. "What are you doing?"

"Drawing your life force into me," he said.

She giggled. "That sounds ominous if it were possible."

"How do you know it's not?" he asked.

"I'm taking a wild guess," she said, turning in his arms.

"Well, damn," he said.

"Well, damn," she echoed, and they kissed. She caressed his mouth and squeezed his body tight. "Kick your brothers' asses down the street like a can and bring them here to Chantaine."

He drew back to meet her gaze. "That's pretty strong language for a princess," he said.

"Just sayin'," she said.

"How cool are you?" he said. "I'll get the job done.

Thanks for sticking with me," he said with a gaze that held all kinds of crazy emotions she was determined to ignore but couldn't. "I'll see you soon," he said.

She kissed him and headed toward the door. "*Ciao,* darling," she said. "Be safe."

Goldie drove her home even though it was 2:00 a.m. He didn't even blink at the time. Pippa took a deep breath and leaned her head back against the seat. "You're kind to drive me back to the apartment at such a crazy hour."

He shrugged. "Crazy is relative," he said.

"You're quite amazing," she said. "With all your skills. Nic and I ate your appetizers and a few bites of your amazing pie last night."

"Cooking relaxes me. I'm glad you enjoyed the food I prepared," he said.

"It was delicious. Is there anything that helps you relax? You spend so much of your time working," she said.

Goldie took a deep breath. "I'm addicted to yoga."

"Really?" Pippa asked. "Does it make that much of a difference?"

"Yes," Goldie said. "Relieves pain, allows me to relax and sleep."

"Do you go to a special studio?" she asked.

"Sometimes," he said. "Otherwise, I use a DVD or cable on TV."

"What station?" she asked.

He smiled. "Eight. You can DVR it. Meditation and acupuncture can help, too."

Pippa thought about the prospect of having needles

stuck inside her and shook her head. "If you say so," she said.

"Take it slow. You will learn your truth," he said.

"Goldie, what do you think of this whole crazy situation with me, Nic, Amelie and Paul?" she said.

"You're more powerful than you know," he said.

She thought about that for a moment. "I hope so, but speaking of power—you are quite powerful and talented. Why do you stay with the Lafittes?" she asked.

"They are my home," he said. "I would do anything for them."

His resolute statements sent chills through her. "I wish I had your talent and your fortitude," she said.

"You have both," he said. "Don't fear them."

Goldie pulled into her apartment complex, flashing a pass, then driving toward her apartment. "I'll escort you upstairs," he said.

"It's not necessary," she said.

"It is for me," he said, pulling to a stop. Stepping outside the car, he opened her door and walked with her to her second-floor apartment. "I'll wait outside. Knock on the door to let me know you're okay."

Pippa ventured inside her apartment. For just a half beat, she felt lonely and insecure. Then she gave a quick walk-through to her bedroom. She realized she was okay and opened the door. "No one here but me," she said to Goldie. "Perhaps I should get a cat."

Goldie chuckled. "Good night, Your Highness," he said.

Pippa spent most of the next day with Amelie. Nic's mother knitted, chatted and dozed on and off throughout the day. Pippa noticed that Amelie's energy came and went in short spurts. Paul lumbered restlessly on crutches. Nic had been correct about his father's need to release pent-up energy. Goldie stepped in and helped occupy Paul.

Pippa remembered Amelie when she'd had so much more energy. She'd been so lively, engaging. Irresistible. She still possessed her charm even when sleeping. Her stubby eyelashes rimmed her eyes. Her face growing more gaunt every day, full of wrinkles, crinkles, hollows and bones, defined her character. Her stubborn chin told the world she would push it to the max, till the very end. Amelie was nothing if not a fighter.

Pippa felt her throat suddenly close shut at the realization that Amelie was going to die, and it would be soon. She'd known all along that Amelie's time was short, but Pippa realized she'd been in denial. Amelie's time was all too close. Pippa left a little later than she'd planned. Goldie gave her a sandwich and followed her home.

Pippa took a shower and fell into a dreamless sleep. She awakened to the sound of her cell phone beeping. Glancing at the caller ID, she saw that Bridget was on the line.

Reluctantly, she accepted the call. "Good morning, Bridget. How are you?"

"When did you move? Why didn't you tell me? I went to your suite and you weren't there. Stefan won't discuss it, but he's clearly furious. How could you do this to us?"

"I moved a few days ago. It took place quickly because I had to do it before I lost my courage. I couldn't continue to live in the palace. I felt so trapped," Pippa said.

"We all feel trapped," Bridget scoffed. "The key is stealing your freedom whenever you can."

"You're a better fighter than I am," Pippa said. "I needed to finish the big fight so there could be peace for me, for everyone."

Silence stretched between them. Bridget gave an audible sigh. "I want to argue with you, but I can't. I obviously haven't had enough coffee." She gave a growl of frustration. "Maybe I'm just jealous that you got out before I did."

Pippa smiled. "You're right on my heels with your ranch in sight. You have Ryder and your boys. I have… genealogy."

"I still may find a man for you," Bridget said.

"Oh, please. If you love me, Bridget, stop," she said and laughed.

"Everyone deserves a second chance," Bridget said.

"Maybe in five years," Pippa said.

"That was cruel," her sister said. "Don't forget, there's a family dinner tonight."

"Lovely," Pippa said. "I'll have the whole table glowering at me."

"Don't be late," Bridget said. "*Ciao,* darling."

Chapter Eleven

"I want to go to the ocean," Amelie said at three-thirty.

Pippa blinked. "The ocean?" Today had been a duplicate of yesterday with Amelie knitting, chatting and sleeping except for this latest request.

"Yes, I want to swim," Amelie said, standing. "I'll put on my suit."

Pippa followed the woman to her feet. "I'm not sure that's wise. I don't think you're supposed to be swimming."

"Why not?" Amelie asked.

"Well, because of your condition," Pippa said.

"Oh, you mean the draining procedure. I'm permitted to swim after five days. I don't suppose you have a suit. I'm not sure mine would fit. Perhaps I should go by myself."

No. "I'll come up with something. Goldie can help me," Pippa said. "Go change into your suit." She wondered if Amelie would tire before they were able to leave. As soon as Amelie walked down the hallway, Pippa called for Goldie. Somehow she ended up with shorts and a tank top.

With surprising energy, Amelie returned wearing a caftan, the strap of her swimsuit peeking through the shoulder sliding over her too-slim frame. "Ready to be a little fish?" she asked with a singsong tone in her voice.

"Ready," Pippa said. "Goldie said he'll drive us."

Amelie frowned. "But what about Paul?"

"He's already given Paul a good workout. Paul is napping in the extra room," Pippa said.

"Excellent," Amelie said. "Let's go. Another adventure."

Heaven help them all, Pippa thought. Moments later, they trudged through the sandy beach toward the ocean. Partway there, Amelie pulled her caftan over her head and dropped her towel on the sand. She lifted her head to the sun and smiled like a child.

Pippa's heart caught. She picked up her cell phone and clicked a photo and another. She was no photographer, but she hoped the photos somehow captured Amelie's love of life.

"Let's go," Amelie called. "Before the water gets too cold."

Pippa tossed her cell phone into her bag and ran toward the ocean with Nic's mother. The water was already cold. Pippa muffled a shriek. "It's a bit nippy."

"Could be worse," Amelie said. "We're lucky it's not winter. The waves are so calm."

Amelie reached for Pippa's hand. "Isn't it lovely?"

Pippa took a deep breath and looked at the beautiful

blue ocean with the slightest caps of white. Both she and Amelie wore water shoes to cushion them from the rocky ground.

Amelie smiled but her teeth chattered. "I always wanted to be a fish or a dolphin," she said. "Or a butterfly."

"You're all of those in one," she said.

Amelie laughed. Her lips were turning blue. "You're such a lovely person. The perfect princess." Her smile fell. "The one thing I'll miss is meeting my grandchildren. You could have my first grandchild."

Pippa stared at Amelie in shock. "Grandchild?" she echoed. She felt her insides clench. Could Amelie sense something? In fact, she was late with her period, but because she wasn't regular, pregnancy wasn't a concern. Nic had worn protection.

"Don't worry, it will all work out. You'll have a beautiful baby," Amelie said.

Pippa wondered for a moment if Nic's mother was suffering from some kind of delusion. "You've grown cold. We should go back."

"Just a moment longer," she said. "I want to feel the water and the waves a moment longer."

Pippa laced her fingers more tightly through Amelie's and began to count. She was torn between protecting Amelie's pleasure and her fragile health. Amelie stumbled, then dipped her shoulders underneath the water.

"Amelie," Pippa said.

Seconds later, Amelie ducked her head beneath, frightening the bloody hell out of Pippa. She tugged on Amelie's hand, pulling her above the surface. "What are you doing?" she asked Nic's mother.

"It was so nice under the water," Amelie said, beaming. "I feel like I'm nine years old again."

Pippa put her arms around Amelie and squeezed her tight. "Let's get our towels. I want you cozy and warm."

Amelie's teeth chattered as Pippa led her to their towels. Goldie rushed out to help them into the car. "Turn on the heat, please," Pippa said.

"But it's—" Goldie broke off and met Pippa's gaze. Understanding flowed between them. For Amelie, it may as well have been winter. Her body was so thin and she'd become chilled in the water.

"I hope she won't get sick from this," Pippa said, scrubbing Amelie's arms.

"She won't," Goldie said. "You did the right thing, Your Highness. She was determined to go to the sea. We're lucky you went with her."

They returned to the cottage and Pippa helped Amelie into cozy pajamas, then into bed. Only after Goldie's promise to frequently check on Amelie did Pippa agree to leave. As she climbed into cab, she noticed the time. Bloody hell. She was going to be late for the family dinner.

Rushing, rushing, rushing, she took a shower, dressed herself and pulled her errant hair into a bun. Forget cosmetics, she told herself. She drove to the palace and raced up to the private dining room and burst inside. Everyone was there, her brother, his child and his pregnant wife, Eve, her sister Bridget, her husband, Ryder, and the twins. For one stunning moment, they were silent. Damn them.

"Hi," she said, forcing a big smile. "I'm so sorry I'm late. Time got away from me." She sank into the empty seat. "How are you feeling, Eve?"

Eve shot her a look of sympathy. "Better, thank you. How are your studies?"

"I'm getting there," Pippa said and glanced at Bridget. "How's the ranch?"

"Well, if we could get the plumbing and the kitchen straight, we'd be most of the way there," Bridget said. "Why is your hair wet?"

"I just took a shower," Pippa said and reached for her glass of water. She eyed the wine, but remembering what Amelie said, she wasn't sure she should do much drinking. She didn't think she was pregnant, but she supposed it was remotely possible.

Her hand shook as she held the glass of water. *Pregnant? No.*

"What's for dinner?" she asked brightly.

"Beef, rare," Eve said, wincing slightly. "Stefan's favorite."

"Mashed potatoes for Eve and anyone else who wants them. It's the only thing she can eat. That, and bread."

With the help of her screaming niece and nephews, Pippa made it through the meal. She gave a sigh of relief as dessert was served. Bananas flambé served with a flourish. She took a few bites, then discreetly motioned for one of the servers to take her plate.

"This had been wonderful, but I should leave. Back to work early tomorrow," she said and pushed back her chair.

"I'd like a word with you," Stefan said. "In my office."

"Our suite," Eve said. "Stephenia would love a bedtime hug and kiss from her aunt Pippa."

A flicker of irritation crossed his face, but he appeared to mask it with a quick nod. "Our suite will be fine." He said good-night to Bridget and her family, then the four of them made their way to Stefan and Eve's suite. Pippa had noticed Stefan had appeared more remote than usual this evening, but she'd just thought he was either still peeved about her move or his mind was on something else altogether.

Once inside the suite, Pippa kneeled down and extended her arms to Stephenia. "Come give me a big hug."

The little girl rushed toward her, her curls bobbing. Laughing, she threw her little body against Pippa. Her uninhibited expression of joy and complete trust tugged at Pippa's heart. "Now that's a hug," Pippa said and kissed the toddler's soft cheek. "You are such a sweet and smart girl. I bet you've been busy today."

Eve nodded with a wry expression on her face. "There'll be an early bedtime for Mamaeve tonight, too. Come along, Stephenia. You need to pick out your book. And Stefan—" she said but stopped.

Pippa saw the silent communication between the two of them and wondered what was going on. Surely he couldn't still be so upset about her move from the palace.

Stefan brushed a kiss over his daughter's cheek. "Sweet dreams," he said, echoing Eve's frequent nighttime wish.

As soon as Eve and Stephenia walked toward the

bedrooms at the other end of the suite, Stefan turned toward Pippa. "How are you?"

"Well, thank you. And you?"

"Also well. Your studies?"

Pippa resisted the urge to squirm. She'd been forced to put her academic work aside during the last week. "Demanding as always."

"You've been quite busy since you returned from Italy," he said. He pulled out a computer tablet and turned it on.

The uneasiness inside her grew. "Moving makes for a busy time." She hesitated to ask but went ahead anyway. "What is your point?"

"Some photographs of you were posted on a social network just before dinner. I'll be surprised if they don't make the rag sheets by morning." He showed her a series of photos of her holding hands with Amelie in the ocean. "The woman looks familiar," he said in a cool voice.

Her stomach knotted, yet at the same time an overwhelming relief swept through her. "Good eye, Your Royal Highness. That's Amelie Lafitte."

Stefan clenched his jaw. "What in hell have you gotten yourself into?"

Pippa sighed. "I got myself involved with a family experiencing a tragedy."

"What tragedy? I'd heard Amelie had been ill for some time, but if she's swimming, she must have recovered."

Pippa shook her head. "Amelie is terminally ill. She's—she's dying."

Surprise crossed his face. "I'm sorry to hear that."

He cleared his throat. “That said, any association with the Lafittes is understandably forbidden. You must stop your involvement at once.”

Pippa shook her head. “Oh, I’m sorry. That’s not possible.”

Stefan tilted his head to one side in disbelief and disapproval. “Pardon me, of course it’s possible. You merely send a message to the Lafittes with your good wishes, but tell them you’re unable to continue the association.”

“I can’t and won’t do that. At this time of all times, I would hate myself for pulling away from them.”

Stefan’s jaw tightened again. “Pippa, after I received these photos, I asked my security detail to investigate the situation with the Lafittes. It has been brought to my attention that you’ve used family connections to secure a cottage for them. Not only that, Paul Lafitte, whose presence in this country is illegal, is living in this cottage. How do you think your cousin Georgina will feel when she learns you’ve used her cottage to house a criminal?”

“He’s not a criminal,” she said, unable to fight a stab of impatience. “He’s a man with a broken foot and he’s about to lose the love of his life.”

“Pippa, this is not up for discussion. What you’ve done is illegal and dishonest.”

“I’m not proud of being dishonest with all of you. I’ve hated every one of the lies I’ve had to tell, but your attitude made it impossible.”

“I don’t think you understand what a black mark this will make on our name. I insist you sever your relationship with the Lafittes," he said. "Please don't force my hand on this."

Pippa fought a sliver of fear, but her anger at his manipulation was stronger. "Are you threatening me? With what? Let's not keep it a mystery."

He paused, then narrowed his eyes. "If you don't stop your association with the Lafittes, I'll be forced to consider revoking your title."

Pippa absorbed the potential loss and made her decision in less than two breaths. "Then do what you have to do. I'll do what I must do. Helping the Lafittes through this painful time is the most important thing I've ever done in my life. If I lose my title over it, then c'est la vie. Good night, Stefan," she said and walked out of his suite.

Her heels clicked against the familiar marble palace floor. It crossed her mind that if Stefan carried through with his threat, this might be the last time she walked these halls. Worse yet, she realized, she might lose her relationship with her family. Her chest tightened with grief. Her hands began to shake and she balled them into fists. As much as her dysfunctional family drove each other crazy at times, Pippa loved them with all her heart. She would never get over losing them.

Deep in her heart, though, she knew that she would hate herself if she turned her back on the Lafittes. Stefan had forced her to make an impossible choice. She prayed she would have the strength to live with the consequences.

The connecting flight from Madrid began its descent into Chantaine just after 8:00 a.m. Nic rubbed his eyes, which felt like sandpaper. He looked at the passengers beside him and behind him. By some miracle, all three of his brothers were on the flight. Alex, his youngest brother, sat beside him gently snoring. Paul Jr., who went by James, and Michael sat across the aisle in the row behind them.

The plane had a bumpy landing. Nic hoped it wasn't a sign of what was to come for the rest of his brothers' visit.

Alex awakened, rubbing his face. He narrowed his eyes at Nic. "Looks like we made it. Are you sure our father isn't in a Chantaine dungeon somewhere?"

"You never know with Paul Lafitte, but he wasn't when I left," Nic said. "Besides, you're not here to see your father. You're here to see your mother," Nic said. "If you're man enough."

Alex scowled, but Nic knew that very same challenge had gotten Alex and Nic's other brothers onto the plane. He'd made a strong, no-holds-barred demand, and thank goodness, his brothers had responded.

"There's a car waiting," Nic said. "When we get to the cottage, you'll have a good meal."

An hour later, the driver drove the limo toward the cottage. The ride was mostly silent, but Nic figured he would be paying the price for the intimidation and manipulation he'd used to bring his brothers to his mother. Despite their anger, their brothers drank in the sight of their mother's island.

"Not bad," James said. "Never visited Chantaine before. Mom always said it was beautiful. She was right."

Alex gave a dry chuckle. "Who says they would have let us on the island?"

"You got on this time," Nic said.

"Because you've donated a ton of money and enhanced Chantaine's economy," Alex said.

"There are worse ways to spend money," Nic said.

The limo pulled into the driveway.

"Quaint," Paul Jr. said.

"A friend helped out," Nic said. He wondered how Pippa was doing. He knew that moving from the palace was a huge change for her. He and his brothers got out of the limo and walked to the front door.

Paul opened the door. On crutches, he looked at his four sons in shock. "Well, I'll be damned."

"We've already done that several times over," Paul Jr. said. "Where's Mom?"

Paul's expression hardened. "She's asleep, and if you can't show her respect and kindness, you can go the hell back where you came from," he said and slammed the door in their faces.

Silence followed.

"Same ol' dad," Michael said.

"Yep, sonofabitch, but he was always protective of her," Alex said.

"When he wasn't in prison," Paul Jr. said.

"This is stupid," Nic said. "Let's just go inside. Dad will have to deal with it. I'm sure Goldie has a great meal for us."

"Who's Goldie?" Paul Jr. asked.

"You'll know soon enough," Nic said and inserted his key into the door and pushed it open.

Paul had apparently hobbled to the back of the house. Nic turned on a baseball game and Goldie immediately showed up with platters of appetizers and sandwiches, along with beer. Beer before lunch may have seemed inappropriate, but in this case, it was for the best. His brothers commented on the food and the game while downing a few beers.

Finally, his mother appeared in the back of the den. "She's here," Nic said, turning off the TV. His mother was gaunt and tired, but clearly delighted to see her sons.

"Am I dreaming?" she asked, lifting her lips in a huge smile.

"Go," Nic said in his brother Michael's ear.

"Me?" Michael asked.

Nic nodded, and half a breath later, Michael sprang to his feet and enveloped his mother in hug. "I'm sorry I haven't—"

"No sorries, no apologies," Amelie said, hugging him in return. "I'm so happy to see you."

A moment later, James rose and pulled her into his arms. "Mom, I've missed you."

Alex finally stood and made his way to his mother. "I'm the worst of your sons," he confessed.

"No," she insisted with a smile. "You are all the best sons any woman could want because you came to see me before—" She broke off, her smile fading. "Before I turn into a butterfly."

Nic's heart wrenched at the sight before him. It had taken an enormous effort to make this happen. He just wished it hadn't been necessary.

His mother pretended to eat and sipped some lemonade while she enjoyed the visit with her sons. Amelie asked each of them about what they were doing. None were married and none had children, much to her disappointment. She encouraged all of them to enjoy Chantaine as much as possible during their visit, but Nic knew his brothers were leaving at 5:00 a.m. the next day.

After a while, Nic could tell she was growing tired. "We should let you rest," he said.

"In a bit. I have something to say first," she said. "You're not going to like this, but I raised you to be extraordinary men, so now's the time for you to man up."

The room turned silent. His brothers grew restless.

"Take a deep breath. Listen. It won't be that long. You can handle it," she said. "The truth is your father broke the rules because he was determined to take care of me. He was determined to keep me in the same way a princess should live because, after all, I could have been a princess. How do you compete with that? How do you produce a lifestyle fit for a princess, even though I didn't ask for it?"

His mother's words sank into him. He'd never realized what a burden his father had taken on when he'd stolen his mother from Prince Edward. It made him think of his current relationship with Pippa.

"Can't deny that was tough," James said. "But he made our life a living hell by destroying the family reputation."

"True," his mother said. "But that was a long time ago. It's time to get over it."

Silence followed.

"Excuse me?" Michael said. "Get over it? His disreputable dealings are the gifts that keep giving. We had to move out of the state to reestablish ourselves."

"Well," his mother said. "It's time for you to get over it. You've reestablished yourselves. Paul is nursing a broken foot. I have two things to ask of you," she said. "Be true brothers. Stand together. Be family. And forgive your father," she added.

Nic felt his brothers close up like locks at Fort Knox. "Love you, Mom," he said and moved toward her to give her a hug.

She embraced him in return. "Thank you," she said. "You made a miracle."

"No, it was you," he said. "I just added a little muscle."

"I'm getting tired. I should go to sleep. Can we get a photo of me with my boys?" she asked.

Goldie took a few photos and his mother went to bed. His brothers sacked out in the guest room and guest quarters. Nic considered calling Pippa, but he was drained. He resolved to call tomorrow afternoon, after his brothers left and he caught up with some rest.

Nic arranged for the limo that took his brothers to the airport in the early predawn morning, then went back to sleep. Hours later, a knock on the door awakened him. Goldie, wearing a tortured expression, dipped his head. "I'm so sorry, sir. Your mother has passed on."

Chapter Twelve

Numb from the news, Nic dialed Pippa's number as he paced his room an hour later.

"Hi. Welcome back," she said.

Her voice was like oxygen to his system. "Thanks," he said. "I have some bad news." He paused a beat because he'd already had to say the same thing several times. "She's gone."

"Oh, Nic, I'm so sorry. I'll be right over," she said.

"Good," he said, feeling a shot of relief that bothered him. Now, more than ever, he needed to keep himself in check. There was just too much to do and his father was a mess.

He made several more calls, unsure what to do about a memorial service. Thank goodness, his mother had made her burial wishes clear in her will. She wanted her ashes spread in Chantaine. Nic suspected his father would fight it.

He heard a vehicle pull into the driveway and immediately went to the door. Pippa stepped from the car and rushed into his arms. "I'm so sorry. How are you?" she asked.

Feeling her in his arms was a balm to his soul. "I'm okay. We knew this was coming."

"But you're never really ready," she said, pulling back to search his face.

"True, but we were more prepared than most," he said and led her into the den.

"How is your father?" she asked.

"Not good," Nic said. "He was having some pain with his foot, so he spent the whole night on the patio. My brothers were sleeping in the guestroom. I think my father must have taken an extra dose of pain reliever because he didn't even wake up when my brothers left early this morning. Goldie went in to take her a croissant and some juice. He was the one who found her. My father was horrified that she died alone." His throat closed up.

Pippa took his hand in hers. "But your brothers, did she see them?"

Nic nodded.

"It's almost as if she was waiting to see them again and that gave her permission. You did a wonderful thing by bringing them here," she said.

"Trust me, I had to be damn ugly to them to make it happen," he said.

"And now there are other things to be done. Arrangements," she said. "How can I help you?"

Nic took a deep breath. "I need one more favor. My mother wanted her ashes spread here in Chantaine."

"And a memorial service, too," she said, her eyebrows furrowing together in concern.

"Yeah," he said.

"I'll do my best. Not sure Stefan is speaking to me at the moment," she added in half jest.

"Why? Is he still upset that you moved out of the palace?" Nic demanded.

Pippa waved her hand in a dismissive gesture. "Stefan's always bothered about something. It's his nature. What about your brothers? You said they'd already left."

"They're on their way back," he said. "I'd like to do this quickly and get my father back to the States. There are too many sad memories for him here and he's going to have to find a new normal for himself."

Pippa nodded. "Okay, I'll go out by the pool area and make a few calls," she said and left him to his list.

Fifteen minutes later, she returned, relief on her face. "I was able to get permission for your mother's service. Because the weather has been good, I wondered if you would like it to take place outdoors. There's a lovely green park on the other side of the island that people use for all kinds of occasions including memorial services. Chairs can be set up for your family."

"That sounds good. Thank you," he said, mentally checking the decision off his list. Nic felt as if he had a million-mile journey in front of him. Pippa made everything feel easier, but soon enough, he would be back in the States and he would be handling everything by himself. Again.

Two days later, Pippa took a seat at the end of a second row of chairs arranged for Amelie Lafitte's memorial service. She didn't want to call attention to herself. By a stroke of luck, or fate, she'd located a minister who had lived in the same orphanage as Amelie. She was pleased that someone who had known Nic's mother would lead the service.

It was a beautiful morning. Amelie would have loved it.

"Excuse me, is that seat taken?" a familiar voice asked her.

Pippa looked up and surprise raced through at the sight of her sister-in-law, Eve, and her sister Bridget. She stood, feeling as if her heart would burst with gratitude. "I don't know what to say," she said. "I can't believe you're here."

"Of course we're here. You're family. This is where we're supposed to be. Stefan didn't come because he didn't want to turn things into a madhouse," Eve said. "But he sends his condolences to you and the Lafittes."

Pippa hugged Eve. "You must have given him a Texas-size lecture because the last I heard, I no longer had a title," she said.

Bridget rolled her eyes. "He's got to make that threat to each of us at some point. He just can't stand not having control sometimes, most times," she added and held out her arms. "Come here. Shame on you for suffering by yourself. Why can't you be more like me and make everyone suffer with you?"

Bridget's remark made her laugh despite how emotional she felt. "I knew none of you would approve," Pippa said. "But I couldn't turn my back on them."

"That's one of the many reasons we love you," Eve said as she took her seat. Bridget also took hers.

Within the next moments, many people arrived, taking seats and crowding around the area. "I didn't know this many people remembered Amelie," Bridget said, surprised at the number of people gathering in the park.

"You would understand if you'd met her. I wish you'd had the opportunity," Pippa said, her eyes suddenly filling with tears. "She was a magical person."

Bridget covered her hand in comfort and the Lafitte men arrived, filing into the front row of chairs reserved for Amelie's family. Seconds later, the minister stood at the front of the group and began to speak.

He delivered a heartfelt message with touches of humor as he described Amelie as a child and how she seemed to have held on to her sense of wonder despite life's trials. Nic then read a message his mother had written for the occasion. The sight of him so strong delivering his mother's last words wrenched at her. She knew he had to be suffering but wouldn't reveal it. Pippa wished with all her heart that she could help him.

As the service drew to a close, Pippa noticed Bebe, the proprietor of Amelie's favorite creperie, move toward the front of the crowd. "Please forgive the interruption, but Amelie was such a joy. We were so thrilled to receive a visit from her a short time ago and she was just as beautiful as ever. Several of us who knew her have asked and received permission to plant some buddleia in her honor. We've planted one already. It's over there," Bebe said, pointing to the flowering bush to the left of the crowd.

Eve gave a loud sniff. "Now that could make even me cry. A butterfly bush."

"And look," Bridget said. "There are butterflies."

Pippa saw the beautiful butterflies fluttering and met Nic's knowing gaze. Amelie had often said she wanted to be a butterfly. In that moment, she felt the bond between Nic and her solidify. They would always remember, together.

Nic asked her to come to the cottage after the service. She had arranged for a catering service to bring food. With all the turmoil of the past few days, Nic, his brothers and his father might have forgotten to eat, but their hunger would remind them soon enough. When she arrived, they were silently eating. Nic introduced her to his brothers and they all responded politely. Moments later, they all scattered except Nic.

"It was a beautiful service. I believe Amelie would have approved," she said.

"Yeah, especially with those butterflies. That caught me by surprise," he said, shoving one of his hands into his pocket. He'd pulled off his necktie and opened his shirt. Dark circles rimmed his eyes. Pippa knew he hadn't gotten much sleep.

"What else can I do for you?" she asked.

He pulled her into his arms. "Oh, hell, Pippa, you've already done more than I could imagine. The rest is up to me. I'll pack up my dad and we'll head out tomorrow."

Surprise rushed through her. She'd known he planned to leave soon, but not this soon. "Tomorrow?"

"Yeah, I need to get him away from Chantaine. I'll send in a team to clean up the cottage," he said.

"I can make those arrangements," she said.

"No, you've already done enough. Too much," he

said and sighed. "When I said fate would bring you and me together, I had no idea it would be for this. Or that it would turn out this way."

Pippa felt a twist of nerves at his words. "What do you mean 'turn out this way'?"

"Well, I've got to leave now. I've got to get my dad straight. There's no one else to do it," he said.

Alarm shot through her. "Are you saying goodbye?"

"No. I'm just saying I'm not free to be here with you right now. When I get my Dad settled, we'll see if you're still interested," he said.

Pippa stared at him in disbelief. "Of course I'll still be interested. Why wouldn't I be?"

"Your family still hates the Lafittes," he said. "In their eyes, I'll never be good enough for you."

"My family is rethinking their stance on the Lafittes. Besides, what's important is how I feel about you, not how they feel about you."

"We'll see, darlin'. You've taken a lot of heat for me. You deserve a break to decide if I'm worth the trouble," he said.

"But, Nic," she began and he covered her mouth with his index finger.

"Trust me. This is for the best," he said and lowered his mouth to kiss her.

Two weeks later when Pippa hadn't heard from Nic, she wasn't at all sure this *break,* or whatever Nic called it, was for the best. Plus, there was the matter of her increasingly regular nausea. When she counted the number of days since her last menstrual period, she broke into a sweat and got sick to her stomach again.

Even though she'd known she was late a couple weeks ago, she figured it was due to stress. After all, Nic had always used protection. So nothing could happen, right? The combination of her symptoms and that strange conversation she'd had with Amelie just before Nic's mother had died gnawed at her.

It took several more days for Pippa to work up the nerve to take a pregnancy test. She even dragged out the old disguise of the hated gray wig and ugly clothes and paid cash at the pharmacy so that no one would recognize her. She nearly fainted at the result. Positive. Perhaps she should get another test. She did, three of them, actually, from different pharmacies. The results were all positive.

She knew she needed to tell Nic, but this wasn't the kind of news she could give over the phone. It wasn't as if she could send a cheery little text saying *Guess who's going to be a daddy?* She knew he must be terribly busy making up for lost time with his businesses and helping his father create a new life, but the lack of contact from him only fueled questions and doubts inside her.

She and Nic had never discussed marriage, and she really didn't like the idea of him proposing just because she was pregnant. She wanted Nic to propose marriage because he didn't want to live without her.

Pippa rolled her eyes at herself. As if Nic Lafitte would ever allow himself to want a woman that much.

Suffering more and more each passing day, she avoided her family. Her older sister Valentina may have gotten pregnant without the benefit of marriage, but she'd had the good sense not to tell Stefan until she was on another continent. Pippa didn't want to even think about how to break the news to her brother.

She plunged herself into her studies and made progress that impressed even her. At the rate she was going, she could wrap up the last of her dissertation within a couple months. She wondered if she would be showing then. Another week passed and she hadn't heard from Nic. What did this mean? Had he forgotten her? The possibility made her ill. What if this had just been a fling for him? What if he hadn't fallen as deeply for her as she had for him? What if she was truly alone? And now with a baby on the way… Even with all the hours she'd been putting in for her dissertation, she was sleeping for only a few hours each night. She avoided looking in the mirror because she knew she was looking more tired and miserable with each passing day.

Pippa had successfully begged off two family dinners, but when Stefan called for an official meeting of all adult Devereauxs, she could no longer hide. The meeting was held in Stefan's office, which indicated potentially serious business. As Pippa entered the office, she noted the additional chairs. Bridget, her older sister Ericka, who lived in Paris, and her younger brother, Jacques, who'd responded to Stefan's missive by leaving his soccer team mid-tour. Ericka and Jacques were both talking on their cell phones.

"Pippa, there you are," Bridget said, then frowned at her. "Oh, my goodness, you look dreadful. What have you been doing to yourself? You need to let me set up a day at the spa for you."

"I've just been trying to make up time on my dissertation. Burning the midnight oil," she said.

"Well, don't burn any more. How are the Lafittes?" Bridget asked. "I apologize for not calling sooner. I've been so busy with the building of our ranch and both the twins got sick."

"I know you're busy. Nic and his father have gone back to the States. They both had a lot to do after Amelie's death," she said.

"Hmm," Bridget said, her mind clearly whirling. "He's been in touch, though, hasn't he? He hasn't just abandoned you after you helped his family."

"He hasn't abandoned me," Pippa said, even though she felt that way. "He's just terribly busy right now. Do you know why Stefan has called the meeting?"

"No," Bridget said.

"It must be big if he insisted that both Jacques and I come immediately," Ericka said and gave Pippa a hug. "I hope no one is ill."

Jacques turned off his phone and approached his sisters. "We're all here except Valentina. I'm stumped about this one. Stefan can go over the top easier than most, but I don't know—"

He broke off as Stefan and Eve entered the room. His assistant closed the door behind him. "Please be seated," Stefan said, his face, devoid of humor.

Pippa's stomach clenched at his expression.

Stefan gave a heavy sigh and sat on the edge of his desk. "As you all know, our father wasn't perfect. We can be thankful to him for our lives, our positions. Nothing will change that. However, he had a mistress for several years. She was a small-time actress. Her name was Ava London."

Pippa felt a stab of surprise, not that her father had

stepped out on her mother, but that Stefan knew the identity of this woman. She slid a sideways glance at Bridget, whose mouth gaped open.

Stefan gave another heavy sigh. "During their affair, Ava gave birth to two children."

Pippa and her siblings gasped in unison. Her mind whirled at the implications.

Stefan nodded. "According to the advisers, this development shouldn't affect succession. The son, Maxwell Carter, is thirty years old and is living in Australia. The daughter, Coco Jordan, is a—" He cleared his throat. "She's a nanny in Texas."

Pippa felt her stomach roll with the news. She couldn't help thinking about her own unborn child. "What else do we know about them? Did Ava raise them? What—"

Stefan shook his head. "Ava made an agreement with my father. He would support her until her death if she gave her children up for adoption and didn't reveal their existence. Ava passed away two weeks ago and her attorney is determined to follow her wishes, which are to ensure that her children know that they have Devereaux blood."

"Great," Bridget muttered. "This sounds like a public relations nightmare."

"It is," Stefan said. "The two children may also have some rights to an inheritance."

Bridget scoffed. "But they haven't had to perform any duties," she protested. "We've spent our life serving."

"True, but our attorneys have not been able to determine the legalities concerning their inheritance," he said.

Pippa skipped over the money issues. She had tried to be aware of economics ever since Stefan had begun to complain about frivolous costs. Her biggest expense had been the cost of her degree and she'd been fortunate to receive scholarships. "What are they like?"

She felt Bridget stare at her. "What do you mean what are they like? They're illegitimate Devereauxs."

"But they're people, human beings," Pippa said. "She's our half sister. He's our half brother."

Eve met her gaze and smiled, giving her a thumbs-up.

"Leave it to Pippa to bring in the human element," Stefan said and gave a half smile. "Both of Coco Jordan's parents have died. She's finishing her education after taking care of her mother during a terminal illness. Her parents left her no inheritance, so we're not sure how she'll respond to the news that she could gain financially from being a Devereaux. The advisers and public relations staff want to control the release of this information, so we will be inviting her to Chantaine as soon as possible."

"Mon Dieu," Ericka said. "You're going to bring her here? Why will you not pay her off and bury this information?"

"Because in a contemporary media environment, we have learned it's impossible to bury this kind of information. Our goal is to take this distressing news and to somehow make it work for us."

"We call that taking lemons and making lemonade," Eve said in her Texas drawl.

"So what's our new *brother* like?" Jacques asked sarcastically. "Knowing our luck, he's a drug dealer or something."

"Not that bad," Stefan conceded. "His adoptive parents live in Ohio. He graduated with a degree in engineering and has been working in Australia for the past few years." He paused a half beat. "He hasn't responded yet to our communications."

"Has the daughter?" Bridget asked.

"Yes," Stefan said. "But she hasn't yet accepted our invitation to come to Chantaine."

"Do you think this is a strategy to make us give her money?" Jacques asked.

"Jacques," Pippa said, "must you be so suspicious? Maybe this has taken her off guard, too. If she stuck with her mother during an illness, she can't be all bad."

The room turned silent because they all knew that Pippa had just helped the Lafittes during their difficult time. Pippa's stomach continued to churn. The realization that her father had denied his own children hit too close to the bone with her. She hadn't been able to talk to Nic yet. How would he respond to the news about her pregnancy?

Suddenly, her feeling of nausea overwhelmed. "Excuse me, I need to leave," she said and ran for the toilet connected to Nic's office. After she was sick, she splashed her face and mouth with water. Glancing into the mirror, she braced herself for what she would face on the other side of her door.

Taking several deep breaths, Pippa opened the door. All of her siblings were standing, waiting. Bridget crossed her arms over her chest, tapping her foot. "Do you have something you want to tell us?" she asked.

Pippa bit her lip. "Not really," she said.

Eve chuckled and the sound eased something inside her.

Stefan narrowed his eyes. "Pippa," he said.

She sighed. "Eve's not the only one who is pregnant," she said.

Stefan's face turned to granite. "Lafitte," he said in disgust. "I'll make him pay."

Her stomach turned again. "No," she said and raced for the toilet again.

Bless her Texan heart, Eve saved Pippa from a grueling discussion with Stefan. Pippa decided she needed to thank the heavens for Eve on a more regular basis. Eve had come through for her in several critical situations.

Pippa returned home and breathed a sigh of relief. She wished, however, that she would hear something, anything, from Nic. She finally gave in, called his cell and left a message. "Hope you and your father are okay," she said. "I need to talk to you when you get a chance."

Less that twenty-four hours later, she got a return call. When she saw the caller ID, her heart hammered so fast she could hardly breathe, let alone speak. "Hi," she said.

"Hey," he said. "It's been nuts here. My father took too many sleeping pills and he's been in the hospital. He's in rehab right now and I'm working on interim housing for him. How are you?"

How could she top his troubles? "I'm fine. I just thought we should touch base," she said, pacing the small den of her apartment.

A short silence followed. “You sound different. Are you sure you’re okay?”

“Yes,” she said. “I’m fine.”

“I would have called you, but I’ve been slammed with my dad’s issues.”

“I understand,” she said, adding as much backbone to her voice as she could muster. “I’m sorry he’s struggling.”

“Yeah. I could have predicted it. The good news is my youngest brother has started checking in on him,” Nic said.

“That’s wonderful. I know your brothers’ relationship with your father has been, well, precarious,” she said.

“That’s a nice way of saying their relationship with him was in the toilet. Flushed repeatedly,” Nic said. “My two other brothers don’t appear to give a rip, but Alex is working at it. There’s hope anyway.”

“That’s good,” she said. “I’m glad.”

Another awkward silence stretched between them. “You sure you’re okay?”

“I’m fine,” she insisted.

“How are the Devereauxs?” he asked.

“In perfect health,” she said.

“Good to hear. Stefan breathing down your throat?” he asked.

“No more than usual,” she said.

“I need to go,” he said. “I’ll call you in a couple of days. I’m glad you called. It’s so good to hear your voice.”

The call was disconnected and it took several seconds before she began to breathe again. His last words vibrated through her. *It's so good to hear your voice.*

He called and left a message the following day. She missed it, damn it, because she was in a meeting with her professor. Three days after that, there was a knock at her door. She looked out the peephole. It was Nic. Her heart hammered against her rib cage. She felt a jolt of nausea rise from her belly.

"Just a moment," Pippa called. She willed her stomach to calm down. Turning away from the door, she took several breaths and told herself she would get through this. She walked to the door and opened it. "Hi," she said.

"Hi," he said, studying her. "Are you okay? You don't look well," he said.

"It's good to see you, too," she said and headed for the toilet. Moments later, she returned to her small den where Nic stood with a brooding expression on his face.

"You're not sick, are you?" he asked.

"Not really," she said. "I've just had some nausea lately."

He frowned. "That was one of my mother's symptoms," he said.

Her heart softened. "Oh, it's not that. I'm not sick that way, Nic."

"How can you be sure?" he asked.

"I just am. Trust me," she said.

He searched her face for a long moment. "Then what is it?"

She took a deep breath. "Why don't we sit down? Would you like water or ginger ale?"

"Ginger ale," he echoed, clearly disgusted.

"Water," she said and laughed. "Have a seat." She filled two glasses with ice and water and brought them into her small den. Giving one of the glasses to him, she sat across from him. "I didn't expect you."

He took several swallows of water. "I didn't like the way you sounded."

She winced. "How is your father?"

"Okay at the moment. Alex is checking in on him." He set his glass down on a coaster on a lamp table. "What the hell is going on? Something's wrong. If you want to dump me, just say it."

Pippa dropped her jaw in astonishment. "That thought hasn't occurred to me."

"Then why are you acting so weird?" he demanded.

"I wasn't aware that I was acting weird," she said.

"Well, you are," he said.

"We haven't seen each other in nearly a month and we didn't talk for almost three weeks," she pointed out.

"I told you what was happening with my father," he said.

"Yes, but that doesn't change the fact that we didn't communicate for three weeks."

He frowned at her. "You're still not telling me what's going on," he said. "Spit it out."

She took a sip of her ice water, hoping the cool hydration would help calm her nerves. "What made you come to Chantaine?"

"You," he said.

She gave a nod, but didn't say anything.

"And I missed you," he admitted.

"That's good to know," she said in a dry voice.

"What the hell—" He broke off. "What's going on?"

"I'd rather not discuss it at the moment," she said. "I'd rather hear your true feelings for me."

He met her gaze for a long moment, then raked his hand through his hair. "You're more important to me than I had planned," he said.

"What had you planned?" she asked.

He shrugged. "I knew we would be together."

"So you planned for a fling, a temporary affair," she said.

"Yes."

His honest answer, which she'd asked for, stabbed at her.

"What had you planned?" he asked.

His question caught her off guard. "I don't know that I made any real plans," she said. "I just knew I couldn't turn away from you. The situation with your mother made it even more intense. I wanted to be with you. I wanted to be there for you." She closed her eyes and allowed the words to tumble from her heart. "I fell in love with you, and now I'm afraid I'm in this all by myself."

"You're not," he said. "But I don't want to be a wedge between you and your family. You would grow to hate me for that."

"It's not right for you to make that decision for me. Don't you see that in another way you're treating me like Stefan does? You're treating me like I don't know my own mind and heart." She clasped her hands together tightly and voiced her worst fear. "Are you sure this isn't some kind of smokescreen to hide the fact that you don't really love me and you don't want to be with me?"

His eyes lit with anger. "That's the most ridiculous thing I've ever heard you say."

"It isn't at all ridiculous to me, and it occurs to me that if I have to extract a commitment from you, then maybe I don't want it after all," she said, feeling a terrible wrenching sensation inside her.

He pulled her against him. "What do you want from me?"

"Not much," she said. "Just undying love, devotion and adoration."

"You've had that for months," he said.

She was afraid to believe him. "Why didn't you tell me?" she asked, her eyes burning with tears.

"I had to wait for you to catch up," he said and cupped her face.

Pippa finally saw everything she'd been afraid to wish for right there in his eyes.

"I love you, Pippa. I just don't want to make your life a living hell. I want to give you an opportunity to—" he shrugged "—come to your senses."

"Too late for that," she said, laughing breathlessly. "Besides, if being without you means I'm coming to my senses, then I don't want to do that." She bit her lip. "But there's something else I have to tell you."

"What?"

"I'm pregnant."

Epilogue

Nic felt as if Pippa had hit him upside the head with a two-by-four. In a way, she had. It took three seconds before his mind moved into high gear. His immediate response was primitive and protective.

"You have to marry me," he said. "Your brother may want to kill me, but our child deserves a father."

Pippa winced. "That was romantic," she said in a wry voice.

Nic sweated bullets. He couldn't lose her. He had to protect her. He had to protect their child. He had to make her see everything he'd tried to hide. "I love you. I want to be with you all the time. Forever. I just didn't know how we could work it out with your family. Cut me some slack. I didn't plan on falling for a princess."

"That's much better," she said and pressed her face against his chest. "I wanted you to want me for me, not just because I'm having your child."

"That was never an issue," he said, stroking her crazy curls with his hand. He couldn't believe his luck. Pippa was pure gold without her title and somehow he'd managed to win her heart. "So am I gonna need to do the pirate thing and steal you away?"

She laughed and the husky sound vibrated against his chest. "No. I think everything will be okay once you talk with Stefan."

Nic anticipated a rough discussion, but was determined to do whatever was necessary for her and their baby. "I'm up for it."

"My family can be difficult," she said.

"You're worth it," he said and sealed his promise to her with a kiss.

Later that day, Nic met with Stefan. Nic didn't blame Stefan for being protective of Pippa. She was worth protecting. If the situation were reversed and Stefan had gotten his sister pregnant, Nic would have knocked him into next week. Nic admired Stefan's physical restraint and did everything he could to reassure the prince that he was devoted to Pippa. Nic suspected it would take a while to win over Pippa's clan, but he would keep chipping away at it.

Despite their differences, Nic and Stefan had a lot in common. One thing they both agreed on was that Nic and Pippa should get married right away. Three weeks later, he pledged everything including his troth, allegiance, love and devotion to Pippa. He was in it for good and he was relieved that she was, too. Nic hadn't known he could love a woman this much, but he'd never met anyone who brought him so much peace and happiness at the same time. He knew it wasn't possible to be any happier than he was with Pippa.

Until Pippa took him to a level he'd never imagined months later, when she gave birth to a beautiful baby girl. Pippa insisted that they name the baby Amelie and Nic had a feeling that the baby was gonna wrap him around her finger the same way her mother had. He was damn sure he didn't deserve all this joy, but he wasn't giving up the treasure he'd been given for anything. Her Highness was stuck with him, and thank God, she seemed to be just as happy about it as he was.

* * * * *